Anatomy

Of

Love

(The Anatomy of Love Trilogy)

Book 1

Dr. Wilson Anderson

A Novel

by Kitty Berry

ASIN: B074MKL5D1

ISBN-13: 978-1985661585

ISBN-10: 1985661586

Warning: This book is for mature readers only. It contains adult themes that are sexual in nature.

Cover Design by Olivia Ryan

"Falling in love has physical effects on our anatomy. A churning in your tummy or a heart that feels like it's going to pound right out of your chest. The feeling of your body betraying you when you want to seem cool, calm and collected in front of the one person who drives your body into a frenzy."

-Unknown

Special Thanks:

From the bottom of my heart, I need to thank two very special people who recently stepped into my author world and completely rocked it!

First is my PA, Rosa McAnulty. I should have known, during that take-over when you showed up live on screen with me, that great things were going to come from it. You are not only fun to work with but also someone who is turning into a wonderful friend. Your honest and positive approach to the book community and the expertise you bring to your work is invaluable. I appreciate all you have done to help me in the short time that we have worked together and I look forward to us spending many years cultivating a lasting friendship.

And now for Vanessa Kelly, a fellow author, who reached out a helping hand to me without being asked and helped me in a way I can never return. I will always remember your wonderful spirit and I can only hope that someday I'll be able to repay you for your kindness and generosity. Friends like you are a real treasure!

"No one who achieves success does so without acknowledging the help of others."

-Author Unknown

Chapter 1

Will takes the stairs of his modest home three at a time. He flies into the foyer greeting his mom as she enters with her key.

"Thanks for rushing over. I hate waking you like this" he says with an affectionate kiss to Milly Anderson's cheek.

"It's that sexy man on the news, isn't it?" Milly asks.

Will laughs then rolls his eyes. His mother knows he'll never break confidentiality and reveal the identity of his patient, especially not someone amid a media shit-storm.

Will knows that his patient has the fight of his life ahead of him, literally, but dealing with the media won't be a walk in the park either. He'll be damned if he'll add to the frenzy. Even telling his mother, whom he could trust to keep it on the down low, would still be wrong.

"You know I'm not going to tell you who my patient is, famous or not, right?"

Milly smiles at her son. "Your father saw it on the news earlier. He told me about it," she tsked. "What they're saying they did to that poor boy. What is wrong with people today?"

"They weren't raised by the best mother in the world."

"They didn't have the best son on the face of the planet" Milly responds. This is their usual banter much to the chagrin over the years of Will's brother and sister. They don't always find it in good humor.

"I'll be home as soon as I can but I have no idea when that will be. Scar is asleep but check on her. She's been sneaking that fuc…sorry, that damn phone," Milly raises an eyebrow at her son then smirks at his correction. "Into her bed to talk to that kid" Will growls.

"Ah, young love."

"Ma!"

Will is not ready to think of his young, innocent daughter as a sexual being, a girl with desires and urges. He's sure she doesn't have them yet. Fuck, she's only fifteen, she'd better not be having urges. But Will knows what teenage boys think about and urges and sexual desires are all they have. And that kid that's been sniffing around his little girl screams bad boy, torn hymens, and heartbreak.

"Oh, stop it. Don't you remember?" Milly asks then when she sees her son's face crumble she engulfs him in her warm embrace. "I'm sorry. You know I didn't mean it like that."

"I know. I gotta go. Scar has dance after school until seven then she's sleeping at Aliana's house, so I just need you to get her off to school. Aliana's mom will get them back and forth to dance. She's staying over there till Sunday night. I should be able to come home by then."

"Of course, honey, go, it's fine. I've done this a million times. No worries," Milly says with a smile. "Now you go save that Damian Stone so the world can enjoy his sexiness."

Will laughs, kisses his mother's forehead this time then bolts into his garage.

It's less than an hour drive so he calls into the hospital to be sure his team will be assembled when he arrives. If his calculations are correct, he'll arrive as Damian Stone's helicopter is landing on the roof of his hospital.

"Sir, don't forget Ellen's last day was yesterday. Your new nurse doesn't begin for a day or...wait, what time is it?" the head nurse on the neurosurgery floor says. "God, I hate working this shift."

"It's two in the morning," Will reports as if he's saying it's two in the afternoon. "Call in anyone, it's fine. I can deal with one surgery without Ellen."

"Sir, you do understand that she's having a baby and not returning to work."

Will growls. "So I've been told."

Will and Ellen have worked together since his first days at the prestigious New York City hospital. He knows it was a difficult decision for her to decide not to return to a job she loves but he understands her reasoning as well. He never had the luxury of choices like that with Scarlett but he would never begrudge them to Ellen.

"I'll call Addison first, she's been looking for more hours."

"Fine. I'll be there in forty minutes. Have them prep the OR in case I need it. I'm going to try to avoid surgery but from what Stone's brother-in-law said, I have a feeling that's not going to be possible. I also need security alerted. I will not have my floor become a media circus. If even one of them makes it to my floor, I will personally shut it down. Understand?"

"Yes, Sir. Um, a Mr. Mac called, maybe that was his first name, I don't know. Anyway, he said his team will be providing added security and he requested to meet with the head of our team. I've made all the calls."

"Thanks. Okay, I'll see you soon" Will says before he disconnects the call.

******

Just as Will is pulling into his reserved parking spot, Milly enters her granddaughter's bedroom to find her father knows his child all too well.

"Young lady, is that light I see from your cell phone?" she scolds.

The teen quickly fades her screen and shoves her cell under her pillow then pretends to snore.

Milly laughs as she remembers her own children at that age doing similar naughty things. Well, all except Wilson. Wilson, her middle child, never gave her an ounce of grief. Not after that medical scare, anyway. Dr. Wilson Anderson hadn't become the best neurosurgeon in the country on accident. When Will was a small child, he'd had a series of seizures that led to the detection of a brain tumor. After multiple surgeries, over the years, and visits with his doctor, Will had decided his career path. It was his proudest moment when Dr. Talbott had offered to take him under his wing.

"I know you're awake, Scarlett Rose Anderson," Milly says with a smirk in her voice. She knows she should scold the child but discipline was never her strong suit. "What if I'd been your father? He would have taken that phone for a month."

Scarlett leaps up and scurries off her bed and into her grandmother's arms. "Grammy, no! Please don't tell daddy. He's being impossible lately. He doesn't like Johnny. He's jealous because he has no life and I'm trying to live mine."

Milly represses a chuckle. Yes, the world through the eyes of a teenage girl. She remembers it well, living it as one then as a mother to the most impossible girl and now she's getting to see it as a grandmother. Years sooner than she thought but she's never regretted a thing about Scarlett.

Milly sighs. That's not true. She wishes Scarlett's mother had been different. Not selfish and self-centered. A woman with an ounce of maternal instinct would have been nice. But instead, Scarlett's mother had flown the coop hours after giving birth, leaving her twenty-two-year-old son, who had just been accepted to the medical school of his dreams, alone and broken, confused and scared. Milly and Charles had swooped in to protect their child, the one that they'd grown overprotective of, and sought legal counsel. They'd helped Will obtain sole custody and ensured that Julia permanently gave up all parental rights over her daughter.

"Was that Johnny on the phone? It's two in the morning, Scarlett."

"IknowIknowIknow," she strings together into one word. "Grammy, I can't help it though, I love him!"

Milly smiles at her granddaughter's declaration of love and knows in her sixty-three-year-old heart that Scarlett means every word she's saying. What the girl doesn't know is those feelings are not permanent. She won't even remember this boy's name in two years when she's in college and realizes that the world is a much bigger place than her small Connecticut hometown.

"Be that as it may, young lady, your father has rules and you need to abide by them. Now, give me your phone and go to sleep. You'll see this Johnny character in school in five hours. I think you'll survive till then without him."

"No!" Scarlett begs. "Please. Daddy won't give it back forever and then how will I talk to Johnny? OMG…or Snap with him?"

Milly has no idea what this 'snapping' is, she's not sure she wants to so she lets it go without question. "I'll return your phone to you in the morning and not tell your father but you need to go to sleep right now and I don't want to hear about you up and on your phone at all hours of the night again."

Scarlett rolls her eyes, the signature move of a teenage girl, but then plops back down in bed. "Fine," she mutters, feeling under her mattress for her iPad mini. If she can't be on her phone with Johnny, it will have to do. "Okay, but I get it back as soon as I wake up, right?"

"After you are ready for school and have had a healthy breakfast. Your father had to rush into surgery. He doesn't know when he'll be home so I'll see you off to school then he said you have dance and plans with Aliana to sleep at her house all weekend?"

Scarlett smiles, remembering her plans for after dance, crossing her fingers that Aliana and she can pull this one off. "Yep, that's the plan. Aliana's mom is getting us to and from dance then I'm staying over there all weekend."

Milly tucks her granddaughter back under her sheets and gives the tip of her adorable button nose a kiss. Before she even has her door closed, Scarlett is on her iPad, looking at Johnny on the screen.

Chapter 2

Will flies through the doors of the roof and covers his head with his hands as he rushes to the helicopter that is landing only a few feet away.

"I'm here, Sir" Addison yells from behind him, her arms flailing in the wind from the chopper. Addison was thrilled when she was called in to serve on Will's team. Addison has wanted desperately to work for Will for ages now. But that's not really all she wants from the drop-dead gorgeous doctor. Addison has been harboring amorous feelings for Will for months but her feelings have gone unnoticed. She hopes after this case, after working closely with Will, he'll finally look at her.

As luck would have it for Addison, just as the doctor turns to acknowledge her presence, she stumbles and trips ass over teakettle and finds herself sprawled out on the concrete. When she looks up, Will is standing over her with a look of annoyance on his face.

"Did we interrupt a night of drinking, Miss Campbell? Because if you're intoxicated, you will not sit on my team" Will scolds.

Addison stutters as her hand touches his. Even mad, Will is a gentleman and has begun to lift her to her feet. "N-n-no, I'm not…I haven't had anything to…I was home in bed when I got the call. Alone."

Addison scrunches her features after unnecessarily adding that she'd been in bed alone. Jeez, she should have told him the whole truth. Could it have been much worse if she had said, "No, Dr. Anderson, I'm not intoxicated. I was in bed thinking of you with seven inches of my rabbit inside me."?

Holy shit! Did she say that out loud?

Will looks at her for a moment as if he couldn't possibly have heard her correctly then clears his throat. "Did you say something about a rabbit?" he asks. "If you have a pet to look after that is more important than sitting on this team, please don't let us keep you from it."

Can nothing go her way?

"No, I don't have any pets, Sir. I'm happy to be on your team. I'm prepared."

"Fine, then act like it. And if this behavior is due to who my patient is, fix it right now or leave. Understand?"

Addison shakes her head in answer this time, afraid of what else might come out of her mouth if she speaks to him.

The doors to the chopper open and a man who must be an ex-Marine with close cut brown hair that matches his cocoa colored skin jumps to the concrete barking orders at everyone around him. He approaches Will with an extended hand. "Mac," he offers. "Mr. Stone's head of security and brother-in-law."

"Will Anderson, neurosurgeon."

The men shake hands as the medical team lowers the stretcher with Damian Stone's body strapped to it. Anyone who knows the man would laugh at the irony of that. Damian Stone is a Sexual Dominant, the one to strap submissive women to the bed, not the other way around.

"The best neurosurgeon, I hear, correct?" Mac demands squeezing Will's hand to emphasize his strength.

"That's correct," Will says, hating to let his ego show but knowing that if he wants this man's respect he hasn't another option. "I was trained by the best and since his retirement, I'd say that title is pretty fitting. My outcomes are better than anyone else's and I'm not timid when I operate."

Mac runs a hand over his head. The man is clearly upset over his brother-in-law's condition. "I'll meet with your security detail as soon as I ensure that my wife and sister-in-law are safe. They'll be here any minute. And Anderson," Mac says over his shoulder as he begins to walk with the medical team. "If you fuck up, your ass is mine."

Will laughs. Who the hell says that to the world leading neurosurgeon?

"I don't fuck up. Ever."

And he doesn't. Not in the operating room that is. In life, in love to be more specific, he's a total fuck up. Will sighs at the thought of his non-existent love and sex life. This case is proving to be stressful and he wishes he had a woman he could blow off some steam with. But Will has never been the type of guy to want a woman just for sex, not like his best friends, Caine and Jessie.

"Dr. Anderson, Sir," Addison says with a gentle touch of her hand on Will's bicep, much too intimate a touch from the nurse only recently assigned to his service. But if Will remembers correctly, during her internship, he'd also thought she was a little too touchy feely. Maybe it's just her nature. She seems like a sweet enough girl. A little too ditzy and clumsy for his liking but she'll have to do until his new nurse arrives. Damn, he's going to miss Ellen and doubts he'll ever find another nurse that he gels with like he did with her.

Pushing his thoughts aside, Will looks down at Addison's hand on his arm and then slowly up at her eyes. She removes her hand and clears her throat. "Um, Sir, everyone is heading inside. Are we going along or do you need another minute out here?"

"What? No, I'm fine. Let's go" Will barks as he storms after the medical team and back into the hospital. He manages to maneuver himself into the front of the pack by the time they reach the elevators. He begins barking orders, in the calmest, kindest way he can, to his medical team. He'd hoped that he could have avoided opening his patient's head up so soon after the trauma of his torture and his surgery to remove the bullet that had barely missed his heart but upon setting eyes on him, he knew that wasn't going to be avoidable. Will knows when the pressure of a swelling brain is getting to the dangerous point and looking at Damian Stone prone on a stretcher in front of him in the elevator, his is well past the point of no return.

"Addison," Will calls. "When this elevator stops you are to immediately alert my floor that I will be taking my patient into surgery. I am not to be disturbed and I swear to fucking god, if I get called out of my operating room because the media has caused a ruckus on my floor, someone will pay. Understand?"

"Yes, Sir."

"You are also to alert your head nurse that you will be scrubbing in and unavailable for the foreseeable future. Have her tell Mr. Stone's family I will speak to them as soon as possible. She is to set them up in the family room on my floor and keep it a private room for them. Have her find another room for the other families and offer them food service for the duration of their stay for the trouble of relocating. Any problems, tell her to work it out."

"Yes, Sir" Addison shakes her head and exits the elevator already running.

"Scrub in now, anyone on my service and make it fast," Will demands as he bolts to do the same. "We're losing precious time. Get him prepped and ready. Someone get a scan as quickly as possible. I'm not about to trust the scans from a hospital that almost let his head explode. Fucking imbeciles!"

******

Surgery went as well as Will could ask for, his patient showed great promise of survival and making a full recovery, cognitively speaking. As for his other injuries, he wasn't so sure.

Will had called his best friend and colleague, Dr. Caine Cabrera, onto his patient's case knowing he'd need the best urologist in the country if he was to ever have a chance at being sexually active again.

Will and Caine had worked in tandem, side by side, in the operating room to minimize the effects of multiple surgeries on an already fragile man. The operating room had been insane and filled with too many people but the duo had barely noticed even each other, focused solely on saving their patient's life.

In the end, they'd been happy with the outcome and had parted ways with Will heading to talk to Damian's wife and family, Caine promising to do the same after checking on another patient who was experiencing complications.

Hours later, Will returns and interrupts the room when he opened the door of the family waiting area, entering in his white doctor's coat. "Mrs. Stone, may I have a moment?" he asks the stunning brunette he had briefly spoken to before entering the operating room. Will knows from his parent's account of living through his surgeries, that the waiting is the hardest part so he never makes the families of his patient's wait. After washing up, he always heads directly to the parent or spouse of his patient, many times before his resident or fellow has even had the chance to finish the sutures.

"Of course. Dr. Anderson, these are our friends and family. Everyone, this is Day's doctor" Sydney makes the introductions.

"Please to meet you all. Please call me Will. I'd like to talk to Mrs. Stone in private then she can update all of you. I won't keep her long" he says as he opens the door and motions Sydney from the room.

Will leads Sydney into his office, a floor above where her husband lays in his hospital bed asleep in a medically induced coma. His office is large and bright, the wall behind his desk looks out onto the city, the New York skyline stunning from this view at night. He has a large mahogany desk and chair, a sofa and coffee table, and a few other pieces of furniture in the space. The walls are a light green, clean and inviting, a neutral color palette to encourage a calm relaxed environment for both the doctor and his patients.

"Please, Mrs. Stone, sit" Will suggests and indicates the sofa upholstered in cream with green pillows to match the walls.

Sydney nods and takes a seat, placing a pillow in her lap and hugging it tight to her body. Will sits beside her instead of taking the seat of power behind his desk. He's always hated the neurosurgeon's reputation of thinking they're a god amongst mortals. He takes her hands in his. His hands are large and strong and he squeezes hers to gain her attention. Sydney looks up into his eyes and sighs.

Will is an attractive man. The kind that looks good in anything, probably better in nothing at all. He's tall and lean, his muscles taunt and tight, like a fitness expert in medical scrubs. There's a going joke amongst the nurses on his duty about the size of his manhood. Apparently, they all live for the days when he wears his scrubs and inadvertently shows off that manhood, his pants not leaving much to the imagination. It doesn't hurt that he's only in his mid-thirties and already an established and well-respected professional in his demanding field. His hair is medium brown, most likely closer to blond in the summers, cut short and tight, the top a little spikey, messy because of the amount of time his hands spend there. He has a kind, gentle face with a thousand-watt smile that lights up a room. But his best feature, other than his impressive physique, are his eyes. They're blue and caring and always focused directly on the person he's speaking with.

"This is a very difficult time for you, Mrs. Stone" he begins.

"Sydney. Please call me Sydney and my husband is Damian, you don't need to be formal with us."

"Sure, and you can call me Will. I guess it's best if we're on a first name basis. I'm doing everything I can for your husband but there's a possibility that he'll have a long road to recovery ahead of him. I'll spend some time with you and his friends in the morning, get to know him a little better" he states as he runs his hand through his hair, confirming why it looks the way it does.

Sydney sighs and looks down into her lap where their hands are joined. She shifts and Will releases his grasp. "What did you want to speak with me about? Did something happen to Damian since we spoke after his surgery?" she asks then clears her throat, her emotions lodged there.

"No, he's stable now. There's been no change. That's not a bad thing though," Will states with a smile for Sydney, tilting his head to make eye contact. "I wouldn't expect a change in his status just yet."

"Oh, okay. Well, I guess that's a good thing then?"

"Yes, it is. I wanted to talk with you about the next couple of days. While he's in the coma."

"Okay."

Will heaves in a deep breath. He loves medicine, loves getting his hands in someone's brain. What he doesn't enjoy about his job is this. Talking to the patient's families, possibly giving them false hope or worse yet, a diagnosis that will destroy their world. "We don't know all that much about what patients hear or understand when in the state we are currently keeping Damian."

"So you don't know if he'll hear us if we talk to him?" Sydney Stone asks.

"I like to believe he will, that's what I've come to speak to you about. I want to encourage you and your friends to spend time with him, talk to him, share memories, tell him about things happening now. Encourage him to come back to you."

A tear leaks from Sydney's eye then she smiles as she remembers that Brook, Damian's cousin, once told her about her birthing experience and how she had crazy dreams while she was unconscious, but she also claims that she heard a lot of what was going on in her hospital room and it helped her to come back.

"Damian's cousin's wife was in a coma once. She said she heard her friends talking."

Will nods and that thousand-watt smile lights up the room again. He pats Sydney on the knee then stands and offers her a hand. "I have plans to meet a friend for dinner but I'll have my cell on if you need me. I'll be back in the morning to talk with you and Damian's friends a bit more. If there's any change in Damian's condition while I'm gone, my nurses will call me. And if you have any questions don't hesitate to contact me."

"Yes, Dr…ah, Will," Sydney blushes. "Thank you. Can I stay with him overnight?"

"Of course. I had a feeling you were going to ask, so I put in special orders with my nurses," he leans in and whispers. "Some of them have a soft spot for me, especially on my scrub days, not sure why but I'll take what I can get."

Sydney nods, she's sure each and every nurse has a soft spot for the handsome doctor.

Will leads Sydney to Damian's room and leaves her with instructions to talk with him about special times they've shared then he heads back to the rest of Damian's family and friends to fill them in on his condition and ask them to be available to speak to him the following day.

Chapter 3

Will walks into the restaurant and scans the tables for his best friend and fellow doctor, Jessie Holt. Jessie is the world's best fertility specialist and gynecologist. It's a specialty area that has earned him both bragging rights and numerous hours of male ribbing.

Just as Will's attention is drawn to a table of women laughing and having a good time, his cell chirps in his pocket with a text from his friend to call him.

"Well, if it isn't the pussy doctor," Will laughs when his friend answers. Yes, male ribbing at its best. Calling Jessie "the pussy doctor" is his and Caine's favorite past time. "I'm just walking in now. Where are you?"

"Fuck, man. Sorry. I'm not gonna make it. My patient went into early labor. I have to head over to the hospital and deliver this baby I helped create" Jessie says, his voice laced with excitement. This is his favorite part of the job. He loves the sound of that first cry then the smile on the face of the parents.

"Fine but what the fuck am I supposed to do now? Scarlett is spending the night with Aliana, I finally have a night off and now I'm alone?"

"Yeah, again, sorry but you're at the restaurant you said so why don't you just eat then check out their bar scene? You need to get laid, man. You're starting to sound on edge. How long has it been?"

Will sighs. The last thing he wants to admit to his friend is the span of time he's gone without a woman. "I don't know. A while" he answers evasively.

"Well, if my calculations are right, I'd say at least a year. I have no fucking idea how in God's name you go that long without pussy."

"I have the amazing hands of a brain surgeon, remember?"

"You're a dick. Eat and then find a hot chick at the bar and take her back to her place and fuck her. If not for you, then please, for the rest of us, for me at least. Please, I'm begging you. If not, I'm taking you to the club with me and handing you over to one of the Dommes. That'll straighten your ass out. Well, after it's red and welting."

"Ah, okay then, Holt. On that note, good luck in the delivery room," Will laughs. "Catch up with you tomorrow." Will knows all about his friend's sexual proclivities but doesn't care to be schooled in them anytime soon. He sees the appeal, the hotness of a little kink but the life of a full-fledged BDSM Master? He could never see himself in that role.

"Later, man. Oh, and don't forget to wrap it up tight. I don't want to be in a delivery room with you anytime soon. Or a free clinic" Jessie laughs.

Will hits the end button without responding to his friend's nonsense and glances around the room once more. Fuck it, he's wanted to eat here for ages, getting another reservation will take at least three months, and he's starving. He huffs in a deep breath and walks to the podium. "Hey," he greets the hostess then leans around her to see what the commotion is coming from that table of women he spotted earlier. "Um, I'm Dr. Anderson. I have a reservation for two that just became one. Hope that's not a problem."

The hostess looks him up and down then smirks. "Not a problem for me at all and can I say, I'm not sure what she was thinking, she must be crazy."

"Oh, no, I wasn't stood up. It was a friend. Another doctor. A guy. He got called into the hospital" he blurts, feeling the need to save face.

The waitress raises an eyebrow at Will.

"Oh...nonono," he slurs together. "I'm not gay. I mean, it's fine if people are. I'm just...not. Really, I…"

"That's what they all say, whatever. This way" the hostess instructs and leads Will to the table next to the group of rowdy women.

"Oh, um," he stutters. "Yeah, can I have a different table?"

"Sorry, full house tonight."

Will nods and takes his seat. The waitress walks away with a smirk and as Will looks up he makes eye contact with a woman from the next table. She smirks and raises her wine glass at him then downs the burgundy liquid. Will checks behind him to be sure she's looking his way and not at someone else, someone more her speed. When he finds a wall to his back he raises a timid hand in her direction then buries his head in the menu.

A moment passes before Will feels the presence of someone standing beside him. Thinking it's his waiter looking for his drink order, he raises his gaze only to find the most beautiful set of eyes studying him.

The woman who had toasted him with her wine.

Shit. Now what? He's going to kick Jessie's ass for leaving him alone tonight.

"What's going on over here?" she asks as if scolding him for some type of bad behavior he's sure he hasn't engaged in tonight or any other for that matter.

"Um, I'm sorry, you must have me confused with…"

"I heard you tell the waitress that you were stood up. I agree with her, she must be nuts."

"Nonono," again he finds himself speaking like his teenage daughter. Fuck, he needs to pull himself together and act like the respectable adult he is. He's a world-renowned brain surgeon for fuck's sake. "I mean, no, I'm not here on a date."

"Well, clearly" the woman says looking at the empty chair at Will's table.

"No, what I mean is a friend blew me off tonight, a guy. I was already here so I figured I'd stay," Will explains then at the raise of the girl's eyebrow he furthers his explanation. "And, no, I'm not gay."

"Me either," she chuckles. "I mean if the situation were right, I might be persuaded to go down on a chick if the guy I was with found it hot but in general, I like dick."

Holy shit this girl. Did she just say she'd go down on a girl? Who says that to a complete stranger in a restaurant? Then Will tries to remember the last time he went down on a girl and comes up empty handed. The thought of going down on the girl in front of him pops into his brain and he shakes his head to clear the thought away before he embarrasses himself with a boner like a teenager.

No luck. We have wood, yep a full-fledged boner in the middle of a high-class restaurant in Manhattan. Jesus Christ, what is wrong with him tonight? Maybe Jessie is right and he needs to get laid.

Will tries his best to nonchalantly adjust the erection that she just made spring up in his pants but when her gaze meets his lap he knows he's been caught. He clears his throat to drag her attention back to his eyes in hopes she'll ignore it. "Um" he says, not knowing what else to say to this girl, that if he's being honest, scares the fuck out of him.

"My friends and I are over there," She begins pointing to the table of giddy women, granting him mercy and not addressing the obvious bulge in his pants. "It's kind of a girl's night out slash bachelorette party thing, the one in white thinks she's getting married in a few weeks. It's not going to happen, mark my words but we're humoring her."

Will nods then studies her features more closely. How could a friend of hers be getting married? Hell, this girl looks like she's barely the legal drinking age. "Is she old enough for that?" sneaks out of his mouth before he can stop and think.

The girl chuckles again and Will finds that it's a sound he likes hearing from her. "We look younger than we are I guess. Good to know."

"How old are you?"

She laughs again. "Old enough to have more college loans than I know what to do with and old enough to drink," she says raising her glass to her lips and taking a sip. "Old enough to have a job in the real world so I can start adulting and old enough to know if a guy will be worth my time in bed. You look like the kind of guy I'd have to clear my schedule for."

At that, Will has to laugh. Outright laughs from the bottom of his belly. "Yeah? I don't know about that" he says. After over a year without a woman, Will is certain he'd pop one off with this girl in record time. He's concerned it could happen right here at this table. In his pants.

"So, either mommy or a girl did a number on you," she picks up his left hand. "No ring so you're not married. No tan line where your ring would have been if you were married but one of those assholes who take their ring off. You're eating in an over-priced, fancy place so I'm guessing not divorced or you'd be eating at a fast food joint and giving the ex every dime."

Again, Will laughs. "What makes you think I'd be broke even if I were supporting an ex-wife?"

The girl shrugs. "Don't know. Come on," she says pulling him to stand. "Hang out with us. It's a buzz kill for me to watch you sitting here all alone after your gay lover stood you up."

"I told you it was just a friend. He's…"

She smirks at him. "Kidding. Relax, I have excellent gaydar. And you are definitely not gay. Metrosexual maybe but that's par for the course here in The Big Apple. You know New York recognizes like thirty genders?"

"Um, no," he stutters. "And I couldn't impose. It's a girl thingy you said. Go eat with your friends. I'll try to not be a buzz kill."

The girl tugs harder on his hand, persistent little thing. Will's mind spins from the whirlwind this girl is sweeping him up into.

"Oh, come on. You're not going to make me go back over there and let them make fun of me because you shot me down now are you? Think of the ridicule I will have to endure. Bullying is real you know, and it's not good for my fragile ego."

Will laughs again. This girl seems to be bringing out his more jovial side somehow. Fragile ego? This girl? Please, she exudes confidence.

"Please, please, please" she begs with her hands coming together as if she's praying for his answer to change. She also bounces on the balls of her feet causing her perky breasts to catch his attention.

"Okay…"

"Yes! Score. Grab your chair, you can put it next to mine. I'll move Amber down. She's annoying me anyway" she says rolling her eyes at him and making a face by sticking out her tongue. Yeah, that's not helping the issue that's still going on in his pants but damn she's cute when she does that.

"Wait, um, I'm Wilson. My friends call me Will. What's your name?" he asks, extending his hand.

"Sloan. My friends call me Forest Gump" she laughs and Will joins in as she bumps her hip against his.

Just as Will is maneuvering his chair at Sloan's table, the waiter arrives and shakes his head. "You can't just rearrange the furniture" he says, his hands flapping around in the air.

"We can and we did" Sloan says then gives him a shooing sign with her hands.

The waiter rolls his eyes. "Fine, whatever but this better be reflected in my tip."

"Oh, it will be now," Sloan says with a smirk then turns towards her friends. "This is Will, you guys. Say hello and be nice, he's a little skittish."

The table laughs and simultaneously says, "Hello, Will."

Will raises a hand then pulls out Sloan's seat for her to sit before he himself gets comfortable. "Have you ordered yet? I don't want to impose on your girl thingy Sloan said you were doing tonight."

"You told him where we're going?" one of the girls whisper shouts across the table.

"Not yet," Sloan admonishes. "I just told you he was skittish."

"Wait, what? Where are you…"

"Let's order," Sloan says. "Where the hell did the waiter go? And by the way, Will, that's gay. The waiter. Totally gay, you? Not so much."

"Are you planning a bank robbery or a diamond heist?" Will asks, still focused on her friend's previous comment.

"What you talking 'bout Willis?" Sloan asks with a laugh.

"Cute, very cute," Will says as the table laughs at Sloan's joke. "How do you even know that show? You're nowhere close to old enough to have ever seen it."

"I was a T.V. junky in college. I watched a ton of reruns."

Will smiles but before he can say another word the waiter reappears and takes the table's order. Will can't wait for his drink to arrive so he can maybe calm his nerves then after that's taken care of maybe he can work on calming down his dick that won't seem to let up in his pants.

During their meal, Will observes the women and their easy banter. They talk about the pretty friend he learns name is Katherine's upcoming nuptials and never once tease or give each other a hard time. It's like watching a more mature version of Scarlett and her friends. He hadn't realized this was the way women behaved, he'd thought his daughter and her friends were acting as girls acted not as how women did. He, Caine, and Jessie could never go a meal without giving each other shit over something, everything as a matter of fact, and even possibly ending up in a friendly scuffle on the floor.

Sloan is in her element, light and funny with her wolf pack. She seems to be the tightest with the bride whom Will learns she lives with. "So will you stay in the apartment when Katherine moves out?" he asks.

"She's not going anywhere" Sloan whispers in his ear and a chill runs down his spine at the feel of her breath on his neck.

"Um, she's getting married. She won't be living with her husband?"

"No, she won't be. Because she won't be getting married."

Will looks perplexed but isn't able to further question Sloan because Katherine stands and commands the attention of the group. "I just texted the driver, he'll be out front in ten minutes so let's get the check and really get this party started."

Will finds himself wanting more time with the charismatic Sloan but doesn't want to ask her to leave her friends. He also doesn't want to get shot down in front of a wild pack of girls either. So, asking her for a date is out of the question. "Dinner's on me. I'll get the check. Thank you for allowing me to join you ladies tonight. It was actually quite fun."

"No way," Sloan says wrapping her arm with his. "You're not getting away from us so fast and you're not paying for dinner either."

"No really, please. I've got it. It's my way of thanking you for the company."

"Just let him pay, Sloan. We need to get to Hard as Stone. Come on. We can argue about it in the car" Amber whines.

Sloan smiles at Will. "Fine, but you're coming with us and we'll pay you back in the car."

Katherine, Amber, and Rose head to the ladies' room to check their faces while Will flags down the waiter and pays their bill. He leaves a tip that makes Sloan raise an eyebrow. "You some big-wig Wall Street guy or something?"

Will laughs. He wouldn't know what to do on Wall Street unless someone began having seizures so severe their brains were in jeopardy of exploding. Then he'd know exactly what to do. He figures those Wall Street money guys wouldn't know what to do in his operating room so whatever. "No, nothing like that" he says as the girls reappear and lead them out to the limo at the curb.

"I should really get home. This was supposed to be an early night for me. You know," he laughs nervously. "To catch up on sleep and all" he lies. Sort of. That's how this night was supposed to end before he'd taken on his famous patient.

"And all?" Sloan asks. "You mean jerk off?"

Will chokes on the air he's trying to suck into his lungs as the girls laugh and elbow one another.

"No, I wasn't going to...I was...I don't get a lot of sleep" he stutters.

"I bet you don't with all that masturbating you do. Jeez, Wills, have some control," Sloan teases as she pulls him towards the limo. "You're coming with us. It's more fun to," she clears her throat, "come in a group than to come alone. Wouldn't you agree, Willy?"

"Ah...I..."

The other girls push him along and before Will knows how to get out of the situation, he's in the back of the limo with his leg pressed firmly against Sloan's.

"Where did you say we were going?" he asks, afraid that he had heard them correctly.

"Hard as Stone," Katherine hoots. "It's a high-class gentleman's club."

The limo explodes with laughter and shrieks from each of the girls and a groan from Will. Yeah, not going to be good for his dick, that's for sure.

"Wait, you do know that it's girls there taking off their clothes, right?"

"Yep, it's on our bucket list" Amber reports.

"Bucket list?"

"Senior year of college, we made a bucket list. You know?" Sloan asks. "Skydive, go to Hawaii, strip club."

"Yeahhhhh," Will says dragging out the word. "I understand the concept of a bucket list, but..."

"I'd rather go with Mike; I hear it's hot, you know as a couple. But he isn't into that kind of thing."

"She means he isn't into doing anything with her," Sloan whispers into his ear and that chill runs down the back of his neck again. What the fuck is that? "He's a fucking douche. Trust me, not making it to the altar."

Will sends her another bewildered glance, his eyebrows furrowed. "Don't say it," Sloan warns. "I'm a great friend. I've warned her a ton of times about him. Even threw the evidence of his wandering dick into her lap. She's in denial, I don't think she even likes him, no one possibly could. She just likes the idea of him. It's a long story."

"We're here!" Rose screams as the limo pulls up in front of the gentleman's club owned by none other than Will's patient, Damian Stone.

Will had done his research on the multi-bazillionaire before he'd agreed to be his doctor. He hadn't had much time but he quickly learned that Damian Stone owned, just to name a few, apartment complexes, an ice cream place, a bar, a restaurant, a strip club, and the most notable, a chain of BDSM resorts across the country.

And here he is at his patient's club with a group of girls he just met and a hard-on for one of them to boot. He laughs at himself. This is not the customary night out for Dr. Wilson Anderson.

Chapter 4

Amber, Rose, and Sloan split the cover for all of them, insisting on paying for the bride and Will. He's sure the amount will set them back a week. Will had forgotten how expensive it was to enter the most upscale gentleman's club in the city. It's been ages since he came here with Caine and Jessie.

The décor looks like it's been done by a famous interior design firm. He knows now that it has been, Damian's wife and best friend being the designers and Damian owning the firm. Since taking on Damian Stone's case, Will has learned a few things about the man. His business ventures being one of them.

There are numerous couches around a few different hardwood stages, the floors of which are smooth and stained dark wood. Some of the stages have your standard stripper pole in the center and some are without. There's a larger main stage in the center of the space and private rooms on the outskirts. In a sleazy place, those rooms would be where you'd go for a hand-job or to get head, here though? Those rooms are used for private parties but no hanky panky is allowed. Damian Stone is a kinky man, possibly more so than even Jessie, but Will knows through his research that he's always protective of the girls who work for him. He'd never allow anything like that to happen in one of his clubs.

Alcohol is not served for obvious reasons but Will sends the girls to their reserved table in front of the main stage while he heads to the bar to get waters and whatever non-alcoholic fruity drinks he can find for them.

When Will arrives back at the table, after a waitress promises to have his drink order sent to them, he finds the only open seat next to Sloan. He sits and leans down to whisper into her ear. "So which one of you added this to the bucket list?"

Sloan wiggles her eyebrows. As if he hadn't known it'd been her.

The music is loud and seductive as the DJ announces the main attraction on the stage in front of their table and Will's eyes briefly go to the dancer before returning to Sloan's.

"Here we go," Katherine says. "Leave now or get out your dollars, bitches."

Sloan laughs. "She's a little drunk and can get carried away. She doesn't get out much because that dick fuck of a fiancé of hers keeps her locked up tight so he can troll the city for pussy and not get caught."

"Wait, what the fuck?" Will asks.

"I know," Sloan says. "Never in a million years would I put up with that shit. And he's got a small dick that he doesn't even know how to use" she states.

Will shoots her a look as if to ask how she'd know.

"Oh God, no! Please. I'd never give that idiot the time of day let alone my...anything, actually. I got her drunk once and she opened up about everything," she explains. "You're not one of those guys that fucks a girl to get off and never bothers to remember she'd like to have an orgasm too, are you?"

"Me? Um, I...no, I..."

"You're cute when you can't form a sentence" Sloan laughs.

"Alright, you ladies know the rules?" Amber asks. "Tell them Will."

"Me?" he questions. "Why do you assume I know the rules of a place like this?"

"I'm sorry, I'm going to need to ask you to either show us your man card or your dick now to prove you actually have one" Sloan chuckles. She's joking but in honesty, she wouldn't mind checking out the goods. From what she spied earlier, he was given more than his fair share from the dick department.

Will blushes bright red, unable to come up with a retort, he leans back in his chair and just smiles. Then he shocks them all when he pushes his chair back slightly, leaning it on the back legs so they can all see his lap. He brazenly glances down into his lap and Sloan follows his gaze. Her eyes widen at the sight of his erection barely contained in his pants. "We're good," she says as she fans herself. "He's packing."

Will nods then laughs at himself, unable to believe he just did that. What the hell has come over him?

He nods then smirks at Sloan who is looking a little flushed in the cheeks.

The lights dim and the music changes to a thumping beat as the DJ's voice comes on introducing the main attraction.

"Pumpkin Delight?" Sloan laughs. "You think that's the name her mama gave her, Wills?"

Will smiles at her use of another nickname for him on her lips. Then, as the women at his table are laughing and watching the dancer slowly remove her clothes in a dance of seduction, his eyes are locked on Sloan. He studies her while she smiles and rolls her eyes at the dancer. Sloan is beautiful, more than beautiful, perfect. She's a tiny, petite girl, youthful looking, like the stress of life and hardships of the world haven't had their time to take a toll on her yet. Or maybe she's just been lucky. Unlike Will.

Will shrugs. Either way she's gorgeous and he can't take his eyes off her. Since they've been here at Hard as Stone, he's found he can't keep his hands to himself either. His arm has been hooked around the top of her chair, a finger lazily brushing her shoulder, since they sat down.

She looks at him and smiles, wondering what he was shrugging about. Her eyes, brown but speckled with hues of green that reflect in the light, when there is light. The room has been darkened for ambiance. But Will knows her chestnut brown hair is hanging on her shoulders, it's silky smooth, he feels it brushing his hand. He knows her cheekbones are high and plump and he wants to kiss them, suck the spot for the briefest of seconds before he moves on to the rest of her.

The rest of her…fuck, the rest of her. It just keeps getting better the more he looks at and discovers things about this girl. Her breasts are perky and round, about an overflowing handful Will thinks with another adjustment of his pants. He bets her nipples have supple little pink tips that she loves to have flicked with a tongue. His tongue.

Jesus, he's in a gentleman's club and the only girl he can see is this one next to him. She's certainly the only girl he's hard for right now.

His eyes roam down to her waist and tight tummy then land on her luscious legs. Legs he wants between more than he's ever wanted anything in his life. Those legs squeezing his head as he goes down on her and makes her come for him then wrapped tightly around his waist while he sinks deep inside her.

"Wait, what?" Will asks. He was lost in those thoughts of Sloan and had missed what she'd said. It sounded a lot like 'lap dance' though.

"I said, and you would have heard me if you weren't perving out on me," She laughs at his expense. "I called her over for a lap dance. Our treat seeing as you paid for dinner and won't take any money."

"Nonono," There he goes again talking like his daughter. "No lap dancing and you paid for me to get in here. We're even."

The table of Sloan's friends chuckle. "Too late" Katherine says as the girl Sloan called over arrives. Sloan raises her eyebrow at Will in a challenge. He groans in acceptance. What else can he do?

Shit. As if his dick isn't ready to cut glass and pound nails already, the girl looks like she's good at what she does. And it's been ages since a woman has touched him. He sends up a silent prayer to the ejaculation gods asking them to not let him come in his pants like a teenage boy in front of this girl and her table of friends.

The dancer, a young blonde, stands about two feet from his seat, with her feet just slightly more than hip-width apart, her toes turned out in a ballet position he's watched Scarlett perfect over the years.

Yes, think of Scarlett. That's it. That'll calm his dick down and save him from embarrassment. Scarlett doing ballet. And bye-bye erection.

But then his eyes look at Sloan and he can tell this is arousing her, watching him is arousing her. And we have lift off again. God damn, his dick pops back to life in record time near this girl.

With her hips, the dancer begins to draw a circle over Will's lap, keeping her long, lean back arched in that perfect way. The way a woman arches her back in the middle of a climax. The way he's picturing Sloan doing while he's between her legs, sliding into her body and finding his own release. Their eyes are still riveted to each other's as he has that thought and Sloan smiles as if having the same idea.

When the dancer slowly bends her knees and begins to grind down as far as is comfortable with the situation in Will's pants, then up again, continually undulating her hips and dancing erotically, Will places his hands behind his head but never even glances at the girl in his lap. His eyes are locked with Sloan's. The look in her eyes is hotter than anything this other girl, a professional erotic dancer, could ever possibly come up with.

She turns slowly, the dancer, and Will barely notices or cares. Why should he? The girl who has the potential to make him embarrass himself in this club and come in his pants is sitting next to him, fucking him with her eyes, not on his lap dry humping him.

The dancer takes a few more small steps, her turn blends into and seamlessly becomes part of her dance. She continues to circle her slim hips, hoovering them over the bulge Will can no longer care enough to hide. She turns her back to him, and with her super long legs held straight, she bends forward slightly, looking back at him coquettishly, as she begins to stroke her tight ass.

Sloan absentmindedly puts her pointer finger on her lips then runs it down her chin and into the top of her cleavage, a path Will pictures his tongue making. Will moans audibly and the table of women catch on that his arousal has nothing to do with the lap dance. "I think he has it bad for Sloan" Rose says to the others.

Will and Sloan hear her but can't take their eyes from each other's to respond. Sloan raises an eyebrow at Will in question and his head falls back momentarily then he smirks at her with a shake of his head to confirm Rose knows exactly what she's talking about.

Still with her back to Will, the dancer gently sways, opening her legs gradually. Slowly, she bends over so that her ass is brazenly pointing at Will. She bends a knee then straightens the other leg out to the side. The dancer begins to glide her hand up the straight leg while she raises her head over her shoulder to look back at Will, but his eyes are on Sloan. The dancer slaps her ass hard to get his attention but it just makes him think about slapping Sloan's plump ass.

His eyes never meet the dancer's.

She gracefully dances herself into the triangle made by Will legs spread wide to accommodate his growing arousal. She stands with her back to him still and her feet together. She's as close to his chair as she can possible get, he can smell the fresh scent of her perfume mixed with what must be the smell of her shampoo. It's pleasant but it's not the scent he wants. He wants to smell Sloan. Every inch of her flesh before he licks her to get a true taste of the woman. At the thought of licking her pussy, his head falls back again and he groans, "Sloan…I…fuck."

The dancer bends her knees, keeping her back straight, and gently puts her hands onto Will's knees. He's thankful it's this dancer touching him and not Sloan. He knows if, hopefully when, Sloan touches him like this, he'll come. Immediately. There will be no way to hold back this release building up inside of him. Not after how long he's gone without a woman and how attracted he is to this one. Fuck, Sloan is sexy and doing something to him like no other woman ever has or, he suspects, ever will.

The dancer lowers her ass towards his lap, barely brushing the bulge in his pants. Both Will and Sloan know she can feel his crotch on her skin. Then, keeping her hands on his knees for support, she grinds down gently, moving her hips in a circular motion. Over her shoulder she looks at Will as he sighs out Sloan's name again.

Sloan bites her lower lip and breathes out Will's name in response.

"Looks like the feeling is mutual," Amber says. "I have money on them fucking in the bathroom the second this dance ends."

"I don't know if he'll make it to the bathroom" Rose laughs.

Facing Will, standing between his legs, still as close to the chair as she can get, the dancer places her knees in the space between his crotch and the edge of the chair. Not much room there with a hard-on the size of his. She gently puts slight pressure against his groin with her knee then leans towards him and blows gently into his ear. She stands up, facing Will, sends Sloan a sly smile then catches one of his knees between hers and gently rubs up and down his thigh.

Sloan looks as if she's reaching her breaking point right alongside Will. Her cheeks are flushed and Will notices that her nipples are tight, peeking through her shirt and pointing right at him.

Standing between his thighs now, the dancer leans forward, placing her hands on the back of Will's chair for support. She puts one knee on each of his thighs, then lifts her torso, sliding her knees into the space in front of his crotch. She slides, slowly, all the way down his body until she's kneeling on the floor in front of him.

Will looks at Sloan with heat in his eyes and she knows he's picturing her on her knees in front of him instead of this dancer. Sloan is too. She sees herself releasing his erection and licking it from root to tip, tasting him on her tongue.

The girl uses Will's knees for support and stands, bringing her ass up first. Then with a flick of her hair in his face, she raises her upper body and plants a gentle kiss on his cheek before sauntering back onto the main stage.

Neither Will nor Sloan know how long they sit there just staring at each other. Amber, Katherine, and Rose are looking from them to each other with their mouths hung open, wondering if they should leave them alone. It feels as if they're watching an extremely intimate moment while surrounded by a room full of people. Amber finally breaks the silence when she clears her throat. Sloan and Will snap out of their fog, barely, and bring their eyes to the others.

"I think it's time to head home," Amber says with a smirk. "I need a shower after watching that. And by that, I don't mean the lap dance."

Sloan shoots her a glare to shut her up as the women rise from their seats.

"Sloan...I...um, I need a minute" Will says looking down at his lap.

Sloan laughs. "That might take more than a minute, pal."

The girls start out to the limo with Sloan looking over her shoulder at Will then turning to blow him a sassy kiss. Will tries to compose himself. Fuck, he doesn't remember the last time he was this hard. Everyone will assume it was from that lap dance, which he admits, was hot but he'd hardly even seen the girl. All he saw was Sloan. The bulge in his pants that won't seem to calm down was all from her.

Will manages to make it to the car, with a slight limp, as the girls are climbing in. He sits in the empty spot next to Sloan, adjusts his dick for comfort, and heaves in a deep gulp of air when her hand brushes his thigh and he feels the warm rush of her breath on his neck. "Amber and Rose are staying at my place tonight. You want to show me yours?"

Will doesn't want the night to end. He can't imagine ever letting this amazing creature leave his sight but he also can't bring her to his house even with Scarlett staying at Aliana's. He's never brought a woman anywhere near Scarlett. Sloan doesn't appear to be crazy but a guy can never be too careful.

"Um," he stutters. "Yeah, I have a better idea. Let's bring them to your place then we can head somewhere, okay?"

Sloan smiles even though that stung. She knows he's going to suggest a hotel to avoid her knowing where he lives. "Sure" she says anyway. She doesn't want this night to end either.

The limo pulls up outside of Stone Towers and Will briefly glances at Sloan. Does she know who he is? The media might have already publicized the famous doctor on Damian Stone's case and she could be playing him, a fame junky looking for a minute in the limelight. But, does she even know the man who owns and lives in her building? There's a chance that she doesn't. A good chance. He doubts that the multi-millionaire socializes with his tenants and she hadn't mentioned knowing him when they were at his club.

"You live here?" he asks.

"Yeah. Katherine is a model at the owner's agency. She holds the lease. I just help with the rent and stuff. I've only been here in the city for a few weeks. I start a job here soon so it made sense not to commute."

"Where are you from?"

"Jersey. Don't say a word" she yarns.

Will laughs and puts his hands in front of his chest to warn off an assault. "Never, Jersey Girl" he laughs.

Before Sloan can smack him, the girls are climbing out of the limo and making wise cracks.

"Have fun" Amber calls.

"Don't do anything I wouldn't do," Rose says.

"That leaves everything wide open for you, girl" Katherine says then ducks to avoid the slap coming her way from her friend.

Sloan waves as they close the door. Then she's alone with Will. "Where you taking me, big boy?"

Will calls out the name of an upscale hotel to the driver then smiles at Sloan. "That okay or…"

"It's fine," she says. "But it better not be a roach motel."

Will laughs. Ah, this girl.

Chapter 5

They arrive at the upscale hotel and Will pauses when he realizes how this will look at the front desk. He glances at Sloan to measure her feelings then bites the bullet and risks it. "Maybe you should have a seat on one of those couches over there," he says nodding at the seating area in the center of the lobby. "I'll get the room."

Sloan nods. She knows he's avoiding questions from the personnel at the hotel. This is not an establishment that rents their rooms for a few hours of fun.

Will offers her a sad smile then approaches the man at the desk. "Hello, I'm..." he looks over his shoulder to be sure Sloan is sitting where he asked her to and not able to hear him. "Dr. Anderson. My apartment building is having an electrical issue and I have surgery in the morning. Might you have a last-minute room I can have?"

The man glances at him briefly then smirks just enough for Will to catch his expression. "Just you or are you going to let the lady come up too?"

Dick.

Will hates lying but hates admitting to having a one night stand even more. "My wife will be joining me. Anything else you need to know about my personal life or can we get to our room and our privacy?"

The man looks ashen as he back pedals. "Sorry, Sir...um, Doctor ah...Yes, of course. Let me get some basic information from you then you can be on your way. I'll have a bottle of complementary champagne sent up for your troubles. A wake-up call?"

"That won't be necessary," Will says as he hands over his credit card and provides the man with his name and information. "I don't want to be disturbed. I need to sleep and get to the hospital, that's all."

"Of course, Sir. Again, my apologies. Have a nice evening, Dr. Anderson, Sir" the man says as Will walks away with the keycard to what he hopes will be a pleasure cove for the remainder of the evening and well into the morning.

"You don't do this, huh?" Sloan asks, sliding her hand in his and twining their fingers together.

Will likes the way their hands feel interlocked.

"What?" he asks. "Stay at a hotel?"

"No," Sloan laughs. "Take a girl to a hotel to fuck for the night. You seem uncomfortable."

Will shrugs. Is he uncomfortable about fucking this girl? Sure. But not for the reason she thinks. Well, not only for the reason she thinks. Sure, he's not experienced with one night stands and he's having way too many feelings way too fast for this girl to even contemplate only having her for tonight. But the other reason for his nerves is his lack of recent sex. Yeah, he knows it's like riding a bike and you don't forget but it's been a long time since his dick has felt anything other than his hand or an occasional toy or two he's tried out on his own, desperate for the tightness of a woman's body. Will is scared shitless of embarrassing himself and disappointing this girl. This girl who he wants more than tonight with.

"Um," he stutters. "I'll admit; I've never done this before."

"You're a virgin?" she asks much too loudly, gaining the attention of the couple they're approaching who are also about to step into the elevator.

"Shhh," he admonishes with a laugh. "No, I'm not a virgin. Jesus, is it that bad? Do I come off like one?"

Sloan chuckles. "Only time will tell."

"See, now that's why I'm uncomfortable."

Sloan looks at him quizzically as the doors to the elevator open and they enter following the other couple inside. Will presses the number for their floor and greets the man and woman.

"It's been a long time for me," he whispers into Sloan's ear, bending down so only she can hear him. "So, I'm a little concerned about…" he clears his throat. "Stamina."

The elevator dings on their floor and Will guides Sloan out of the doors with a nod to the couple still inside the box. His hand remains on her lower back as he guides her down the hall to their room. He swipes the keycard then holds the door open for her. "Ladies first" he says.

"Just remember that when we're having sex and you'll have nothing to worry about."

Will laughs at her forwardness and she blows him another one of her kisses over her shoulder.

"Have a look around," he suggests. "I'm going to pop into the bathroom really quick. I'll only be a minute."

"Don't rub one out in there thinking it'll help you last longer. That doesn't work."

Will looks shocked that she knew what he was planning and what the hell does she mean that doesn't work? Of course it does. If he can just jack off quick and release the tension, when she touches him he won't go off like a rocket.

"I wasn't…I just need to use…"

"Yeah you were, pal. Don't. Let me, okay?" Will heaves in a deep breath as she saunters towards him. "Bet I can give you a better lap dance than that girl at the club."

Will groans, he's certain of it. If Sloan does half of what that girl did to him, he's sure he'll disappoint her and come way too quickly. Probably before his dick even gets out of his pants.

She pushes him, her two hands on his hard pectoral muscles, and he finds himself sitting on the edge of the bed.

"Now, be a good boy and no touching unless you're given permission."

"Bossy" he says, his voice rough with desire and his hands already touching her.

She laughs as she snuggles her body in between his legs, forcing his open wide. His hands instinctively go to her hips and pull her in closer.

"No, no, no. Don't touch, bad boy" she scolds.

Will smiles and shakes his head then places his hands behind it like he had at the club.

Sloan unbuttons the top three buttons of her shirt revealing her ample cleavage then her hands cup her breasts and raise them an inch from his mouth. Her thumbs swipe over her nipples and she groans.

"Slo…" he begins to moan her name but his plea is swallowed up by her mouth. Her lips descend to his and open. His hands fly to her, one going into her hair, the other cups her neck tenderly. He opens his mouth for her to gain entry and her tongue swirls around his. His dick twitches in his pants between them and he feels her muscles tense. Knowing Sloan must also feel her pussy clench for him is driving him out of his mind insane. Then as quickly as she kissed him, she pulls back.

"Hands" she warns.

Will laughs. "You've got to be fucking joking. I need to touch you. Please," he begs.

"Not yet. My turn. Remember, Ladies first."

"I thought you had something else in mind."

Sloan straddles his lap, the heat from her core radiating against his hardened dick then she leans back slightly, placing her hands on his knees.

Will feels as if he might explode at any second but he can't take his eyes off her. They travel up and down her body but don't know where to stay. Every inch of her is beautiful. Her full breasts only an inch from his lips, her tight belly that he can see fluttering under her shirt. Her thighs, gripping him tight. Christ, maybe his luck has changed for the better because in this moment, he's the luckiest bastard in the world.

She extends her legs, one at a time, until her ankles are resting on one of his shoulders and his hands are cupping her ass.

"Fuck," he sighs as his head falls back and his breathing accelerates. "Sloan, that feels so fucking good but I…"

"Shhh, it's fine," she says. "We have all night. Let me do this."

Will nods knowing that once she starts to grind against him, he'll pop one off in his pants for sure. Jesus, and they both still have all their clothes on.

Sloan starts to pump her ass back and forth at a speed that makes them both moan aloud. She rides him like that until her legs begin to tremble then she lowers her legs back to the ground and he sighs with relief. That is until she takes her shirt off then unhooks her bra to expose her luscious breasts to him. She grabs his hands and cups her breasts with them. His thumbs brush against her nipples before he lowers his head to catch one in his mouth.

"Oh my God," she moans. "Use your teeth. Lightly," she requests and Will obliges with a moan of delight. "Yes!"

"Sloan" he sighs before he captures her mouth in another heated kiss. His tongue swipes over her top lip before his teeth graze then bite the lower one.

That's all the encouragement she needs to begin to work him over again.

Sloan begins to move her hips then her whole body as if he's inside her and she's reaching for her climax. Her hot, wet core rubs against his erection, he feels the heat and moisture through their clothes. Fuck, she must be soaked. He can't wait to feel her, slick and hot for him. But he's too close now to hold back so he knows that must wait for round two.

He breaks their kiss just long enough to warn her of his impending orgasm. "Sloan, baby, you're about to make me come. Let me take off…"

She seals her lips over his again and rubs her pussy back and forth against his aching cock as she moans in his mouth.

"Fuckkkk," he groans as he spurts his release, his hands gripping her ass, his lips crashing back onto hers. Sloan lets him ride his climax out, rubbing back and forth slowly until he stills and breaks their kiss, his mouth going to her neck. "I came in my pants like a teenager" he laughs.

"You have no idea how hot that sounds," she breathes. "Well, not the teenager part but…"

Will doesn't let her finish that sentence. He flips her onto the bed and pulls the button on his pants loose. She spreads her legs and lets him slide between them. His hands grab for her pants next and he works the button open and the zipper down, giving his hand access to slide inside. He exhales a lungful of air when his fingers find her panties. "Shit, you're soaked, Sloan. Take these off for me while I clean up quick. I'll be right back."

"No, don't go," she begs. "Let me...I'll..." she begins as she undoes his zipper then releases his wet cock. Her hand slides along his length and she moans at the weight and size of his manhood, marveling in its slickness from his release.

Will is lost in the pleasure zipping through his body as he heaves his pants off and flings them across the room. He hadn't been sure if he'd be able to get hard again so quickly but with Sloan, he had barely grown soft after he came.

Sloan's tongue snakes out and licks the tip of his cock where a dollop of his release has pooled. He rips his shirt over his head and pulls back her auburn hair to watch her lips surround him. "Jesus Christ, baby, your mouth is amazing."

Sloan's tiny fingers surround his base and begin to work in tandem with her mouth, jerking him off while she gives him the best head he's ever had. Her lips slide up and down his shaft in a rhythm that makes him insane. On every swipe up his dick, she releases it from her mouth so her thumb can rub over his sensitive head. As her mouth comes back down and makes contact with him, her tongue flicks the same spot and Will's eyes begin to roll from the sensations raking through his system. He tries to pull back as he grows harder, his dick swelling to epic proportions, but she grabs his ass with her free hand and holds him close. "Sloan, stop, baby. Let me...it's your turn," he says. "I promised ladies first and I've already fucked that up."

"After you come in my mouth you can do whatever you want to me. I just want to taste you first."

Holy fuck this girl is a wet dream come true. She's already made him come in his pants once and now he's about to come down her throat, hard. All before he's even had the chance to get her off once. He'll really have to bring his A game now.

"You don't have to..." he begins and tries to pull back again when he feels his balls tightening with his approaching second orgasm. Jesus, he never would have thought this was possible. Not at his age, anyway, but here he is, approaching his second release in under thirty minutes. "Sloan, stop now if you don't want me come in your mouth because I can't hold back much longer. Fuck, you're amazing at that."

She sucks him deeper, relaxing her throat muscles and taking him in almost to the root. A task no other woman has even contemplated with his size or girth. Her eyes look up and lock with his, holding his gaze, sealing his fate.

With his eyes remaining on hers, Will comes again, somehow harder than he did the first time only thirty minutes prior. He releases stream after stream, each with a tortured growl and a thrust of his hips. His hands remain on her head until he rides out his pleasure and begins to slow his thrusts.

Sloan pulls back after he settles but before she can catch her breath, he captures her mouth again, tasting his release on her tongue. She smiles into the kiss and he releases her lips to ask, "What?"

"I like that you wanted to taste yourself on my tongue. Most guys would never. But it's hot, kinky even. I like it a little dirty, you know, Willis?"

"Oh, Sloan," he moans as he leans down to kiss her again. "I need to feel you now, taste you. Take your pants off and show me your pussy, sweetheart. Let me see how badly you want to come. It's your turn and I owe you big fucking time."

Sloan slowly removes her pants and panties as Will grasps his dick in his hand and pumps it back to life. Shit, this must be a world record hard-on this girl has given him because he's still hard as steel and ready to fuck her into next week. But he stops himself. He knows he owes her a little pleasure of her own and if she's going to take him, as hard as he wants to go at her, he knows he should get her ready.

His eyes rake over her body and stop when they fall to her pussy. She's bare, waxed smooth. A sight he's never seen in the flesh. His dick throbs at the thought of sliding between her soft, glistening lips and he sucks in a deep breath. Damn, he'd never have imagined how hot this would be. He always kind of thought the bare look on a woman would flip him out, remind him too much of a little girl he knows. But not with Sloan. With her, all thoughts of his daughter are tucked away in a safe corner of his mind and her bare pussy is the best thing he's seen in an eternity.

"What?" she asks, suddenly self-conscious, worried that he doesn't like what he sees.

"You're bare," he states. "You wax?"

"Um, yeah. Sorry if you don't like it. It's just…"

"Your pussy is so pretty, so pink and I can see," he slides his finger over her glistening lips. "how wet you are."

"Oh" she sighs and relaxes back on the bed.

"That's a good girl. Lay back and relax. It's your turn now, baby. Let me take care of you. I can't wait to watch you come, taste you on my lips."

"Yes, Will, please" she begs as she raises her pussy, offering him a taste.

He chuckles then inhales her arousal and it goes straight to his dick. "I have never in my life been this hard. I just came twice in under an hour and I can't wait to get inside this tight pussy and come again. But first…"

And then without finishing his sentence, Will begins to warm her up by caressing her inner thighs with his hands then trailing his tongue in their wake. He breathes against her flesh so she can feel his breath on her clit and Sloan squirms from the anticipation. Before she has time to call out a plea for more, he begins licking her like an ice cream cone, in long, thick strokes that cover the entire area of her pussy held open by his thumbs. The taste of her on his tongue captivates him and Will's moans grow louder.

His mouth comes together with Sloan's pubic area in such a way that it maximizes the pleasure she instantly begins to experience as he begins his mouthy ministrations. This is a man who may not have one night stands but he definitely knows his way around a woman's body.

Will latches on to her and connects with the center of her pubic bone, where it needs to be for the maximum stimulation of Sloan's clitoris. She cries out in pleasure when he sucks the bud into his mouth, her body jolting from the bed. He smiles and lowers her back down, using his hands on her hips, making her take every second of the pleasure she deserves. Her hips raise off the bed again and with an evil smirk in her direction, he holds her hips down harder and makes her accept the pleasure he plans on delivering.

As a sheen of sweat begins to coat her skin, his licks gradually build up in intensity before plunging in fully, his tongue exploring her outside and in. Her taste hits his system once more and drives him to the brink of his own madness. He pulls back momentarily to inhale her scent again then he licks her arousal from his lips and savors her taste.

Sloan thrusts her hips at him once more at the sight, arching her back and making little kitten sounds of approval. "That feel good, honey?" he asks.

"Oh, my God, yes. Christ, you're good at that. You should hold a seminar for the rest of the men in the world because…" Sloan is cut off as Will dives back into her, quickly reaching a rhythm, then mixing things up when she's right on the brink of a mind shattering climax.

"No!" she protests.

To keep her on the edge but not allowing her to fly over into a world of relief and ecstasy, Will uses his lips to kiss her most intimate parts, alternating soft kisses with wet smooches on her thighs, her knee, then her mound right above her sensitive clit. He lightly nibbles and then sucks on entire bits of her skin, paying special attention to the flesh behind a knee. When he finally clasps onto her clit once more, the gentle suction feels incredible and she mewls as her body begins to tremble from the orgasm building inside. Will blows softly across her skin, teasing her with the new sensation of coldness on her exposed flesh.

"I want you to come for me, beautiful. Use my tongue to get off and come in my mouth" he instructs.

"Yessssss" she purrs.

Will presses his flat, still tongue against her pussy and waits until she begins to move her hips so he can synch his movements with her rhythm. Sloan begins to push and grind against his tongue, unable to delay her release much longer. Will is close to out of his mind but he forces himself to take it all in, remain still while she seeks out her pleasure, showing him the speed and pressure she needs to climax.

Once he knows what she needs, he springs back to life with a series of fast vertical and diagonal tongue strokes. He licks her senseless with a short burst of energy. Sloan continues to ride his face, chasing her pleasure until he returns to the flat, still tongue.

She cries out in a series of protests until he springs back to life at the most opportune moment and her entire body is seized in a climax so strong it lifts her from the bed. She cries out his name and shakes as spasm after spasm course through her system.

She's mindless as her orgasm continues to flow through her but Will is there the whole time with soothing sounds and soft, gentle licks to her pussy. As she begins to settle and return to her body, she realizes that he's moaning and savoring her release. The sight of him, between her legs, licking at her almost makes her come again.

He smiles at her then pulls back, taking one long swipe of his tongue across his lips to get every bit of her essence that he can.

"You are stunning when you climax and I have never tasted anything better than your pussy on my tongue."

"Fuck, Will," she sighs. "I need you inside of me. Can you go again so soon?"

He laughs as he grips his dick and glances down at his erection. "I don't think I can not go again."

"Other girls have told you how big you are, right?"

He shrugs. "Maybe one or two. I'll be gentle and go slow. If it hurts, tell me and we can stop, okay? I don't want to hurt you."

Sloan nods then grabs his arm as he goes to leave the bed to get protection. "Before we do this…"

"What do you need? You want to talk for a bit? We can call room service and get a bite to eat, a snack or something and talk. We don't have to do this right away or ever if you're having second thoughts."

Wow! A real man who is cognizant of a women's feelings instead of only worrying about getting himself off. Sloan can't for the life of her understand how or why this man is single.

"What are you thinking? You have a strange look on your face all of a sudden."

"I was wondering how in the hell you're sing…oh my fucking God! Are you married? I mean, you don't have a ring and there's no tan line but…"

"Shhh," he eases her into his arms and places her head on his chest as he lays them down on the bed. "I'm single. I swear. No wife, no girlfriend. I haven't even been on a date in over a year."

"Oh, okay" she yawns.

"You're tired. It's late. Maybe we should go to sleep."

She nods and snuggles closer to Will as he reaches for and pulls the blankets over their naked bodies. He kisses the top of her head and whispers, "Good night" but Sloan is already asleep in his arms, a place where she fits perfectly. In the morning, he plans to tell her that piece of information but right now his eyes are heavy and his breathing is falling into suit with hers. The last thing Will thinks about as he falls asleep is how good it feels to have her soft, warm body next to him. It's a feeling he could get used to.

Chapter 6

Will wakes after a few hours of sleep to a raging erection. He thought the two orgasms Sloan had given him a few hours ago would have been enough to quench his thirst for a while. He was wrong.

He glances over to see if she's still sleeping and when he finds her still and silent he props himself on an elbow, his bicep strong. He flexes it for a moment in case she opens her eyes. He laughs at himself wondering if he'll ever think like an adult and not a teenage boy.

But Sloan is out cold, her lips slightly spread and her breathing steady and slow. Will sits up for a better view and rakes his eyes over her beautiful form. The sheet has bunched around her waist in sleep, her naked back exposed, the curve of the side of her breast taunting him. His hand rubs over his hardness and he moans before dragging himself from the bed to use the bathroom.

Will brushes his teeth with the complimentary necessities and tries his best to force his dick to cooperate so he can use the toilet and get back to the woman in the bed just outside the door. The woman he needs to get inside of.

He returns to the bed and glances at the clock. Shit, he's been gone from the hospital longer than he likes but he can't leave until he's had this girl.

Will snuggles back into bed and runs his hand over her back, down to her ass that he cups and lightly squeezes making her stir. Then a sly smile crosses her face. "Whatcha doing there, Willis?"

"You know that's not my name, right?"

"I know. But you didn't answer my question. You looking for something I can help you with?"

"I um…I need to um…I need to go soon," he stutters. "Work, you understand."

Sloan sits up and glances at the clock on the bedside table. The screen reads 3:32am. Work or a wife she wonders because who goes to work at four in the morning? Well, her actually. But Will doesn't strike her as a nurse like she is or will be once she starts this new job in a few hours, her workaholic doctor requesting that she begin on a Saturday. She might be in for crazy long hours but Sloan can't wait to start.

She chuckles, blowing her suspicions of a wife off. If the man was married, it's too late now, they'd done enough for her to already hate herself so why not finish it off right? And she needs to feel him inside of her. "And you want morning or," she checks the clock again. "Middle of the night sex before you go?"

"No" he says. "Well yes, but I mean…"

"Give me a second," she says cutting him off as she rises, naked and unashamed from the bed, and heads towards the bathroom. "I'm not letting you leave here without having that monster inside me."

Will laughs. This girl is the best ego stroke he's ever had. Monster, ha! Yeah, he wishes. Then he looks down at his raging hard-on and can see what she means. He knows, anatomically speaking, that he's well-endowed but he's seen enough dicks to know that so are others. Could he really be the first man of size a girl like Sloan has ever been with? He pushes that thought aside. Thinking about her with another man pisses him off.

"Starting without me?" Sloan asks as she saunters back towards the bed.

Will looks down to find himself, dick in hand, stroking his erection. "Oh, I, um…huh? I hadn't noticed I was doing that."

"Mmmm," she hums. "I did and it's a glorious sight. If I didn't want you to fuck me so bad right now, I'd tell you to finish while I watched."

"Come here," he says, his voice dripping with need. "I want you too."

Sloan crawls up his body, rubbing her flesh against his along the way until she is laying flush with him, all the right parts lined up.

"I need to grab a condom" he says even though the last thing he wants is a barrier between them.

Sloan nods and rolls to the bed, allowing him to retrieve what he needs from his wallet. She giggles to herself or she thought it was internally until he raises an eyebrow in question at her.

"I was just wondering if they made them big enough" she explains.

"You're good for my ego, sweetheart, but you know there are a lot of guys the same size, maybe bigger."

"Really? Cuz' I've been around the block a time or two and uh, you win the prize. The best cock award goes to…drum roll…"

Will closes his mouth over hers and devours her, licking and kissing, sucking and biting, He makes her forget all thoughts of other men, every thought except for her need for him. "I don't want to think about another guy touching you and I certainly don't want you to be having those thoughts when we're about to…do this" he states as he pulls back only long enough to roll the condom down his length.

"Will?"

"Shhh," he soothes. "You ready, baby? This might pinch a little at first but I'll go as slow as I can. I don't want to hurt you."

Sloan nods. "God, yes. Please."

Will grasps the base of his dick, now harder than he thought was humanly possible, and gently rubs the swollen head along her slick folds. "So wet for me" he states as sparks ignite in his brain. "You'll be able to take me just fine, sweetheart."

"Please" she begs raising her hips in a plea for penetration.

"I want to savor this, baby, but I can't wait another second. Open for me" he demands as his free hand places her leg on his shoulder. Will lines his erection up to her opening then, with his eyes locked on her and a strangled groan slipping from his lips, he thrusts inside her. Just the tip slips in, anything more he'll have to push with more force to make it through her tightness.

"Yes" she cries out. Sloan's hips raise slightly to give him better access.

"Fuck," he moans on the second thrust that gains him an inch more of access. "You're tight, Sloan. Let me in, sweetheart. Take all of me. You can do it, breathe and relax."

She shakes her head. "No, you're so thick. But, ohhhh, it feels so gooooood" she moans as Will gains another few inches into her body.

"Hold still," he pants. "Just for a second, baby. I can't come yet. Please. You feel too good but I'm already getting close and I need to get it all inside you. And I want you there with me."

Will lets his head fall back as he pushes in, harder this time then the last few pushes, to gain complete access to her tightness. When he feels her wetness coat him through the condom he loses his mind and knows he can't hold back no matter how much he wants to. He just prays he can get her off as fast as he's about to get there himself.

His finger quickly finds and begins to circle her clit with the perfect amount of pressure. Sometimes it pays to have a best friend who knows women's bodies better than anyone. Yes, he owes Dr. Jessie Holt, a.k.a. "The Pussy Doctor" for this one. And to think, Will and Caine had laughed off that night in the bar when Jessie had given them the inside knowledge of a gynecologist. He'd have to kiss the man for it now.

Will continues to press down and rub Sloan's clit as he thrusts inside her, his pushes growing harder and faster. Then he pulls back and smiles at her. She's close, he can feel her walls clenching around him and her sounds are ratcheting up his arousal. He knows this next move should get her there. He prays it does because it's going to get him there too.

Will thrusts in hard to the hilt and Sloan cries out, her nails biting into his back. Along the way he rubs against her tight, wet walls then begins tiny thrusts of his dick so that the head continues to rub along her most sensitive internal spot making her pant, unable to catch her breath.

Sloan's losing her mind. She pants, incoherent pleas and moans escape her lips until Will rears back one last time. He leans down and plants a gentle kiss to her lips then whispers in her ear, "Come with me, Sloan. You're so fucking sexy and I'm going to come inside you. I'm coming right now, sweetheart. All for you."

"Yessssss" she cries out as Will begins thrusting again then she shatters around him, her walls milking him as he releases inside her.

The world momentarily goes black for each of them.

"Wow!" he says when he gains control over his body.

"What the hell was that?" she asks.

Will smiles. "Yeah, to be honest, I've always heard about how awesome it is if you can come together," he shrugs. "I guess I just never connected with anyone like that before."

"Me either. Jesus. Do that again" she begs with a wiggle of her hips.

He laughs. "I wish I could but I need to take the condom off before it slips and I don't have any others."

"Oh" she sighs.

"Hey," he says as he slides out of her body then lifts her chin with his finger. "Let me toss this and clean up then I want to hold you, okay?"

Sloan nods and snuggles under the covers as she watches Will slip into the bathroom. Then the panic sets in. What if he isn't feeling the things she is? What if what he's saying to her are only words? She can't take that kind of let down. Not again. She's had one too many one night stands or guys that showed an initial interest only to leave her in a few days, disappointed and questioning what was wrong with her.

So, in that moment, Sloan decides to protect her heart as much as she can.

She flings herself from the bed, quickly grabbing her clothes and throwing on only the most necessary of garments, shoving her bra into her pocket. She can't find her panties but she doesn't have any more time to look. She'd have to shower at home and change anyway in the next few hours before she's due at her new job, her first real job. She has enough panties; she'll never miss this one pair. She scribbles her number on a piece of paper and flies out the door. If he calls her, great. If not, at least she wouldn't have to see the look of pity she knows he'd have in his eyes if he had to lie to her face and promise to call. Will seems like a nice guy, genuine, but, in the end, even the nice ones can be a dick the morning after.

She's descending in the elevator before Will steps out of the bathroom to find her gone. His eyes fall to the paper with her number on it left on the bed where they'd just made love and shared a moment so strong he can't for the life of him understand why she'd leave.

Then the old insecurities set in. Why wouldn't she leave? Not even Scarlett had kept Julia from leaving. What was there to hold this incredible girl to him? Nothing.

He sighs and pockets the number, figuring he'll decide if he should call her later. It's getting late and he needs to get back to his patient then meet this new nurse of his that is replacing Ellen. She'd been pissy, he was told, over beginning on the weekend so maybe she won't even show up. He'll do what he always does, what he learned to do as a kid who had to deal with brain surgery, he'll compartmentalize this and deal with it later. Maybe when he calls the number, she'll answer and he can ask her out on a real date. Maybe he'll be sent to a recording telling him he'd been a fool to believe she felt the same for him. Or, maybe he wouldn't call at all. Maybe he'd protect his heart and just use this memory as another addition to his spank bank. Either way, he didn't have time now to dwell on it. He needed to get back to the hospital, check on Damian Stone then try to grab a shower before he met his new nurse. He knows it would be in poor taste to do so smelling of sex.

Will begins to throw on his clothes and while he's looking for a lone sock he sees a piece of material sticking out from the blankets.

Black. Lace. Her panties.

He lifts them to his nose and inhales. Her scent makes his mind go wild and his dick harden again. Talk about spank bank. These would come in handy if the number she left him was a dead end.

He pulls on his shoes and leaves with one last look over his shoulder at the bed he'd shared for a few hours with Sloan, a woman who has managed to sneak in and begin the defrosting process of his heart. Then he pulls the door closed and leaves.

Chapter 7

Will enters his patient's room and finds him laying peacefully in bed, his wife tucked into his side. Will sighs at the sight then pushes his feelings aside and approaches Damian's bedside. Thinking about lying in bed with Sloan in his arms right now can't happen. Not the time or place but Will can't help where his mind takes him.

Sydney Stone, his patient's wife, startles awake, looking sad and lost as the realization of where she is and why sets in.

Will knows falling asleep only to wake up and remember what's happened is the worst. He's seen more families suffer through this pain than he ever cares to remember. It wasn't the same thing with him but Wilson knows what it's like to wake up and have a moment's peace before you realize that your whole world has come crashing down around you.

He holds out a hand to the beautiful Sydney Stone and helps her to sit up. She clears her throat and looks sadly at her husband lying motionless next to her, the man beaten and tortured who managed to survive not only that but a bullet to the chest and two surgeries, one at the hands of Will.

"I must have fallen asleep" she admits.

"You need your rest. You and the baby" Will says nodding at Sydney's expanding belly.

"I know but…"

"You should go home for a few hours. Try to get some rest and you need to eat. He's not going to wake up while you're gone. His body needs more time."

"I know. It's just he wouldn't…"

"He wouldn't leave you? Probably not but he also wouldn't want you to put your health or the baby's in jeopardy."

He knows if that were him lying there and Sloan was carrying his child, he'd want his doctor to send her home to take care of herself and their child.

What the hell?

He spent a few hours in a hotel room with the girl and he's already got her pregnant in his mind. He needs to tamp this shit down and quick if he wants to ever see her again. He's planning on calling her once he gets his shit together. He can't call her if his mind is going to things like her carrying their child because God only knows what he'll say. He's sure whatever it is would scare her off for good this time. He questions what spooked her in the hotel room and tried to remember if he'd said or done anything that would have made her leave. Coming up empty-handed, Will smiles at his patient's wife.

"I know," Sydney admits. "Okay, I'll see if Mac and Drea want to head back with me. Damian's sister is pregnant too. She should get something to eat and have a rest as well."

Will smiles at his patient's wife. "I'll stay with him. I want to get to know him a little better anyway."

Sydney smiles at that. "Thanks. Call me if…"

"Absolutely."

Will turns and fiddles with Damian's chart to give Sydney a few moments to say goodbye to her husband. When he glances back to the bed, Sydney is gently stroking her husband's hair and whispering into his ear.

"I told him my favorite story about us last night," she reports. "It was a bit dirty."

"I'm sure he loved hearing it. I actually have a pretty good one I'm about to share with him myself."

Sydney raises an eyebrow at Will then kisses him chastely on the cheek before exiting the room. "Thank you for everything."

She looks back sadly one last time before the door closes.

Will pulls up a chair and sits down, placing his feet gently on the edge of Damian's bed. "You'll never guess where I ended up last night. Quite a coincidence" Will laughs.

He tells Damian about winding up at a restaurant alone and sitting down to enjoy a quiet meal only to get himself wrapped up with a group of rambunctious girls out on the town for a night of bridesmaid debauchery. He opens up to the silent man, able to tell him about the insanity of his growing feelings for a girl he just met. He'd never hear the end of it if this were Caine or Jessie he was talking to. No, the unconscious Damian Stone is the perfect person to spill out his heart to.

Will can't believe his own feelings as he begins to voice them to his patient. He hadn't realized how deep he was in until he began to speak about Sloan aloud.

Shit, he was in trouble. Big. Time. Trouble.

He turns, at the moment he admits being in a gentleman's club, to find Tate Taylor and his wife in the doorway. Tate is his patient's cousin and a famous music producer. His wife, Brook, is his daughter's obsession. Scarlett has been driving him insane about taking one of the choreographer's workshops. Hell, if Scarlett isn't going on about that damn Johnny kid, she's talking about dancing for Brook Taylor.

"Sorry, we can come back if you need to…" Tate trails off.

"No, I was just getting to know him a little. I know it sounds weird but I really believe that patients can hear when…"

Brook interrupts. "Yes, they can. Trust me" she says with a smile as her husband pulls her into his side. Brook had heard her friends around her bed when she was in a coma after having her twins. She might have twisted up some of what they were saying but she heard them alright.

"I'll let you two visit for a while. I'm glad you're here actually. I told Sydney I'd stay with him so she could go home and rest for a bit. She needs to take care of herself and the baby. But I need to go get cleaned up. I have a new nurse coming on my duty in," he checks his watch. "Shit! Sorry. She'll be here in half an hour and I haven't even showered or had a minute to go home."

Brook smiles, a naughty gleam in her eye. "Well, I'd shower if I were you. You never know when you'll meet "The one.""

Will laughs. "Yeah, "The one.""

He'd thought he'd met her once but he'd been wrong. He hasn't really been looking ever since he learned his hard lesson about women and love at an early age. He'd had Scarlett to look after but now that she was older maybe it was time.

Tate leans in and whispers so his wife, who has sat on Damian's bed wouldn't hear, "And if you were doing what I assume you were at his club, I'd say a shower was in order."

Will looks at Tate and blushes slightly. "I've never been there before," he stutters. "I kind of got dragged there."

Tate raises his eyebrows at the embarrassed doctor. "Any way you like it, man" Tate laughs then pats him on the back and heads to his cousin's bedside.

The door to Damian's room opens again and the head nurse on the floor enters. "Dr. Anderson, your new nurse has arrived. She's waiting for you in your office."

"Fuck" he curses under his breath then glances back and nods at the Taylors before exiting his patient's room.

His daughter is going to die when he tells her that he met Brooklynn Taylor. Then she's going to kill him for not getting her autograph or begging her to allow Scarlett to audition for her dance company. All things he'll have to deal with later. Right now, he needs to rush to his office to meet this new nurse of his who is a half hour early. Why did Ellen have to have a baby and leave him?

Will hates change. Ellen had been his nurse since he began performing surgeries on his own. She knows his little intricacies and his own medical history, how it drives him to be a successful and aggressive brain surgeon. Not a wild cowboy by any means but never a pussy in the operating room. No tumor will get the best of him, damn it. His own hadn't and he'll be damned if he'll let one take his patient down without a fight.

He's been criticized in the community for this tactic but let the other doctors say what they will. It's not his fault they're too afraid to cut sometimes. An inoperable tumor? That's not a term that's in his vocabulary. And all that matters to him are his patients and their families. No mother of a child with a brain tumor will ever criticized him for being too aggressive with the scalpel and saving her child.

So fuck everyone else.

Now he just hopes this new nurse isn't going to question his methods. As he runs through the halls and weaves between doctors and nurses he hopes she's not an old battleax set in her ways either. The last thing he needs is to have to hold another round of interviews because this one doesn't work out.

After weeks of sitting through appointment after appointment, Will had finally been saved when he was called away to assist a fellow surgeon on the other side of the country. He'd been glad to allow his secretary to conduct the last of the interviews then went with the candidate she suggested. With the approval of his board, of course.

Will takes a deep breath before he opens his office door. Then he sucks in enough air to choke an elephant when the woman waiting for him turns to greet him.

Chapter 8

"Sloan!" Will says. "How did you know where I work?"

Sloan is speechless. She stares at the man she spent a night of passion with unable to believe her bad luck. She'd finally landed her dream job as a nurse and then she'd slept with the doctor, ultimately her boss, the night before. Fuck her life!

"Sloan?" Will asks again, the reality of the situation starting to pull at his mind.

Sloan clears her throat then extends her hand. "Dr. Anderson," she greets. "I'm Sloan Hale. Your new nurse. It's a pleasure to meet you, sir."

"What the fuck?"

No, really, what the holy fuck?

"Sir?"

"Stop with the 'sir' shit, Sloan. Answer my question. What the fuck?"

"Don't 'what the fuck?' me. What the fuck you, Will?"

Wilson runs his hand through his thick hair. When he pulls it out, his short tresses are even more mussed than when Sloan had seen him last and it had been her hands that had caused that sexy as fuck look on the doctor. "I-I-I had no idea who you were" he stumbles over his words still trying to make sense of the situation at hand.

"Bullshit. You've had my file for weeks now. You want me to believe that you haven't once opened it and looked inside. I'm sure there's a picture of me in there."

Will raises his hands in front of his chest to ward off the assault Sloan looks about ready to rain down on him. "I haven't looked at a thing. I wasn't even here when you were hired. My secretary must have met with you like I asked then I went on the recommendation of the board."

Will's eyes rake over her and land directly on her ample breasts, the memory of her hard, pink nipples force him to adjust himself in his trousers, a garment, he imagines, that is leaving nothing to the imagination.

"Don't look at me like that" Sloan demands.

"What?"

"Like that," she points at him. "Like your dick is in my mouth."

"I enjoyed my dick in your mouth. It's all I've been thinking about since."

"This is completely inappropriate."

Will smiles then laughs at the predicament he's in. She's right. This is completely inappropriate but for once in his life he doesn't care. He gives zero fucks about what others will think or say. He wants this damn girl and her being here right now, as his nurse or otherwise, must be a sign from above. From a god or the force, whatever, he doesn't care as long as he can have her.

"Sloan, listen," he begins.

"No! Fuck, I needed this job."

"And it's yours, sweetheart. We can…"

"Really?" she questions. "You just called me 'sweetheart'. You planning on doing that in the OR?"

"Shit. Sorry, no, I'll try harder to…"

"Good-bye Wilson" she says as she grabs her purse with plans to leave.

At first, Will thinks about letting her go. Honestly, this sticky situation can turn out to be more than it's worth. He should just let her go, have his secretary call the candidate that was second choice and tell them they start tomorrow. But as her hand is reaching for the doorknob he springs into action.

Will takes two long strides and reaches for her hand before it lands on the knob of the door. If she wants to put her hand on a knob, he's got one for her alright. It's trying to burst out of his pants to reach her right now. She can touch his knob all she wants, hell he'll encourage it, but he needs her hand off his door. He needs her to stay with him.

He quickly turns her and before she knows what's about to happen his mouth is on hers, owning her, making her melt into his touch. His tongue licks at her lips then bites her bottom one. "Sloan" he moans as he presses his erection into her belly.

She pulls back, looks down at her feet to gain the courage then says, "Last night didn't happen. I'll keep this job because I need it and working for you is a coveted position but that can't happen again."

Will looks stricken. He wants to talk some sense into her but she's ashen and way too skittish right now to agree to anything. He'll have to take what he can get and at the moment he's thrilled to at least have her as his nurse. He'll wear her down and make her his in every way soon enough. Hell, the chase might even be fun.

"I know what you're thinking" she says.

Will raises his eyebrow at her. "Yeah?"

"You're thinking the chase might be fun. It can't happen, Dr. Anderson. If the situation were different," she shrugs. "I don't know, maybe but it's not and we can't so we're not."

"We can and we should" he says as he slowly closes the space between them.

"Maybe you can, but I can't," she says. "I have to meet with the supervising nurse now."

"Sloan" he tries to stop her before she walks out on him again.

She holds up a hand to quiet him. "Don't."

Sloan leaves and Will falls into the chair behind his desk. His mind is a whirlwind of activity. He knows he should calm down but Christ, she riles him up. He thinks about calling Caine or Jessie to get some perspective but he knows what the pair of them will say. Well, after they spend ten minutes laughing at his expense that is.

He looks down into his lap and groans at the erection he developed just from being in the same room as Sloan. Maybe she's right, maybe this just can't work. He certainly cannot walk around like this in the hospital and if he's going to be near her all day, this looks like his reality.

He stands to pace his office, hoping the effort will calm his dick down. So much for that thought when he shoves his hands into his pockets and finds her panties.

Just as he's lifting them to his face to inhale her scent, his office door opens and Sloan walks back in. She can't help but smile when she sees what he has in his hands. "What were you planning to do with those?" she asks.

"My plan was to put them on my face so I can smell the scent of your sweet pussy while I jerked off behind my desk," he admits with a raised eyebrow. "Care to watch, Miss Hale...or help?"

Sloan leaps into his arms, her mouth clasping over his. He opens for her and their tongues swirl. "We can't do this, Dr. Anderson" she states as she pauses for air and Will begins to kiss her neck.

"Of course not, Miss Hale" he says as she untucks his shirt and pulls. She's too short to get it over his head so he helps. He flings the shirt across the room then reaches for her blouse and starts on the buttons. He'd like to just rip the damn garment open and get to her breasts as quickly as possible but he knows she doesn't have any other clothes. He'll be sure to fix that problem as soon as he can, he'll have a full wardrobe delivered for her so he can rip every single one of them from her body before he spreads her across his desk, an activity he plans on doing numerous times a day.

He smiles at himself at the thought. Who is he? This is not the refined Dr. Wilson Anderson he knows but he likes this new version of himself much better.

Sloan had been busy while he was lost in his head because when his eyes rake over her again, she's in nothing but her bra and panties and reaching for the button on his pants. He can't wait for her tiny fingers to do their job so he yanks on the zipper. In any other state, his pants would have fallen to the floor but with a hard-on raging like this one is, they remain on his hips.

Sloan looks down and smiles as she lowers to her knees in front of him and reaches for his waistband. She pulls it out and over his dick, making sure to torture him with a brush of her finger along the way. "Sloan," he moans. He watches as she parts her lips and her wicked tongue darts out to lick his tip. "Fuck."

Sloan smiles at him from under her lashes then sucks his length into her mouth. She doesn't bother to start off slow, she goes to town on him, bobbing her head and using her hand to take him to the edge. She gets him there in record time and he's forced to pull back before he comes in her mouth. Again. "Sweetheart," he warns. "I don't want to come yet."

She stands in front of him, silent, a plea on the tip of her tongue.

"Sit on the desk and open your legs. Give me your panties first" he orders.

"Starting a collection?"

"Hmmm" he laughs.

He watches as she lowers her panties to the floor then unable to wait, his hands surround her waist and he lifts her to his desk. "Brace yourself on your elbows and watch me" he demands.

"Yessss" she purrs as his tongue gently brushes over her hardened clit.

Will is learning her body. He remembers every second of last night. He knows the sounds she makes when she needs him to go at her harder and the sounds she makes when he's getting her close. The purring sounds he hears now tell him she's right on the edge.

"You gonna come for me, you naughty little nurse, right on my desk?"

"Christ," she sighs. "Please."

Will stands and leans over her body, kissing her mouth as he rifles through his desk drawer with a hand in search of a condom.

"You keep condoms in your desk?" she asks. "At work?"

He just smiles.

"Do you do this often? You didn't seem like the type last night."

"Never done this before," he states. "You're taking my work sex virginity."

"That shouldn't sound as hot as it does. Jesus, Will, fuck me."

"Oh, now it's Will?" he asks as he slides the condom down his length.

As he begins to thrust into her, she defiantly calls out his name again.

"Fuck," he curses as he increases his thrusting. "I can feel your pussy clamping down on me, Miss Hale. You ready to give it up for me this quickly?"

"Yes," she sighs. "Make me come."

"With pleasure, sweetheart. Grip the desk for me and don't let go."

Will begins thrusting harder and deeper into her than he did last night and Sloan's orgasm reaches the pinnacle in record speed. "I'm coming" she cries right before his lips crash onto hers and he grunts and moans into her mouth.

"Me too, baby, come on my dick."

"Yessssss" she calls out as he thrusts into her then pauses before rearing back and filling her to the hilt as his dick swells and he comes with her.

Will's body crashes down on hers and he nips at her ear. "Coming together twice in one day? That must be a world's record."

"Dr. Anderson," they hear as his secretary knocks on his door. "Is everything okay in there?"

"Did you lock the door?" he whispers and Sloan shakes her head. She'd been too anxious to get to this part to remember they could get caught. She closes her eyes, afraid to see the look of horror on his secretary's face if she opens the door.

"Yes, fine, thank you," Will calls out.

"Okay, sir."

"That was close," Sloan says. "See, this is why this won't work. I never should have…"

Will cuts her off with a heated kiss. "Shhh…get dressed. We need to check on one of my," he clears his throat. "I mean our patients then you're going to dinner with me tonight."

Sloan nods. She knows they have a job to do but switching gears that quickly isn't that easy for her.

Will sees the look on her face and knows he's fucked up somehow. "Um…that was good. Are you okay? Did I hurt you? Were you too sore from last night. Jesus, I should have thought of that before I…"

"I'm fine," she says as she pulls her bra on and looks for her panties. She can't possibly have misplaced two pairs in one day. Then she remembers Will had asked for them. "Have you seen my panties?"

He smirks as he tucks his dick into his pants then shrugs on his white lab coat. He places a hand in each pocket then produces a pair of her panties in each hand.

"Will" she admonishes.

"That's Dr. Anderson, sweetheart. Now let's go."

Chapter 9

Will flies through the door of his patient's room with Sloan at his heels to find that Damian's heartrate has increased and is causing the machines to beep at an alarming pace. Beside him, nurses are flying into the room.

"Is he okay?" A man that Will knows is Sydney's dad, Damian's father-in-law, asks. "I didn't mean to upset him. I was just telling him that he needs to beat this for my daughter" Stan states.

Will barks a few orders at the nurses in the room, ignoring Sloan's presence all together. If she wasn't so scared in the moment, her first as a real nurse, she'd be pissed. But she heaves in a deep breath and thanks her lucky stars that he hadn't placed any responsibilities on her shoulders yet. She stands back and watches as the others spring into action and follow his every command.

Will does a quick assessment of his patient then places a gentle hand on the man concerned over his loved one's health. "He's going to be fine," Will says, still looking flushed and disheveled from the earlier activities he engaged in with Sloan. "I actually like that he's showed a response to what you've said. That's very promising" he states as he briefly glances over at Sloan. Stan follows his gaze and Will knows that the man sees that Sloan looks just as flushed and disheveled as he knows he must. Stan smirks at his son-in-law's doctor and Will guesses that the man is laughing to himself. It's clear that he and Sloan had shared a moment together before bursting through this hospital room door. Will's just glad the other nurses, especially Addison, don't seem to have noticed. He'll have to be more careful in the future for Sloan's sake.

"Miss Hale," Will says as he nods towards the door then he turns to the other two nurses in the room. "Monitor him, contact me with any changes."

"Yes, Dr. Anderson. Would you like me to call you if…" Addison begins but is interrupted by Will.

"Have me paged" he replies curtly.

Will catches a look cross over Sloan's features and he quickly leads her out of his patient's room before Addison says or does something else that Sloan can misinterpret. Addison has clearly been trying to gain his attention for more than professional reasons and the last thing Will wants is to have Sloan think that he sleeps with all of his nurses. He's not Caine or Jessie, for Christ's sake.

They make it down the hallway before he notices the change in her coloring. "What's wrong?" Will asks.

"That was Damian Stone."

"And is that a problem?"

"No. I just...holy shit! Damian Stone is our patient?"

"Well, technically mine, but yes. You'll be assisting me on his case. You understand the confidentiality laws I assume?"

"No, I mean yes, of course. I won't say a thing," she sighs. "Is he going to be okay? I heard on the news what happened. He owns my building, you know. I've talked to him a few times. His wife is really sweet and those babies of theirs are too cute."

"On the neuro end of things, time will tell but I predict a full recovery. My friend is his urologist, that end of things might prove to be more complicated. I'm excellent at what I do and so is Caine. Would you agree, Miss Hale? About me being good at what I do?" Will smirks at her. "Now about the dinner I'm taking you to."

But before Sloan has a chance to answer, a voice shrieks over the hospital's PA system. At the same time Will and Sloan's beepers go off. "Dr. Anderson to OR 2," the voice calls. "Dr. Anderson OR 2 STAT."

"Let's go" Will orders Sloan and reaches for her hand to hurry her along.

*****

By the next day, Will is coming down off the adrenaline rush from a four-hour emergency surgery as he exits the OR area after having cleaned up. He hears choking, possibly vomiting and the moans of a female he recognizes. The sounds are familiar, only when he heard them last they were from her pleasure. Now they sound like they're from the opposite of enjoyment.

He turns the corner to find Sloan slumped over a garbage can, heaving into the receptacle, her hair in her red, blotchy face. "Sloan," he calls out, unable to mask his emotions and growing feelings for this girl when he thinks that she's sick or hurt. "What's wrong?" he demands. "Are you ill?"

"Shit," she mutters under her breath and wipes at her mouth. "Nothing's wrong, Dr. Anderson. I'm fine."

"Like hell you are. Let's go."

"What? Wait, I'm not going anywhere. Let me just stay here for a second. I'll be fine."

"And let someone see you like this? They'll judge you, the new nurse, puking after her first surgery. I won't have anyone thinking less of you than you deserve. Those were a rough couple of surgeries and I'm sure not easy as your first. But you did good in there. You did" he reiterates when he sees the doubt on her face.

Sloan nods then turns and finishes emptying her stomach into the garbage can. Will holds her hair out of her face and rubs soothing circles across her back until she settles. Once she does, he lifts her in his arms and carries her in the direction of his office.

"Put me down," she demands. "I can walk. If people see…"

"Shhh. There's no one here. I'm taking you to my office to clean up."

Sloan finally gives in to the warmth of his body and rests her head on his firm chest. Her hands curl around his neck and her fingers lace together. "Mmmm" she purrs without thought.

"Almost there, sweetheart."

"You called me sweetheart again" she whispers.

"Sorry, I'll try harder when we're around the other doctors or nurses but when we're alone, all bets are off. We're here" Will says as he kicks open his office door.

Sloan is thankful that his secretary isn't there to witness this. She's long gone for the night as are many of the staff. It feels eerily quiet in the hospital at this late hour and Sloan wants to just grab her things and go home to regroup until she needs to be back here in a few hours.

"I need to go to the nurses' room to get my stuff, Will. I'm fine now, really. I just want to go home and go to bed."

Will looks at his watch. He's been gone forever and knows Scarlett will be home in a few hours from her weekend sleepover at Aliana's and he needs a shower and take a nap. He'd love to take Sloan to her place and cuddle up with her in bed, rub her back and tell her she'll be fine. Or, take her to his place and bathe her in his tub, soothing her sore, aching muscles then make sweet love to her until she's boneless. But he knows he can't do either of those things so instead he just nods and mumbles something about seeing her in the morning.

"Goodnight, Dr. Anderson. Or good afternoon, this schedule is going to take some getting used to" she says as she slips out of his office.

When Will arrives home he's agitated. He showers and decides on a quick drink to calm his nerves so he can sleep for a few hours before it's Monday morning and he needs to head back in and do the rounds on his patients. He pours himself a calming few fingers of his finest Scotch to settle his emotions then plunks down in his favorite chair to wait for Scarlett to get home.

Never in a million years did he expect the sight of his daughter, not more than a child, to be the cause of more stress, but when the teenager strolls through the door and he gets a glimpse at her clothes, tight shirt and short skirt, then a closer look revealing love bites covering her neck, Will loses his ever loving mind. "What the fuck?" he yells. "That little fucking prick, when I get my hands…"

"Daddy calm down!"

"Calm down? Scarlett Rose you have hickies covering the better part of your neck. Did Ellie see those?"

"No" Scarlett begins to cry.

"Well, I can't see how not. Sit down right there and don't move. I'm calling her," he warns then mumbles, "I don't know how the fuck..."

"No!" Scarlett cries. "You can't call her. She didn't see them. I don't want her to think you're mad at her because of me. She's the closest thing I have to a..."

"Oh Scarlett, honey, I'm sorry," Will says as he goes to his daughter planning to engulf her in his arms but is stopped in his tracks when she folds her arms across her chest. "I can't tell you enough times how sorry I am about that, but Julia..." Will is forced to heave in a deep breath at the sound of her name on his lips. It's a sound he tries to never hear.

He tries to approach her again, take her into his arms like he did when she was a little girl and had fallen and scraped a knee but Scarlett holds him off, this time with a strong hand raised in his direction.

"I know, I know, I know," Scarlett says, her voice agitated and snippy like only a fifteen-year-old girl's voice can be.

Will is still trying to calm himself down, because he realizes that silently planning the death of a teenage boy is probably not a good thing, when his cell bleeps with a text from Ellie, Aliana's mother.

Ellie: *Girls played us. Told me they were with you. Guessing they told you they were here. Aliana is spilling the details now. You're not going to like where they were or who they were with. Frank has lost his mind. I'm sure you can hear him from there.*

Will's response to the woman who has been his neighbor and friend for many years, always there for him to lend a hand with Scarlett, is simple and to the point.

Will: *Get bail money ready. Tell Frank to meet me outside in*

Then he turns to Scarlett and sees red. His little girl marked by some pompous asshole who thinks, because he can dribble a fucking basketball in high school, that he has the right to treat his daughter like nothing more than a cheap piece of ass. He remembers the type well from his days in school. He's always despised the guys who think they're entitled to any girl just because of their social status and can't for the life of him figure out what the hell his daughter sees in this kid. He thought he'd done a better job of raising her and teaching her how to make good decisions. He's guessing now that he was wrong.

Maybe it wasn't all his fault. Maybe some of it was just because the poor girl needed her mother not her best friend's mother or her grandmother. But wasn't that his fault too? Hadn't it been his fault that Julia left them? It was, it had to be. What mother would leave their child unless she couldn't stand to even look at the father of that baby?

Damn it, this is all his fault.

Will turns at the sound of Scarlett crying into her hands. He tries not to let his rage at her or himself take over but it's a losing battle. "I can't fucking believe that you lied to me and your grandmother. You and Aliana went behind our backs and Ellie and Frank's. Where the hell have you been since Ellie picked you up from dance on Friday night?"

Scarlett tries to speak through her tears but now that she's caught she can't control her emotions. She hates upsetting her father, she's always tried to be a good girl for him. She knows how much he sacrifices for her. His own life, friends, women. Scarlett's not dumb. She knows her dad is a young, rich and attractive doctor who could probably date any woman he wanted to but instead, to shield her feelings, he's never had a girlfriend. Scarlett knows that's her fault.

"We were with Johnny and Jack. He loves me daddy. You just don't understand. You don't get it."

Will sees red and pictures himself snapping the kid's neck. He knows exactly where to strike too, right at the brain stem. It'd be over in a second. He downs another finger of his Scotch and tries to speak calmly to the daughter he's about to place on house arrest until she's twenty-one at the earliest.

"Oh, baby girl, listen to me, honey. There's a secret to finding a good guy, a nice one. It's the shy ones, the boys who no one notices right now because guys like Johnny are too busy hogging all the limelight. Those shy ones, the boys who want to hang out in their rooms all weekend and play video games online with their friends, build forts and still go camping with the guys, the boys that no one sees yet, those are the ones that are going to turn into men one day. Boys like Johnny stay boys forever."

"You don't even know him" Scarlett yells as she hops out of the chair she had been hankering down on.

"Baby, I do. I know the type and he's not the kind of boy who deserves a girl like you. You need a boy who will respect you for who you are and not what they can get from you. This Johnny kid is using you, Scarlett. He thinks he owns the world and can do whatever he wants because he's some high school super star. That is not the kind of boy that will grow up to be the kind of man to take you for a walk under the stars and just lay there and hold your hand. You want a guy that will take you to the movies, cuddle with you, hold your hand and fall asleep with you in their arms. This kid would be out of there before he even had his pants up."

"That sounds like what you want daddy. Maybe that's not what I want. Maybe I don't want to end up with a guy like you."

Will looks stricken as her words set in and Scarlett immediately wishes she could take them back. "Daddy, I didn't…"

Will raises his hand to stop her. "If I find out you're having sex with this kid, I won't be held responsible for what I do when I find him. Think about that Scarlett because like the kind of man I am or not, I am your father and I will do anything and everything to keep you safe. You are grounded and not to leave this house other than for school and dance if you're lucky. If I catch you with that little prick again…"

Will is cut off as his daughter storms out of the room screaming that she hates him and wishes she could live with her grandparents. He thinks about telling her he'll gladly drive her to them now and they can start that arrangement pronto but he manages to hold back.

With a grunt, he heads out to his front lawn to see if Aliana's father, Frank, is waiting for him. Frank is heading up his driveway when Will opens the door. The man has two beers in his hand and hands one over to Will then downs his own in two quick swigs. "We might need more" Frank says as he extends his hand to his neighbor.

"I have harder stuff inside. You want some Scotch?"

"Let's talk about what the girls pulled out here first then maybe. You're going to need to be out here so you won't punch a hole through your wall. Trust me, I have the drywall guy coming tomorrow" Frank says, showing Will his swollen knuckles.

Will examines them and nods. "You'll live."

"I might, but that kid my daughter thinks is the shit might not."

"Friend of that Johnny douche my daughter thinks is the best thing to ever walk the face of the earth?"

"Yep, best friend from what Aliana says. Claims they're so smart and come from nice families. They play basketball and would never do anything to hurt them," Frank says in the voice he's perfected when imitating his overdramatic daughter. "They're in love don't you know?"

"Fucking-a, man. Christ, when did they start up with boys?"

"I don't know," Frank says. "I let Ellie deal with that shit," he says then pauses when he realizes that Will doesn't have that luxury. "Sorry. I didn't mean to…"

"Nah, no worries. I knew she had a 'boyfriend' but I never thought it was something I had to worry about yet. Where were they all weekend?"

"From what Ellie and I got out of Aliana, they were at Johnny's. His parents took his oldest sister back to college and left him in charge. I guess the dad's brother was supposed to stop by to be sure they didn't throw a party or whatever but he got called into work and couldn't make it over there."

"I'm having Jessie do an exam. If he fucked my daughter, I'm going to jail."

Frank sighs, removes his glasses to rub his sore, tired eyes, then places them back on. "Ellie told Aliana she's taking her to her doctor too. The little snot just rolled her eyes. I thought my wife was going to rip her head off."

Will nods then reaches for his cell and taps out a text to Jessie Holt, his friend and gynecologist.

Will: *I need you to exam Scar. She spent the weekend with some kid. If he fucked her, I need to know and you should be prepared to help hide the body*

Not more than ten seconds pass before Jessie's response pings on Will's cell.

Jessie: *I am not examining your daughter! I will be over in thirty minutes with Cindy, she'll do the exam while we hide the motherfucker's body! WTF?*

Will spends the next thirty or so minutes listening to Frank fill him in on his daughter's weekend exploits. Per Aliana, they're all friends and stay together as a group, the girls never alone with the boys. She insists that they're not having sex with them, that they've only kissed. Apparently, Johnny likes to let his lips travel around his daughter's body a little more than his buddy Jack does.

"Well, whatever, it's done now. Scarlett is not leaving this motherfucking house unless she's going to school or dance. I even thought about cutting dance off but...I don't know. I'm afraid that would make things worse. I met that choreographer the girls are dying to audition for. I wasn't going to tell her. I was going to wait to surprise her with an autograph, maybe even ask her if she'd let the girls go see her studio. Now, I'm thinking about rubbing it in Scar's face just to piss her off."

Frank pats Will on the back. "Listen, we just need to check in with one another whenever they say they're going somewhere. It sucks that we can't trust them but until they prove we can," Frank shrugs. "Why give them the opportunity to pull this shit again, right?"

Will nods as a car pulls into his circular driveway. He waves at Jessie and Cindy then turns back to Frank. "I'll let you know what happens?"

"Yeah. Call me later, man." And with that Frank waves at Jessie and the other doctor then heads back down the street to his own shit-show.

Jessie is out of the car and demanding an explanation before Cindy can grab her bag from the backseat and approach the men. "What the fuck happened to my little girl? If someone hurt her Will, I can't be held responsible" Jessie says, as protective of Scarlett as her father is.

"It's that Johnny kid. The girls lied to us and spent the weekend with him and his friend at his house. Unsupervised. Scarlett walked in covered in motherfucking hickies!"

"Oh fuck, no. Where's this little prick live?"

Will sighs. He appreciates the support he knew Jessie would offer but the last thing he needs right now is any encouragement. "I'm not even sure. Let's see what Cindy says first. I've already warned Scarlett that if he's having sex with her, I'm kicking his sorry ass."

Jessie nods and runs a hand through his hair. "Yeah, yeah, that's good. Did you call Caine?"

Will shakes his head. "I called you first for obvious reasons. You can text him," Will says as he turns to Cindy. "Cindy, thanks for doing this. Scarlett's in her room. Can you examine her there?"

"Sure but Will, listen, she's a teenage girl with a boyfriend. If it hasn't happened already, it's going to in the not so far off future. I think it's a good idea to get her on birth control just to be safe. I'll do the exam and make up some reason why she needs it, okay? You gave her the vaccine, right?"

Will nods. "Yeah. Fuck, I can't handle this shit."

Cindy smiles then nods sadly at her partner's best friend. "Let's just see what we're dealing with first, okay?"

"Yeah, sure. This way" Will says as he leads Dr. Cindy Baxter into his house.

"I hear you're treating Damian Stone," she states as they enter the foyer. "We um, know each other."

Will raises an eyebrow. Damian Stone either knows a woman because, before he met his wife, he'd fucked her or…well, that's really the only option with the man. "Know each other?"

Cindy blushes and shyly nods. "I was Brook Taylor's OB in California. I…um…I met him when he was there visiting her," she lies to hide the fact that she's a sexual submissive and one of Damian's past subs. "Is he going to be okay?"

"Caine is on his case too. We're the best at what we do so I think so. All confidential, Cindy, okay?"

"Yeah, yeah, sure. I know, please, you don't have to worry about me."

Will isn't sure. He only knows the other doctor through Jessie. Jessie had been looking to add another doctor to his practice a while ago and had thought of his old classmate who had been living in California. One call from him and she'd relocated to the East Coast which had caused Caine and Will some concern. They tried to warn their friend that a woman would only do that for a man she had feelings for but Jessie had just smiled and shrugged them off.

Cindy stops Will at the top of the stairs with a gentle hand to his forearm. "Will, you're a doctor, I'm sure you understand that this is not what should motivate a parent to get their child sexual healthcare. I get it, Scarlett is your daughter but she's going to likely be very angry with you over this regardless of the outcome."

"I know," Will admits. "I'm just not sure what else to do. I've been planning on taking her to a gynecologist for a year or so but…it's tough for her without a mom and my mother, I…"

"You don't need to explain or justify this with me Will, but Scarlett is another thing. You need to be very sure about this before I go in there."

Will nods and shoves his hands into his pockets.

"You also need to know that any doctor who has any kind of knowledge of the female anatomy will look to the state of the hymen to tell them about a woman's sexual activity, but also know that the hymen can break from other causes. And I'm sure I don't need to tell you that not all sex is about vaginal entry. I can't tell you if they've done...other things. And often, intercourse won't fully tear a hymen completely the first time. Especially if he's not that large or didn't enter her roughly. My guess is if they did it, it was probably his first time too and there's a chance that he was barely inside her before he ejaculated. He could have entered her but not reached her hymen."

Will moans and runs his hand through his hair. "Fuck, I can't even think of my daughter..."

"I know," Cindy says. "The teenage years are difficult. You're a good dad, Will. I'll see what I can do, okay? Maybe talk to her a little?"

"Yeah, that'd be great. But ah, what do you need to..." Will asks nervously, not wanting the details of the exam he's ordering to put his daughter through but knowing he'll need to have the information if she ever comes to him to discuss it.

"The test typically involves a check for the presence of an intact hymen but, like I just said, the condition of the hymen alone is often inconclusive. I'll also check the vaginal muscles," Cindy begins to explain as Will leans his back against the wall for support. "I'll need to insert a finger or two into her vagina to check the tightness, that will tell me if she's habituated to sexual intercourse. But if it's only happened once..."

"I get it," Will says, holding up a hand to stop Cindy from providing more details. "What else?"

"Well, vaginal laxity and the absence of a hymen can both be caused by other factors. You understand that the tearing of the hymen may have been the result of some other event? It's a misconception that the hymen always tears when a girl loses her virginity or that intercourse is required to rupture the hymen. Sometimes, once puberty begins, with or without sexual activity, the hymen starts to wear away due to a girl's period, hormones, physical activity like dancing which I know Scarlett does, sometimes even tampon use, as well as from," Cindy clears her throat, "Masturbation."

"Fuck," Will moans as he braces himself on the wall. "Okay, let me know if you need me. I'll stay out here."

"Will, you need to tell her who I am and what I'm going to do. I also plan on doing a full exam and running an STD screen."

Will sighs deeply as he knocks on his daughter's door, only briefly waiting to open it and enters. He and Cindy find Scarlett with her phone in hand.

"I thought I told you that you were grounded. Is that Johnny?" Will asks as Scarlett disconnects the call and quickly erases her call history. "Give me the phone."

"Daddy, no! Please. I promise I won't leave the house but I need my phone. I can't believe you're doing this to me."

"Yeah, well there's a lot of things I can't believe you've been doing either. Scarlett, this is a friend, a colleague, Dr. Baxter. She's here to talk to you and do an exam."

"An exam?" Scarlett asks. "Daddy, I don't need brain surgery because I like a boy."

"Scarlett, I'm a gynecologist" Cindy states with a smile.

"Oh."

"I'll ah…I'll be outside if there's anything…okay then" Will stammers as he leaves the room.

He leans against the wall again for support for what feels like hours before Jessie and Caine appear on the landing of his second floor.

"Jessie called me," Caine begins. "I have the shovel in the car whenever you're ready."

Will knows Caine is most likely joking but he also knows that if he was honestly planning to kill anyone, it would be these two men digging the hole for the body alongside him.

"Thanks," Will says. "Maybe we should wait downstairs?"

The trio move to the living space and each pour themselves their drinks of choice. Scotch for Will, a beer for Caine and gin for Jessie.

"How old is the fucker?" Caine asks.

"Her age, I think."

"Sounds about right. I lost my virginity around that time, man. I know it sucks that it's our baby girl but…" Will shoots Caine a scathing glare and he stops midsentence. "Okay, too soon."

"Let's talk about something else to get your mind off this for a minute. How's the new nurse?" Jessie asks.

Will rolls his eyes and sighs. "Another problem I'm currently having."

Caine and Jessie smirk at each other then send Will a look that says they're on to him.

"Do tell" Caine says.

"Yes, and don't omit any of the details," Jessie says. "It's not every day you get laid."

"It's all your fault, asshole. You left me in that restaurant alone" Will says.

Jessie raises an eyebrow at his friend. "Wait, what does me not making dinner the other night have to do with your new nurse?"

Will shares every detail, well, almost every one. He conveniently leaves out the orgasm Sloan had made him have in his pants because really, his friends don't need that kind of ammunition to hold over him. As he's explaining how they parted ways, Will heading home, unclear as to where he stands with Sloan, Cindy descends the stairs and enters the living space.

The three men hurl themselves to their feet, all demanding information at the same time.

"Can you all take a seat please," Cindy asks. "You're making me nervous all demanding answers like that."

"Sorry," Jessie says. "Go ahead, we'll be quiet."

"Will," Cindy asks. "Can I speak freely in front of them?"

"Of course, Scar is like a daughter to them. I tell them everything."

Cindy nods then takes a seat and accepts the water Jessie has poured for her. She looks up at him and smiles. She could get used to being taken care of like this. If only Jessie saw her as more than a friend. She clears her throat to bring herself back to the issue at hand. Her love life will have to wait.

"Okay, so you're all doctors and have a general knowledge of a woman's body" Cindy begins.

"Excuse me," Caine interrupts. "I won't speak for the two of them but I have way more than a 'general understanding' of a woman's body."

Cindy rolls her eyes then looks at Jessie when she feels his stare. He smirks as if he'd like to do something about that bratty habit of hers. She nervously wipes her palms on her thighs, clears her throat again, and continues. "What I meant was…"

Caine laughs. "Yes?"

"Ugh," Cindy moans. "Just listen. The hymen is a ring of fleshy tissue that sits just inside the vaginal opening."

"Yes, it is" Caine laughs again.

Cindy sends him a warning glare. "Normal variations range from thin and stretchy to thick and somewhat rigid. It's not always easy to determine if it's intact exactly."

"I've found a few," Caine says. He catches the glares of the others and asks, "What?"

"Okay, well is Scarlett's intact or not?" Will asks.

"Somewhat is the best answer I can give you but as I warned you before I did the exam, with dance and…"

"Fuck!" Will moans.

"Let her finish," Jessie interjects. "Were there other signs of…activity?"

"I can't listen to this," Will says. "Did he take her virginity or not? I need to know if I need to just scare this kid or kick his ass."

"Okay so for sure, if she'd done anything last night, I would have a good idea if she'd had some kind of sex or not. If she'd had vaginal intercourse with him without using a condom and he ejaculated, there would be traces of ejaculate."

"Jesus fucking Christ" Caine swears.

"And her vaginal tissue might look a little redder or pronounced, but that could be the case from masturbation as well so it's hard to tell. Scarlett had a lot of questions that I promised not to share with you. She didn't protest when I told her I was going to order her birth control pills. My best guess is," Cindy pauses to be sure these three otherwise strong males can hear this. "There's been…um…manual stimulation. Either on her own, with the boyfriend, or both."

Will, Caine, and Jessie moan in unison then each gulp down their drinks.

"Son of a fucking bitch" Jessie says.

"She had a lot of questions about different sex acts so I think they've been talking about experimenting. It's good she's had the vaccine and now she'll be protected against unwanted pregnancy. They'll need condoms to protect against STDs."

"I can't deal with this" Will says, hand shooting to his forehead, a headache beginning low below the surface.

"We knew she'd become a woman one day," Caine says. "I just never thought it would happen so soon."

"She's not a woman, dickhead. She's not even sixteen," Will says. "What the fuck do I do now?"

"You be her dad. Let her know she can talk to you and you won't explode again like you've been doing since she got home today," Cindy says.

Will huffs with a roll of his tight shoulders and a twist of his neck. The kink settling into his neck is going to send him to the chiropractor by the end of the week.

"Tell her she can contact me at any time and I'll be more than happy to answer her questions or provide her with whatever she needs."

The sound of an emergency alert has them all reaching for their pockets, Jessie pulling out his cell first to find it's him being paged by the hospital. "That's me. I gotta go. Cindy?"

"I'll ride in with you. I have patients to check in on. Can you give me a ride home later, though?"

"Sure" Jessie says then turns to pat Will on the shoulder. "Call me if you need help lugging the body."

"Thanks," Will says with an eye roll. "Later. And Cindy, thank you. I can't tell you how much I appreciate you coming over here and doing this today."

Cindy nods. "No problem. Talk to her, Will. She's an amazing young woman. You've done a great job with her but she still needs her daddy, okay?"

"Yeah," Will says. "I will."

Not a minute later, Will's cell goes off with a 911 alert about the patient he had just operated on.

"Fuck, I have to go in too. Can you?" he asks Caine.

"Of course. I'll call Milly and put her on standby in case you're not back by the time I have to leave."

"Thanks" Will says as he takes the stairs two at a time to tell his daughter he'll be home as soon as he can and that she's to stay at home with her Uncle Caine until he returns. No questions asked.

Chapter 10

After another close call in the OR, Sloan had soared out of there. Will is worried over her ability to acclimate into the job but it's still early days. He knows if she can't hack the pressure, the situations that he faces during surgery, he'll have to find himself another nurse.

But that's not really what his issue is, pissing her off is. If he must reassign her, he knows she'll never let their budding romance get off the ground. She's been acting skittish around him already. He plans to change that with another dinner invitation as soon as he checks in on Damian Stone and his family.

The only one in the family room that Will had had assigned to the Stone Family is Brook Taylor, the very person he was hoping to find.

"Hey" he says in greeting, heading over to shake the very attractive dancer's hand.

"Dr. Anderson, how's our patient today?"

"I'm heading in to see him now. I wanted to check in with the family first, see if you had any questions."

"Well, it's just me for now, Tate went to get me a coffee. It's my secret pleasure. Some of the others went home to grab a quick shower and Syd and her mom are in with Day."

"Actually, I wanted to talk to you so I'm glad you're here" Will admits.

Brook raises an eyebrow. "You want to ask me about my coma?"

"Um, well, yeah I guess I'd love to talk about that but that's not what I was going to ask you," Will says indicating she should sit back down in her chair. She had gotten up to shake his hand. He sits next to her and angles himself so he's facing Brook. "It's about my daughter."

"Let me guess, she's a dancer, right?"

Will smiles sadly, he doesn't want to bother Brook with this, he feels weird doing it but he doesn't know what else to do to help Scarlett. Maybe if she was dancing in Brook's workshop, she'd have less time and inclination to be with Johnny. "And your biggest fan" he offers with a weak smile and a little chuckle.

Brook smiles kindly. "You saved Damian's life, Dr. Anderson. Tell me what you want and I'll see to it."

"My daughter and her best friend have wanted to audition for your workshop for over a year…"

"My-my workshop? You understand that's by invitation only?"

"I do. It's all Scar talks about. Well, until that Johnny kid came along."

Will fills Brook in on Scarlett's dance background then the saga of her new favorite activity. Brook laughs when Will shares that Johnny is the star basketball player at Scarlett's school. "They sound like Tate and I. Where do they go to school?"

Will names off Scarlett's Connecticut high school and laughs when Brook tells him that's where she and Tate attended and that Tate has been meaning to go watch Johnny play, Johnny getting close to a school record or two held by Tate. "We live in the same town, Dr. Anderson and I would love to help you out but I can't promise Scarlett a spot until I see her dance. Where does she study?"

Will had known that Brook and Tate grew up in his hometown. They'd graduating not long before he, Caine, and Jessie has entered.

Will gives Brook Scarlett's studio schedule then reluctantly asks her to also consider Aliana.

"Well, now that's going to cost you. I have twins. I'll drop them by this weekend then we'll call it even."

Will laughs but agrees to rearrange his schedule to watch Zach and Zoe.

"I was joking, Dr. Anderson" Brook laughs even though a few hours alone with Tate sounds wonderful.

"Will, please, call me Will."

"Fine. Will," Brook smiles. "I'll get to one of their classes this week. Take my cell and call me if their schedules change. And Will," Brook calls as he's edging towards the door. "Good luck with that boyfriend. From what I hear, he's the second coming of Tate Taylor. And take it from me, that could be trouble for a teenage girl."

Will groans then nods and heads towards Damian's room.

As Will enters his patient's room he finds Damian's wife and mother-in-law on either side of his bed. Damian appears to be covered in a sheen of sweat and he's twitching and moaning. Will listens as Samantha Blake Cooper explains how Damian had cried out during his climax one night in her hotel room. He had heard the rumors and had done a little research after taking Damian on as his patient. He hadn't believed the tabloids, assumed the stories were fabricated to sell the rags but now, hearing Samantha describe the events, he figures he was wrong.

He can't imagine finding out that he'd slept with the mother of a girl he was in love with and insistently, Sloan comes to mind. Shit, is he already having feelings that strong for her? Yep, he knows full well that he is, has been since the second he'd laid eyes on her.

Before Will can understand his feelings for Sloan, Damian cries out in pain or maybe ecstasy, it's hard to tell but what is obvious to Will, because it had just happened to him, is that Damian Stone has just had an orgasm in his pants or in his state or dress, hospital gown. Before Will springs into action he allows himself to revel in the situation. If a guy like Damian can be brought to an orgasm while unconscious, then maybe there wasn't any shame in how Sloan had made him come that first night. Not that he plans to tell anyone, but it does help his ego.

As Will stands and watches his patient come long and hard, his eyes flying open, filled with pain, pleasure, and utter confusion, he raises an eyebrow at Sydney Stone then her mother. Damian Stone looks just as confused as he is by the events.

"Fuck!" Damian cries, his body lifting from the bed then crashing back down. His eyes roll into the back of his head and Sydney cries out.

"No!"

Samantha wraps her arms around her daughter as the machines attached to Damian begin to beep and sound alarms. The medical team flies in the room and Will finally springs into action and begins shouting orders. "Call Dr. Cabrera," he demands. "Tell him there's been an," he clears his throat and knowingly glances at Sydney. "Event."

Will thanks his lucky stars that his friend and colleague is Dr. Caine Cabrera, a world renown urologist and the specialist on his patient's case, is as good at his job as Will is at his because if he's going to have a full recovery, Damian Stone needs the best doctors.

*****

While Will is with Damian, Sloan enters the nurse's room to try to hold back another vomit session. No such luck. She lunges into the stall and empties her stomach. Well, at least she won't have to worry about a diet while working here. She should drop five pounds by the end of her first week. She slumps down on the floor, thankful that the place is kept meticulously clean and sterile, and practices her deep breathing techniques from her yoga classes.

"Hey," a voice calls. "You okay?"

"I'm, um...I'm fine. Just had some bad sushi last night, I guess. Um, thanks for asking" Sloan answers.

"Come on out. You don't want to sit on the floor. I'll get you a cold, wet cloth."

"Okay, um thanks," Sloan says as she heaves herself up off the floor and opens the bathroom stall. "Hi," she says to the kind nurse. "I'm Sloan Hale, Dr. Anderson's new nurse."

Sloan thinks she sees something cross the face of the other woman, some emotion she can't quite put her finger on, but she brushes it off as low blood sugar from vomiting that is making her see things that aren't really there.

"Addison," she says. "I'm one of the nurses here too. I work the ER. I fill in for the doctors when they need an extra nurse from time to time. Congrats on the job. We'd all heard Wilson was getting a newbie. I guess I can see why he picked you."

Sloan doesn't know what to say to that. Why does that 'getting a newbie' comment not sit right with her? And why did he pick her? Well, he hadn't really, had he? No, he'd let his secretary and board decide. "Um, yeah, it's my first real job as a nurse" she admits. No sense in hiding the truth.

"It's strange how the best neurosurgeon in the country, possibly the world, would take on a nurse who has no experience in the field, don't you think? I mean other than the obvious."

"Um," Sloan stammers, getting the feeling that maybe this Addison chick isn't as nice as she had originally thought. "I'm not sure."

Addison smiles a smile too big, too fake for Sloan's liking and if this interaction had occurred outside of the work environment, Sloan would have put this girl in her place. But here, at the hospital, she needs to earn her dues and bide her time. She's the low woman on the totem pole and creating waves isn't the way to go.

"Well, be careful with him. I'm sure you've heard the stories already" Addison says with a smile and a shrug of one shoulder.

Sloan clears her throat and takes the cold, wet cloth Addison offers. "Stories?" she asks.

Addison laughs. "Not from the city are you? Okay listen, here's the thing, this is not some small-time backwoods hospital. The doctors here are the best at what they do and they have the egos to show it. The word 'no' is not something they hear often. Dr. Anderson and his pals, Doctors Cabrera and Holt are the perfect example. Between the three of them, they've slept with every female in this hospital, some of them simultaneously, none of them twice. I even hear they're into really hardcore kinky shit like your patient, Damian Stone."

"Oh" Sloan says. That would make sense she figures. Maybe Damian had chosen this hospital for that very reason. No. His family had decided on his treatment as he was incapable of making any decisions and they'd gone with the best. Will was the best.

"Well, just watch yourself. It's a big hospital but we all know what goes on. You'd be best served if you did your job and kept your legs closed around Dr. Anderson."

Sloan sucks in a quick breath, nods, and feels her stomach churn again. "Excuse me" she gasps as she flies back into the stall to puke once more.

She doesn't see the evil smile that crosses Addison's face before she leaves the nurse's room.

*****

After finally giving up on his search through the hospital for Sloan, Will finds Caine and once again goes to check in on Damian Stone. But as soon as he's done with his patient, if he can't find the damn girl, he's having her paged to his office. Fuck it, she's his nurse, it shouldn't raise suspicions. Hell, Ellen was in his office alone with him all the time. Okay, so maybe he wants Sloan in his office for much different reasons but whatever.

"Day," Sydney Stone begins the introductions. "This is Dr. Wilson Anderson. He's a neurosurgeon. He saved your life when they brought you in here."

"Nice to meet you, Mr. Stone," Will says. "I've heard a lot about you. This is Dr. Caine Cabrera, your urologist."

Caine, in dark blue scrubs, reaches out to shake his hand first then Will reaches out and smiles warmly into their embrace.

Damian glances at his wife and his look says it all. "You hired the best looking doctors the hospital had to offer I see. Something we'll discuss when we get home."

Sydney laughs. "As if I can even see them with you in the room."

She brings her lips to Damian's and offers him a gentle kiss. Will watches as Damian briefly hardens their kiss, opening her lips with a slight brush of his tongue. It reminds him of Sloan. Fuck. He needs to pull his head out of his ass and focus on his patient instead of his dick. Speaking of that, he shifts in his pants, already growing hard thinking about Sloan.

Damian pulls back and raises an eyebrow at Will and Caine who have been watching the couple's reunion. "And we'll be dealing with you almost dying on me first," Sydney states before kissing her husband's nose then turning to Will and Caine. "I'd apologize and say he wasn't himself but…" Sydney begins to say to Will and Caine but is cut off by Will who is admittedly in a hurry to find Sloan and ask her to dinner.

"No need for apologies. I'm just thrilled that he's awake and talking," Will says. "You gave us a scare when you first woke up. Is there anything I can get you? Are you in any pain?"

Damian pauses for a moment. "I'm thirsty and probably need a toothbrush."

Will smiles as he reaches for the water pitcher and a cup on the table near Damian's bed. "I'll call my nurse and have her help you in a bit. One of your friends brought you items from home."

Good, this will give Will an excuse to locate the illusive Sloan Hale and ask her to help their patient then grant him the pleasure of her company at dinner. If all goes well, after that maybe he'll ask her to join him in bed.

Damian looks at Sydney as he reaches for the glass of water Will hands him.

"Alex" Sydney says, referencing Damian's best friend since the first day of college and explaining who brought his toothbrush and other belongings to the hospital.

"And pain?" Will inquires again.

"In the head you're worried about? No, not really. But um, the one that's his specialty?" Damian says with a look in Caine's direction. "Yeah, kind of. It's weird. Painful, raw, I guess, tingly and…" he trails off as he looks to his wife.

"What?" she asks.

Damian shifts uncomfortably, not wanting to ask his wife to leave but also not sure about what is happening in his pants and what her reaction might be.

"Don't even think about asking me to leave because the answer is no."

Damian smiles again at the sass in his wife's voice. "I'm fucking hard and it kills" he admits.

"Okay," Caine states. "Let me do a full exam and see what we're dealing with. I've checked you over a few times and I'm pleased with the responses I've gotten and the healing process your body has already begun. The erection might be from," he clears his throat and glances at Sydney, still in her husband's arms, and remembers how they were laying together in bed when he'd entered the room with Will. "Natural causes."

Sydney smiles as she raises her eyebrows at her husband. Damian tickles her side then says, "Yeah, I tend to be hard around her all the time."

Caine nods in complete bewilderment, the doctor never with one woman for more than a night and never for more than just sex. Hot, wet, dirty sex. "Would you like her to stay then for the exam?"

"I'm not going anywhere" Sydney says with a hand going to her rounded abdomen.

"Hey," Damian exclaims. "You okay, baby?"

"Yeah, I'm fine. The baby is just kicking around. It's nothing, Day. Trust me, I've had three babies already. I know labor pains when I feel them and this is not that."

"Okay, she can stay," Damian says to Caine then turns towards his wife. "If you can handle seeing...I'm not sure what..."

"Shhh," Sydney soothes. "I've been in here through every one of your exams. I've seen it. It's fine, Day, really. It's okay, don't be scared. You're going to be fine and I'm with you, by your side through everything."

Damian is brought to tears again and he cuddles Sydney close to his body then kisses her temple and inhales her hair.

"I'll give you some privacy," Will says, uncomfortable with the emotions he's feeling from watching the couple and the fact that he's placing himself and Sloan in their roles. "I'll send my nurse in to help you with your personal care in a few minutes."

That is as soon as he finds her, kisses her senseless then makes her agree to dinner and...after.

"Thank you. For everything, thank you" Damian says with tears filing his eyes.

Will smiles and nods as he leaves the room in search of the woman who he can't seem to get out of his mind. After a quick circuit through the hospital, Will finds himself in front of the nurses' room door contemplating if he should go in or not. Just as he's about to open the door, a group of nurses exit. When they see him they stop talking as if he'd been their topic of conversation. Then they chuckle and he knows the chances that he was right were very good. He just hopes their gossiping didn't include Sloan.

"Miss Dentin," he says grabbing one of the young nurse's arm. "Have you seen Miss Hale? I need to speak to her about my patient and I can't seem to locate her anywhere."

The other nurses chuckle and Will sends them a warning glare over Nurse Dentin's head.

"Um, yeah. She's in there. I don't think she feels well. Do you want me to…"

Will is through the door before the nurse can offer to get Sloan for him. When he rounds the corner, he's stopped short at the sight in front of him. Sloan in scrubs on her bottom half, her torso bare. "Sloan" he moans.

Sloan covers her exposed breasts then turns her back on him. "Dr. Anderson! What are you doing?"

"I was looking for you. Amanda said you were in here and sick? Are you okay?"

"I'm fine. What did you need?"

Will tries to approach her but she fastens her bra, pulls on a top and grabs her bag to leave before he can get within a foot of her. "I…I, um…Damian needs assistance."

What a chicken-shit he is.

"Fine, then my shift is over and I'll be going home."

"Yeah, sure. Um…I also thought that maybe…" Will begins but stops as he's chasing her to the bank of elevators and can't now ask her to dinner in front of the group of doctors waiting to climb in.

Will steps in behind Sloan and three other doctors follow them.

"Are you going to follow me to his room? I assure you I can handle giving a patient a sponge bath and a bedpan."

Will smiles at her spunk. He's well aware of how good a sponge bath from Sloan Hale would be and he's sure Damian Stone will appreciate that fact as well. His wife, maybe not so much.

When the elevator makes its first stop, the other doctors exit leaving Will alone with Sloan. "I've been wanting to go to Damian's restaurant for some time now, check it out. You want to…"

"Maybe Doctors Cabrera and Holt would like to go with you" she says.

Will frowns. "Um, yeah. I'd like you to come with me instead."

"I'm not going out with you, Dr. Anderson. You're my boss and whatever happened in the past, before I knew that fact, is over."

"Before you knew? What about the other…"

"It's over, okay? I'm not having sex with you."

"Did I ask you to have sex with me? I don't think I said anything about sex, just a meal. But do you want to have sex with me again?"

"I-I-I…Ugh!" Sloan moans. "We need to set boundaries, Dr. Anderson."

Will backs her up against the wall then traps her between his strong arms. "Limits, rules are made to be broken, Miss Hale."

"We need to agree and understand each other. You need to respect my wishes. I will not be another of your plaything nurses for you to share with your pals," she seethes. "What was it the other night, my audition? Did I pass and now you want another try with Cabrera or Holt, both maybe?"

Will recoils. The thought of anyone, especially his two best friends, being intimate with this girl makes him want to hit things. Hard. And what the hell was she talking about? He'd never had a 'plaything' in his life. He wouldn't know the first thing about that. Caine and Jessie, maybe, but how the fuck did they even become a part of this conversation?

"What the hell are you talking…"

The elevator doors open and Will is forced to remain silent in front of the group of doctors that enter and nod in his direction. "Anderson," Dr. Oliver Felstead, Chief of Pediatrics, says. "And is this your new nurse that I've been hearing about?" he asks.

Will loathes this man. He doesn't hate many people but Ollie, yeah, Ollie he hates. Hates his stupid name, his practical jokes, his hair and those ridiculous childish scrubs he wears claiming they're for his young patients. Bullshit, they're for attention and nothing else.

Will rolls his eyes but is forced to make the introduction. "Sloan Hale, this is Dr. Felstead, peds. Felstead, Miss Hale, *my* nurse." Had he stressed the word my? He fucking hopes so.

Ollie extends his hand and when Sloan reaches out he turns hers over and plants a gentle kiss to the inside of her wrist. "You can call me Ollie, sugar. Welcome."

"Seriously, Felstead, tone it down," Will warns. "This is a hospital not the nightclub district."

"Someone is very protective of their new nurse," Ollie teases. "Better watch out for this one, Miss Hale. He might try to put the moves on you in his office" Ollie laughs, thinking that Will has no game and would never proposition a woman, let alone his subordinate in his office.

Little does he know. Asshole.

The elevator arrives on Damian Stone's floor and Will leads Sloan out with a hand to the dip of her back, marking his territory. Fuck it, if Ollie knows it. He wants the dick to know all about his claim on his girl so he'll keep his distance.

Sloan bats his hand away and begins to walk with a purpose to their patient's room.

Will should have known better than to think that his claim on Sloan would have deterred Ollie or that Sloan would have allowed it.

"Miss Hale, I'll be in the cafeteria if you'd care to join me when you finish up with Dr. Willie" Ollie calls out before the doors can close.

"Really?" Will asks. "Glass houses, man."

Ollie smiles as the doors close. "Pleasure, Miss Hale."

Will looks at Sloan and frowns at her expression. Was she thinking about meeting him after she's finished with Damian?

"Well, he seems nice. Are you two close?"

"Sloan, stay away from him. He's trouble."

"Hmmm…sounds familiar."

"What are you…"

Sloan opens Damian Stone's door and Will is forced to follow her inside. "Hey Damian!" she says. "Syd!"

"Hey Sloan, what are you doing here?" Damian asks.

"I work for Dr. Anderson now."

Damian smirks as he raises his eyes to his doctor. Then he out and out chuckles as he watches Will run a frustrated hand through his hair. "Oh, man!"

Sydney jumps in to the rescue. "Listen Sloan, if you can just get us what we need and set up, I'll be fine to bathe him."

"No, no, no," Damian says with a smirk in his doctor's direction. "You're my wife, baby, you shouldn't have to be my caretaker. It can affect the magic. Let Nurse Sloan here do her new job."

Sydney knows what Damian is up to. She picked up on the sexual tension between Sloan and Will the minute the door opened, she knows it's not something her husband missed. She knows Damian is just giving his doctor a hard time and she's happy to see her husband's personality hasn't been affected by the trauma he experienced. She also knows, he'd never make Sloan, one of his tenants, bathe him. Any woman for that matter.

"Sloan, maybe you should listen to Sydney. I hadn't thought about you living in his apartment building when I told you to…"

"Yeah," Sloan interrupts. "I'm kind of hungry anyway. Maybe I'll head down to the cafeteria for a quick bite to eat before I head home. Is there anything I can grab for you while I'm there?" she asks Damian.

"Wait," Will says. "I thought your shift was done? Head home now and get some rest. I told you I wanted to go to…"

Syd and Damian look at each other, not really sure what's going on between Will and Sloan but enjoying every moment.

"Okay," Sloan interrupts Will. "See you guys later. Glad you're okay, by the way" she says with a quick wave to the amused couple.

"Sloan," Will calls. "Wait up," He turns towards his patient. "I'll send another nurse to help you. Just give me a minute."

Damian laughs. "You got your hands full, go deal with that one. My wife is not about to let another woman, nurse or not, see me naked. And the thought of Syd playing nurse has many possibilities."

Sydney blushes as Will races from Damian's room to catch Sloan. He chases her down the hall to the elevator but she's already securely inside and the door closes in his face.

Was that a smirk on hers that he saw as the doors closed?

Will growls. This woman is impossible.

Chapter 11

Will can't explain what the hell has gotten into him as he approaches the front desk of Stone Towers and introduces himself as the owner's doctor.

"How is Mr. Stone? We're all very worried" Pedro asks. Pedro is a kind looking man who seems to genuinely be concerned over his boss's well-being.

"He's recovering nicely. I expect him to be home in just another day or two."

Pedro nods. "So what can I help you with today, Dr. Anderson?"

"Um, my nurse. S-Sh-She's um...she's new and working with me on Mr. Stone's case. I'm worried about her and came over to check to be sure she's, um, that she's okay. It's a hard job, you understand?"

"Of course, sir. I'll call to her apartment and tell her you're here. What's her..."

"No!" Will cries out. He can't alert Sloan to his presence or she might not allow him to head up to see her.

He chuckles to alleviate the tension he just created by bursting out with that last response of his. Fuck, he was losing his shit and quick. "I mean," another light chuckle so the man won't think he's a serial killer. "Sorry. It's just she's nervous about this new job and I'm afraid she won't want me to see her crying over her fears. I just need to reassure her that she's doing great. She's amazing, actually."

That last part just sort of slipped out and Pedro smiles at the doctor. "I'm sure she is. Just let me call up to Mac and have him okay you. You understand, I'm sure? Security in this building must remain in place especially after what's just happened with Mr. Stone."

"No, I mean, yes of course. Mac will approve me. Uh, her name is Sloan. Sloan Hale."

"Oh, Miss Hale. Yes, she's a pretty one. Lives with Katherine. She's a doll that one too but that boyfriend of hers," Pedro says making a face of distaste. "Now him, I don't like. You, I like, Dr. Anderson."

Will smiles but wonders why he keeps hearing that this boyfriend of Sloan's friend is such a jerk. Why would a girl like Katherine put up with shit from any guy? She's smart and beautiful and funny. Sloan seems worried over her and Will doesn't like that at all. Will also certainly can't see Sloan putting up with anything of the sort from a man. Hell, she seemed to have her panties in a bunch earlier over something he's sure he didn't do. What that is, he'd love to know sooner than later in case he needs to prepare for a hit to the family jewels. Yeah, Sloan Hale is definitely a girl who fights dirty.

"Dr. Anderson?"

Will looks at Pedro. Had he been speaking to him? Christ, Sloan has done a job on him. "Yes, sorry. Just thinking about a case."

Pedro nods. "Mac cleared you. Sloan's in apartment 1A. First floor."

"Thanks."

"Oh, and Dr. Anderson?"

"Yeah," Will asks as he turns to look over his shoulder.

"Mac says 'Good luck' and trust me, with that spitfire, you're going to need it."

Will nods and heads to the stairwell, opens the door calmly then, once out of sight, he flies up the stairs three at a time and bursts through the door to the first floor. He realizes, a bit too late, that the apartment building's entry is open, from the lobby you can see each floor and Pedro has just witnessed him catapulting himself through the door to Sloan's hallway. The kind man laughs and sends Will a salute. Will shakes his head. He's caught and there's nothing he can do about it but laugh at himself.

He makes his way to Sloan's apartment and stops short when he hears a squealing sound coming from the other side of her door. Jesus, he hadn't thought about coming here and finding her squealing. Who the hell was in there with her making her squeal like that? It had better not be Oliver Fucking Felstead or so help him God. You know what? It had better not be any guy. None.

Then he hears her voice and it gets worse.

"Yes, that feels good, baby, doesn't it?" she asks in a sing song voice.

More squealing.

And yes, he only hears this because his ear is pressed to her door by now.

More squealing. And…wait, was that a snort?

Jesus Christ, what the fuck was she doing? And he'd heard her voice so the squeals weren't coming from her. Fuck, what the hell was she doing in there to Ollie to illicit those sounds from him? The man is such a fucking pig so God only knows. Then Will remembers what she did to him with her tongue in that hotel room. He's sure he made a similar sound. Maybe he's a pig too.

"Hold still, we're almost done" she says.

That's it. Will bangs on her door. "Sloan, open the door."

"Will?" Sloan asks as she flings open her door. "What the hell?"

Before Will can speak, he feels something wet on his ankle, looks down, and squeals himself. "Is that a pig?"

Thank fucking God it's a pig and not a man in here with her.

"A teacup pig, yes."

"Teacup?" Will questions. Teacup, coffee mug, fucking thermos, as long as it was not a man making those sounds while Sloan got him off, he can care less. Will adjusts himself in his scrubs that leave nothing to the imagination and clears his throat.

"Yes, she's a teacup pig not a Wilbur turn into b-a-c-o-n pig."

"You just spelled bacon," Will says as another pink pig comes leaping in his direction. "How many of these pigs do you have in here?"

"Three," Sloan says and on cue the third of the three little pigs makes a showing. "That's Polly," she says pointing to the first pig who is still running her nose on the exposed flesh at Will's ankle. "And that's Poppy. Oh, no here's my baby. This one is Petunia."

"Polly, Poppy, and Petunia?" he asks. "The three little pigs?"

"Yes, Polly, Poppy, and Petunia. Did you come here to critique the names of my pigs?"

Will chuckles. "No, I did not but the fact that you have pigs is very…"

"What?"

"I really don't know yet but it's definitely something, Sloan. I can tell you that. It's definitely something."

Sloan reaches down and rustles up her trio of pigs then cuddles them close to her chest like a protective mother who has just spied the big bad wolf.

"Hmmmm" she hums.

Will reaches out a hand to the pig trio only to pull his prized extremity back as they protest his peace offering. Loudly.

"Sorry, they're not used to men. The only guy they've ever been around really is Mike and I think I've already explained that he's a dick."

"Speaking of which, why the hell is Katherine marrying him if he's such an asshole?"

"She's not going to marry him" Sloan says as she walks over to a dog bed, made for a Chihuahua, and places the three little pigs down.

Will laughs.

"What?"

"I can't help but think of them as the three little pigs."

"Well, maybe that's because you're the big bad wolf" Sloan says with a defiant raise of her chin.

"Me?" Will laughs again. "You have somehow gotten the wrong idea about me."

"Is that so?" she asks. "You can come in, you know. You don't need to hover in the doorway. They're little, they're not going to maul you."

"Maybe I want to be mauled" he says as he stalks her.

"Will, I…"

"Come to dinner with me, Sloan" Will says as he reaches to place his hands on her waist and pull her in close to him.

"I just ate lunch" she whispers, a little out of breath with him so close.

Will rolls his eyes and steps back then his hand pulls its way through his hair. "With that douchebag?"

"Will we can't date. You're my…"

"So we can have elevator make out sessions and sex in my office but you can't date me because I'm your boss? Oh, and it's fine for you to date Ollie?"

Polly squeals, thinking Will just said her name. He raises an eyebrow at Sloan. "What?" she asks. "They're very intelligent pets."

Will moans. "Sloan, please," he begs. "It's just dinner and we don't need to go now," He looks down at his watch. "I can come back at say, 8pm and pick you up."

Will's cell rings and he glances down at the caller ID to see that it's his mother who he knows must have Scarlett in her care, Caine needing to have been at the hospital hours ago.

"Sorry," he apologizes. "I need to take this" Will walks a few steps away from Sloan but in the open space there's no privacy so he'll have to make this short. "Hey, Ma, everything good?"

"Uh, not really. You should probably head home if you can. I've dealt with the situation but I know you're going to want to discipline her your way."

"What happened?"

"I found that boy with Scarlett in her room."

"Fuck!" he swears. "Sorry, yeah hold tight. I'll be right there" Will says and ends the call. He looks at Sloan. "Sorry, I have to run. Um, rain check on tonight, okay?"

"I already told you, I'm not dating my boss."

"We'll talk about this tomorrow. Sorry" Will says as he runs from her apartment as quickly as he ran to it.

God damn teenagers!

And nurses.

Women in general.

Chapter 12

Will makes it back to Connecticut in record time and flies through his front door. "Fucking shit," he sputters as he stubs his toe on the damn side table where he always throws his keys. And without fail, always stubs his toe.

"Wilson," his mother scolds. "That mouth!"

"Sorry. Where is she and what the hell happened?" he asks as he hops on one foot and rubs the other with his hand.

"She's in her room crying and I'm sure listing all the reasons why she hates me right now. Embarrassing her in front of Johnny is top on the list from what I can gather through her tears."

Will hates this. Hates that his mother can't just be grandma and enjoy Scarlett. Milly is forced to play mother with Scarlett from time to time, today being one of them, and Will knows it upsets her. "I'm sorry, Ma. I'll tell her you were only acting under my strict orders. She hates me already."

Milly smiles. "She doesn't hate you."

Will laughs.

"Okay, she hates you right now but she won't for long" Milly states with confidence and experience.

"How long?"

"Well, your sister hated me until she left for college then she came around."

"Great," Will mutters. "So what happened?"

Milly explains the afternoon she's had to her son, glossing over a few of the finer points. There's no reason she should include that when she walked into Scarlett's room she and Johnny had been attached at the lips. They did have their books out and he seemed like a polite boy, all red in the face with a pillow in his lap. She shuttered to think why then shuttered again when she remembered finding her own boys like that numerous times.

It seems that Scarlett decided to ignore Will's wishes and had asked Johnny to come over and climb up a ladder into her window to help her with her Spanish homework. Now, after getting caught red-handed, she was in her room crying hysterically because she knew Milly had had to call Will and tell him.

"Thanks, Ma and I'm sorry again. I'll call you later" Will says as Milly waves from her car.

Will closes the front door then bellows to his daughter. "Scarlett Rose, down here. NOW!"

He hears movement from the second floor then the standard issue door slam of a teenage girl. Damn this strong-willed child of his. She's making him wait, having first going into the bathroom? Will tries counting to ten and taking deep breaths but by the time Scarlett is standing in front of him, he's no calmer than he was when he'd heard the door slamming vibrate through the house.

"Sit down," he demands. "And don't say a word. You're going to listen to me first then you can defend your case, which I have to warn you, doesn't sound very strong."

"Daddy, I-I-I…"

"What did I say? Shhh."

When Will is done dealing with Scarlett, he's going to need a twenty-hour nap followed by some good old fashion testosterone time with the guys. All these women in his life are giving him an ulcer.

The eye roll comes next as Scarlett plops herself on the sofa and squeezes a pillow into her stomach.

"Sneaking into your room, Scar? Up a ladder?"

"Daddy, I need help with…"

Will raises a hand. He didn't want to know what it was she had told this horny boy she'd needed help with that made him shimmy up the side of his two-story house. Will can do the math and figure it out. Or, as Scarlett insists, the Spanish.

"You are already grounded. I told you I did not want you to see this kid and this is what you do? And you will call Grammy later and apologize for whatever you said to her. She left here very upset."

Will sighs. He hates fighting with his daughter. He can't help but see the adorable two-year-old with that dusting of freckles covering her nose or the ten-year-old in a cast when she'd sprained her ankle at dance and had cried all night in his bed because she would miss her dance recital the following day.

Ah, to go back to the days when Scarlett was an infant and wouldn't sleep. Will had just graduated from college and should have been drunk and celebrating his acceptance into medical school at the time. Instead, he was knee deep in diapers and so sleep deprived he hadn't even known his own name. But he'd take those days back in a heartbeat because discussing boys and sex with his now fifteen-year-old daughter is not a memory he wants to create.

"Was I not clear the other night, Scarlett? Because I specifically remember saying that you were grounded and not to leave this house other than for school and dance if you were lucky. And I warned you if I caught you with that little prick again..."

"Would you stop calling him that," she demands. "You don't even know him and he's not a little prick."

Will thinks he hears her mumble something about not having a little one either but he's too flabbergasted at her sassy mouth to fully process her snide comment just yet. It doesn't take long though. "What the hell did you just mumble?"

"Nothing" Scarlett rolls her eyes again. Eyes so blue they look like glass, eyes exactly like her mother's. Will sighs at the thought of Julia and momentarily wishes he had someone to do all this with. But it's not the woman who gave his daughter her eyes that he wants by his side at times like these.

Shit, now is not the time for Sloan to pop into his head.

"Scarlett," Will sighs. "Honey, talk to me, okay? Enough arguing and sneaking around. We need to figure this out."

"There's nothing to figure out. I love Johnny, he loves me and you think he's a little prick because you can't deal with the fact that I'm not a baby anymore and you have no life of your own so you're jealous of mine" Scarlett manages to say all in one breath.

Will smiles. He actually remembers his sister, probably Scarlett's age at the time, saying the exact same thing to his mother. Well, almost. He doesn't remember 'little prick' entering the conversation twenty years ago. And it wasn't true then. Milly has always had a full life. Will suspects that Scarlett's words sting as badly as they do because there is truth behind them.

"I have a life Scarlett," he defends. "You, our family, my job, Caine and Jessie but that's not the point."

"No, that is the point. Me, family, your job, your friends? You need to get laid then maybe you wouldn't be so obsessed about my sex life."

"Sex life?" he questions. "Fuck! My sex life is not and never will be up for discussion. And you'd better not have a God damn sex life, Scarlett. Have you not heard a word I've said?"

Scarlett heaves in a deep sigh. "Whatever. One of us needs to have one."

"Hey! That's enough. Shut it and listen before you dig yourself in deeper and I change my mind and ground you until high school graduation. Now, here's the deal. Invite the little..." Will stops himself and clears his throat. "This Johnny kid over for dinner so I can meet him properly. If he thinks he's so grown up, he can act like a man and ring my doorbell and shake my hand. After he looks me in the eye and introduces himself and I spend time with him, we'll discuss you spending time with him."

Scarlett leaps into Will's arms like she did as a child and wraps her legs around him like a baby koala. She plants kisses over his face and squeezes his cheeks between her hands the way he used to do to her, making his lips pucker. She giggles when he says, "Boochie Baby!"

"I love you, Daddy!"

Ah, the emotional roller coaster of girls.

"I love you too, baby, but not so fast," Will says. "I have other things to say. Some you're going to like and some, not so much."

Scarlett sits nice and quiet now that she thinks she's getting her way and waits patiently for Will to gather his thoughts.

"First, this one you're going to like. Flip actually," he states. "So, I have this patient that let's just say is related to your idol. Who. I. Met."

Scarlett screams and covers her face, her bottom bouncing on the sofa. "You met Brooklynn Taylor and waited how long to tell me? Oh. My. God. That's so not fair. We've lived in this town my whole life and I have never, not once seen her anywhere."

Will smiles at the return of the daughter he knows and loves. The one who loves dance and...him, not boys. "I asked her about her workshop and she agreed to come to one of your classes this week to watch you and Aliana. If she thinks you're up for the challenge, she said she'll invite you to audition."

Will barely has time to cover his ears before the dog-whistle level of screeching ensues and he's certain he has suffered a profound hearing loss. When Scarlett finally stops screaming and bouncing around the room like a kangaroo in the wild, Will warns her that he's not done.

"I have to call Al and tell her" she whines.

"I already called Ellie. You're grounded, remember? No phone calls," he states. "Now, I need to finish talking to you Scar, and this part, you're not going to like. And trust me, I'm not thrilled either."

"You're going to give me another sex talk, aren't you? I still haven't recovered from the one you and Uncle Jessie gave me about getting my period" she shivers.

Will grimaces. Yeah, that'd been rough. Jessie using the words vagina, tampon, and blood flow with his daughter was an experience he'd love to forget.

"Are you having sex with him, Scar? Have you, I mean?"

"Daddy, I don't want to talk to you about this."

"You need to talk to someone. I hate times like this, baby. I'm sorry I'm all you have."

Scarlett crawls into his lap and wraps her hands around his neck. "You're all I need," she says and kisses him on his nose. "I talked to Cindy though and I'm good."

"Scar..."

"I'm not having sex with him, Daddy. I mean, I haven't. We haven't. Yet," she looks up at Will with a sad smile on her face. Will knows she's struggling with wanting to remain a child while, at the same time, wanting to become a woman. "He's not like that. You'll see when you meet him. He likes me. Is that so hard for you to believe?"

"Oh, baby, no, of course not. I think you're amazing and any boy would be lucky to have you. There's not one that deserves you though. It's just…I know what teenage boys are like and…"

"Just meet him first, okay? And keep an open mind. He's going to be nervous. He thinks you want to kill him."

Will groans. Smart kid.

"I'll behave," he promises. "One more thing, you're still grounded from your weekend shenanigans and today's little party has tacked on another week. No phone when you're in the house, you'll only use your tablet or laptop down here for homework where someone can see you and I don't ever want to find out Johnny snuck in here again. Even if it was to do homework. And just so we're clear on that. I'm not that dumb. I know that you were not just doing homework behind your closed bedroom door. For Christ's sake, Scar, you have a higher GPA than I did at your age. You don't need help with Spanish."

Scarlett growls and climbs off Will's lap. "Whatever" she says and ambles back up to her room and slams the door.

Ah, the return of the teenager.

Chapter 13

The following day, Will is apprehensive to approach Sloan when he sees her at the bank of elevators. He contemplated calling or texting her last night after he'd settled things with Scarlett but then he'd chickened out and instead found himself jerking off to thoughts of her in the shower before falling, exhausted, into his bed. He'd slept through the night but had woken up just as bewildered as he was when he'd fallen asleep.

He can't get her snide comments out of his head. Sloan is, for some insane reason, under the impression that he's a player and that Caine and Jessie are along for the wild ride. He'll give her the fact that his two best friends can be considered playboys. But him? Even the thought makes him laugh. He's determined to get to the bottom of that nonsense today but not with an audience. He'll have to bide his time and wait till he can get the beautiful girl, who has consumed his every thought since he met her, alone.

Will stands and watches her smirk as she types a text and misses the elevator. He longs for it to be him that puts that look on her face. When he hears another elevator dig, he snaps out of his fantasies and rushes into the elevator with her.

And then they're alone.

"Miss Hale," Will greets. "Just the person I was looking for."

"Dr. Anderson" she says in her most professional voice, tucking her phone into her pocket.

"I need to clear something up with you. You seem to have the wrong impression about me. I assure you, whatever you're thinking about me, it's not correct."

"Oh? And what exactly am I thinking?"

"I'm not really sure, Miss Hale but somewhere along the way it would appear that you got the idea that I'm some sort of player and that Caine and Jessie are somehow involved. I can assure you, Miss Hale, I don't know the first thing about being a player of any kind and as for my friends, well…let's just say, the antics they get up to are activities done without me."

Sloan laughs. "Yeah, right. Addison told me all about…"

"Addison? Jesus! Don't listen to Addison. Is that what this is all about? I don't even know her outside of the hospital. To be honest, she scares me. Klutzy and jumpy, that one. I've suspected she takes meds from the closet when no one is watching for some time now."

"What?" Sloan laughs.

"I'm serious. I've spoken to her superior and asked her to keep a watch out. She didn't seem to take me all that serious and mumbled something about it being my fault on my scrub days which I don't see how that plays into…"

Sloan propels herself at Will, hikes her leg on his hip and notches her sweet warmth against his already growing erection. He returns her enthusiasm and turns her into the wall, his hands flying into her hair and his tongue seeking entry to her mouth.

Then, all of a sudden, the elevator stops to let a few others in and the couple is forced to break apart, Will looking shocked and disheveled, Sloan looking mussed and in need of a good fucking.

Damn it, he shifts to try to hide his erection in the damn scrubs he's wearing. They're the most comfortable item of clothing unless, of course, you find yourself with an erection strong enough to pound nails into concrete like the one Will currently has.

"Um," Sloan laughs, looking down at the tenting of his scrubs and sliding in front of him before the other doctors take notice. "Do you understand the scrubs comment now?"

Will looks down then up at Sloan. As realization dawns, his eyes grow as big as saucers and a blush covers his cheeks. "Fuck" he sighs as he runs a hand through his short hair.

Sloan lets out another giggle and the elevator stops to let the others out. Will pulls her into his body and rubs his excitement on her thigh. "Will that be happening again?"

"It's not happening again," she laughs. "At least not any time soon."

"Oh, it's happening again. I'll be prepared the next time, give it my best efforts to remain under control."

"It's not happening again. You're my boss, Dr. Anderson" she says as she casually but not so innocently brushes her hand across the tip of his erection making him hiss, his head rolling back.

"Fuck," he groans. "See, it's happening again" he says as he tries to shift in his scrubs for comfort.

"So, what Addison said about you, Caine, and Jessie sleeping with every woman in this hospital isn't true? She said you even had," Sloan lowers her voice to a whisper. "Ménage a trois together."

"Oh, no. It's true. About Caine and Jessie, I mean. But I swear to you Sloan, I hadn't been with anyone for at least a year before that night with you. Which I think I very embarrassingly demonstrated," he chuckles at the memory of the first orgasm he had with her. "I've never been a player. I don't really have the time. And as for the together part? I see the hotness in theory and trust me, their stories could crack a monk and make him rethink his celibacy, but for me, in reality, it's just not my thing."

"Hmmm" she sighs then after another second's thought she's mounting him again and rubbing her moist heat on the bulge in his scrubs.

"Mmmm," he moans as he grinds against her. "Jesus, you feel so fucking good. This is exactly what I was thinking about last night."

"Last night?" she breathes between kisses.

"Yeah. I jerked off harder than I did as a teenager thinking about you rubbing that sweet pus…"

The elevator stops again and the doors open.

Will groans and Sloan flings her feet to the floor and smiles as Will tries to cover his excitement with his lab coat. "See you for rounds, Dr. Anderson" she says as she exits the elevator, leaving him with an erection so hard he won't be able to walk for hours. He tries to smile at the other doctors who are standing next to him with knowing smirks but only manages a frustrated moan.

Still shocked that she left him in this condition in an elevator filled with his colleagues, Will reaches into his pocket and sends Sloan a text.

Will: *I think I need medical assistance. Know anyone who can help me with the condition I'm currently in?*

Sloan's response comes through immediately.

Sloan: *I'm never getting into an elevator with you again! And your BFF is a urologist, maybe give him a call. I hear you guys are familiar with each other's junk*

Will sends her one more as he waits for the others to exit the elevator so he can ride back down to the proper floor.

Will: *Oh, I plan on having you in an elevator again very soon, Miss Hale and you will finish what you started. But for now, meet me in Damian's room to discharge him. If Caine isn't there yet, have him paged. He doesn't do well in the mornings...don't ask! And no, it has nothing to do with him and my dick!*

Sloan enters Damian's room to wait for Will and finds his room packed to well over capacity, Dr. Caine Cabrera squeezed into the corner with a cup of strong coffee. Sloan makes her way over to the doctor.

"Dr. Anderson will be here in a moment. He got off on the wrong floor."

"I'm well aware of where he last got off, Miss Hale" Caine says with a smirk.

Sloan stares slacked jawed at the doctor who, when paired with Will and Jessie Holt pushes the hotness factor into the heavens. Man, this guy is gorgeous. She might not be into threesomes but she can see how the thought of Caine and Jessie together could entice a woman into bed.

Will said Caine's a player, Sloan's mind begins to think that maybe she can get him to distract Katherine long enough so she'll come to her senses and ditch that asshole she's scheduled to marry in less than a week. Hmmm, or maybe him and Jessie. Sloan giggles to herself. After having one or two nights with a pair of guys, Sloan knows firsthand that Katherine would probably die. Yeah, maybe she should just go for one of them to start off with. Once she gets Katherine to see she's worth so much more than that dickhead, Mike, she can figure it out for herself. And if Katherine enjoys one or both of Will's friends, at least Sloan can enjoy the stories because some woman should be enjoying this man in front of her and often. They should also share the stories of his sexual prowess, that Sloan knows will be good, with their friends so everyone can enjoy.

Before a plan has time to take root in her mind, Sloan watches Will enter the room and speak to Brook Taylor, Damian's cousin's wife then make his way over to his patient.

Hmmm, that's weird. That feeling she just got when she watched Will lean down and speak softly into another woman's ear. Even if that woman was happily married and her husband was not more than a foot away from her. Jealousy? Could it be? Shit!

"Caine and I have cleared you," Will begins snapping Sloan out of her head as Caine walks to Will's side. "You're free to go. I'll have Sloan arrange for a home visit in a day or two. We don't mind stopping in to check you out to cut down on the media if that's good with you."

"Great, thanks. I can never thank you enough. Either of you" Damian says as he squeezes his wife's hand.

"No," Caine clears his throat. "Um, activity until I've okayed it. Understand?"

Damian moans. "Yeah, I got it. My dick has other ideas though."

The women in the room moan. Drea, Damian's sister, rolls her eyes and leads the pack out of his room. "You're such an ass" she says before she leaves with a smirk in her husband's direction, the ex-Marine rolls his eyes then winks at his pregnant wife.

"I'll meet you next door," Sloan whispers to Will. "Bye everybody" she says as she scurries off to their next patient's room.

"Home visit?" Damian asks. "Because of the media, huh?"

"Leave him alone, Day," Sydney warns. "They are adorable together."

"She is smokin' hot, man," Caine says. "If I had a nurse that looked like that, half my patients would be dead by now."

"Hey!" Damian laughs. "Thanks a lot."

Will and Caine laugh with Damian for a moment then promise to see him by the end of the week before they exit his room with farewells to his clan of friends and family.

"Drinks tonight?" Will asks. "Jessie too. I got shit with Scar I need to fill you guys in on and then, well, you see what I'm dealing with. I'm so over my head with this girl, I've got no clue what the fuck is happening."

Caine laughs. "Yeah, I'll set it up. Jessie's been evasive lately, he mentioned a girl. He's up to something. I've never heard him sound like he did about a woman. He'll drop whatever bullshit it is when I mention Scar though."

"Text me later" Will says as he waves to his friend and enters his next patient's room to find Sloan pulled into the young, attractive, professional football player's arms. Her body is prone on his and her lips are swallowed up by his mouth.

"Hey!" he shouts and Sloan wiggles free.

"Ugh!" she sputters. "What the hell?"

"Exactly, Will smirks. "So now you make out with patients?"

"Jealous, Dr. Anderson?" she asks.

"As a matter of fact," he begins then turns towards his patient. "Drew, we've discussed this."

"Sorry Doc," the athlete says with a smirk.

Will makes the introductions explaining to Sloan that their patient recently suffered another serious concussion that has left his judgement clouded and his impulsivity null.

"Don't let it happen again or I can arrange to have those hands of yours tied to the bed."

"Will," Sloan admonishes. "Um, I mean, Dr. Anderson!"

"Will, huh?" Drew asks. "So when are you letting me bounce out of here, man?"

"After that stunt? Probably sooner than I should."

Will and Sloan spend the next hour working side by side, visiting each of their patients and speaking with the families. As they exit the last room, Will grabs her elbow and tugs her into an empty hallway. "Go out with me?" he asks.

"I'm not going out with you. We've been over this. You're my boss and it's inappropriate. And, anyway, it's just the chase."

"The chase?"

"Your ego. All this is is your ego. You chase me, it's fun, a power trip. You get me, you'll be done. Your ego," she explains.

"I want you and I can promise that I will not be done with you anytime soon. And might I remind you, Miss Hale, I've already had you. A few times if memory serves."

"It's against the rules," she breathes heavily. "We can't do this, you're my boss."

"But it's fun, Miss Hale. Don't you like to have fun?" Will asks as his finger reaches out to run down the length of her arm. "I like to have fun and before you came along, it was so long since I had any. I need to make up for lost time."

The call system sounds through the hospital calling them into action and they're forced to once again push their growing feelings for one another under the surface and do their jobs.

After hours in another grueling surgery, Will goes in search of Sloan to be sure she's okay and just before he gets to the nurses' room a group chat comes through between Caine, Jessie, and him.

Caine: *Stone gave us carte blanche at any and all of his places*

Jessie: *VIP at Hard as Stone?*

Caine: *Sure. 8pm? Meet there.*

Jessie: *Yep with a smile and a hard-on.*

Will: *You are both children. Make it Stone Faced and I'll be there.*

Jessie: *Fine and BTW, you're pussy whipped already. Pathetic, man.*

Caine: *Have you seen her? I'm pussy whipped and I haven't had her pussy...YET!*

Will: *One more word about her or her pussy and one of you dies. Remember, I know where your brain stem is. I can make it a slow death!*

Caine: *Want to know where my dick is? I'll give you a hint...Oh, Nurse Hale, you're so tight.*

Jessie: *Oh, Nurse Hale, your mouth is so wet. #KiddingNotKidding*

Will: *FUCK YOU BOTH*

Jessie: *Your girl is right now; you'll have to wait in line*

Will: *I HATE YOU!*

Caine: *8pm See you guys later*

Still shaking his head over his friends' antics, Will reaches the door to the nurses' room. He stands there for a moment and weighs his options. Hell, he's a doctor, he can go in there to find his nurse if he needs to. It's not designated as a women's only area. There are a lot of male nurses in the hospital who go in there all the time. So why is he hesitant?

Well, the last time he'd gone in there he'd found her with her perfect breasts exposed, her nipples begging to be sucked and flicked with the tip of his tongue. Jesus, how many hard-ons was he going to pop at work in one day? He's certain he has reached an unhealthy amount hours ago.

Then he hears her scream and he's done thinking about entering the room. Will is through the door in the blink of an eye and what he finds when he gets in there changes him from Dr. Jekyll into Mr. Hyde.

George Tinkerman, the male nurse who apparently doesn't understand the word 'no' has Sloan against the row of lockers. Her shirt is off again but at least she's wearing a bra this time. George is trying to get his tongue down her throat and she's pushing him away at his shoulders.

"Give it up, Hale, we all know you've been putting out for all the doctors around here. What, I'm not good enough for you because I don't have the bank account of a neurosurgeon?"

Will grabs George by his shoulders and hauls him off Sloan, spinning him around and punching him in the jaw with a loud crack. George lowers his shoulders and plows into Will's middle taking him to the floor. Will hears Sloan scream and then takes a hit to the eye when he loses his concentration and looks her way.

Will responds to the hit with a knee in George's gut then, with a swift move, fit for a ninja, Will is on his feet ready to ruin the douchebag.

Sloan is still screaming when Caine and Jessie, having walked by and hearing a scuffle, storm in the room.

"Fuck" Caine says when he figures out what's happening and his best friend is in the middle of the action.

"Will" Jessie warns as he grabs his friend around the waist and hauls him away from the male nurse who had no chance on getting the best of Will in this fight.

Caine backs George up against the lockers with an arm to his windpipe. "Go ahead and make a move cuz' I'd love to do this" he warns.

"What the fuck is going on?" Jessie asks.

Sloan is trying her best to hold back tears when her eyes meet Will's. "Nothing," she says. "It was a misunderstanding."

George laughs. "Yeah, listen to her. A misunderstanding. Now, if you three can leave, it's my turn."

With that comment, Jessie lets Will go as Caine plows a fist into George's belly, taking him to the ground then heaving him back up. "I'll let you get one more in for that comment then I'm taking him out of here. He's not worth it" Caine says.

Just as Will is about to clock the asshole one last time he hears Sloan's quiet whisper and he turns to her. "Don't," she begs, her voice low and timid. "He's not worth it. Your hands are worth so much more than he is."

Will's eyes never leave Sloan's as he says to Caine, "Get him the fuck out of here and have him fired. Make sure he never works in a hospital again."

As Caine drags George from the nurses' room in a chokehold, Jessie tries to approach Will. Will stops him short with a hand. "I'm fine. Leave us alone," he says. "I'll see you at eight."

Jessie silently nods and leaves Will and Sloan alone.

"You okay?" Will asks without moving a muscle, afraid to scare Sloan more than she already appears to be. "Did he hurt you?"

She shakes her head.

"Can I come closer?" Will asks.

Another head nod, this one a yes.

Will opens his arms and walks slowly to Sloan. She closes the space with him and sighs when her face is buried in his chest. She heaves in a deep breath to fill her lungs with his scent, clean and masculine, sexy.

"What the fuck happened?" he asks.

"George is a dick. He's always hitting on the nurses, making comments when we get changed in here. We try to never be in here alone with him but..."

"Why hasn't anyone reported him?"

Sloan shrugs. "I don't know all the details, just what some of the other nurses have told me."

"What did he...did he try to...Jesus, baby," Will says as he squeezes her tighter and plants a kiss on her forehead. "Let me check you out, okay?"

"You look worse than me. Maybe I should check you out," she tries to lighten the mood. "You might have a shiner there."

Will shrugs her concern off and does a quick once over to be sure she's not physically injured.

"He didn't hurt me but I'd like to go puke now. The thought of his tongue in my mouth is making me sick."

Yeah, he knows the feeling. When Will walked in and saw that sight, he'd almost tossed his cookies too but then his adrenaline kicked in and kicking the guy's ass seemed like a better idea. "I can fix that, if you'd let me."

Will looks at her lips then up at her eyes. "Sloan" he questions and she nods. Her permission granted has Will plunging his hands into her hair and pulling her mouth towards his. Before he makes contact he asks, "Was that comment about us? About me?"

Sloan shrugs and Will gently swipes his lips over hers.

"Sloan?" he asks then kisses her harder, his tongue running over her bottom lip.

"I had lunch in the cafeteria that day with Oliver. You might have been right about him."

"Did you…"

"No! I didn't sleep with him. I don't make it a habit of sleeping with the doctors I work with," Sloan sighs. "He asked if I needed a ride home after lunch and I agreed. I was exhausted and the thought of the subway or the bus wasn't really a pleasing prospect."

Will releases his hold on her and runs a hand through his hair. His eye is starting to throb and the side of his body is already sore. "I will speak to him."

"Will" she warns.

"This isn't a game," he states. "This isn't a game for me, Sloan. You and I, we're not a game."

Sloan nods, understanding his intentions but not sure if she's ready for what they mean. "Then what?" she asks. "if it's not a game, Will, then what is it?"

Will wraps her in his arms again, pulling her hips flush to his body. "It's your eyes, sweetheart. The smell of your hair, these lips," Will kisses her gently. "You're bossy, I like the way you keep me in line. You're funny, adorable, dedicated to your job. Honestly, I don't think there's a negative thing about you."

Sloan blushes. "I'm still not going out with you" she says with a smile in her voice.

"We'll see," Will laughs, for the first time he allows himself to enjoy this part, the chase as she calls it. Because Will knows it's only a matter of time before this girl will be his. He'll just have to up his game. And by up it, he means get some game. Maybe

Caine and Jessie can give him a tip or two tonight. "So, I should go get some ice. You, okay?"

Sloan laughs. "I'm fine, Willie."

Will moans then smiles as he walks out of the room backward to keep eye contact with her for as long as possible.

Chapter 14

"I can't believe he blew us off," Will says. "What the fuck is going on with him?"

"Fuck if I know," Caine says as they're shown to the VIP table at Damian Stone's nightclub. "Nice shiner, man" Caine laughs.

"Thanks for that earlier."

"Anytime."

"So, seriously, what's going on with Jessie?" Will inquires.

"I haven't seen him anymore than you have these last few weeks. He did mention something about a chick fucking with his head but that can't be it. I'm sure it was just an extra bratty subbie girl at Stone's club that he was annoyed over."

Will raises his eyebrow as Caine checks out the waitress from the back.

"What?" Caine asks. "You do realize I hook up with chicks without him, right?"

Will laughs. "Yeah, I guess. Actually, I try not to think about it too much. But, speaking of that topic, you should know that Addison mentioned something about it to Sloan."

"Are you fucking kidding me?" Caine sighs then smiles as he realizes the waitress is waiting for his order. "Oh, sorry. I'll have a Scotch, best in the house, just the one. And a beer but keep those coming."

"Same for me on the Scotch. No beer and just the one. Thanks."

Caine runs a hand through his hair. "I told Jessie that one was a fucking head case. She was more into hearing about you than anything we were offering to do for her" Caine says, describing the night he and Jessie had spent with Addison a few months ago.

"Me? What the fuck does she want with me?"

"Best guess, pal? Your dick" Caine laughs.

Will grimaces. He's always suspected there was something up with that nurse. He just never thought it was that. That's all he needs with Sloan acting as skittish as she is about starting a relationship with him.

Not wanting to spend any more time talking about the quirky nurse, Caine and Will spend the next hour or so shooting the shit and trying to figure out what the hell Jessie is up to.

"A new sub?" Caine wonders.

"Maybe," Will says. "He doesn't really talk to me about that stuff so I wouldn't know."

"He usually fills me in on it and he's been tight lipped all week."

"Hmmm, maybe it's more about a case then a girl," Will throws out there. "Since he's taken on Cindy, he's had more time on his hands. Maybe he's raking his brain over one of his past cases that didn't end well?"

"Yeah, that sounds exactly like him. You know he's never gotten over the Bradley case. That first patient he lost was hard on him. Maybe," Caine says. "He's researching amniotic fluid embolisms? Who knows. He'll tell us when he's ready. Now fill me in on our little girl."

Will tells Caine about Scarlett and Johnny and how the kid is coming over for dinner to meet him.

"Please let me come too" Caine begs.

"No! Scarlett would kill me. I can handle it alone."

"Call me if you need a shovel" Caine laughs.

"Yep" Will says with a far-off look into the crowd of girls on the dance floor.

"What?" Caine asks following his gaze. "Well, look who we have here. Go dance with her."

"I don't..."

"Go," Caine orders. "I'm right behind you. The friend is fucking hot. What's her story?"

Will smiles. This might work out perfectly. Sloan has been insistent that Katherine should call off her wedding. If anyone can get a girl to fall head over heels at first sight and call off a wedding, it's Caine Cabrera. "That's Katherine, the best friend and roommate. She's a model at Stone's agency and she's getting married to some asshole named Mike that Sloan keeps insisting she won't marry when the time comes."

"I love a good challenge. Lead the way" Caine says.

Will walks hesitantly in Sloan's direction. She turns just as he's about to tap her shoulder and they're face to face. Only inches apart. If he was to take just one step his lips could devour hers. "Miss Hale," Will greets her with a sly smirk. "You know Dr. Cabrera."

"Stalking me, Willis?"

"You do know that my name is Wilson, right?"

"I do indeed, Willis" Sloan says with a giggle.

Will reaches out his hand to Katherine. "Nice to see you again, Katherine. This is my friend Caine."

"Willis over here tells me that you and Sloan live together?" Caine says as he leans in to plant a hello kiss on Katherine's cheek. "Not far from me."

Katherine nods but remains speechless.

"Come on, Willie, let's dance" Sloan says.

"I-I-I don't dance."

"I beg to differ. I've seen you move. You can dance" Sloan says.

"I'm gonna sit this one out" Katherine announces as she turns to head to the bar. Caine is quick to grab her elbow and lead her in the direction of the private table he and Will have for the evening, the best in the house with a private waitress to take care of their every need.

Sloan raises an eyebrow at Will then smirks. "I hope that works out the way I have planned."

"You planned this?"

"Well, not this," Sloan says. "I had no idea you'd be here tonight and with Dr. McFuckable to boot but…"

"Mc what?"

"It's a girl thing," she laughs. "From a medical show," Sloan looks at Will for understanding but when she sees none she shrugs. "Forget it."

"Do you have a name for me too?"

"Yeah."

"You gonna tell me?"

"No."

Will growls but Sloan laughs then turns and notches her ass into his crotch as she begins to grind her hips. Will's hands immediately go to her hips and pull her tighter to him as he keeps time with her swaying body. "You're playing with fire, Miss Hale" he warns.

"I'm a nurse, I know how to treat a burn."

Will raises her arms above her head and it slides to the side giving him complete access to her neck. He dives in and licks a trail from her ear to her jaw where he then plants a few sweet kisses. "Mmmm, salty and sweet," he moans. "The way I remember you tasting on my tongue."

"Will" she moans then Sloan takes him by the hand and leads him off the dance floor.

"Where are you going?" he asks. "My table's over there."

"Yeah, I know," Sloan says with a flirtatious smile over her shoulder. She leads Will to a dark area off to the side of the dance floor. "But it's more private here don't you think?"

"And what might we need privacy for, Miss Hale? The last time we had a discussion about kissing, I remember you saying it wasn't going to happen again so I'm wondering what it is you're planning on doing to me in this dark corner."

Sloan hiccups then giggles.

"Are you drunk, Miss Hale?"

"Maybe a smidge but not enough to forget what I'm about to do."

"And what might that be?" Will asks with a tap from his pointer finger to her button nose.

"This" she says as she pushes Will's back against the wall and kisses him, her hand reaching down to cup his aching balls.

"Sloan," he hisses. "Fuck, sweetheart. We can't do this here and I can't do this with you drunk."

But then her lips find his again and Will spins them around so Sloan's back is the one against the wall, forgetting all about what they can and cannot do in a public place. She jumps, wrapping her legs around his middle and throws her head back. "Please," she begs. "We won't fuck or anything. Just...this. Okay?"

Will shakes his head and dives back in. His lips devour hers, their tongues dance together in a tango so naughty a porn star would blush if they saw the two of them. Will braces himself with his hands on the wall on either side of her face. If he doesn't hold on, he's sure his knees will buckle and they'll both crash to the floor.

"Mmmmm," she purrs. "Maybe just a little more."

"Anymore sweetheart and I won't be able to stop myself," Will warns. He pulls back briefly and glances at his watch. "It's getting late and we have an early start tomorrow so..."

"The perfect gentleman" she sighs.

"Yeah. My dick will make me pay for this later, don't worry."

"Send me a video," she says through a yawn.

Sloan lowers her legs and with one last sweet kiss to her lips, Will takes her hand and leads her back to Caine and Katherine.

The men put them in a car and wave as it pulls away from the curb.

"You have lipstick on your shirt, man" Caine says through a stifled chuckle and omitting the fact that his friend's lips are a very nice shade of bubble gum pink.

Will smiles but leaves the evidence of his make out session in place. "So, what did you and Katherine talk about?"

"Sloan's right, she's not getting married."

Will raises an eyebrow and smirks at his long-time confirmed bachelor friend. "Is that right?"

"Yeah," Caine says confidently. "It is."

"And she told you this?" Will asks as he opens the door to his car.

"I'm planning on looking into this Mike asshole. Stone's brother-in-law said if there was ever anything we needed."

Will laughs. "So you're going to have his ass kicked?"

"If it comes to that. He's done a job on her self-esteem and could use a lesson in manners," Caine says. "I'll catch you later."

Will closes his car door as Caine disappears underground.

*****

Will opens the door to his house and smiles when he sees Scarlett asleep on the sofa in their living room. This is exactly how he used to find her almost every night that he got stuck at the hospital. That is until lately when she'd been too concerned over talking on the phone in private to Johnny to try to wait up for her daddy to come home.

"Hey, baby girl," he whispers. "You waiting up for me like old times?"

"Hey daddy," she mumbles, unable to fully wake.

Will heaves her into his arms and carries her up the flight of stairs to her room like he's done a million times. He pauses at the guest room door and glances inside to see his parents asleep in the bed they use on occasions like this.

"Brook came to my classes tonight."

"She did? Honey, that's great."

"I hope. She said she'd call you tomorrow."

"Okay," Will says as he leans down and places his sleepy daughter securely in her bed. "Sweet dreams."

"Daddy?"

"Yeah, baby?"

"You smell nice."

Will laughs. "Thank you?"

"Yeah, like perfume. And I love that shade of lipstick on you."

Chapter 15

Will stops at the fancy gourmet coffee shop just outside the hospital and gets himself and Sloan a beverage. He'd much prefer the famous chain with the pink and brown awning a few doors down but he's trying to impress the girl not show her what an average Joe he is. And anyway, if he's being honest, what he'd really prefer is breakfast in bed with the sassy nurse who has stormed into his life and rocked his world.

Maybe tomorrow.

He enters the hospital, coffees in hand, and heads to his office. If he's lucky, today won't include surgery, just a new patient and a few follow up visits with his current ones before he can call it an early day. He needs to prepare himself to meet this Johnny kid who is hell bent on deflowering his innocent daughter. Little prick. Yeah, he'll also need to figure out a way not to call him that in front of Scarlett. Not. Going. To. Be. Easy.

Sloan is sitting at his desk when he walks into the office. "Miss Hale, don't you look comfy?"

Sloan laughs then winces.

"Headache?"

"Little bit. Shhh, Willis, you're shouting."

Will laughs at the name she insists on calling him then sticks out his hand to her and offers her a coffee.

"For me? How romantic."

Will smiles. "I prefer Dunkin but I wasn't sure what you like."

"I'm with you on that but thanks. Today, anything will help. I hope."

"I'd prefer to take you to breakfast in the cafeteria."

"Be still my heart, Wills, the cafeteria? How so *very* romantic" she laughs after using yet another silly name for him. Amazing, but they're all growing on him and fast.

"Actually, when I was getting the coffees, I was thinking the best option would be breakfast in bed. With you naked."

Sloan laughs. "We've been through this, Dr. Anderson. I work for you. It's not happening again."

"Oh, we're back to Dr. now, huh? And you keep saying that, Miss Hale, but it keeps happening."

Will's cell chirps in his pocket and he sees Brook Taylor's name on the screen. "Um…I kind of need to…"

Sloan raises from his desk chair and saunters to the door. On the way past Will, she runs her hand over his bicep. "Thanks for the java, Doc. I'll see you in thirty. We have a new patient consult."

Will nods and answers his phone. "Hey, glad you were able to reach me" he says as Sloan quietly closes his door.

"Me too. Sorry it's so early but ever since the twins, it feels like ten in the morning is really four in the afternoon" Brook laughs.

"Ah, not great sleepers, huh? Scar was a nightmare for a long time. In my bed, insisting there were monsters under hers, needed umpteen-thousand drinks of water and at least six billion stories."

"Does she babysit?"

Will laughs. "For you, she'd probably do damn near anything."

Brook chuckles. "She's really good, Will, Aliana too. I'm not sure how they weren't on my radar. I can't believe we live in the same town and their names never came up."

"Aliana's parents and I tried to keep them out of the competitive stuff for as long as we could. This is only their second year competing."

Brook sighs, hating that part of her business. The cut-throat competitions and the dance moms. Well, in Scarlett's case, it seems like dance dad. "Can I be nosy for a minute?"

"Sure" Will laughs.

"Scarlett's mom?"

"No clue. The last I saw of her was her back leaving the hospital when Scarlett was two hours old."

Brook heaves in a breath. She can't imagine leaving a child like that. She'd almost left her own sure but it was no fault of hers. Brook had almost died in child birth but had fought her way back from a coma for those babies. And Tate.

"I'm sorry."

"Me too but it's been a long time. I'm over it. Scarlett, I'm not so sure about."

"Maybe I can help," Brook offers. "I'd like them to join my workshop. Train with me for a few weeks, maybe a few months. They're very raw, which is good, no bad habits that are unbreakable yet. Then after that, we'll see. And I'm serious about the babysitting. Maybe a night or two a month so Tate and I can catch a movie or something?"

Will smiles, his pride unable to be contained. His daughter is going to flip and he had a hand in it.

"Will?" Brook asks. "You still there?"

Will laughs. "Yeah, just…Wow! That's great! Scar is going to flip and Aliana too."

"I'll have Heidi send you the details," Brook says referring to her long-time assistant and friend. "I'll work with them locally at my Connecticut studio but I'll need them in the city on the weekends then in California at the end of the workshop."

"Oh, ah, yeah…hmmm…well, alright. I'll work it out."

Brook says her good-byes with promises to also call Scarlett, after Will has a chance to tell her the good news that is, and ask her to babysit. There was something about the girl that spoke to Brook when she saw her. Sure, she was a beautiful dancer with raw talent and spot-on form but it was more than that. Brook hates to think of this girl without a mother to guide her. She doesn't need a babysitter but she'd like to give Scarlett a woman she's comfortable talking to. Having her in her home, playing with her children, might help make her feel more comfortable. Brook knows the importance of a strong psyche in her field. She can't in good conscience throw this young teenage girl into the mix until she knows she can handle it.

After hanging up with Brook, Will heads to his first appointment of the day and finds Sloan in the exam room. He loses his breath when he opens the door and sees her playing with the toddler. He stands in the doorway, an arm on the jam and watches. Her maternal instincts are obvious and strong, nothing like Julia's, and he smiles as she cuddles the child, giggling along with her. The little girl has her hair in pigtails, just like Scarlett used to request almost every day, and by the look of Sloan's hair, she must have been playing hairdresser before he arrived because Sloan is now also sporting the same style. He wishes he could say that his thoughts stayed as innocent as the little girl's but when he saw those pigtails on Sloan, he'd had to shift in his pants. Thank God he was in dress slacks and not those damn scrubs that he's catching on might be the root of a few of his troubles with the nurses.

"I'm Dr. Anderson," he introduces himself to the parents. "But please, call me Will. I see you've met Sloan."

The father shakes his hand then the mother says, "Kathy and Bob Dempsy. Nice to meet you."

Will smiles and approaches the little girl. "And who do we have here?" he asks.

"Lydia," the mom says. "She's two and a little apprehensive of doctors since this all started."

Will smiles as he approaches the toddler, confident in his skills with tiny little girls like this one, like Scarlett used to be. He makes a funny face as he pretends to stumble. Lydia chuckles from deep in her belly.

"You silly man" she says and Will's face lights up at the toddler speech he misses so much. It's way better than talk about sex and boyfriends.

"I am silly. Want to see a trick I know?"

Lydia excitedly shakes her head and Will pulls a latex glove from the box on the wall. Before Lydia can shriek away in fear of a painful procedure coming her way, Will has air in the glove and has let it go so it fizzles around the room. "You want to try?" he asks her.

Lydia shakes her head and takes the glove Will hands her. Now that she's busy concentrating on her task, Will turns towards her parents. "We have a playroom adjacent to the waiting area with a child life specialist. Why don't you take Lydia in there and if she's comfortable enough she can stay while you come to my office so we can talk. I'll examine her after, right before we take her down for a scan, so if she becomes upset she can have a break after I'm done. Sound good?"

Kathy Dempsy smiles sadly and nods as Will waves good-bye to Lydia, promising to play with her again later, with his other hand in the dip of Sloan's back to lead her to his office.

Sloan sits in awe of Dr. Wilson Anderson, the world's leading pediatric brain surgeon, as he sits on a sofa, not behind his great big mahogany desk, and reads through a week's worth of notes Kathy had kept documenting Lydia's days.

It's funny how Sloan thinks of him as Dr. Anderson in this moment when only a few minutes ago, with his warm hand in the dip of her back, she thought of him as Will, the sexy guy that brings her body endless levels of pleasure. Now, in her mind, his hands are still magic, but of a much different variety.

Sloan sits riveted for the hour that Will spends with his patient's parents. He looks them in the eye and listens to every word they say. He holds Kathy's hand and comforts her through her tears. He explains his training and expertise, but never boasts about his skills. Hell, the man has removed half a child's brain before but he says it like it's just a simple fact, something to calm these scared parents down. In comparison to that, removing a small tumor must seem minor to them. Will is an expert in his field, his expertise in the smallest of patients, their brains much more delicate than the adult version. Will takes on adult patients, like Damian Stone and athletes, he's more than capable of treating the adult brain, but his love is this. Saving a child. And those high-profile cases he takes on helps to pay for cases like these, if the parents don't have the means. Will has never once turned away a patient because their parents weren't financially capable of paying his fee or that of the hospital's.

Sloan snaps out of her mind, her thoughts of this amazing man, when she hears Will say, "Here's my cell. Call me anytime day or night. There is no silly question or reason for you to worry over something when I'm only a phone call away and can ease your mind.

And I mean it, if I didn't, I wouldn't give out my number, okay? So, use it if you need to."

Bob stands and envelopes Will in his arms, thanking him for helping his daughter before Will's even laid a finger on the little girl.

Will is able to examine Lydia without a problem, the toddler already won over by his charms as strongly as Sloan is. She even allows Will to put a face mask on her, after he put it on himself of course, to deliver the anesthesia she'll need to remain still during her MRI. Sloan is blown away by Will once again when he carries the toddler himself into the scanning room, insists on doing her IV, then allows Kathy to remain in the room while Lydia is in having her scan. He leads Bob to the technician's room and he and Sloan remain there with him. Will spends the next forty-five minutes explaining everything Bob sees on the screen.

When the scan is complete, Will turns to Sloan. "Miss Hale," he asks. "Can you head up to the patient floor and start charting for me? I'll be up in a minute."

"Yes, sure" she says then says her good-byes to Lydia's parents.

Will growls under his breath when he sees his neuro-radiologist stare at Sloan's ass as she walks away. Bob laughs, "You know you were doing the same thing, right?"

Will smiles at the man but sends the other doctor a death stare.

By the time Will finally makes it back up to the patient floor to check on Sloan, he finds her asleep at the nurses' station, her head on a pile of charts.

"You okay?" he asks with a soft hand to that sexy dip in her back.

"I'm fine" she says, her voice groggy from her little cat nap.

"You're not looking fine, Miss Hale. You're looking like you need a meal and a nap," he says aloud then leans down and whispers for only Sloan to hear. "And maybe an orgasm…or three" he says with a wiggle of his eyebrows.

Sloan moans as she feels her inner walls clench at the mere thought of Will and his orgasm abilities. "Mmmmm," she moans. Then to be sassy includes, "Yeah, a meal sounds great."

"Smartass," he says. "Let me take you to grab a quick bite to eat."

"I can't. Not tonight, rehearsal dinner for Katherine's wedding. I need to leave as soon as I finish these up."

"I thought you said she wouldn't get married?"

"Oh, she's still not. Mark my words. That shit will be over before you know it."

Will laughs. "Runaway bride?"

"I'll make sure of it."

"You sound like trouble with a capital T, Miss Hale."

"That I am, Dr. Anderson, that I am," Will turns to leave her to her task so she can get to Katherine's festivities but Sloan stops him with her words. "You were really great with Lydia today. You'll make an awesome dad one day."

Knowing these are one of those times in the world where he's faced with a decision that can alter the course of his life, Will panics and lets the opportunity to tell Sloan about Scarlett pass. "Yeah, one day" he says instead.

As soon as the words are out of his mouth he wishes he could take them back, tell Sloan they need to talk and open up to her. He wants to share every heartache, every great moment with her but he's afraid she'll pull a Julia and hightail it out of his life faster than he knows what hit him. So, Will just turns and walks away, knowing in his heart he's made the wrong decision and that it will eventually come back to bite him in the ass.

Chapter 16

Will heads back to Connecticut and stops at the over-priced gourmet grocery store that's all the rage for drinks and snacks before picking up the meal he ordered from Scarlett's favorite Italian place. He still can't believe he has to deal with this shit tonight. A teenage boy with hormones raging for his little girl. How the fuck did he let this happen? The last time Will had checked; Scarlett was an adorable five-year-old with a lisp. But if he's being honest with himself, he's noticed the changes in her recently, the breasts and hips, the pouty lips and her sassy attitude. Fuck, his little girl was growing up. Fast.

Will is barely in the kitchen when he hears the doorbell ring.

Johnny.

And he'll have the boy all to himself for a little while. Will had made arrangements with Frank to pick up the girls from dance and conveniently make a quick stop that takes longer than he thought. Will wants to size this kid up and feel him out without his daughter there to intervene. He'd thought about letting Caine and Jessie come over but then he decided against it. He wanted to feel the kid out, maybe scare him a little. He didn't want the poor kid reduced to a puddle of tears and piss.

"Coming" Will yells as he places his groceries on the counter and heads to the front door. He heaves in a deep breath before opening it to find the cleanest cut, most handsome looking teenage boy he may have ever seen. Standing on his doorstep, Johnny looks nervous as hell and like he's about to piss himself even without the influence of Caine and Jessie.

"Um," Johnny clears his throat. "Mr. ah, I mean, Dr. Anderson, sir, I'm Johnny Macello" The boy extends his sweaty hand for Will to shake. Which he does after giving it a death grip and right around the same time as thinking about where that hand might have been on his daughter's body.

"Johnny," Will says. "Come in."

Will holds the door open and Johnny's eyes instantly scan the room for support. "Ah, where's Scar?"

Will smiles and can't contain his laughter. "She'll be here in a bit. There was some traffic on her way home from dance so it's just us guys for now. You want a soda? I assume you don't drink beer, right Johnny?"

Johnny clears his throat. "No, um, yeah," he stutters. "I mean, yeah, I'll have a soda, sir and no, I don't drink beer."

"Hmmm" Will says as he sizes the kid up.

Johnny lets out an audible sigh as Will turns to walk into the kitchen. "Come on," Will orders. "Follow me."

When they enter the kitchen, Will nods to a stool at the island. "Have a seat. I just need to put this in the oven to stay warm."

"Uh, yeah, s-s-sure" Johnny stammers as he wipes his sweaty palms on his jeans.

"So, Scarlett tells me that you're an athlete. Some big man on campus."

Johnny's face lights up at the news that Scarlett thinks he's important, good at what he does. "I play football, basketball, and run outdoor track, sir. But I guess basketball is my best sport though. I don't know, that's what college is looking at me for. But I wouldn't say I'm the big man...what did you call it?" he asks.

"Never mind" Will growls, annoyed that the kid hadn't tooted his own horn like an obnoxious little prick. Shit, what the fuck is Will going to do if Johnny is actually a nice kid like Scarlett insists?

Johnny takes a sip from his soda then chokes when it goes up his nose and down the wrong pipe at Will's next question. "Are you having sex with my daughter?"

He hadn't meant to ask that. Well, not yet anyway but he'd felt his phone vibrate in his pocket and knew it was Frank giving him a ten-minute warning. He didn't have time for further pleasantries. He needed to know what this kid was planning to do with his little girl.

"Sorry," Johnny apologizes. "Went down the wrong pipe."

"You're fine. Answer my question."

"Sir, I...shouldn't you talk to Scar about..."

"Answer my question" Will demands with a raised eyebrow.

"No. I mean…not no, I won't answer your question. I, ah…no," Johnny runs his hands through his hair. "We haven't had sex, sir."

"*We* haven't?" Will asks. "But *you* have before? With someone else? How old are you?"

"Dr. Anderson, I-I-I don't really think…" Will raises a challenging eyebrow and Johnny caves under the pressure. "I'm seventeen, I'll be eighteen in January. Scarlett and I have not had sex but yes, I have before. I had a girlfriend last school year and we…um, yeah."

"So just the one?"

"Sir, I ah, I don't really see how my…"

"How what?" Will demands as he removes a knife from the kitchen drawer and starts cutting up a tomato for the salad. Yeah, that's why he pulled out the knife at this very minute. "How your sexual history effects my daughter?"

Johnny sighs. "No, I understand that, it's just…do I really need to talk to you about this? And that knife is kind of freaking me out."

Will laughs. "Yeah, this is much bigger than the scalpel I'm used to using to make incisions. So, you're not in Scarlett's grade turning eighteen then are you?"

Johnny's eyes grow wide then he sighs. "Okay, fine. I've been with a handful of girls. I know that looks bad but Scarlett knows and um, no, I'm a Senior this year," he says before he tries to take another sip of his soda but then abandons the idea. "But it's not like that with Scar. I haven't tried…I mean we've talked about…but," Johnny mumbles under his breath, "Fuck!"

Will smiles behind his hand now covering his face. "So you've tried to talk my daughter, my fifteen-year-old daughter, into having sex with you?"

"No!" Johnny runs his hands through his hair again. "I swear, sir, honestly, I…she's so much more to me than that. The other girls," Johnny sighs. "Okay, listen, I'll be straight up with you because you're scaring the shit out of me with that knife and this whole conversation and when is Scar going to be back?"

"Don't worry about Scarlett," Will demands. "Talk. Now!"

Johnny covers his face with his hands and runs them down to his chin. He spends the next five minutes stumbling over the story of his glory as a high school athlete and the handful of girls who have thrown themselves at him. He admits to taking advantage of his social status and having sex with girls he barely knew and certainly didn't have feelings for. He tells Will, it wasn't until Scarlett, that he realized how badly he was behaving.

"Scarlett would be out of her mind to think that she was equal to any guy, sir. She deserves far better than anyone I know, me included but I..."

"You what?" Will demands.

"I think I love her. I mean...I've never had feelings for a girl before like I do with Scar and it's not about sex. I swear. We've kissed and stuff but nothing...shit" he mutters.

"Nothing what?"

"You know...just innocent stuff. And it's not about that. I like talking to her and hanging out. The way her hair smells makes me dizzy and when she giggles? Jesus, that giggle makes my heart feel like it's going to explode."

Will stands still and stares at this kid in his kitchen describing his feelings for his daughter. Feelings that are very much like Will's for a certain nurse.

"Oh, thank God" Johnny breathes when he hears Scarlett bound through the side entrance and come bouncing into the kitchen.

She pulls up short when she sees her father with a knife cutting vegetables and Johnny looking ashen and scared to death. "You're ridiculous" Scarlett says to Will before she hugs Johnny.

Will notices that Johnny quickly withdraws his hands from around her waist when he sees Will's gaze fall to them.

"Where's my hug?" Will asks.

Scarlett rolls her eyes then approaches her dad for a hug. Will bends down to reach her and Scarlett whispers into his ear. "I know you asked Frank to take forever to get me home so you could interrogate him."

Will hugs Scarlett then stands up with a smile and a shrug. "You two can go sit down, food's ready."

Will spends the next hour being won over by the teenage boy as he watches his daughter smile and laugh in Johnny's presence. Will doesn't think he's ever seen her happier or more alive. And Johnny? Damn it if the kid isn't great. An honor student and athlete who has been nothing but respectful and pleasant to him. By the end of the night, Will has to admit, even to himself, that he likes the kid.

Scarlett walks Johnny out to his car a little before eleven so he'll make his curfew and Will begins to clean up the soda cans and mess left over from their evening. He heads out to toss the garbage in the garage and decides to say one last good-bye to the boy who has clearly won his daughter's heart.

He stands stuck in place and watches as Scarlett and Johnny kiss in his car. Johnny gently places a hand on her face and pulls her to him, their lips slowly meeting and melt into one another's. Innocent enough but not something any father wants to watch. But as Will goes to turn away, he sees Scarlett attempt to shimmy herself across the seat and straddle the boy.

Will approaches the car and taps on Johnny's window just as Scarlett's hands are pulling his hair. Johnny jumps and curses as he tries to lift Scarlett from his lap, realizing a second too late what a mistake that was. Will growls at him as the boy tries to shift in his pants.

Will opens the car door. "Go to bed," he snarls at his daughter then turns to Johnny. "Don't you have a curfew to make?"

"Um, yes, sir. I was just…"

"Mmmm, I'm aware of what you were just doing."

"Sir, I…Ugh!" he moans. "I'm sorry, we were just saying good-bye and I can't help…," Johnny decides not to explain his excitement over his girlfriend to the doctor. "Anyway," he says clearing his throat. "It was nice meeting you and I hope you won't try to kill me for saying this but I like Scarlett. A lot. I hope you'll accept that we're together."

Will growls again then offers Johnny his hand to shake. "Just keep it in your pants and we'll be okay. For now," Will turns and walks into his house where he can already hear Scarlett on the phone with Aliana, telling her everything about the night.

Will grabs his own phone and heads to his room. The autumn weather starting to cool the air at night has Will changing into a pair of loose fitting sweats that hang low on his hips. He removes his shirt and climbs into bed with a book. By the end of the first page, that he's read at least three times with no clue as to one word on it, he throws it down and gives in to what he really wants to be doing.

He reaches for his phone and texts the girl that has been distracting him from everything in his life since the day he laid eyes on her.

Sloan Hale.

Will: *How was the dinner? Katherine a runaway bride yet?*

It takes a few minutes but Will's phone chirps with an incoming text just as he's about to feel sorry for himself.

Sloan: *What you talkin' 'bout Willis?*

This girl makes him laugh every time.

Will: *Do you honestly not know my name?*

Sloan: *I know your name but I like pulling your chain. Hey, I rhyme and I'm funny!*

Is she drunk? Fuck, he hopes she's alone. And what the hell? Is she taking a date to this wedding or what? He decides to bite the bullet and find out.

Will: *So, are you taking a date to the wedding tomorrow?*

Sloan: *Why? Would you be jealous if I said yes?*

Jealous is a gross understatement.

Will: *Tremendously!*

Sloan: *Why would I take a date to something that is not going to happen?*

Will: *So, you don't have a date?*

Jesus, she's fucking killing him.

Sloan: *No date, no wedding. You'll see. Have you talked to Dr. Cabrera?*

Will: *What has he done?*

Sloan: *Helped the cause with his thick hair, bulging muscles and testosterone. Excuse me a minute, I need to be alone.*

WILL: *SLOAN!*

Oh, hell no! Not while thinking of his best friend.

Sloan: *LOL! Jealous again?*

Will: *Are you asking if I'm jealous of Caine or your fingers? And right now, yeah...both!*

Sloan: *My fingers? Hmmm, why would you be jealous of them?*

Gee, maybe because they're in the warmest, tightest little slice of heaven here on earth.

Will: *Where are they right now?*

Sloan: *Wrapped firmly around my rabbit. Have you ever used one of those on a girl? Oh. God....I...YES!*

Will: *I'm calling you. Answer your phone!*

Will dials her number and Sloan answers with a moan on the first ring. "Jesus, you weren't kidding about masturbating?"

"Oh, don't be so clinical, Doc! And no, I wasn't kidding about getting off. Fuck, your voice...I'm close already."

Will groans and puts his phone on speaker then shoves his pants down, his erection popping free. "Talk to me, get me there with you," he demands as he fists himself and begins to pump his hand. "It won't take long, I promise."

"I may regret this in the morning but I'm drunk and horny and your voice...I can't explain it. It just does something to me," Sloan admits. "I'm in bed. I'm naked, Will...and I was picturing you inside me while I fucked myself with my vibrator."

"Fuck, Sloan...damn, I'm so fucking hard over you, I need to see you. Be alone with you, be inside you again."

Sloan lets out a purr fit for a kitten. "I'm going to come, Will. Right now while you listen to me. Don't make me come alone" she begs.

Will pumps his hand faster, knowing he's already there with her, and moans as he feels the tingling sensation creep up his spine. "Oh, sweetheart. I'm right there with you. Go ahead, let me hear you. Say my name when you come."

It only takes another heartbeat for Sloan to moan his name and another after that for Will to call out hers.

"Thanks for helping, Dr. Anderson," Sloan chuckles. "Sweet dreams."

"Sloan, I..."

Will hears the line go silent long before he wants it to but he smiles to himself, he has to admit, this part, the chase, is pretty fun.

Chapter 17

Saturday morning arrives with Will finding himself laying in his bed, crusty from the activities of the night before, as he awakes from the ruckus in his kitchen. Figuring its Scarlett and Aliana making a mess while cooking up some crazy concoction they found online, Will heads into his shower to clean up. He dresses in a pair of casual jeans and a quarter-zip, runs a hand through his wet hair then descends the stairs to see what delicacy the girls have made for breakfast.

When Will steps into his kitchen he's faced with a much different scene then he expected. Johnny is leaning against the kitchen counter with Scarlett wrapped up in his arms, her body flush against his. Scarlett is giggling as he presses kisses to her neck.

Will clears his throat and watches as Johnny tries to make some space between him and Scarlett but his daughter brazenly holds steady. "Good morning, daddy. Johnny stopped over to bring me a coffee and take me apple picking. Can I go? Please," she begs then in the same breath adds, "And Brook called me and asked me to babysit her twins tomorrow morning. She has a party tonight and said her and her husband might need to take a nap so she asked me if I'd watch Zach and Zoe before going to the workshop orientation."

Before Will can answer about the apple orchard, Johnny's voice catches his attention. "I brought you a coffee too, sir," Johnny says as he hands Will a large cup of his favorite brew. "And I can um, I'll bring Scar to the Taylor's tomorrow. I kind of want an excuse to run into Mr. Taylor."

"Wait, so you got your license when?" Will questions.

Johnny clears his throat. "Um, over a year ago. I can drive friends. I swear, I'd never risk getting Scar in trouble."

"I don't know about…"

"Daddy" Scarlett wails.

Johnny tucks her under his arm like it's his job to comfort Will's little girl. But as Will watches Scarlett soften under Johnny's touch, he has to admit the boy has the moves. But they don't seem like moves. The kid does seem to be genuine. Maybe he wasn't with the girls in his past, but with Scarlett, he seems to be.

With no real reason to say no, Will is forced to watch Scarlett bounce out the door to go apple picking alone with her first boyfriend.

Her first older boyfriend.

Her first older boyfriend who drives a car.

Her first older boyfriend who is going to drive his car to an apple orchard where they can easily hide behind a tree and do any number of things.

Or take that car to a hotel room and do exactly what he had done the night he went to one with Sloan.

"Johnny," Will calls needing to take care of something before the kid takes off with his little girl. "Scarlett, go get in the car and buckle up. I just want to have a quick chat with Johnny about the speed limit."

Scarlett rolls her eyes then blows Johnny a kiss.

"Sir, I swear I won't speed. I'm a really good driver and I'll make sure she wears her…"

"Don't move" Will demands as he bounds out of the room and up the stairs. He returns a few minutes later and hands a roll of foil packets to Johnny.

"What the…"

"Yeah, trust me, the last thing I want to do is hand you my daughter on a silver platter but I also remember what it was like at your age to walk into a store and buy condoms. I don't want you to have sex with her but if it's going to happen," Will huffs in a deep sigh. "Then I need her to be safe. I won't ever ask you to see those again so you don't have to worry that this is a set up to see if you use them or not."

"Sir, I'd never think you were…"

Will cuts him off again. "Call me Will and don't hurt my daughter" he begs.

Johnny nods and smiles. "I won't hurt her. I promise and um, thanks for the…well, you know. I swear, I don't need them but if we did, to keep her safe, I'd deal with the embarrassment in the store. I mean I have before, um, yeah so…" Johnny sighs. "But we're going apple picking, really. Her idea," he rolls his eyes. "But being with her, even apple picking, is better than not being with her."

Will sighs again. "You're alright, kid. Let's keep it that way, okay?"

Johnny laughs. "Sure, sir…I mean Will. Um, yeah. That might take some getting used to."

"Yeah, cry me a river" Will says as he nods to the door then watches Johnny tuck the foil wrappers into his wallet as he heads towards Scarlett in a fast jog.

Will runs a hand through his hair and downs half of the coffee Johnny brought him. He smiles when he tastes it. The kid was good, exactly the way he likes it. Before he's done with his coffee and trying to figure out how in the world his daughter has a boyfriend with his condoms in his pocket, driving around in a car, his phone chirps.

Will looks down to see Caine's face and hits the answer button. Before he can say hello, Caine begins an incoherent rant that Will cannot make heads or tails out of. "Are you drunk?" Will asks. "It's ten in the morning. What the hell is wrong with you?"

"Is Sloan at the weed…wed…wedding?" he slurs.

"Katherine's?" Will asks. "Yeah, I guess. And you are drunk. Why do you care about the wedding, what's this…" Then Will remembers Sloan mentioning Caine in reference to Katherine. Will had asked her what the hell his friend had done but then got lost in Sloan and never followed through on his question.

"She's won't marry him" Caine slurs with a sigh, still not forming sentences correctly.

"Yeah, Sloan insists the same thing but what's it to you?"

"Long story. I's go. I gotta hit the gym or that fucking douchebag she's about to...Fuck me," Caine curses as something in the background breaks on the floor. "I see you later. I'll come to you and we go together."

With that, Will stares at his phone wondering what the hell is going on.

He spends the day sending texts to Sloan to see what she knows but she doesn't respond.

Will: *Caine just called to ask me if the wedding was still on.*

No response.

He tries asking if she wants to meet up after the wedding.

Nothing.

He sends one last text saying something about calling him if she needs anything.

Lame and of course she doesn't respond to that one.

Will wastes away the day alternating between worrying about Scarlett out in a car with a boy, an inexperienced driver but one who clearly has a lively sex drive, and Sloan, possibly at a wedding with some overeager guy sitting at her table trying to chat her up.

By the time Scarlett is bounding back in the house to grab a quick shower, Caine is texting him that he'll be there in thirty minutes to head to Stone's party in the city.

"What's up Scar?" Will asks when she enters the living room looking pretty and smelling sweet as flowers. "You made plans for tonight?"

"Yeah, Aliana and I are going out with Johnny and Jack for pizza then back to her house. I swear Frank and Ellie are going to be home. You can call them. They know you're going to a party."

"I know," Will says. "I talked to Frank about two hours ago."

Scarlett rolls her eyes.

Will hates that he must check up on her and annoy her like this but it's what being a parent is all about. Loving the person you created so much that you want to protect them from every hurtful possibility in the world. Loving them so fiercely that you hand their boyfriend a line of condoms and beg him to use them if he has sex with your little girl. Fuck, being a parent sucks sometimes.

She stares at her father for a few more minutes then her pretty features soften. "You look really nice, dad. Are there going to be girls at this party that you and Uncle Caine are going to?"

Will smiles. "Actually, it's at Brook and Tate's cousin's."

"I know," Scarlett says smugly. "Brook told me she'd see you there tonight."

Will nods. "Have fun tonight and remember the rules, Scar. Don't make me regret trusting Johnny, understand?"

"Yes, I understand. You have fun too. Bye, daddy," she says as she reaches the door then as Caine is entering and she's exiting, she adds, "Oh, is that new nurse of yours going to be there tonight?"

"What?" Will asks, his cheeks reddening and giving him away. "What are you…"

"Well, if she is, I hope those weren't your last ones that you gave Johnny. And by the way…nice. Good for you, dad." Scarlett laughs as she kisses Caine on the cheek and leaves with a wave over her head.

"What the hell was that?" Caine asks.

"I-I think she just congratulated me on the size of my dick."

"The fuck?" Caine demands looking a bit haggard after a day of binge drinking.

Will explains the extra-large condoms he gave to Johnny after spending last night with the kid and feeling better about entrusting his daughter with him but still needing to be sure that Scarlett was safe. "Scarlett is dancing for Brook Taylor; she must have mentioned something about Sloan" Will deduces.

"Speaking of, have you heard from her yet? And answer in one of those inside voices we used to tell Scarlett to use. I have a motherfucking headache."

"No," Will whispers. "I haven't heard from her. Now, are you ready to tell me what's going on with you and Katherine?"

Caine lifts a shoulder. "Not yet. Maybe after a few more. You called the car service, right? I had my brother drop me off."

"Nope," Will says looking at his watch. "I'll drive. Ready? And you look like you've had more than enough already. You drinking with your brother in the afternoon at your old hang out can only mean one thing. This girl has gotten to you somehow, hasn't she?"

"Yep," Caine says. "And yes, I have had more than enough but I ain't done yet."

Caine spends the next hour filling his best friend in on Katherine, who may or may not be a married woman, and his interactions over the past few days since he met her. Will tries his best to keep Caine distracted from the liquor, talking about Katherine is keeping him busy but it's clear to Will that she's the cause of his friend's binge drinking.

"I can't believe what I'm hearing from you, Caine Cabrera, a confirmed bachelor and to be quite honest, a fucking man-whore."

Caine laughs. "Yeah, we all fall, some just make a louder crash on the ground."

"So that was the earthquake I felt last week?" Will teases as they step out of the car and enter Stone Towers.

"I'll meet you up there," Caine says. "I just need to check, okay?"

Will offers him a sad smile. "I'll come with you, but you know the chance that she's here is slim to nil, right?"

"Yeah, I know."

After finding apartment 1A silent, not even a squeal from the three little pigs, Will leads Caine up to the penthouse suite.

"Well, you seem to be feeling better" Will says when he sees his patient looking even better in his home than he had the day he was released from the hospital.

"By the looks of that," Caine laughs then clears his throat. "You seem to be doing just fine."

Damian shifts his growing erection in his pants then laughs at the doctors who he invited to his welcome home party.

"Any pain?" Caine asks his patient with a nod to his manhood.

"None out of the ordinary. And if you'd let me fuck my wife, Cabrera, I'd have none at all."

"All in good time" Caine chuckles. He can sympathize with the man. He's been walking around with blue balls himself since he met Katherine Mills. He'd thought by now that problem would be resolved. He'd also thought the situation with the woman causing the issue would have remedied itself as well, but that doesn't appear to be the case. Instead, Caine is standing in his patient's penthouse while the girl, who is driving him out of his mind, is probably on an airplane heading to her honeymoon with another man.

Damian growls at Caine then smirks in his direction before he leads Sydney into the center of the room. Caine and Will watch as Damian reaches for a glass of champagne that's being passed around and clinks his glass to gain the attention of the room. Will brushes the waiter off when he offers a glass to Caine, saying that he's well over his limit and done for the time being. Caine sends him a look and an eye roll but doesn't press the issue any further.

Everyone grows silent and turns to face the guest of honor. Damian delivers a heartfelt speech and accepts hugs and well wishes from his family and friends in the room before returning to his doctors. "I almost forgot to mention it," he begins. "Sloan came by early this morning and asked for a favor."

Will raises his eyebrow. "What kind of favor?"

Will's mind hits the gutter. A sexual favor? Then all he can think is that maybe she asked for a loan from the bizillionaire so she could move and start over somewhere where she can avoid him. She'd find a new hospital and a new doctor to work for. One who she'd want to have a relationship with.

Damian brings Will out of his head when he responds. "She asked if she could use my cabin in the woods. Syd had showed her pictures one day and promised to have a girls' weekend there soon."

"Yeah?" Will asks.

Sure, she'd probably wanted it for the weekend to celebrate with the date she lied about taking to Katherine's wedding. Wait. Katherine's wedding.

"Did she say anything else?"

Damian laughs. "She asked if she could also have one of my drivers on standby. What's the problem? You're acting like she asked me to provide her with cock for the weekend."

Caine, unable to contain himself another second, jumps in. If anyone is providing Katherine with a cock-filled weekend, it's going to be him, damn it. And he knows if Sloan is at this cabin in the woods, Katherine must be there too. And if Katherine is there, then she isn't on her honeymoon. If she isn't on her honeymoon, then she isn't married. "What about Katherine?" Caine asks, trying to keep his growing agitation out of his voice and failing miserably.

Damian laughs. "Here's the thing, Cabrera," he smirks. "I might know some things that would interest you both but until my wife is told, by you, both of you," Damian says pointing to each of his doctors. "That I can fuck her, long, hard, and as often as I want, she won't let me. And when I'm being cut off from my wife's pussy…I tend to forget things."

Caine growls, "Let's go. I'll examine you again. If I think you're okay, I'll give you the green light and warn Sydney what she's in for. God help her. But, if you're not okay for sex, I can't do that so instead it looks like I'll be kicking your ass to get whatever you know about Katherine out of you."

Damian laughs again. "Maybe Mac should come with us for this exam then."

Will rolls his eyes. "Would you both stop acting like fucking children. We'll examine you, then regardless of the outcome, you're telling us what's going on with the girls."

They enter Damian's master bedroom suite and lock the door. Will conducts his neuro exam first then checks his patient's heart rate. He runs his finger over his incision, that is now nothing but a minor scar hidden under his thick hair, and steps back giving Caine the green light to step in.

"He's good on my end," Will states then turns to Caine. "You're up and no bullshitting."

Caine shoots Will a look. "You know me better than that, man."

"Not after the story I heard in the car I don't. Just check him out."

Damian spends the exam with a smirk on his face. He has every intention of telling them what he knows about Sloan and Katherine. He's just having a little fun with the good doctors and if he gets to start fucking his wife again out of this, all the better.

"Take off your pants" Caine orders.

"No foreplay?" Damian jokes.

"How long have your erections been lasting?"

"Too long because my wife won't let me do anything about them. My dick is fucking killing me as bad as it was when I first met her."

Caine moans. "Sorry, I know the feeling."

As Damian drops his pants and lies down he says, "You got a hard-on over Katherine, huh?"

Will laughs. "He's had a hard-on over anything in a skirt since we were fourteen."

"It's not like that this time."

"The ground came up out of nowhere, right?" Damian asks. "Trust me, I fell harder and faster than anyone when I met Sydney."

Caine completes his exam and apologizes for making Damian suffer through the last few days without access to his wife. "You're cleared but take it easy. Start out slow and make it quick. I'd prefer if you masturbated first to see how it feels then move on to her hand. No delayed gratification, no holding off to get her there first. Got it?"

"Yeah, send her in, Doc" Damian says with a wicked smile.

Caine and Will both chuckle.

"And let's limit the activity and orgasms to one or two a day until I see you again. And no intercourse yet. Just manual and oral stimulation till next week. I'll see you next Monday in my office or I'll stop by here and if everything is going well, I'll clear you one hundred percent."

"Thanks, Doc. And, um...about Sloan and Katherine," Damian says as he pulls up his pants. "I was just giving you guys a hard time. I would have told you everything either way."

Caine nods. "Yeah. Spill then."

Damian nods towards a bar in the corner but Will waves him off. Caine has had more than he should have already.

"So, Sydney and I own a house in the woods upstate, a getaway from the noise and media here in the city. She told Sloan and Katherine about it one night when they were talking and I guess Sloan remembered. She came to see me today and asked if she could hide out there with Katherine."

"So she didn't go through with the wedding?" Caine asks.

"I don't know," Damian admits. "Sloan was here first thing this morning. Before the wedding. She said she was hoping that Katherine would come to her senses and if she did, they'd need a place to hide out till things settled down."

"She could have called me" Will says.

Damian puts a hand on his back. "Some of them fight it till the end, man. Sloan's a strong girl, she's not going to submit to you without a fight. Just keep at it. She's got it bad for you, trust me. I've seen how she looks at you. I think she's just protecting herself because she works for you."

Will nods and sighs. "Here's hoping" he says as he helps himself to a much-needed drink.

"So, I gave her the keys and the code to get in and told her a driver would be on stand-by but I never checked to see if they used him. I can have Mac..."

"Please" Caine says.

Damian nods and sends a text to his brother-in-law. Within two minutes a smile crosses his face. "My driver dropped off two girls and three little pigs about two hours ago. One was wearing a wedding dress, the other had on the veil. They drank the whole ride and there was a lot of laughing but more crying so I don't know what you two will be walking in on. May the force be with you," Damian laughs. "Mac's coming in now," he says as he unlocks the door. "He'll need your fingerprints for access to the house and he'll give you the address. Or do you need a driver?"

"No," Wil says. "I'll drive; he's wasted" he says nodding at Caine.

"Yeah, man," Damian says to Caine. "I'd tamper that down if you want your dick to work when you get there."

"Very funny, Stone. My dick works just fine."

Mac opens the master bedroom door after a quick knock knowing that Damian is expecting him and not in there with his wife. "Can you two come with me to the office, please," he asks Will and Caine. "I'll need some info from each of you and I'll need to fingerprint you both. It's an easy ride. I'll give you directions if you'll be driving or I can call for a car."

Mac leads the doctors out of the room and then the three men laugh as they hear Damian yelling for his wife.

Chapter 18

Will and Caine make good time from the city into upstate New York even in the mist that turns to rain then into a full out downpour only to finally settle on a steady drizzle. Will finds Damian's cabin in the woods and parks the car alongside the standalone garage that is off to the side of the cabin. Mac had told them it'd be where he'd park if he didn't want the two girls inside to know he was there before he had a chance to be sure they were alone. Mac's a good man.

As they climb out of the car and come together to stand and scope out the situation, Will laughs that Damian refers to what he's looking at as a cabin. The house is amazing and as night has darkened the sky, the woods surrounding it gives it the feeling of being engulfed by an enchanted forest. As Will scans the grounds for any sign of Sloan or Katherine he marvels at the sky glowing from the moonlight and sprinkled with stars.

Romance personified. Now if he only had Sloan in his arms.

"This is romantic, right? That's what you're thinking?" Caine asks.

"Yup, go ahead and call me a pussy, but sitting on that porch on that swing with Sloan in my arms…totally romantic and exactly what a girl like her deserves. Katherine too, man, so if you're at all serious about shit with her, especially after her coming off whatever the hell went down today, you'd better pull your head out of your ass and warn your dick what it's in for. One girl, one pussy, romance."

Caine scoffs. "I wasn't going to call you a pussy. Jessie would have," Caine laughs. "But I was actually having very similar thoughts about that swing. Katherine may have been straddling me and bouncing on my cock but…old habits and all that, you know" Caine sends his friend a mischievous grin.

The men try to decipher if Sloan and Katherine are inside, alone or otherwise but even though the cabin glows from the lights, in what appears to be the main living space, there's no sign of life from within the house.

"Maybe they already left?" Will guesses.

Caine pauses to listen with a finger to his lips as if he's a boy scout and has any idea what he's doing in the wilderness. "You hear that?" he asks Will.

Will listens more closely to the environmental sounds, the local wildlife starting up its nightly chorus. Then he pauses too when he hears the faint sound of music then female laughter. "Yeah," he says smiling. "They're playing music inside and that was Sloan laughing."

He'd know that sound anywhere but why was she laughing? Was she inside with another man who was eliciting that alluring sound from her? The thought makes him see red and want to charge into that cabin and throw her over his shoulder like a caveman.

Before they can discuss their plan, the front door opens and like an angel with a glow backlighting her hair, Sloan emerges into the darkness of the wraparound porch. She's wearing what appears to be Katherine's veil on her head and not much else on her body. She's never looked more perfect to Will than right at this moment.

Fuck, she looks hot too, sexy, and drunk. Not necessarily in that order.

Will and Caine stand stock-still. They want to watch this scene play out for a minute and regroup before they make any sudden moves to alert the girls of their presence. As Katherine exits the house and comes to stand on the porch beside her friend, Caine asks, "The fuck am I looking at, man?"

"Well, it better not be Sloan in nothing but a bra and those fucking see through white panties."

Caine laughs. "What? Yeah, calm down. If I'm looking at anyone, it's Katherine in that damn wedding dress that's pissing me off but she looks hot as fuck with the back pulled up between her legs and tucked into her cleavage making it more like some kind of an adult onesie than a gown. But I'm talking about them," he nods with his head at the reason the girls moved their drunken, half-naked dance party to the porch. "Are those skinned kittens?"

Will laughs from deep in his belly. "No, those are the three little pigs."

"The three little pigs?" Caine asks. "I'm apparently more drunk than I thought."

"They're Sloan's teacup pigs. Polly, Poppy, and Petunia."

"If I wasn't so enthralled with Katherine, Jesus, she's fucking sexy," Caine moans and adjusts himself. "I would ask, but right now, whatever, man."

By now, Will barely registers Caine's presence let alone his words. Sloan has begun swaying to the music, her hips making circles and her breasts slowly bouncing up and down in that push-up bra that is highlighting one of her best features. She's holding a bottle of beer and every few rotations of her hips she takes in a slow pull of the ale.

The pigs must have needed to be taken outside because once they're done doing their business, they scurry back up to the porch squealing to get back inside and out of the rain. Sloan opens the door but before her and Katherine can follow the three little pigs inside, Will calls out to her. "Hey," he says. "If I had known clothes were optional, I wouldn't have gotten so dressed up."

Sloan looks at him and smiles, the corner of one side of her lip raising. "Well, Doc, you can always lose an item or two on your way over here."

Katherine's eyes meet Caine's and Will follows his friend as he heads in the direction of the cabin, Caine's only goal to reach Katherine and get her into his arms as quickly as possible. Will wishes he could watch that scene, the great playboy, Caine Cabrera, falling to his knees for a woman, but he's too worried about reaching his own girl.

As Will steps up onto the modern style cabin's wraparound porch that appears to run the entire front of the house and continue to the back, he comes to stand in front of Sloan. He takes her hand and leads her to the two rocking chairs near a small table. He sits and pulls her into his lap as Caine lets Katherine lead him into the quaint cabin.

"Whatcha doin' here, Willis?" Sloan asks.

Will chuckles. "That never gets old for you, does it?"

"Nope" she says with a giggle that Will silences when his hands plunge into her hair and he pulls her mouth to his. She relaxes in his arms and opens, allowing him full access to her mouth.

"You looked so beautiful dancing in the rain" Will moans into her mouth then dives back in and deepens their kiss. He pulls back when a shiver runs through her body. "You're freezing," he says. "It's way too cold up here at this time of year to be outside dancing in the rain in a bra and panties."

"I had to take my dress off," she giggles, still a little drunk. "There was blood on it."

"See, now a week ago or with any other woman, I'd be concerned and checking them over for injuries, but with you?" he laughs. "It wasn't your blood was it, sweetheart?"

"Nope. The motherfucker had it coming! Threatening to make b-a-c-o-n out of my three little pigs. That was the last straw."

Will laughs from deep in his gut as he stands with Sloan in his arms. "Let's get you inside and into a warm bath then you need something to eat. You can tell me the story from the start inside."

Sloan buries her face in Will's chest and inhales his familiar scent. She closes her eyes and lets him take care of her, too tired and too drunk to fight her feelings for the man. On the way, Will tells Sloan about Stone's party and how Caine seemed to need to see for himself that Katherine had possibly not gone through with the wedding. He didn't include that he was just as anxious to reach her to be sure she wasn't snuggled up with a date in the cabin.

They enter the large open space that includes the living room and kitchen. A huge flat screen television is on one wall and a floor to ceiling stone fireplace on the other. There's a loft space above, opening the upper floor to the lower. The upper floor houses a master suite and three other smaller suites complete with their own bathrooms. They hear noise from one of the guest rooms where they assume Caine and Katherine have bunkered down so they head in the direction of another room.

Will closes the door with a push of his toe and walks Sloan straight into what he assumes must be the bathroom. He keeps her in his arms as he begins the tub for her bath then places her on the vanity to go in search of bubbles. He adds the luxurious foam to the water and the scent of flowers fills the room. He clicks on the switch on the wall to heat the floors then adds two plush towels to the heating rack.

Will turns to Sloan. "Do you need a minute or two alone?"

"A minute? Why Will, are you planning on getting into that tub with me?"

"Damn straight I am. You can have a minute to use the toilet but that's about all the time I can give you. I-I...if I were a stronger man, I'd be able to walk away from this."

"Yes you would."

"Is that what you want, Miss Hale? For me to be a better man and walk away?"

"Yes, n-no...I don't, I don't know...I-I...no. Stay. Please."

Will nods. "Good choice because walking away at this point really isn't an option for me. I'll give you a..." Will stops short and laughs as Sloan pulls her panties off and sits on the toilet and pees in front of him. It's the first time a woman has ever done that and the sight screams of domesticity, something he's always craved but been too afraid after Julia to go after.

His eyes must be bulging out of his head because Sloan begins to laugh. "Have you never seen a girl pee before, Wills?"

He shakes his head. "No, I...sure I have just not..."

"I get it and um, I'm sorry I called you a prick" she confesses.

Will nods to the toilet that Sloan has left unflushed waiting for him to use. She nods back and as Will steps out of his pants and takes himself in hand to have his turn he says, "What? You didn't call me a prick."

"Oh, yeah I did. You just weren't there to hear it. I called you a dick too. A few times. And a few other things too."

Will raises an eyebrow then removes his shirt and approaches Sloan. He turns her around without a word and unclasps her bra, his hands quickly going to her front to support the weight of her breasts. His thumbs seek out her nipples as they harden for him and he feels another shiver run the length of her body as he takes her hand and helps her into the tub. He steps in behind her and sits then pulls her back to his front, opening his legs and placing her between them. Sloan moans when she feels his erection, already solid for her, against her back.

Will's head rolls back and he has to fight the urge to sink deep inside her.

"Why did you call me a dick?" he asks.

Sloan laughs. "I was drunk and Katherine and I were sort of male bashing. You just got dragged into the crossfire. I don't really think you're a dick."

Will nods and smiles to himself. "So, tell me about the runaway bride and what the fuck she's doing with my best friend."

"Let's save that story for when you feed me," she suggests. "Right now I just want to forget everything and relax in your arms."

"I'd love nothing more, sweetheart" he says as his hands begin to roam across her body, massaging her tense muscles and lighting a flame between her legs. He reaches for the exfoliation scrub on the ledge of the tub knowing that it'll rev up Sloan's circulation and stimulate her sensory receptors. Understanding the brain can come in handy at times like this.

He warms some of the sea salt scrub between his palms before touching her skin with it. When he comes into contact with her flesh, he tries his best to use a gentle touch, circular strokes to massage it into her body. It's not easy. He wants to devour this girl but he knows she needs this instead. He sits her up, away from his body and he instantly misses her warmth. His hands rub her shoulders then her back and Sloan's head falls instinctively to the side. Will takes that as a sign that she wants that beautiful neck of hers given some attention too.

First, he cups her neck in his hands and rubs the scrub into her skin, feeling how slick and smooth it's making it, reminding him of another spot on her body that gets slick for him. Sloan moans and Will loses his focus for a minute as his lips begin to suck the skin at her neck. He briefly feels like a teenager marking his girl but he pushes aside all thoughts of the teenagers in his life who may have done this same thing and instead he follows his natural instincts and sucks her flesh until there's a mark. Fuck it, who cares what people say or think at the hospital. He plans on making their status perfectly clear as soon as they walk through the door on Monday. Together.

Sloan is too relaxed to catch on to what he's just done. He knows there might be hell to pay for this later, but Will doesn't give a fuck in the moment.

He moves on to her arms and legs, both firm and toned. He feels her muscles flex as he kneads out the tension that lays there from her days spent on her legs in the OR or from standing at the nurses' station writing in his patient's charts. Her feet come next and he shifts them in the tub for better access. He brings her legs between his and pops her big toe into his mouth to suck. His tongue making an arousing rotation of the digit. He smiles when he sees the expression of total relaxation on her face when his thumbs find her arches and begin to stroke them one at a time until Sloan is a puddle of mush.

Will props himself on his knees in front of her, hovering over her. He watches her eyes dilate at the anticipation of him entering her.

Ah, silly girl. No time soon, sweetheart. He has plans to make her so needy for his cock that she'll beg with that dirty little mouth of hers.

Now he moves on to massage her belly then her breasts and nipples. His hands and fingers stroking her heated flesh make Sloan arch out of the water. "Please," she begs. "I need to come, Will. You're making me crazy."

Will laughs as he skirts his fingers over her taunt tummy. If she thinks he's making her crazy now, wait till his fingers delve inside her. "I know," he chuckles. "All in good time though. Now lay back and relax for me. This is about to get good."

"About to?" Sloan laughs on a deep sigh of contentment.

Music to Will's ears.

He begins to circle his fingers around her nipples, careful not to stroke the hard tips. His dick aches and bounces when a moan fit for a princess escapes her. "You want me to touch your nipples, don't you sweetheart?"

"Fuck, yes!"

Will leans down and draws first one then the other into his warm mouth. His tongue laves them, flicking and swirling until he feels his dick make a demand. "Either pull back or get me inside this girl. Now!" it says.

Will shifts them again, back to their original position and at first Sloan's sounds speak of her disapproval. Then, confident that her skin can't get any smoother, Will starts in on her head. "People don't realize what an erogenous zone the scalp is," he whispers into her ear as his fingers begin to massage her temples. "Feels nice though doesn't it, sweetheart?"

"Yes" she moans as her body softens to a near sleep like trance against his body.

Will reaches for a hand towel and submerges it into the water. Using his fingertips, Will makes slow, small circular strokes, stimulating the point between her nose and upper lip, then he works his way outward and upward along her high cheekbones, back to her temples, and landing on her forehead. "You hold a lot of tension here," Will states. "Keep your eyes closed."

Will places the hot towel over her face to create a tension-relieving face mask as he washes her hair. He drizzles a generous helping of the sweet smelling shampoo he finds on the built-in shelf into his hand and rubs before he places his hands on her scalp again. Now, Will interlaces his fingers and places his hands on top of her head, his palms are above Sloan's ears. He begins to gently press and rub the bottom of his large palms against Sloan's scalp, then works his way down the back of her head, back up towards the top again, then all the way to her forehead. By the time Will has turned the shampoo into a super sudsy froth, Sloan is fast asleep against his chest, her breathing steady and slow.

Will continues to massage her long after her breathing has evened out and she's fallen into a deep contented slumber. He gently tugs and kneads her earlobes when he's done with her scalp. Then, lowering his head, his tongue swipes her lobe to rouse her from sleep. He whispers softly into her ear. "Time to rinse the suds off, sweetheart. Keep those beautiful eyes closed for me."

Will fills the small pitcher he finds near the shampoo bottle with warm water, he gently tilts her head further back, then rinses out the bulk of the shampoo. To get her completely rinsed, he'll have to shower her before they head to the bedroom.

Once her hair is reasonably suds free, Will moves on to condition her long locks in the same manner he had shampooed them. By the time he's rinsing out as much of the conditioner as he can, Sloan begins to raise her hips, seeking attention in the one area Will has been careful to avoid.

He removes the towel from Sloan's face and sighs as she blinks her eyes and smiles at him over her shoulder. "You're an amazing man, Dr. Anderson."

"Dr. Anderson?" he questions. "Really?"

Sloan just laughs. "I love giving you a hard time."

"I'll show you hard" Will says as he presses his hips up letting Sloan have a better feel of his erection.

"Will" she pants and he cracks. He needs inside this girl and pronto.

Will slides out from under her and steps out of the tub. He reaches back in and lifts her into his arms. Will walks into the open shower and, with his back to the water to protect Sloan, he turns on the jets. Once he's satisfied that the temperature is right, he places Sloan on her feet and begins to rinse them both off.

"I need to get you on a bed, spread open," Will says. "And my tongue inside you then my cock."

Sloan shakes her head urgently and Will turns the jets off and grabs for a towel. He quickly wraps it around his waist then retrieves another. He quickly dries Sloan's hair as much as the towel will absorb then grabs another to dry her body. "I'm dry," she says. "Take me to bed."

"Let's hope that's the last time I hear that tonight."

Sloan laughs. "Okay, my skin is dry."

"And what's wet, Sloan. For me, what's wet?"

"My pussy," she moans. "My pussy is wet. For you. Will. Please."

Will doesn't hesitate a minute longer. He takes Sloan by the hands and walks backward into the bedroom so his eyes don't ever have to leave hers. He pulls her to the bed then turns them around so he can lay her down. Will nods to the bed and Sloan moves to climb up. "Not so fast, Miss Hale," Will says with a grin and a laugh. "Lose the towel. I want you to prop yourself on your arms and watch me. The whole time. Eyes open and on me. Understand?"

"Yes, Dr. Anderson," she taunts. "I understand."

Sloan climbs onto the bed and props herself on her elbows so she has a clear view down her body. Then with a grin of her own, she lets her knees fall open.

Will hisses in air through his teeth at the sight laid out before him. "My name when you come," is all he says before he covers her pussy with his mouth. Sloan cries out and her head falls back at the first swipe of his tongue over her sensitive flesh. "Eyes," he warns. "Watch me make you come."

And she isn't far away. A few more licks in the right place, at the right speed, with the right pressure, as only Will knows how to do to her body, and she's going to be flying off the bed into a world of pleasure so strong she's not sure she'll ever come down.

Sloan pulls in her bottom lip with her teeth and moans his name as her body crashes over the edge into orgasmic bliss and her cries grow louder. Will smiles into her pussy but never removes his mouth from her core. He moans and laps at her through her high, keeping her there for as long as she can take before he eases her back down with a few long, slow licks to her flesh.

"I love how you taste, sweetheart. I can't get your flavor out of my head, the sounds you make when you come. Fuck, Sloan...I need to be inside you right now."

Sloan nods and lies back, waiting for him to climb up her body and ease inside but Will laughs a playful laugh as he reaches for and flips her body saying, "Let's try this on your knees this time. I've been dying to see your ass up in the air for me."

"You're a surprise around every corner, Wilson Anderson."

Will laughs. If she only knew it all.

"What do you mean?" he asks.

"The clean cut, distinguished doctor who acts years beyond his age in public has a naughty side."

Will slaps her ass for that one then raises his eyebrow at her. "You've only seen the tip of the iceberg, sweetheart."

"I want more than just your tip, Willie," she says, her eyes growing glassy as she watches him sheath himself with a condom then continue to stroke his swelling flesh. "Give me all seven."

Will smiles, he loves that she wants to take him all in but he can't help but correct this sassy girl. "I have at least eight for you, you want them all or should I keep an inch or two to myself?"

Sloan moans as she feels him at her entrance. "I want every single one," she begs. "I've never been good with measurements."

With another swat to her firm ass, Will sinks deep inside her warm heat. He laughs again as she pushes back into him knowing full well he only gave her half of what he has on that first slide.

"Don't tease me, Wills" she warns.

"Fuck!" he groans as his hands slide under her ass cheeks and raise them up, giving him deeper access to her body. "I thought you weren't good with measurements?"

"I know when you're only giving me half of that cock. I've had it all before, remember? Twice actually."

Will sinks in deeper. "That better?" he asks as he watches himself disappear to the root.

Sloan's head rolls to the side and her back arches. "Yes!" she cries out. "More."

Will sets his pace and watches her closely for any signs of discomfort. He wants to give her what she asks for but he doesn't want to hurt her. He's not being macho, he knows his size and facts are facts. He did nothing to get lucky in the dick department, that was all Mother Nature but he'll be damned if he wastes any of it. If she wants it, that is. And by her cries and pleas, his girl wants it all.

Will luxuriates in the feeling of her tight pussy, hot and wet around him. He takes his time and slides slowly in and out of her body, he's trying to buy himself a few extra strokes. But she's liquid heat all around him, it's like fucking through warm honey and Will knows he'll reach his climax quickly. What is it about this girl that makes me go off like a schoolboy on his first time?

Sloan moans a contented sound.

"Feel good, sweetheart?" he asks.

"Yes," she pants. "I'm close, Will. Do you…"

Will moans on a chuckle. "Do I what?" he asks. "Do I love the way you feel strangling my cock so fucking tight, I've been holding back since the first stroke?"

"I'm coming" Sloan says as her body crashes over from his words. Her body shivers, her pussy tightens and when Will feels her soften and she somehow manages to grow slicker still, he raises her ass in his hands and pumps hard and fast. He chases his climax, coming hard and long inside her before crashing down on her body.

And once again, he understands the hype of simulated orgasms.

He recovers before he suffocates her and flips them around, pulling Sloan into his side. He strokes her hair out of her beautiful face and kisses her temple. They laugh when they hear their friends in the next room giggling.

"Do you think they heard that?" Sloan asks.

Will shrugs. "If they weren't doing the same thing, I'm sure they did," Will picks up on a look that crosses her features. "What?"

"It's just that I'm your nurse and it looks bad."

"Hey, stop," Will demands and pulls her closer. "First, he's my best friend. He's not going to judge you. And second, I don't give a fuck what anyone thinks."

"You don't have to. You're the famous doctor and the guy. That makes me the slutty nurse."

Will growls then sits up to look Sloan in the eyes. "And if I hear anyone refer to you as such…well, I think I may have already given you a sneak peek at that already."

She chuckles then her belly protests her lack of food since the day before. When he hears Sloan's belly rumble, Will raises an eyebrow and she giggles, forced to admit to not having anything other than a liquid diet in the recent hours.

"Let's get you fed then we can go to sleep, you look exhausted."

"Oh, pulling out all the romance now, huh?"

Will slaps her ass with a smile then rises from the bed to look for his discarded clothes.

"My dress is disgusting; blood remember?"

"How I would have loved to have seen that," Will laughs. "I'm sure Sydney has something in a closet somewhere. I'll go look in the master bedroom."

Will pulls on his pants, leaving the rest of his clothing on the floor. He has no plans to have any of them on for long so why bother with more items. He's going to forage for something for Sloan to wear then make her a quick meal, after that, he plans on being right back in bed with her. Naked.

On his way to find Sloan some clothes he encounters the three little pigs who each grunt their disapproval of the debauchery he had just finished with their owner. He reaches down and pets them, allowing each of them to smell his hand and get used to his scent. They snort at him at the smell of their owner on his hand and Will smiles down at them as they follow him into the master bedroom then back to the guest room.

Will and the three little pigs return to the guest room with a pair of sweats and a top for Sloan that he slips over her head. The action reminds him of his days dressing Scarlett and he knows he needs to call and check in on her. "Hey, um," he stammers looking for a reason to have a few minutes alone. "Why don't you freshen up and I'll find something for us in the kitchen? Meet me in there?"

Sloan smiles and nods her head as she reaches out for the comfy pants in Will's hand. "Sure. I'll be right out. And I see you found my babies along the way."

Will leaves the guest room with a smile in Sloan's direction then enters the kitchen. He immediately notices that it leads to the lower deck in the back of the house and he quietly steps outside. He shivers at the cool, crisp autumn air and he spies a Jacuzzi hot tub, hammock, and outdoor kitchen, all three giving him an idea. He quickly pops back inside to look for options in the fridge and cabinets, grabs a coat from a hook to cover his bare chest, then returns outside to begin cooking while calling Ellie to check in on Scarlett.

Ellie's phone going to voicemail has him trying Frank's then realizing it's an ungodly hour on a Sunday morning. Needing to be sure his daughter is safe and knows he'll be home before nightfall, he texts Scarlett's cell phone.

Will: *Uncle Caine and I had an unexpected trip pop up. We're in the woods upstate. Be home by dinner. I'll grab a pizza.*

Will isn't surprised to see that Scarlett responds instantly. She's been attached to that phone morning, noon, and night ever since Johnny hit the scene.

Scarlett: *I'm fine dad! At Aliana's. Why are you texting so early?*

Will: *Okay, stay there till I get home or call Grammy.*

Scarlett: *Making breakfast in bed? LOL!*

Will: *Go back to sleep!*

Scarlett: *I'd tell you the same but…*

Will growls at her insinuation. How the fuck is she old enough to have an inkling about what he's been up to? And furthermore, when did she become bold enough to talk so openly with him about his sex life? Maybe it was him giving condoms to Johnny or maybe it was just the simple fact that he's never had a sex life before. Either way, he doesn't like that his little girl is growing up.

"Smells great," Sloan's voice makes him jump. "Whatcha making?"

Will pockets his cell and walks over to Sloan to inhale her neck. "You smell great but the eggs I have cooking with a few surprises inside aren't so bad either."

Sloan checks him out head to toe. "What are you wearing?"

Will looks down at himself. "I grabbed this coat before I came out here. It's a little nippy."

"Maybe we should eat inside?"

"Nah, we're tough, rugged, country folk now. We'll be fine and um," Will looks in the direction of the hot tub. "I want to get you into that. Sit" he orders as he plates the hangover egg and pepper omelets on plates.

"What's that and where did you learn to cook like this?"

"It's my famous hangover omelet. My mom taught me how to cook a few things. But this is something Caine, Jessie, and I concocted one morning after a particularly rough evening."

Sloan raises an eyebrow. "What's in it?"

"Well, I had to make do with what was in the kitchen but you know Stone, it was pretty well stocked. So, hmmm, let me see. There's eggs, of course," Will says as he lifts a forkful from his plate and offers it to Sloan. "Peppered bacon and a bunch of different bell peppers."

Sloan opens her mouth for a taste, letting the fork slide across her upper lip on the way out. When her tongue snakes out to lick her lips and she closes her eyes and moans at the flavor, Will is forced to adjust himself in his pants.

"Mmmmm," she moans. "So, good."

Will takes a bite for himself then offers her another.

"I can feed myself," Will ignores her comment and nods to the second forkful he's extending to her. "Where's the kick coming from?" she asks.

Will laughs. "Sorry, too spicy?" he asks but not offering her an explanation why he's liked his food spicy since he was a small child. Chemo had damaged his taste buds so Will always eats his food with a little kick.

"Not at all, just wondering."

"Cayenne, whiskey, some of the cheeses," He eats another forkful then offers her a third. "Drink some coffee and your juice."

Will and Sloan clear their plates and finish their coffees before Will takes her hand and leads her to the hot tub. He flips on the switch and Sloan bounces on her toes when the pool of water begins to bubble and a light blue hue illuminates the water.

"Clothes off, climb in" Will instructs.

"What if Caine and Katherine see us?"

"We'll be covered under the water. They'll catch on quick and go back inside."

Sloan is hesitant to do his bidding, still hung up on something about his being her boss no doubt. After a few minutes of contemplation though, she pulls the string on her pants. Letting them fall to the ground, she steps out of them then lifts her shirt over her head. Will drops his pants and shrugs off the jacket he'd found on a hook near the door. He extends his hand and helps her climb into the tub.

As Sloan sinks under the water to cover her naked body, in the chance that Caine and Katherine should emerge from their own love cave, Will climbs in behind her and cups her breasts in his hands, his thumbs hardening her nipples. Sloan relaxes enough to place her head on his shoulder and sighs at his touch.

He continues to stimulate her nipples, closely watching her body's reaction. She begins to arch into his touch and as her breathing accelerates Will pinches both of her nipples. He wasn't sure of the reaction he was in for but he couldn't have asked for a better one.

Sloan calls out his name in a plea for more as her hips begin to undulate in his lap. Will's lips find her earlobe and begin to suck, his tongue running the length of the shell. "Shhh," he soothes. "I'll take care of you, sweetheart but after I make you come in my hand, we're going back to bed so I can fuck you properly."

"Fuck me here" she begs having since forgotten about her concern over Caine's judgement.

"Can't," Will says shaking his head. "No condom out here."

"I'm clean, I swear," she promises. "And on the pill but if you don't trust…."

"I trust you. I'm clean too but," he sighs. "It can complicate things. Let's give this a little more time, okay?"

Sloan shakes her head agreeing but Will can see the disappointment written all over her face. He hates that he's caused that but he can't help it. The one and only time he hadn't used a condom, too caught up in the moment, Scarlett had been the result. Yes, that day in his old apartment, he pulled out well before he came, laying his cock on Julia's belly and watching as it pulsed out his orgasm. But, nine months later, he was still a single father and had learned his lesson. He loves his daughter but he can admit how she had complicated his life. Still does to this day.

Take for example his relationship with Sloan. He can't jump in head over heels like another guy his age. He has to take things slow, be sure she's right before he can even let Scarlett know he has an interest in her. Then he'll need to know for certain that she's open to the fact that he has a daughter. He knows not all young women Sloan's age want a ready-made family. Then there's the issue of more children for him. Does he want to start over again when Scarlett is almost ready to be out on her own? He's not sure. Even if it means losing Sloan, he's honestly not sure.

Will trails his hand over her flesh and smiles as her skin pebbles for him. She's under the water and warm, her shivers are all for him and he knows it. "Relax," he instructs. "I'm going to make this quick then I'll take you inside."

Sloan moans as his fingers open her, finding her slick and ready for him even under the water. Will can't help but let out a moan of his own at the discovery. He lets one then another finger slide inside her, his thumb beginning its circular pattern on her clit. "Your pussy feels so good, sweetheart. I can't wait till that's my cock it's squeezing like that."

"Yessss," she hisses. "I'm close already."

Will laughs at his luck. Where has this girl been his whole life? A few swipes of a finger or his tongue and she's going off like a rocket for him. With most girls, it had taken him at least three go arounds, all ending in them pissed off that he'd come and they hadn't. Before he'd even figured out how they liked to be touched, hard or soft, up and down or left to right, they'd been over and he hadn't had the chance to prove himself in bed. With her, it's been so easy. From the first touch, his body somehow just knew what hers needed.

"Go ahead, sweetheart. Let me feel you come for me."

The water sloshes over the side as Sloan's body throbs and her orgasm pulses through her system. All the while, Will is there helping her ride it out, making her take every last ounce of her pleasure. But then he reaches the end of his restraint and climbs out of the tub, scooping her relaxed, limp body into his arms. Will walks into the house and heads to the room they've claimed as theirs with purpose, Sloan and he dripping water on the floor along the way as they go.

When he gets to the door he kicks it closed and tosses her to the bed. "Sit on the edge for me?" he asks. "I want you to lick me but don't let me come. No matter how delirious you make me, even if I beg, okay?"

"Mmmm, so I get to torture you a little?" Sloan asks as Will throws a towel from earlier, that he finds on the floor, over her shoulders to keep her warm and help her to dry off.

Will wraps a hand into her long hair and pulls her face closer to his body. "I'm all yours to torture, baby. Show me no mercy."

Sloan licks her lips as her eyes meet his from under her lashes. She smiles when he moans before she's even touched him. His dick is hard, the head swollen and moist at the tip and Sloan can't help but swipe her tongue over it for a taste.

"Fuck, yes," he moans when he feels her tongue then again when Sloan moans at the taste of him in her mouth. "Now all the way up and down, all around me but no sucking, just that amazing fucking tongue of yours. And still be careful," he warns. "Because trust me, that tongue is more than enough to make me come in your mouth right now."

Sloan flattens her tongue and licks him from root to tip, first on his underside then all around. When she circles back to the underside and flicks at his sweet spot, Will's hips buck and his head falls back. "So fucking good," he sighs. "Now lay back for me before you make me come. I want that pussy."

"Will" she begs, scooting up the bed as she watches him slide on a condom. His earlier refusal to take her bare had stung but she knows it's for the best. He is right, that kind of intimacy can change and complicate things and she wasn't sure where, if anywhere, this was heading.

"I got you, sweetheart," he promises and hopes it's one he can keep. "But get there quick for me then we'll take our time on round two."

Will sinks deep inside her on the first thrust, finding her soft and slick from her earlier orgasm in the hot tub. He reaches down and grabs her legs, placing them on his shoulders, Will sinks in deeper than he's ever been inside her.

"Oh. My. God!" she cries. "So good. Fuck me, move just a little and I'll come for you."

"I love that dirty mouth. Yes," he says as he begins to move. His hips pounding into her as he chases his own orgasm. "You're going to make me fucking come too, sweetheart. Play with your clit while I watch" he begs as he pulls out and flings the condom off. He fists himself and jerks off as he watches her orgasm slam through her. And then he's right behind her, spurting his hot release onto her taunt belly and nipples, careful not to coat her pussy with it even though that's exactly what he craves to do.

Sloan catches her breath first and reaches a hand to her stomach to swirl in his ejaculation then a finger finds its way into her mouth with a moan escaping her. Will continues to stroke himself as he comes down from his high, all the while revving back up as he watches her put that finger, covered in his come, in her mouth.

"You keep doing that and I'm going to be back inside you before you even know what's happening."

"Is that a promise?"

"Oh, baby…stay right there" he warns as he reaches for a wad of tissues to clean up and another condom. He sheaths himself again then lays back down on the bed.

He nods at Sloan and she climbs on top of him, sliding her pussy over his cock. "No teasing this time, just fucking ride me."

Sloan begins to slowly move over his body, her lips finding his and swallowing his moans. She scoots up on her feet, his hands slide under and cup her ass, and then she's moving again. Up and down, so slow he's ready to take over and pound out another orgasm for each of them but then he decides it feels way too good so he settles into the bed and lets her set the agonizing pace. "You're fucking killing me" he admits.

"Death by pussy," she laughs. "That's definitely one for the medical books."

Sloan rides him, slowly up and down his cock until she feels her orgasm building then she increases her speed and Will jumps in to help. His hips raise and fall in time with her body until they're calling out each other's names and coming undone together once again.

"Fuck that was good" Will sighs, contented as he pulls her achy and tired body into his arms to settle down for a much-needed rest before they'll have to head back to the city.

"Yeah," she agrees. "You probably won't believe me but I usually can't um," she clears her throat. "You know…finish with a guy."

"Really?" he asks, shocked. "You're the easiest girl to make come that I've ever met."

She lifts an eyebrow and frowns at him.

"I didn't mean it that way. You're not easy like slutty easy," he laughs, "It's just, I don't know. Usually it takes me a few times to get a rhythm going and figure a girl out. Even then, most times I've wondered if they'd faked it."

Sloan laughs then covers her yawn. "I'm too tired to even address that right now but trust me Will, you're better than good in bed. I highly doubt any one of the many girls you've been with has faked anything."

"Many?" he laughs. "There haven't been that many, trust me."

"We all quantify things differently. You know how I have the problem with measurements," she laughs. "I'm sure to you the hundreds that you've probably had," she yawns again. "Aren't that many. To me, that's many."

He strokes her eyebrows as she gently closes her eyes and begins to doze off.

"Twelve," he says on his own yawn. "You're number twelve."

Sloan pretends to be out cold, not responding to the fact that this perfect man in his mid-thirties has only slept with eleven other women. How is that possible? She tries to do the math. Maybe he lost his virginity late. But late for a guy would be what? Sixteen at the most. So, okay, maybe he'd only been with two or three girls in high school. But then college, she'd assume he'd had a ton of girls. But if she's really only his twelfth, then she'd guess that maybe he'd had a few steady girlfriends during those years. Alright, so maybe add another five or six during those years and you have maybe seven to nine. But that only leaves two to four more for medical school and since he graduated. It just doesn't seem possible. Unless…

It's another red flag that pops up in her mind. They've been doing that lately. Her best guess, he's either currently married or was for many years to hold such a small number of women on his list of fucks.

As she's truly losing her battle with sleep, she thinks she hears him say, "And thirteen is an unlucky number so it's a good thing I'm stopping at twelve."

Chapter 19

"Daddy," Scarlett excitedly greets Will as he walks into his living room to find his daughter and his parents looking comfy on his sofa waiting for him to arrive home with pizzas. He'd called them after he and Caine had dropped the girls off in Manhattan and alerted Damian Stone about Katherine's jilted lover's threats. Damian had promised to get Mac on security for their apartment. He laughed at Sloan's request that the three little pigs also have security but then when he realized she was serious; he'd agreed to get Mac on that as well. That'd be a first for the ex-Marine.

"Hey, baby girl," Will returns. "Hey dad, ma."

Will's mother reaches for the pizzas in her son's arms then plants a soft kiss to his cheek. She smiles when she smells Sloan's scent on his skin. "Did you boys have a nice weekend?" she asks with a knowing smirk.

Caine leans in for Milly to give him his kiss then he shakes Charles' hand. "Hey, Owl" he calls to Scarlett using her nickname. He's called her that since she was a baby and had the hugest eyes he'd ever seen.

"Hey Uncle Caine," she returns. "I'm starving. Uncle Jessie is in the kitchen, he had to take a call in private."

Will and Caine glance at each other. Neither of them can figure out what their friend has going on. Caine can't remember the last time they'd gone out together, let alone the last woman they'd shared in bed. Good thing too, because he has no plans on sharing Katherine with Jessie or anyone else. He'd have to have a conversation with Jessie about that once the Andersons left and Scarlett went off to her room.

Scarlett talks almost nonstop through their meal, the adults barely getting a word in edgewise. She tells them every last detail about Johnny's football season and how he's already training for his upcoming basketball one. Caine and Jessie give Will a few good digs during that conversation. Then she switches topics and goes on and on about Brook Taylor and her new dance workshop. Caine and Jessie grow as quiet as Will when she tells them that she'll be going to California with that workshop the day after Christmas and will be gone for a few weeks.

Before she bounds up the stairs to call Johnny from her room, Scarlett makes them promise that they'll all go to watch Johnny play in the homecoming game on Thanksgiving Day.

Milly and Charles say their good-byes at the door, Milly leaning in to both Will and Caine to whisper, "You both smell like perfume. I expect names and details the next time we talk. And Jessie has himself a girl too. He's being very secretive about it but I can tell. A mother knows these things."

The two men look shocked for a second then nod in agreeance, knowing there is no reason to fight it. They're caught red-handed and Milly will be like a dog with a bone until they confess the whole story. Well, maybe they'll leave out the sex bits but the fact that they spent a weekend in a cabin in the woods, each with a woman who is more than a quick fuck, they'll be forced to share. They can't wait to hear what Milly thinks she knows about Jessie and his new girl.

*****

Will enters the hospital with two coffees in hand and approaches the bank of elevators with sweet anticipation at seeing Sloan. He's pleased to see he won't have to wait another second when the doors open to reveal her, back against the far wall with Caine and Jessie standing in front of her, both with shit eating grins on their faces when they see their friend.

Will enters the elevator and greets them all. "Miss Hale, for you," he says as he hands her the coffee he purchased her with his own. Then he turns to his friends. "Gentlemen," he greets the duo.

"Wow, that's really nice, dude," Jessie scoffs. "Where the fuck is ours?"

"You two make a decent salary. Buy your own" Will laughs as he bats Caine's hand away from stealing his.

He glances at Sloan and notices that she's wearing a shirt that she keeps tugging high up on her neck to cover his love bite from the day before. "Is your shirt causing you discomfort, Miss Hale?"

"Maybe he'll take it off for you" Caine whispers with a chuckle as Jessie leans over and hits the button for the next floor. "Hey! What the fuck?" Caine asks.

"We'll walk" Jessie says.

"Up ten flights of stairs?" Caine complains.

Jessie pats Caine's flat, toned stomach. "You can use the exercise, old man. You're the one who fell for a younger woman."

Sloan raises an eyebrow then smirks about Caine and Katherine. Her plan to get her best friend away from the toxic man she was planning on marrying has worked perfectly.

The elevator stops and Caine and Jessie, still bickering like brothers, exit, the doors close and Will and Sloan find themselves alone once again in the space. Sloan, wasting no time, attacks Will. Her lips crash over his as he opens for her and lets her sink deep inside. He tastes like coffee and trouble and the thought that this well put together doctor could be trouble makes Sloan smile into the kiss. Will returns her delight then pulls her bottom lip with his teeth. He's rewarded with Sloan hiking her leg up on his hip.

"I can feel your hot pussy against me," Will says. "What are you doing?"

"I'm riding an elevator with you" Sloan says, using their old banter.

The elevator dings and they're forced to break apart as the doors open to a few other doctors who raise their eyebrows at the sight of Will and Sloan looking disheveled and flushed. They wave them along, not wanting to climb aboard with the doctor and his nurse who are clearly sharing a private moment. Or at least it should be private but Will and Sloan seem to find themselves in this public elevator more times than they know is appropriate.

The doors close again and Will kisses her this time, his tongue running along her bottom lip that is swelled from his earlier bite. "You look so fucking hot like that."

"Are you sexually harassing me again, Dr. Anderson?" Sloan jokes.

Returning their banter from earlier, Will responds. "I'm riding an elevator with you. You're the one who mounted and then kissed me, Miss Hale. Again."

Before Sloan even has time to giggle, a sound that can harden Will to concrete in a nanosecond, he grabs her and wraps both her legs around his waist, notching his growing hardness into her sweet spot. He thrusts, gently rubbing in the right place. "Okay, now maybe I'm sexually harassing you."

"Don't stop," she begs.

"Mmmm, that sounds amazing on your lips. I believe I heard you saying the same thing this weekend. More times than one, Miss Hale."

The elevator dings again and they break apart, having arrived on their floor and needing to begin rounds. "I'll take you back to your apartment at the end of the day, sweetheart. Just giving you the day to prepare" Will says with a smile as he readjusts himself in his scrubs before walking in the direction of their first patient's door.

Chapter 20

Will and Sloan fall into a comfortable routine throughout autumn. Will brings her a coffee each morning and every night after they're done for the day, he drives her to her apartment. Some nights, the ones where his parents or Ellie and Frank take Scarlett, he stays over. The nights that he needs to get back to Connecticut, he knows disappoint Sloan but she never questions him.

By Thanksgiving, when she leaves to head home to visit her family for the long weekend, Will begins thinking it's time to come clean and tell her about Scarlett. He hates the idea of being away from her, he'd much rather have her with him at his parent's house with Caine, Jessie, and his daughter.

He never meant to wait this long and he knows the longer he does the worse it will be when he is finally honest with her. He should have told her months ago that he had a daughter. He's not entirely sure why he didn't but he promises himself he'll sit Sloan down and open up about everything from Julia to Scarlett and what it means to their relationship that he's a single father. That is as soon as he figures that shit out for himself.

Caine and Jessie arrive at Will's to head to the Thanksgiving game at Scarlett's high school dressed like models who just stepped out of a magazine. Will watches his friends from his picture window approach his front door. Neither stops to knock, Caine opens the door and they step inside. Will loves their familiarity, wishes that were Sloan walking into his home unannounced. But, if it were her doing so, wouldn't it be their home? It'd sure as hell feel like it.

"You ready?" Caine asks looking around. "Where's Owl?"

"She left with Aliana about an hour ago," Will says. "Something about being there to see Johnny go into the clubhouse or some shit. I'm sure the last thing she wants is to be seen with three old guys."

"Speak for yourself, man," Jessie says. "I'm fucking hot!" He pulls his phone from his pocket and smiles when he glances at the screen.

"Something on there to be thankful for, hot *old* man?" Will asks.

"One hundred percent," Jessie says with a grin. "Better than what one of those dumbass millenniums could tap, that's for sure."

"Tap?" Will laughs. "So you're in college again?"

Jessie flips him off as he smiles at his phone then responds to the text that is obviously holding his attention better than his friends.

Neither Caine nor Will push him for further explanation, Will afraid of what might be on that screen but certain that it is female related after Jessie's crude comment. The trio head out in comfortable silence to spend the early afternoon watching a football game before heading to Charles and Milly's for their customary Thanksgiving feast. Will wishes that Tommy and Chrissy were scheduled to be there this year.

His older sister, Chrissy, is married to a lawyer and living in Texas. They only come to Thanksgiving every other year. This one is being spent at Brandon's parent's house in Georgia. Because of that, Will's younger brother Tommy, has decided to spend this holiday abroad in Italy with his new Italian model girlfriend. Will has seen pictures and he can't blame the guy. So, he's glad to have his two best friends by his side where they have always been.

The game is exactly what Will had expected it to be. A bunch of loud teenagers yelling and screaming and parents who were even worse. A group of moms sitting behind him, Caine, and Jessie have spent the last hour ogling them and making comments just loud enough for them to hear. Caine and Jessie, of course, love the attention. Will not so much. But his ears pick up when the women start talking about the star quarterback that's dating his daughter.

"I can't believe Johnny is taking her to the Harvest Ball" one of them says.

Oh, they had better not make a negative comment about his little girl. If they do, Will is prepared to put these sex starved cougars in their place.

"He's always been close with her" another says.

Caine glances at Will from his left then Jessie does the same from his right before turning to catch Caine's eye as well. Something unspoken passes between Caine and Jessie but Will is too busy listening to the women to take notice.

"I thought she just met him this school year?" Caine asks.

Will holds up a hand to silence Caine so he can hear the busy-bodied women.

"Yeah but come on," a third chimes in. "Mary? I mean, I get it, I guess but..."

The horns start blasting and powder flies up in the air at a touchdown, cutting the gossipy women off. Will looks at Caine for a clue as to what is unfolding. "Should we ask them for details or wait till we get our hands on the little prick?" Caine asks.

"I vote we wait for his sorry ass to explain" Jessie says.

Will moans. "This is going to kill Scar and," he sighs. "I can't believe I fell for his shit."

"Do you think he used those condoms you gave him?" Jessie asks. "I mean with Scarlett? I told you that was a dumbass move, dude."

"What should I have done?" Will asks as they stand to leave the bleachers. "Let her get knocked up at fifteen and continue the cycle?"

"Will..." Caine warns.

Will puts up a hand to silence his friend. "You know what I mean."

Caine and Jessie had known Will since they were boys. They knew he didn't perceive Scarlett as a mistake but they also lived through every hardship he had to face as a young single dad. It was the least they could do considering the secret they've spent years harboring.

That final touchdown won the game and the guys try to locate Johnny to warn him to stay far away from Scarlett. They find him walking on the field in the direction of the clubhouse. He looks worried over something, not celebrating with his team on the win. Maybe he's worried over Scarlett finding out about his cheating ways. The guys remember what the high school rumor mill is like. If those busy-bodied mothers knew about Johnny's date for the dance, they're sure it won't be long before Scarlett finds out.

"Hey," Will calls out when he sees his daughter's boyfriend. "Get over here!"

Johnny turns towards Will at his voice. "Hey, Doct….ah, I mean Will."

"How dare you?" Will begins as Johnny approaches. Caine places a hand on Will's shoulder to calm him down. Doesn't work. "I was right about you all along, you little prick. How could you do this to Scarlett?"

"Sir," Johnny defends himself. "I don't know…"

Will interrupts him as Scarlett comes bounding up to Johnny and jumps into his arms. "Get your hands off my daughter."

"Daddy!" Scarlett scolds as another attractive teenage girl, wearing a hat, approaches them and Johnny's face shows the tension his body had displayed earlier.

"Hey," he says to her. "You okay?"

Will barley takes the time to glance at the other girl before he rips into Johnny. "Have you told your "girlfriend" about your date for the dance, huh?" he begins making air quotes about his relationship status with Scarlett. "Why don't you tell my daughter the truth for once? Your using her to add to your list of girls and once you get what you want you're going to toss her aside. Are you sleeping with them both? Others too? Who do you think you are, playing with girls like this?"

"Will" Jessie tries to halt his rant.

Will brushes him off and continues, crazy on his daughter's behalf. "No! And if you have already…you know…with my little girl, I swear to God, I'm not going to be able to control myself."

"Sir, I…" Johnny tries to explain. "This is…"

Will sends a quick glance to the girl who now has tears running down her face, caught in her affair with another girl's boyfriend. "Oh, so this is Mary then, huh?" Will asks. "Well, perfect. Scarlett, are you aware that Johnny is taking her to some dance?"

As Scarlett is beginning to answer, Will finally takes a better look at Mary and starts to wish he'd never come to this damn game.

"Yes, daddy," Scarlett snarls. "I'm well aware that Johnny is taking Mary to the Harvest Ball."

"I...Johnny, I..." Will tries to form words for what he's just done.

"Shut up, daddy! You've said enough."

"Owl," Caine warns. "Don't."

Scarlett rolls her eyes as Johnny pulls her into his side and reaches for Mary's hand. "Sir," he says to Will. "We should have explained so there wouldn't be any misunderstandings. We just never thought...how did you even hear?" Johnny asks then says, "It doesn't matter. This is Mary, she's been my neighbor my whole life," he says with a smile to the girl. "We've been best friends forever, she's like the sister I never had," Johnny bumps her hip. "She can be a pain in the ass like one too."

Mary sends him a shy smile but remains timid and quiet. Scarlett holds her hand up again to silence Will as he tries to apologize before Johnny says what he sees coming.

"Mary had a boyfriend and a date to the dance until last week when the douche, that claimed to be her boyfriend, dumped her because her hair fell out from chemo. Mary has leukemia, Dr. Anderson," Johnny admits. "So after I beat the shit out of him, I asked her to the dance. She had her dress and everything. The dance is all she's been talking about for months. Well, that and the asshole she insisted on not listening to me about. Mary told me no, even though Scarlett said she was okay with it, but I told her it wasn't up for discussion. So, I'm taking her this year, I can take Scarlett next year when it's her dance. I hope you understand."

Will huffs in a deep sigh and looks to Caine and Jessie for help to get out of the mess he's stepped into. They both send him a sad smile, unable to do anything to assist the friend they protect from the topic of cancer as much as they can, which in Will's line of work, is not an easy task. But it's something they've always tried their best to do. And they always will. It's a pact they made when they were kids and Will had thought his own cancer had returned.

Those were rough days, another brain surgery, days absent from school and his own high school social scene. But Caine and Jessie were there for him through every step of the way. Will's cancer had thankfully not returned, it had only been scar tissue that formed after many years, boggling the minds of the medical community still to this day. But had he needed treatment, Caine and Jessie had their electric razors ready to go.

"Well, dad," Scarlett says, her voice dripping with sarcasm. "Do you understand?"

"Oh my God, Johnny, I am so sorry and Mary," he says turning to the young girl who, before cancer, was probably not this timid shell of a person he's seeing before him now. "I don't know what to say. I overheard some mothers talking about Johnny taking another girl to the dance and I jumped to the wrong conclusion. It's been Scarlett and me, just us, for a long time and I'm trying to figure this new us out, you know?" he asks running a defeated hand through his hair. "I just wanted to protect her. I never meant to hurt your feelings and of course I understand."

The rest of the group gathered around remains silent and waits to see if Will has plans to apologize to Johnny as well. "Johnny," he begins, always a man to do the right thing. "I owe you the biggest apology ever given. I am so very sorry and I hope you can forgive me. You really are a good kid. Actually, you seem like your turning into a pretty decent man already. I should be, and I am, proud that my daughter likes you. I promise I'm going to try better to keep my emotions over you and Scar in check moving forward. You've never done anything to lose my trust. I need to have some faith in her judgement and she seems to like you so…"

Johnny laughs. "It's okay, Doct…um, Will. I tell Scar all the time, when I'm a dad, I'm going to be exactly like you. I know you love her and you're just looking out for her. You don't really know me yet, but I promise, I'm not going to hurt her."

Before Will can respond, a group of guys with a leader of the pack saunter by laughing. Will catches a remark or too but doesn't react at first. His mind is still reeling over his own inappropriate actions. But when Caine hears the ring leader call Mary "cue ball" he's had enough and steps in front of the kid. He was just in the nick of time too because Johnny was ready to pummel the dude into the ground by the looks of the vein bulging in his neck and the cries from Scarlett and Mary to calm down.

"Shut the fuck up, asshole. Didn't learn your lesson from the first beating I gave you?" Johnny yells. "Great, 'cuz I'd love to do it again."

"Hey," Will steps in front of Johnny. "Calm down. That him?"

"Yeah," Johnny huffs in a deep breath. "That's the fucking pussy."

"You think you're funny, kid? Huh?" Caine asks. "Let me tell you a little something about what you're doing. You're making yourself look like the biggest douche in this high school. If you think any girl is every going to look at you again after the way you're treating Mary, you've got another thing coming. And pussy? Ha!" Caine laughs. "Shit like this gets around and will follow you to college. You'll be jacking off the rest of your life. Now, stop being an asshole to a girl who is scared to death right now and trying her hardest to be brave. What do you think? Huh? You think she wants to be sick? She doesn't. She didn't ask for this. She didn't want to lose her hair. She didn't want her boyfriend to dump her because she has cancer. Any decent human being, a kid or not, would never have treated her like what I just witnessed. You should be ashamed of yourself and your parents should be mortified over your behavior. I plan on being in the office speaking to your principal first thing on Monday so I suggest you start making amends real fucking quick."

Dustin laughs. Stands there and laughs in Caine's face then sneers, "Whatever, old guy. Fuck you. I got what I wanted from her and don't worry about me, I get all the pussy I need." He makes a V with his fingers and flicks his tongue between them as he and his group of assholes laugh and walk away.

Will, Caine, and Jessie stand still and watch Johnny draw Mary into his arms and hold her close to his chest. "Shhh," he comforts her. "He's not worth it, you deserve the best and he's not it." Scarlett rubs the other girl's back.

"Scarlett knows how to pick them, man. We did good with her, huh?" Jessie asks.

Will nods his head then walks over to Mary. "Um, so, I had cancer too. Brain tumor when I was a kid." He bends down to show Mary and Johnny his surgical scar, covered now by his hair. He glances at Scarlett who covers her mouth with her hand and cries. She knows her father doesn't share this information with many people. "Then in high school they thought it was back and I had another surgery. I missed some school and when I went back some kids made fun of me because I had had my head shaved and they saw the scar."

Mary nods and more tears flow from her eyes.

"I broke a few noses" Jessie says.

"Hey, I'm the one that almost got suspended when I broke that asshole's ribs in the bathroom" Caine reminisces.

Johnny laughs. "I kind of wish you guys were in high school now."

Jessie and Caine look around at the students on the field. "Nah," Jessie says with a shiver. "I did this shit once, that's enough."

"Who's your doctor?" Caine asks and is pleased to hear that Mary is being treated by one of the best in the country. Her doctor happens to also be their colleague at the hospital.

"We're all doctors," Jessie says. "At the same hospital so if there is anything you need when you're there, you let us know. Anything. We'll sneak in visitors and outside food. The food there sucks."

Mary chuckles. "Thanks. I, um, I go in on Monday for another round."

"Okay," Caine says. "We'll stop by and introduce ourselves to your parents. They stay with you?"

Mary shrugs. "As much as they can but they have to work and I have siblings that need them too."

The guys look at each other. They remember what is was like when Will had had his surgery as a teen. Milly had taken a leave of absence from work and money had gotten tight. Charles spread himself so thin between work, Chrissy, Tommy, and the hospital that he almost wound up in the bed next to his son. Caine and Jessie had skipped school some days and stayed with Will so Milly could shower and grab a coffee without worrying that Will was alone.

"Okay well, we'll be by first thing to check on you" Jessie says.

"Thanks."

"I'm sorry again" Will says to the teenagers.

"It's alright, dad. I'll see you at Grammy's, okay?"

"Sure," Will says then turns and extends his hand to his daughter's boyfriend. "Johnny?"

He and Johnny shake and make things right then Will smiles at Mary before turning to lead Caine and Jessie back to his car.

"I can't wait to rat out that motherfucker on Monday," Caine says. "I was serious about that shit."

The guys spend a pleasant day with Charles, Milly, and Scarlett. Well, other than the good natured ribbing they give to Will. He's glad for it though because he had been worried that his mother was going to want to interrogate him on the woman she knew he'd recently spent a night with. Instead, she was distracted over the story of Mary.

Autumn quickly turns to winter, the weather cold and brutal. Will and Sloan continue on their course without much fanfare until one morning before Christmas. Holidays just weren't on Will's side.

"Why are you always here?" Sloan asks as she steps out of the shower and watches Will shave in the mirror.

"Do you not like me here?"

"No, I like you here just fine. I'm just wondering why we're always here. You aren't homeless, are you?"

And there it was. Will had known Sloan was bothered by his lack of an invitation to his house but he still wasn't ready to involve Scarlett yet. She'd been through enough recently, more than enough. Mary and Johnny had gone to the dance together and the way Scarlett and Johnny tell the story, they'd had a great time. But not long after, Mary had taken a turn for the worse and has been hospitalized ever since. Will knows all too well that sometimes the treatments can be worse than the disease.

Will, Caine, and Jessie have kept their promise and visit her as often as their schedules allow. Even if they can't sit and hang out with the sick teen, they make sure there is nothing she needs whether it's food, which she barely eats anymore, entertainment, which doesn't seem to hold her attention, or anything she might request.

Will has been trying to delicately prepare both Scarlett and Johnny for heartbreak if Mary loses her fight with the disease that's eating away at her tiny body.

Scarlett was leaving in a week, the day after Christmas, to go to California with Brook Taylor. Will would have a month without his daughter. He wasn't sure what he was going to do without her. Well, except fuck Sloan on every available surface in his house. Then by the time Scarlett returns, he'll be ready to introduce them and accept the fallout from both ends. He's not sure which female is going to be more pissed off at him over the scenario and his lies by omission but he'll deal with them when the time comes.

"Hmm," Will hums. "Funny you should say that. I was hoping that you'd agree to spend some time with me after the holidays. At my place. You fly back in on the twenty-seventh, right?"

"Yeah, my flight arrives at JFK around noon, I think."

"Great. That gives us two full weeks' vacation time pending an emergency patient. We can spend it at my house in Connecticut, be away from the hustle and bustle of the city, regroup, maybe plan some future things."

"Aren't you vague this morning."

Will chuckles. "I like to keep the mystery alive, sweetheart."

"You've seen me pee!" Sloan laughs.

Will grabs her around the waist and slides her between his body and the vanity. He leans down and nuzzles her neck, getting shaving cream on her face as he delights in her squeals and then those of the three little pigs as they come barreling into the bathroom to protect their caretaker.

Will bends down and pats them each on the head. "That's enough now," he laughs. "Your mommy is fine."

"I'd be better if I felt like I knew something about you. I need details, Dr. Anderson."

"I'm a surgeon, I don't really have much of a life to acquire many more details than that."

"Fine, let's play twenty questions" she suggests.

"Only if it's like strip poker and it ends with you naked."

Will wipes his face then pulls her in by the top of her towel, the section tucked around her body. His hands go to her face to hold her still as his lips ease hers open. He walks her back into her bedroom and gently pushes her onto the bed. His hands pull the towel from around her body as she tumbles to the mattress. "You three might want to sit this one out" Will says to the pink triplets that are now settled into their piggy bed only a few feet away.

Sloan laughs. "Fine, this is how we'll play. I'll ask a question, if I'm satisfied with the answer, you'll get a reward. If I'm not, no prize for you and we move on to the next question. Deal?"

Will huffs in a breath. He's not sure what information she's fishing for but what's the worst that can happen? If she doesn't like his answer or if he refuses to answer one or two, she'll try to refrain from giving him his ultimate goal in this game. She'll try, but she'll fail. He knows once he gets her body going, she'll submit to his evil ways.

"Okay," she begins as she wraps herself in the sheet to cover her lady parts. "Question one. Where did you grow up?"

She's starting off with the easy ones.

"Connecticut," he states. "Where I live now."

She cocks an eyebrow and Will knows that answer is too vague to get him any action so he quickly supplies the city and the fact that his parents still live in his hometown as well. Then for extra credit and because he's feeling generous, he throws in the fact that Caine and Jessie grew up there too.

It works. Sloan, with the sheet still tightly wrapped around her body, sits on Will's lap and straddles his waist. That would have been reward enough but then she begins to stroke his neck and earlobe with her tongue.

"Mmmm," he moans as he hardens under her. "I like this part of the game. Let's skip the questions and do more of this."

Sloan laughs then pulls away. "Yeah, no," she says. "Question two. Do you have siblings?"

Well, okay. Not as easy but still not overly personal yet.

"Yes" he states with a smirk.

"And for that smartass answer you'll get nothing," she states. "Moving on. Question…"

"No, no, no," he begs. "Wait, I'll elaborate."

She motions her hand to indicate that he has the stage.

"I have two. An older sister who still thinks she's in charge of us and a younger brother who still has no common sense."

"Very good, now onto question three…"

"Wait," Will demands. "Where's my reward for that one?"

"You didn't answer when you were asked so no reward. If you want what I would have given you for that one then you better answer this next one lickety split" she demands.

"Oh, I see how it is. We're playing dirty. Fine. Continue" he says as he raises his hips and nudges at her core.

Sloan sucks air in between her teeth and almost forgets they were playing her little game. As Will pulls back though, she remembers her goal. "Don't mess with me, Willy," she warns. "Now answer the question right away or nada for you. Got it?"

Will sighs then shakes his head with an eye roll.

"Firsts," she states.

"That's not a question."

"Semantics, my good friend. You know what I mean. Tell me your firsts. First kiss, first drink, first smoke, losing your virginity…I want them all."

Will laughs then tosses her to the bed and positions himself between her legs, notching her knee up on his waist. "Fine, but I'm not giving you all that for one reward. I want a kiss for a description of my first one, I'll throw in the first drink, smoke, and maybe even another tidbit for free but then," he smiles a wicked smile. "I want inside for my virginity story. Actually, I think I'll be staying there while we talk about it."

Sloan shakes her head, accepting his terms. Hey, she's a nurse, not a negotiator.

"I had my first kiss when I was fourteen. Her name was Maddie. It was at a school dance. Our lips touched and she moaned. I almost came right there. As I showed you on that first night, I can have a bit of a quick trigger. I pulled my lower half away from her, for obvious reasons, then tried to slip her some tongue. I hadn't a clue and ended up poking her in the eye with it."

Sloan starts belly laughing and Will begins to tickle her sides. "You laughing at me, sweetheart?"

"Yes," she says. "Yes, I am," Then Sloan raises her head slightly to give him better access to her lips. "And now I'm kissing you."

She kisses him soft and gentle at first but as he moans and rocks his hips up to meet her heat, she opens for him and allows Will to have control. He liked the slow, gentleness of her kisses but he needed more and made sure she knew it. She accepted his dominance, the trait he only seems to display in his job and in bed with her, until he pulled away and smirked. "A deal is a deal," he says. "I smoked my first cigarette when I was about fifteen. Caine and Jessie were with me. We choked and damn near died, my chest felt like it was on fire and honestly, none of us ever went back for a second try. I did my first drug when I was barely old enough to walk. Yes, I know that's opening up a can of worms and trust me, I'm more shocked than you are that I'm willing to share it," Will holds up a hand to push aside her questions so he can finish with the more meaningless trivia before he delves into the important stuff. "I drank my first beer also at fifteen and also with Caine and Jessie. We got drunk and puked in the woods where we were drinking. Luckily, we were alone and only we ever found out what lightweights we were," Will heaves in a deep breath. "Now for the virginity story. I think I told you my conditions on that one."

Will grabs a condom from the bedside table and slides it over his erection, giving himself a few good pumps for relief along the way. Sloan lets her legs slide open a bit more, welcoming him home. Will pushes the sheet that she has wrapped around her body aside and slips in. Her eyes are set on his, clearly trying to process his 'drugs as a baby' comment. He'll address it in a minute. First, he needs to expel some of his nervous energy and what better way than this?

After a few inches, Will begins with the other story he'd promised to tell to gain this reward. "Her name was Rhonda. Funny, right? You don't hear that name a lot. We were sixteen and dated for like a year. Fuck, you're so tight, baby."

A few more inches slide through her folds on a grunt and a moan, the grunting from Will, the moans all Sloan's. Then Will slides home the rest of the way with his own moan and a sigh as Sloan arches under him, her nails raking over his back. "Will, yes," she begs. "Fuck, yes."

Will smiles. "Yeah, sweetheart?"

"Mmmm. More."

"More story or…" he trails off as he nudges in deeper to finish his question.

"More story and more cock."

"I love that fucking dirty mouth you have in bed."

Will obliges and gives her a few hard thrusts to ramp her up closer to a climax, his own isn't all that far from the horizon either. He takes her mouth and forgets his story for a moment, luxuriating in her wet heat.

"I'm about to come" she admits.

"Not something I heard with Rhonda, I'm afraid," he continues his story, pulling back on the intensity of his thrusts to hold Sloan in limbo. "I'll be honest; I was never sure if we'd really done it or not. It was over before it started, you know?"

"Did you wear a condom?"

Will laughs. "Of course. One would have thought that barrier to full on friction would have helped some but not so much. I came on the second push, not even sure, like I said, if I was in," Will laughs. "Anyway, I came and jumped off her like there was a fire. We were at Jessie's, in his basement, so I ran into the bathroom and cleaned up. Caine and Jessie each had one of her friends with them in other corners of the room. It was dark and I almost broke my nose on the bathroom door when I went barreling in there, pants around my ankles."

Sloan laughs. "I feel sad for Rhonda. She missed my favorite time with you."

Will stares at her with a questioning look on his face.

"Cuddling with you after sex is almost as good as the sex."

"Oh, really? Well then" Will teases and goes to extricate himself from her body. Sloan grabs his ass.

"Whatcha' doing Willis?"

Will laughs then leans down and takes her mouth again. He doesn't release her until they're both yelling each other's names through their climaxes.

Will pulls Sloan into his arms and kisses her temple. "I love this too."

Wow, that was close to 'I love you, too' and it flips Sloan's belly upside down.

Wanting to know more about his earlier comment, but not wanting to push him, Sloan says, "You don't have to tell me if you don't want to. I mean, it was just a silly game. It's not…"

"Shhh," he soothes her heavy mind. "I want to. It's time."

Sloan tries to move from his arms, thinking it best if they're dressed for the heavy conversation but Will holds her in place until she gives up the fight. "Stay in my arms. It'll be easier for me like that, okay?"

Sloan nods against his chest then plants a few kisses over his heart. Will sighs and runs his hands through his hair then begins. "I became a brain surgeon because brain surgery was all I ever knew. My mentor, Rick Talbott, was also my doctor, Sloan. I was diagnosed with brain cancer when I was two."

Sloan heaves in a shocked breath as tears slip from her eyes. She tries to swipe them away before he notices but he feels them fall onto his chest. "I'm…I don't know what to say" she admits.

"Just listen for now, okay?"

Sloan nods again and remains silent for the rest of Will's story.

"So, I started having seizures one day and my mom took me to the E.R. They accused her of being neglectful, said I had gotten into some chemicals. They were too busy calling the authorities to question her to order a fucking scan. Luckily, my mom is no nonsense and told them pretty much to fuck off. She had me at my doctor's office first thing on Monday. They listened to her, as a doctor should, and ordered a scan. Within a week I was in surgery. A week later, pathology came back. It was cancer. So, I was taking drugs to save my life by the time I was a little over two. Other than that chemo, I've never done another drug. Not weed, not coke, nothing. Trust me, the chemo was enough."

Sloan sits up and takes his hands into hers. "Thank you for sharing that with me. You didn't have to…"

"I did and I'm glad for it. There's more though."

Sloan nods giving him the green light to continue.

"So after my treatment, I was great for years, then out of the blue, at one of my yearly scans, it was back. Rick went back in to find it was only scar tissue, but as a teenager it had scared the living fuck out of me. Caine and Jessie stood by me the whole time. They even promised to shave their heads if I went bald. The two of them are like brothers to me. And before you ask, yes my real brother and sister would have shaved their heads too. I'm close with Tommy and Chrissy."

Sloan holds his face in her hands and gently kisses his lips. When she pulls back and looks down, she chuckles. "That looks disgusting, just sayin'. Maybe you had the right idea with Rhonda."

Will looks at his placid penis, the filled condom slipping off, and laughs. "Give me a second?"

Sloan nods knowing he needs a second more to compose himself than to remove the condom. She'd felt his heart rate speed up as he talked about having cancer then felt the tear that had also escaped one of his eyes.

Will returns and sits on the edge of the bed, his back to her. "So, that's why I do what I do. Rick saved my life, more times than one, and growing up with that fucking tumor hanging over my head…I don't know. It motivated me to want to save every child in the world from that feeling."

Sloan sits up behind him and wraps her arms around his waist, her chin going to his shoulder.

"There's a lot more to say but…"

"Another time," Sloan suggests. "I feel like I know you better than anyone else already."

"What if you're wrong about me, though?"

"I'm never wrong. I'm always spot on, dude."

Will laughs and plants a kiss on her hand that he lifts to his lips. "Trusting your instincts, Miss Hale?"

"Something like that."

Will gently pushes her back down onto the bed and hoovers over her still bare body. Will had slipped on boxers after extricating the condom and cleaning up. "What are we doing, Sloan? I mean, is this a relationship?"

Sloan smiles. "I think some people would say this is a relationship."

"Are you one of them? There's so much more I need to tell you…"

"Shhh," she stops him. "All in good time. The most fun is in finding all this stuff out, you know? One step at a time. I'm in no hurry, I mean, you're not that old."

Will shows her his evil grin before he tickles her. "I guess I'd agree," he states as she giggles and he keeps tickling her. "My toothbrush is here with yours, some clothes, a few other things. Maybe I'll bring my dentures and cane over soon," he teases. "But yeah, I'd say this is a relationship. I mean, right? I know the code to your apartment. Are there any other guys that can say that?"

"Just the three others that I am currently fucking."

"Oh, you're going to pay for that one," Will says. "Take it back."

"I take it back," Sloan smiles. "So, that's all I'm going to learn for now then? The rest I'll just have to wait for?"

"Yup," Will says. "All part of the fun, sweetheart."

Chapter 21

Will exits Sloan's apartment, ready to head home, basking in the glow of her acceptance of a relationship with him. Now that he's her boyfriend the tension has lessened. He is her boyfriend now, right? I mean, that's what their talk was about, wasn't it? Shit, he runs his hand through his unruly hair, they hadn't really talked about that at all.

As he composes himself and begins to head for the stairwell, he doesn't expect to feel like a co-ed doing the walk of shame but when he bumps into Addison, the nurse from the hospital that has been rumored to want more from him than to be on his service, that's exactly how he feels.

"Dr. Anderson," she says as a peculiar expression crosses her face, one that clearly means she's about to make trouble for him. "Visiting Sloan and Katherine?"

"Um, yeah," he stammers, clearly caught off guard by the jumpy, klutzy nurse that he's still convinced is doing drugs. No one is that on edge all the time. "I needed to drop something off for Slo," Will clears his throat catching himself. "Um, Miss Hale. Documents to review before a tricky surgery we have coming up. You live here too?"

"Yeah, I just moved in with someone from the hospital last week. My other place was a roach motel."

He'd have to talk to his patient and owner of this building about that. He doesn't trust Addison with that kind of access to Sloan. At the hospital, he's more confident that he can keep Sloan safe from her manipulative ways. Will shakes his head then continues to the stairs with a wave. "See you at the hospital" he says as he pulls out his cell to call Damian Stone and get her out of the building by the end of the week.

"Yes, you will" Addison says with an evil smile to Will's departing back before she heads back to her place to do the search on the doctor she's been meaning to do for ages. Ollie will just have to wait for his damn bagel, they had bigger fish to fry and had wasted enough time in breaking up the happy couple.

*****

Will arrives home to find Milly and Charles caught up in the hustle and bustle of decorating for the upcoming holiday season with Scarlett and Johnny in the mix. Scarlett is holding a ladder as Johnny stretches to hang crisp, white lights around the doorframe. He sees his parents inside setting up the train village in the picture window and waves with an added smile.

"Be careful," Will warns Johnny. "Don't you have a record of Tate Taylor's to break?"

Johnny sighs. "Don't remind me. The pressure is nearly killing me. According to Scar, he's coming to the game on Friday."

"I thought you were over there with her last night watching the twins?" Will asks. "Didn't you see him."

"Yeah," Johnny sighs. "But he won't talk to me. He doesn't seem happy about me taking the school record away from him. And there's this issue about my sweet spot."

Will laughs. "Nah, he's just giving you a hard time. He's a successful guy, I doubt he's that invested in the past," Will clears his throat, a tad afraid to ask his next question. "What's this about your 'sweet spot'?"

Dear Jesus, let that be some kind of basketball term and not what is going through his head at the moment.

"I don't know," Johnny says as he climbs down the ladder and kisses the top of Scarlett's head. "Tate gives huge money to the school for athletics. We get a new court like every couple of years but on one condition. There's this spot that he insists on staying the same. The wood cannot be changed and there are letters, FLO, engraved with a date from 1990."

Scarlett jumps in with romance eyes. "The rumor is that Tate and Brook," she clears her throat and smiles at her father. "Shared a very special moment on that spot when they were a couple back in high school."

"It was Tate's sweet spot too. As a player, the place on the court he liked to sink his threes from. He's not so thrilled that I'm about to beat his record from his spot. A big part of my game hinges on the exact three-point-shot he favored."

Yes, Will inwardly cheers. A three-point-shot, that's basketball not anything to do with sex and his daughter. "Yeah, let's have that be all you take away from him on that spot" Will growls with an arm around Johnny. He had to add that in just in case.

Johnny laughs then pulls Scarlett in for another kiss to the top of her head. It's funny how Johnny's outwardly affectionate nature with Scarlett no longer pisses Will off. "Do you think the rumor is true?" Johnny asks.

Will laughs. "I've met the family. Trust me, your sweet spot was one hundred percent Tate Taylor's sweet spot in more ways than one. But let's keep you focused on what's important on the court, got it?"

Johnny wiggles his eyebrows at Scarlett as he tickles her waist and nuzzles her neck. She takes off running and Johnny follows her into the house, leaving Will with the job of decorating the large tree by himself as he wonders how familiar Scarlett is with Johnny's sweet spot off the court.

A few days later, decorations all in place, Will, Caine, and Jessie find themselves in the stands at Scarlett's high school again. This time it's basketball season and Tate and Brook have invited the guys to join them with Damian and Sydney.

"So," Will says with a smile that Damian picks up on. "What's up with the sweet spot rumor I heard about."

"Ohhhhh," Damian laughs. "Big man on campus kissing and telling! Christ, it only took you almost thirty years to grow a pair."

Brook shoots Damian a look that Sydney reacts to and elbows her husband in the gut for. Then Brook turns on her husband. "I can't believe you. I mean, really? After all this time?"

Tate shrugs. "I've never told the high school why I insist on keeping that spot in its original state or why I had 'FLO' engraved there."

Brook smiles, clearly remembering the true reason that spot on the court is special to the man she's been with her whole life.

"You're such a whipped pussy, man" Damian chuckles as he pulls Sydney close to his side to escape another elbow.

The group laughs out loud at the irony. Damian Stone had been the biggest man-whore New York City had ever seen until Sydney Cooper had fallen at his feet, literally, and turned his world upside down. Now, Will would bet, Damian wouldn't see another woman even if she were standing in front of him naked.

"Says the pot, douche" Tate retorts.

"What do the initials mean?" Caine asks, the curiosity getting to him first.

Tate smiles at his wife who toys with a locket around her neck. "My first, last, and only."

"Pussy" Damian pretend coughs, ribbing his cousin.

Tate leans over his wife and pummels Damian in the arm a few times until Brook interrupts their horse-play. "You are both children. Stop!" she demands in her authoritative mommy voice. The men halt and smile innocently up at her. "Tate and I had sex on the court. Right there," she points in the direction of Tate's old sweet spot that Johnny claims is now his. "We were in here alone before a game. He needed to calm down, I helped. End of story. Now everyone shut up and watch the game."

"It was so much more than that, baby" Tate says with complete confidence.

"Shhh, of course it was" Brook confirms.

Since Brook and Tate are clearly caught up in each other and no longer paying anyone else much attention, Jessie elbows Caine to egg him on and the pair start in on Will. "Huh, that's hilarious. That's Johnny's sweet spot too, you say?" Caine begins.

"I wonder why that is, Will?" Jessie adds.

"Shut the fuck up, both of you!" Will demands. "Are you saying that maybe my daughter helps to relieve his pre-game stress? You know, the girl who is also like a daughter to both of you?"

Caine and Jessie both go ashen as a look passes between them. Will watches as they each shiver then nod an apology once they realize what they've insinuated. But as Will growls and runs a frustrated hand through his hair, they laugh along with the rest of the group, that look that passed between them hidden again.

Brook breaks the silence. "He's a great kid, Will. They're teenagers in love for the first time. Chances are, they're having sex. I mean, look at the boy! Talk about the next Tate Taylor" she laughs knowing she'll get a response from her husband for that one.

"Baby," Tate begins. "Maybe we should go for a walk around campus for old time's sake" he suggests with a wave of his palm.

Brook laughs. "Maybe later, Taters."

"Taters!" Damian mouths with a smirk to his cousin who flips him the one finger salute.

The game ends with Johnny only two baskets short of breaking Tate's three-point-shot record. He's sure to hold the honor by the end of the first quarter of the next game. Tate heads into the locker room to give the kid a hard time and then congratulate him. What Johnny doesn't know is that Tate has been his biggest fan for a long time and has already put in a good word for him at his dream school. Like Tate, Johnny bleeds blue, Carolina Blue. The kid might not be able to go there to play, the game has changed since Tate's day, but he's smart enough to attend the public Ivy League school. Tate will make sure their eighteen percent out-of-state acceptance rate doesn't affect Johnny. He'd be a huge asset to the team with his knowledge of the game and his intelligence. At the very least, they could use him on their bench doing stats.

"Scarlett ready to head to California?" Brook asks Will as they wait for the rest of their party to make their way out of the crowded gym.

"I think so. She's never been away from me, though. She's a little worried but she'll have you and Aliana and her cell, right?"

"Sounds like you're more worried than she is."

Will smiles. "It's not easy. Any of it, is it?"

"What?" Brook asks smiling at Will. "Being a parent?"

"Yeah. And trust me, doing it alone," he sighs. "I don't know. I made some bad decisions I guess. I just hope she doesn't hate me because of them."

"You did great with her. She's a phenomenal dancer, she's smart and kind, she's a beautiful girl inside and out. I don't think you have anything to worry about."

Will huffs in a breath as the others approach. "Thanks. These two helped a little."

Brook laughs at Caine and Jessie jumping on each other and nudging Will for attention.

"What are you telling her about us?" Jessie asks.

"He gave you two credit for helping with Scarlett. She's a great girl, you guys did a good job with her," Brook says. "You two are going to have to take care of him while she's gone. Will seems to be having a hard time over her absence and she's not gone yet."

Will sees that look pass between his two best friends again but then as quick as it happened it was gone and Will leaves it alone.

"He'll be fine once he gets Sloan in his bed" Caine teases.

Brook raises an eyebrow. "Your nurse?"

Will nods.

"I knew it. So, it's more than a fling then?"

"Yeah," Will admits as he smiles. "It's more. Scar still doesn't know yet but I'm planning on introducing them when she gets back from the workshop."

"Oh, Tate owes me big time" Brook laughs.

Chapter 22

Christmas is perfect except for Sloan's absence in his life. She left the day before the holiday to spend time with her family and Will regrets not asking her to stay with him. He knows the time has come to tell her about Scarlett and he plans on doing that as soon as he picks her up at the airport. Sloan will be returning early from her annual family holiday vacation in the sun.

Caine and Jessie spent the holiday with the Andersons as usual and Will was glad to have Tommy and Chrissy home for a few days but by the time he's driving them to the airport with Scarlett, he's ready for his time alone with the woman he's been craving all week. Will had scheduled Scarlett's flight to coordinate with his siblings and was now on the way to the airport.

His SUV is filled with luggage from the travelers and a passenger in every seat, Caine and Jessie coming along for the ride to see Scarlett off and of course, Johnny too.

Will parks and they walk Chrissy and Brandon to their gate and say their goodbyes first. She promises to send pictures of her first sonogram to Will. Her and Brandon had shared the news of their first child with the family at Christmas.

After the soon-to-be parents are off, the group heads to Tommy's flight and Will pulls him aside for a one on one before he leaves.

"I didn't want to bring it up in front of the others but when Bianca didn't show," Will pauses, testing the waters. "I saw the tabloids, man."

Tommy laughs. "And you believe everything you read?"

Will sends him his best older brother look and Tommy crumbles.

"Alright, fine. We're trying to work some shit out. We decided to take a break over the holidays. I'm here, she's in Aspen."

"With him?"

Tommy shrugs.

"You love this girl or what, man?"

"She's fucking hot, Will. You've seen pictures. And trust me, compared to what she does in bed, those pictures suck ass. But, do I love her? I don't fucking know. It wasn't supposed to be…whatever."

Will knows exactly what his little brother is going through. He hopes he can share some wisdom but with his track record, should Will expect Tommy to listen to a word he says?

"I'm not really a great example and I'm not going to give you a lecture but if you love this girl, Tommy…if you love her, you need to fight for her. Tell her how you feel and man the fuck up and figure your shit out."

Tommy sighs when his flight is called. "I'll call you, okay? I'll think about it but after she…whatever. I mean, you're clearly with someone and she wasn't there either this week. Does Scar even know about her? Does this girl know you have a daughter? I gotta go dude, but think about what you just said. It sounds like you should take your own advice."

Tommy leans in and man hugs his brother before he heads to the gate with a wave to everyone else.

"Dad," Scarlett calls bringing him out of his trance. Tommy was right. Will needs to follow his own advice and man the fuck up too. He should have introduced his daughter to the woman in his life and vice versa a long time ago. "Let's go! Aliana just texted me, they called the first boarding on my flight."

Will heaves in a deep breath, he's not ready to watch his little girl board a plane and leave him for a month. But he agreed to this trip months ago and he can't go back on his word now. He also knows he deserves these days alone to work out his own shit with Sloan.

He runs to catch up with the others just in time to watch Johnny slide his hands into his daughter's hair and pull her close for a kiss that turns into a full contact make-out session in front of his eyes. When they break apart he tries to ignore the teen readjusting himself as he sinks into a seat, burying his head in his hands, sad to see his girlfriend leave.

Scarlett smiles at her father and opens her arms for a hug and a kiss then she says good-bye to her honorary uncles before returning to Will again. She turns to leave as Will wipes a tear falling from his eye then she runs and jumps into Johnny's outstretched arms, not Will's. It stings at first but Will knows she's growing up and there are things that she'll need someone else to provide for her. He's glad it's a kid like Johnny that she's chosen for them.

Will, Caine, Jessie, and Johnny walk to the parking lot with Frank and Ellie, Will sad to see his daughter leave but excited to return here tomorrow to pick up Sloan.

*****

As Will had figured, Sloan's plane is delayed, adding to his anxiety. He paces in the terminal and types and deletes his umpteenth thousandth text of the day to Scarlett. The time difference is going to be an issue as are their schedules. He browses the news and media sites on his phone for an update on Tommy's love life then finally plunks down in a chair to wait, his foot tapping out a beat on the floor. Will must have closed his eyes and drifted off because before he knows it, he hears the announcement of the arrival of her flight. He straightens himself up and eagerly awaits the first sight of her.

Sloan's face lights up when she sees him and Will can't stop his nerves from pushing a worrying hand through his already messy hair.

"You're a sight for sore eyes, Dr. Anderson."

Will responds physically, unable to hold back. He plunges his hands into her hair and hauls her tight against his body. He smiles down at her as he gently rocks his hips. "God, I fucking missed you. You look extra sexy with this tan," he says. "There better be tan lines under here."

"Mmmm, feels like your dick missed me too. And there might be a line or two for you to run your tongue over."

"So much," Will says. "He missed you so, so much."

Sloan takes his hand and they walk to the baggage claim area. "I just might have to show him some mercy in the car then" she teases.

He thinks she's teasing. But oh, please dear God, please let her be serious. A blowjob, even a handjob in the car is exactly what he needs to settle down.

"You seem nervous," Sloan states, picking up on his energy. "Scared to have me living with you for a few weeks with no work to distract us?"

Will moans. It's now or never. "We'll end up with work. It's inevitable, happens every time but..." Will sighs for the tenth time and again his hand plunges through his crazy locks. "There are some things we need to talk about. Things I haven't told you that might," he clears his throat. "That will," he corrects. "Change things between us. I've been waiting for the right time but I'm afraid I may have waited too long."

Sloan tries to hold back the expression of concern from her features but fails miserably as they reach the baggage carousel and wait for her things to come around.

"Um," she stammers. "Okay, you have me worried now. Let's just get my stuff and head to your place. It sounds like it's better if we talk this through in private."

Will nods in agreeance and grabs a bag, tossing it over his shoulder then pulling the handle out of a second to roll behind him. He reaches out with his free hand and leads Sloan to the visitor parking section where he parked.

They drive most of the way in silence, Will asking if she needed to stop for anything, wanted to grab a coffee or find any other possible way to stall what he knew it was time, past time, to do.

"Wow!" Sloan teases. "This must really be bad. Like I have a wife and I'm a convicted killer kind of news."

Will laughs. "Well, now that you've said that, I guess what I have to talk to you about will seem like nothing. And I've never been arrested."

Sloan raises an eyebrow. But has he been married, is he married? He must notice the look on her face because Will looks just as ashen as Sloan guesses she is.

"Hey, hey," he commands her attention. "It's nothing like that, relax. It's good. Well, I hope you'll think it's good. Oh, fuck...I don't know."

"Instead of that coffee maybe we should stop at the local bar and get hammered first."

Will chuckles. "It's barely three in the afternoon."

"It's happy hour somewhere" Sloan laughs, making Will smile.

They pull up in front of his house and Sloan whistles her approval. "Nice digs, Doc."

Will beams, proud of his home. "I've been here a long time. My parents live around the block. This house used to be theirs but they wanted to downsize so I bought them the place where they live now and took over the mortgage they had here."

"Are you raising circus acts or something?" Sloan teases again to lighten the heavy mood. "What do you need this much space for?"

Will chuckles. Scarlett feels like a circus act at times. Lord knows he wouldn't know what to do with elephants and clowns any more than he does a teenage girl. "No," he finally answers. "But the three little pigs are loving the place. I got them yesterday. They seemed annoyed that I was alone, by the way."

Sloan squeals, almost like the pink trio, and claps her hands, excited to see her pets after being away for a few days. Will had offered to grab them from her apartment so Katherine wouldn't have to watch them while Sloan spent the next few weeks in Connecticut. Caine had seemed sad to see them go, the pigs having grown on him. Will had even caught him looking up breeders to get some for Katherine to call her own.

"Are you sure?" she asks. "This place looks way too nice for the likes of them. What if they ruin something? Did you leave them in their crate while you came to get me?"

"Nah, they have the run of a room or two. They can't get into anything."

Sloan laughs. "Oh, you silly man. Wait."

Will looks nervously at her then they smile and start to laugh thinking about what they'll find when they get inside.

"I warned them," Will jokes. "If I came home to any nonsense, I'd be making you bacon and eggs."

"You looking to bleed, Wills?"

"Funny, Polly asked the same thing."

"If she could talk, that bitch would" Sloan admits.

Will grabs her things from the trunk and leads her in through the kitchen, the garage leading into his house. Sloan looks around the bright, open space and smiles when she hears Polly, Poppy, and Petunia snorting for attention from the cornered off mudroom. She laughs. "Putting my pigs in the mudroom? That's classic, Wills."

"I thought it was fitting. They seemed happy in there until they saw you."

Sloan steps over the baby gate, left over from Scarlett's toddler years that Will had hauled up from the basement. She holds the troublesome trio inside and cuddles them to her bosom, one at a time, before she pats their heads and scratches behind their ears. "They smell good. Did you give them a bath?"

Will laughs remembering that experience last night. "I did. It was…interesting."

"I bet," Sloan laughs. "Okay, give me the tour, they'll be fine in here for a little while longer."

Will tosses them each a treat to snack on so they won't complain about being alone for a few more minutes then he leads Sloan by the hand for the grand tour. He walks her quickly through the main living space where there are endless pictures of Scarlett and leads her straight to his room. "First, let's check out my bedroom then I'll show you the rest" he suggests with a waggle of his eyebrows as Sloan sneaks a glance at his watch.

"You've got about twenty minutes before the pigs plot their escape."

"I can do this quick, remember?"

Sloan laughs remembering their first time together but knowing that Will can also last as long as it takes to make her a very satisfied woman.

Will closes his bedroom door behind them then grabs Sloan and playfully tosses her to his bed. He'd long ago removed all pictures of his daughter from his room. It was just too weird jerking off with her face anywhere near him, so he knows his secret is safe until after he's had Sloan in his bed.

"I've been thinking about what I'd do to you once I got you in my bed."

Sloan rolls her head to the side to give him better access to her neck. "What took you so long?"

"Hmmm, later. First I need that pussy. I've jerked off more these last few days then I did as a teenager. I missed you."

"Sounds more like you missed my pussy, dude" Sloan says only half joking.

"Sloan," Will admonishes. "You know I'm just joking. I mean, yeah, I jerked off hard but…"

"I know. Let's…"

"Yeah" Will says. "This…then we talk about a few things, okay?"

Sloan nods. She reaches for the hem of her shirt and pulls it over her head revealing her pink lace bra. Will moans and runs a hand absentmindedly over his growing and hardening bulge before following suit and removing his own shirt.

"Come here" he demands even though she's already in his arms.

Will pops the snap on his jeans then lowers his zipper. "I won't last long, just warning you."

Sloan chuckles. "I hope I won't either."

"I'll do my best" Will says as he pushes his jeans to his ankles then kicks them aside after toeing off his shoes. He reaches for Sloan's waist and pulls her mouth to his, devouring her with a heated kiss. His hands working quickly to rid her of her jeans. Once gone, he pushes her back to enjoy the sight of her in nothing but her pink lace bra and panties.

Will's phone vibrates on the bedside table and he reaches to retrieve it. When he sees Scarlett's face he momentarily panics and without thinking answers the call. "Are you okay?" he asks. "What's wrong?"

"Hey Dad!" Scarlett's voice is happy and excited. Nothing for Will to have been worried over then.

"You sound happy" Will says realizing Sloan is watching his every move, contemplating her own no doubt after his rude behavior.

Will holds a finger up to Sloan and listens to his daughter. Scarlett tells Will she was just calling to tell him that she was fine and that she was going to send him some video clips and she didn't want him to freak out over them the way Johnny had when she'd sent them to him. Something about a lyrical routine and a partner that's gay anyway but Johnny needs calming down and it would be great if Will could ask him over for pizza and calm him down for her. Typical teenage girl stuff he's been dealing with these last few years.

Looking at the woman laying half naked next to him brings Will back to the present and he tells Scarlett he'll try his best with Johnny soon and asks her to call again before bed.

"I love you, daddy" Scarlett says, a sentiment she doesn't offer all that much anymore and he can't pass up the opportunity for anything. Not even to spare Sloan's feelings. He'll fix that in a minute.

"I love you, too" he says then disconnects the call.

He turns to Sloan who is wearing a look of confusion on her face and getting up to reach for her clothes.

"Hey," Will halts her. "What are you doing?"

"I haven't a fucking clue, Will," she says. "What the fuck was that? And don't tell me it was your mother!"

Will heaves in a massive breath and, knowing the time has come, holds his hand out to Sloan. "Let me explain. Please. It's not what you think. Come with me?"

Sloan sighs, her jeans now covering her legs. Will retrieves his own and steps into them before leading her back out into the hall. They walk hand in hand to another door and Will gently kisses her before opening it. "I should have told you a long time ago but this is all new to me and I wasn't sure what to do. Please don't be mad."

Sloan steps into a room that clearly belongs to a teenage girl. The walls are a bright minty green color and the furniture sitting on the hardwood flooring is white. There are pictures of a striking girl with a boy, so handsome it should be illegal at his age, spread throughout the space. Ballet shoes hang from a vanity that is covered in cosmetics and hair products.

Sloan looks at Will. "I don't understand" she says.

"Sloan, this is Scarlett's room. I have a fifteen-year-old daughter."

Sloan remains silent but starts for the biggest picture of the girl and her boyfriend that sits on the bedside table. She picks it up and studies it. She kind of looks like Will, his smile, but not his coloring, and her eyes are someone else's. Her mother's maybe.

"What are you thinking?" Will asks.

"I don't know," Sloan is honest. Why lie at this point? "Her eyes. They're not yours."

Will takes her hand, not sure if they should stay in Scarlett's room for this discussion or not. He doesn't tug her though; he waits to see her reaction.

"No, they're not. Scarlett has her mother's eyes."

"I need a drink," she says. "Can we go…"

"Yeah," Will says and leads her back to his main living space.

Will pours them each a drink then meets Sloan on the couch. "Please tell me what you're thinking. How badly did I fuck this up, Sloan?"

"I'm not sure. I…I don't know what to say."

"Just tell me what you're thinking, please."

"Are you married? Is that it? Why we were always at my place until today? Is your wife away with your daughter and I'm just here to fill in?"

Will lets out the breath he hadn't known he was holding in and smiles sadly at Sloan. "Come here" he requests, trying to pull her into his lap.

"I think it might be better if I stayed here till you answer the question. Are you married?"

"No" Will simply states.

Sloan nods. "But there is someone. Her mom?"

"No. It's been just Scarlett and I since about two hours after she was born."

Sloan looks at Will wondering why that is and hoping that this sweet man is not about to tell her that his wife died two hours after having their daughter and that she's the only woman he'll ever love. But what other explanation can there be? No woman in her right mind would leave their child and a man like Will.

"Did your wife," Sloan clears her throat. "Die?"

"I never had a wife and no, Julia didn't die."

"Julia" Sloan tries the other woman's name out on her tongue for the first time. The other woman. She knew something like this was going to happen. Hell, it's why she didn't want to start this in the first place. Love and relationships were fucked up and ones with your boss were the worst kind. Now she'd be out of a job and loveless all in one swoop.

Will hands her another drink. "It looks like you can use this," he says as he downs his own. "This isn't how I saw our staycation starting off."

"Hmmm" she moans and sinks back into the plush sofa letting the liquid burn its way to the pit of her stomach.

"Sloan, please. Stop thinking the worst and let me explain."

She nods but pulls her hand back when Will tries to take it. "Maybe you should talk without touching me. I...I'm sorry. I just need to understand what I've gotten myself tangled up in first then...I don't know."

Will tells Sloan about meeting Julia in college his senior year, falling in love, or what he had thought was love at the time, and then throwing caution to the wind and taking a chance. A chance that turned him into a single father while on his way to medical school at the age of twenty-two.

"I was stupid. I'll never regret having my daughter but...Until you, it was just Scar and I and I was okay with that."

"And now you feel different?"

"Yeah," Will sighs. "I told you how I had cancer, remember?"

Sloan gives him a look that says nothing but, "Duh!" and he continues.

"Well, one night my mother decided to finally tell me about a possible long-term side effect. She hadn't wanted to have the conversation with me before then, for obvious reasons, but knowing I was going to med school and smart enough to figure it out, she decided she'd waited long enough. She told me that there was a chance I could never father children."

Sloan covers her mouth with her hand to try to hide her reaction but fails. So, based on that reaction, now Will knows that she wants to have children. Another layer to complicate things more. He's still not sure what his feelings are on that topic.

Will sends her a sad smile then continues. "She said she'd set up an appointment with a specialist and we'd figure it out. Going to the doctor with my mother and jerking off in a cup wasn't high on my list so I blew it off but I couldn't stop thinking about it. Then one night Julia and I…well, things got started and I didn't have a condom. We'd been together a long time and I knew she wasn't sleeping around. She was on the pill and I promised to pull out."

"Yeah, that doesn't always work."

Will laughs. "No, it doesn't. Nine months later I had a screaming bundle of girl to prove that fact. She blamed me for the pregnancy and as her due date got closer she changed. Dramatically."

Will goes on to explain that Julia left him and Scarlett in the hospital only hours after giving birth. Not knowing what else he could say, Will asks Sloan if she wants to ask him anything else. She shakes her head, still trying to digest what she's already heard.

"Maybe we should get something to eat," he suggests. "Or do you want to turn in early?"

"Why didn't you tell me?" she asks, changing her mind. "I mean, I get why you didn't say anything maybe that first night but why not till now? The night we played twenty-questions…"

"Would have been the perfect time," Will finishes her sentence. "Yeah, I know. I panicked. I didn't tell you at first because, to be honest, I was afraid it would have chased you off. I also didn't want the pressure if you asked to meet her. I don't bring women around her. I promised myself a long time ago that if I ever did, it would be a woman I was serious about."

"So you're serious about me now?"

"I am, yes. I'm sorry, Sloan. I…"

Will is cut off when Sloan's lips crash over his and her arms wrap around his neck. He pulls back. "So you want to meet my daughter then?"

"Yeah," Sloan says smiling. "I want to meet your daughter. But first" she begins with a smirk as she pulls him back in the direction of his bedroom.

Chapter 23

Will and Sloan do not get three uninterrupted weeks as he knew they wouldn't. They're called into two emergency surgeries during the first week. Then on the second, Will receives the call from Johnny that he's been dreading.

"Hey, Doc…Yeah, ah Will" Johnny stammers when Will answers.

"Hey Johnny," he says pulling Sloan onto his lap in the kitchen where they were just about to sit down for a snack to keep up their energy. This was a day they planned as a marathon sex romp. A fun activity for a single father who finally has a house to himself to behave in any way he wants. Or so he had thought. "What's up? Scar okay?"

"Ah, yeah. I talked to her last night. But um, it's Mary. Something seems wrong but I don't think she wants me to know. Can you see what's going on for me? She went into the hospital last night but she's not due for treatment."

Will looks at Sloan as he stands her back up on her feet so he can rise and pace the room. He disconnects Johnny's call and fills Sloan in before calling into the hospital to find out what's happening. He and Sloan both know before he places that call.

Johnny was right, Mary isn't due for a treatment and her cancer is responding well to it but most times that's not the issue. The problem is that her immune system is non-existent and she has pneumonia.

With their plans ruined by the somber moment and their concerns over the young girl, Sloan and Will head to the hospital to see Mary. While speaking to her parents in the hall, they are both taken aback when Ollie and Addison walk by looking more friendly with one another than appropriate in the workplace. Yeah, they're not ones to talk but still.

"Excuse us a minute," Will asks Mary's parents and they head back into their daughter's room. Will and Sloan wait as what looks like a happy, albeit deranged couple, approaches them.

"Well, well, well," Ollie begins. "Looks like it was just me you didn't want to sleep with because you two are on vacation but here you are together. Are you fucking the good doctor, Miss Hale?"

"Shut your fucking mouth, Oliver. Seriously. You're looking more than," Will eyes Ollie and Addison up and down. "Comfortable with her so I'd walk away and drop it if I were you."

Ollie smirks at Will then slides his hand to Addison's ass. "Funniest thing happened. I wonder if you could help me out, friend," Ollie sneers. "I'm in need of a new place. Seems your patient is buying out my lease but now I need to find a place to stay. It's a shame too, Addison had just moved in and we were so close to Sloan."

Will lunges, not thinking his actions through but the movement is enough to shut Ollie up. Addison takes him by the hand and leads him down the hall. Then she stops and turns back around. "See you at the hospital gala. You are going aren't you, Dr. Anderson? It's to benefit your department this year."

Will slowly nods once then turns and places a hand on Sloan's lower back and leads her to Mary's room. What the hell? Will rolls his eyes at Sloan and suggests that she stay far away from both of them.

Later that night, Will calls Johnny and explains the seriousness of Mary's complications and tries to warn the boy that things can get much worse and fast or stabilize just as quickly but he wants the teen to be prepared for the worst. He suggests that Johnny call her, Mary's in isolation and even with his pull, Will can't get the boy in. It's for Mary's safety that she not have visitors.

Upon arriving home, Will and Sloan head up to bed early, their day of planned fun foiled but they snuggle together for a private moment under the sheets.

"What was Addison talking about today?" Sloan asks through a yawn as Will gently strokes her nipple with the pad of his thumb.

"What?" he asks. "The gala?"

"Uh, huh," she moans. "Mmmmm, that feels good" she admits as her back arches into his touch.

Will lowers his lips and plants a soft kiss to hers before taking her nipple into his mouth and running the pad of his thumb over the other. "How's that?"

"Even better but…the gala?"

"Oh, yeah," Will says as he begins to kiss his way down her body, his tongue circling her naval. "It's a huge party to raise money for the hospital."

Sloan pulls in a gasp when she feels his tongue run up her pussy and circles her clit.

"Fuck," she sighs. "I know what it is. I mean…"

Will sucks her clit into his mouth and his hands find and tweak her nipples again. "You taste so good, sweetheart. Are you close?"

"Oh, my God," she moans. "Please. So close."

Will lowers his tongue back to her core and licks her to a mind-blowing orgasm. He sits up and holds her gaze as he shamelessly licks his lips then leans down to claim hers and give her a taste of her own sweetness. He hovers over her body, supports himself on one arm to sheath himself in a condom before gently sliding inside her. "Jesus, you're so wet."

"Yes. For you. All for you."

Will begins to pump his hips as he claims her mouth. He thrusts in and out at the pace he knows they both need to climax. As he grows closer, he breaks their kiss and asks, "Sloan, will you be my date to the gala?"

She moans her response then cries out her second release.

"Fuck, I'm going to come too, sweetheart. Let me see those eyes while your pussy makes me come."

Sloan and Will lock stares as he empties himself into the condom with a growl and a final deep, hard thrust. He rolls off her body, removes and disposes of the condom then pulls a sleepy Sloan into his side. She rests her head on his chest. "When is it?" she asks.

"Day after Scarlett gets home. She's coming this year. I'm sorry, I should have asked you sooner but this thing between us scares me when it comes to my daughter. I hope you can understand that. And so, that's why I hadn't asked you yet then I forgot all about it until Addison brought it up today."

"Hmmm, yeah, why is that?"

Will shrugs. "I think she's on the planning committee and she's fucking nuts sooo…" Will lets the rest hang in the air as he kisses Sloan's eyelids and watches her start to doze off. He's not sure what the crazy nurse's motivation is for mentioning the event. Maybe she thought he hadn't asked Sloan and her mentioning it would drive a rift between them? God only knows what that girl has going on in her head.

"I'll call Katherine in the morning. Maybe her and I can go shopping then meet up with you and Caine for lunch? Wait," She pauses. "Does Katherine know about your daughter?"

Will had had this conversation with Caine not long after he'd started dating Sloan's best friend. Caine wasn't happy keeping something from the first girl he was in a relationship with but Will had given him no choice. In the end, Caine's loyalty to his best friend had won out and he'd agreed not to tell Katherine about Scarlett until Will had a chance to come clean with Sloan.

"I asked Caine not to mention it. He wasn't happy about it but understood my reasoning and agreed not to mention Scarlett to Katherine until I found the right time to talk to you."

Sloan nods. "He's protective of you."

"Yes he is. Jessie too. We're all protective of one another."

"I'm glad. Katherine and I, Rose and Amber, we're like that too. That's why I had to get Kat away from Mike. Anyway," Sloan sighs. "I'll call her in the morning. You can tell Caine he doesn't have to keep your daughter a secret anymore."

"Sounds great, sweetheart. I'll give you my credit card."

"I can…"

"Not happening. I'm buying your dress. I'm sure Caine is buying Katherine's. I'll call him in the morning to be sure we don't open a can of worms we don't want to be a part of. I'll tell him that you and I have spoken about Scar."

"Fine but I could pay for a dress" she laughs as she snuggles in, her back to his chest.

"No!"

"Bossy" she says with a smile.

"Good Night, Miss Hale."

Chapter 24

"Would you calm down, please, you're making me freak out" Sloan begs as she checks herself in the mirror for the hundredth time in less than ten minutes.

"They'll be here any minute," Will says with a kiss to her temple. "And you look flawless. I'm not nervous over you, sweetheart. I'm nervous over Scarlett."

Sloan looks at Will's reflection in the mirror. "What do you mean?"

Will sighs. "It's been just her and I forever. Well, my parents are great and Caine and Jessie for sure helped me with her more than anyone should have, but at the end of the day, it's been just us. Now she's got Johnny and I have you. Things are changing fast. Teenagers don't always do so well in the face of change and I just don't want your feelings to get hurt by how she might react."

"Oh," Sloan says. "So, you don't think she's going to like me?"

"I think she's going to have a lot of questions and I'm one hundred percent positive she's going to grow to love you."

"I'm not stupid, Will. I know she's not going to call me mommy and throw her arms around me in the airport. I just don't want her to be threatened by me, by us, okay?"

Will nods and the doorbell chimes as the door opens and the pack of people he invited along arrive.

Caine strolls in with a casual arm slung around Katherine's shoulder with Johnny laughing behind them. "Thank God I'm out of their car," he says to Will then raises an eyebrow when he sees Sloan holding his hand. "I thought he was going to kill us driving with one hand. I won't mention where I'm sure the other one was. He's a great role model for your daughter's boyfriend by the way."

Will shoots Caine a look. "You realize a teenage boy thinks you're ridiculous? A. Teenage. Boy!"

Caine chuckles. "It was only one finger; it's not like I made her come in front of him" he jokes and gets a slap on the bicep from Katherine for it.

"Hey, Will" Katherine says with a kiss to his cheek then she pulls Sloan in for a hug. "You doing okay? You look a little green, honey."

"Thanks," Sloan sighs. "Just what I wanted to hear."

Will introduces Johnny to Sloan and makes the boy promise not to text Scarlett and tell her that her father has a girlfriend. "I want to introduce them, okay?" Will says.

"Yeah, sure. Scarlett will be happy for you. She's thought you've had a girlfriend for a while now, you know?"

"Really?"

"Yup" Johnny says with a smile.

"Well," Will says pulling Sloan in for a kiss to her lips. "I guess I'm not as smooth as I think I am."

The room laughs. All except Jessie who is too busy with his phone to interact with the group until Will calls him out on his less than stellar behavior. "You going to put that phone down or are you in competition with him," Will points to Caine. "Over who can act more like a teenager than the actual one we have here?"

"Sorry," Jessie apologizes. "Work shit."

"Mmmm" Caine and Will hum together knowing when their friend is bullshitting them.

The door opens again and in walks Frank and Ellie with Charles and Milly. Milly bounds into the house like an excited teenager and wraps Sloan in a huge embrace before Will even has the chance to make introductions. He'd told his parents about her when he asked them to come along to retrieve Scarlett from her trip. He'd been excited for his parents to meet Sloan today for this very reason right here. Milly Anderson can make anyone feel safe and secure, welcomed. Even a woman about to meet her boyfriend's teenage daughter for the first time.

"You're shaking like a leaf, sweetie," Milly says to Sloan as she releases her. "I'm Wilson's mother, Milly. This is Charles. Relax, it's going to be okay. Scarlett is going to love you."

Sloan shakes hands with Charles and Milly pulls her back in for another hug.

"Mom," Will says. "She's going to think you're a little off if you keep hugging her."

Milly smacks Will on the chest then smiles at Sloan. "She's beautiful" Milly whispers to her son loud enough for the whole room to hear and to make Sloan blush.

Will pulls Sloan into his side for a squeeze and a kiss to the top of her head. "Yes she is," he says. "Now are we ready to go?"

They discuss the driving arrangements and the gang decides to take a few cars as Caine and Katherine are planning on leaving from the airport to go out to dinner and Jessie says he's going to hitch a ride back into the city with them. Frank and Ellie want to have their own car as well so Will agrees to drive himself, Sloan, his parents, and Johnny. With the plan in place, they motorcade to the airport.

On the drive, Sloan gets to know Will's parents a little as well as Johnny. It calms her nerves over meeting Scarlett. A little.

The entourage is assembled together at the gate when Scarlett arrives with Aliana and the Taylors, Brook and Tate each with a twin in their arms. Johnny races up to his girlfriend and lifts her giggling body into the air then kisses her senseless, no longer afraid to show his affections for the girl in front of her father.

Will pulls Sloan in closer to his side when he feels the anxiety seeping off her. "She's going to love you, relax," he states. "If she ever comes up for air. Jesus," he moans. "That doesn't get easier to watch."

Caine pats Johnny on the back so he and Scarlett will ease up on the PDA behavior only teens can pull off. "Will's about to combust, man" Caine laughs.

"Sorry," Johnny apologizes but then, unable to help himself, goes in for one more heated kiss before releasing Scarlett to hug her dad and meet Sloan.

Scarlett pulls back and searches the group for her dad. When she sees him with a beautiful woman pulled tightly into his side she smiles and rushes to him. Scarlett leaps into his arms and covers his face with kisses like she did as a child, her legs wrapped around his middle.

Sloan stands back and watches the scene, knowing Will has a daughter and seeing him in the role of daddy are two different things. It takes her breath away. She'd like to say that it wasn't a hot sight but she'd be lying. If she's being honest, there's a good chance she just ovulated at the sight of Will smothering his daughter in kisses and accepting hers.

Sloan is in deep thought over children, current and future, and she doesn't notice that Will has placed Scarlett on the floor and he's speaking to her. "Oh!" she says when she realizes. "I'm…sorry. I was just…forget it. Hi," she extends a hand to Scarlett. "I'm Sloan Hale. I um, your dad and I work together and um…yeah."

"Hey," Scarlett responds with a giggle. "I'm Scarlett, his daughter."

Sloan nods and Will smiles at his two favorite girls in all the world meeting for the first time. "Ah, Scar," Will begins. "Sloan and I have been seeing each other for a while now. She works with me and I thought it was time for you to know and meet one another."

"You're sleeping with your nurse?" Scarlett says but before Will can reprimand her she says, "Nice, Dad!"

"Scarlett," Will warns. "I'm introducing you to a woman I'm serious about for the first time in my life because she's the only woman who has ever been worthy of meeting you, but my sex life will never be up for discussion, understand?"

Scarlett laughs. "I've seen the condoms, dad, remember?" Scarlett laughs. "I'm not stupid. Did you think I'd assume you had them laying around in case you wanted to make water bombs one rainy day?"

Will runs a hand through his hair and Sloan laughs. "She's a spitfire."

"Seems to be a quality I like in my girls," Will teases with a kiss to her temple then turns to his daughter. "Let's go home and get you unpacked and you can get to know Sloan, okay?"

"Yeah, sounds good. Let me say good-bye to Tate and Brook and the kids first."

Will approaches the couple with their kids alongside his daughter and thanks them for taking care of her while in California. He beams when Brook tells him that Scarlett shows great potential in her dancing.

After saying good-bye to everyone, the group splits apart and Will finds himself behind the driver's seat of his car with Sloan seated next to him, his parents in the middle row and somehow his daughter has managed to get herself in the far back where she is snuggled up to Johnny. The six talk comfortably, with Will chancing a few glances to be sure his daughter and Johnny aren't up to anything indecent. Once back in town, they stop for pizza before finally dropping Johnny then his parents off.

"Are we bringing Sloan home too, Dad?" Scarlett asks.

"Um, she lives in the city. She's been…"

"Sleeping at our house while I was gone" Scarlett finishes with mirth in her voice.

Will looks at his daughter in the rearview mirror.

"Scarlett, I don't have to stay," Sloan begins. "I mean, I can get my things and take a train back into the city. Will, maybe it's a good idea if I…"

"Will it make you uncomfortable if she stays with us for a few more nights until we go back to work, Scar? We have the fundraiser so it'd be easier if she stayed but…"

Scarlett shrugs. "I guess not. It's just weird to think about you…you know?"

"Yeah, I know the feeling and don't think about that, please. Jesus, don't think about that!"

Scarlett laughs. "Okay dad but you better promise to be quiet."

Sloan chuckles as Will rolls his eyes at his daughter and pulls into his driveway. "I'll try my best. Go unpack and then maybe we can play a game or watch a movie?"

"I'm kind of tired. The time change and traveling. I think I'm going to call Johnny then just go to bed early. Can we go for breakfast in the morning though?"

"Sure" Will says as he places Scarlett's bags down in the foyer but then the three little pigs squeal from their spot in the mudroom and Scarlett perks right back up.

"Did I just hear a pig? What the hell have you two been doing since I left?"

Sloan looks at Will with a raised brow. If the girl only knew that her room was the only space they hadn't desecrated. She clears her throat. "Oh yeah, I have three little pigs. You want to see them?"

"Are you for real?" Scarlett asks. "I love pigs. Oh. My. God! I've been telling Johnny forever that I want one and you have three? Wait till Aliana sees them!"

Will smiles then looks at the two most important girls in his life. "I'm going to head upstairs and catch up on some research. Why don't you introduce Scar to the triplets?"

"Yes! Yes! Yes!" Scarlett says bouncing on her feet. "I'm not tired anymore. Let's go!" Scarlett grabs Sloan's hand and drags her in the direction of the squealing like they've been besties their whole lives. "What are their names? Are they pink? I want a pink one. Why do you have three?"

Sloan laughs as they walk through the kitchen and head towards the pig's makeshift living quarters. "They're all girls. I didn't want to deal with any hanky-panky," Sloan laughs. "Their names are Polly, Poppy, and Petunia and yes, they're pink. I got three because I didn't want only one. They'd be lonely. But when I went to pick up the two I ordered there was only one other pig left. I couldn't leave Petunia all alone, so I have three."

Scarlett begins to squeal louder than the three little pigs when she sees them and climbs over the gate to sit on the floor and let them maul her. They jump into her lap and bump her cheek with their noses.

"They like you," Sloan says. "They don't always take to new people right away."

"OhmygodIlovethem," Scarlett says, the sentiment coming out as one long word. "I want to keep them and love them all day long!"

Sloan laughs. "They can be a handful. I think it's kind of why we get along."

"Why?" Scarlett asks. "Are you a handful too? I think I am sometimes. Johnny says I am, my uncles too."

"Your father talks about you like you're the best thing since sliced bread so I doubt he thinks you're a handful."

"He does?" she asks. "I think I've been freaking him out lately."

"Why?"

Scarlett shrugs her shoulders and Sloan drops the topic, thinking it might be too early for a heart to heart with the young girl and not exactly ready for this herself. So instead she changes the subject and tells Scarlett about the pigs and then about her dress for the fundraiser.

The conversation continues with Scarlett holding the pigs, who fall asleep in her lap, while Sloan makes them each a sandwich and grabs some chips. "Snack is ready," she says. "You can put them on their bed. They're pretty conked out after all that loving you gave them. Come sit."

Scarlett climbs onto the chair next to Sloan and thanks her for the turkey and cheese with pickles, both of their favorite, and heaves in a deep sigh. Sloan knows the girl has something on her mind and wants to share it but isn't sure she should.

Scarlett looks at her phone that just vibrated and smiles at a text then she sighs again as she responds and puts her phone back in her pocket.

"Something you want to talk about?" Sloan asks. "I can be a great listener, you know?"

"Yeah but you'll tell my dad."

"Only if it's something that puts you in danger. Girl talk can stay between us, okay?"

Scarlett nods and gathers her thoughts. "I don't have a mom, you know. Did my dad tell you that?"

"He did."

"I never met her. She left us at the hospital. She didn't want me."

Sloan frowns then offers Scarlett a smile. "But your dad did, honey. He loves you. I'm sorry about your mom. Sometimes people do things we don't understand. She must have had her reasons."

"Yeah, I'm sorry about it too but I have my grandmother and I tell her lots of things. Or at least I did. It's different now, you know? I…talking to her about certain things is weird."

"Sex things?" Sloan correctly guesses.

Scarlett nods. "Ellie is great too. She treats me like a daughter. She's taken me to all the sex talks and even showed me how to use a tampon but Aliana gets pissed when I talk to her about things now because she says that Ellie then assumes she's doing them too and lectures her non-stop."

"So you have some questions?"

"Well, I talked to that doctor friend of Uncle Jessie's a few months back."

"Doctor friend?" Sloan asks then figures out who she's referring to. "Oh, you mean Dr. Baxter? Cindy?"

"Yeah, I guess," Scarlett says. "Uncle Jessie is so tapping that. My dad and uncles dragged her over here to give me an exam to make sure I was still a virgin then put me on the pill in case Johnny and I started having sex."

Sloan rolls her eyes, appalled that Scarlett is most likely right and Dr. Jessie Holt is 'tapping' his new partner but also that Will and his friends ordered a pelvic for this girl just to be sure she was a virgin. "Oh! My! God! Of course, they did. Jesus, Scar. If I'd…"

"Yeah, the three of them are handfuls," she laughs then clears her throat. "So, can I ask you something?"

"Sure."

"Um, so Johnny has had sex before with a few girls. I…I'm still a…a virgin."

Sloan nods to encourage her to continue, relieved that the girl is opening up to her and being honest.

"Yeah, I mean, we've done sex stuff before. Well, you know, like everything else except that."

"Wait, what?" Sloan almost chokes on her bite of sandwich. "Everything?"

Scarlett nods shyly then buries her face in her hands, clearly embarrassed with the topic.

"Wait a minute, like anal?" Sloan asks then slaps a hand to cover her mouth when she realizes that she just asked her boyfriend's teenage daughter about anal sex. And she hadn't meant to ask that so loudly. If Will heard her, he'll be down here in a flash flipping his lid.

"What?" Scarlett asks. "God, no! Shhh," she warns and checks to be sure Will hasn't heard and come running downstairs. "Wait, why? Have you and my dad…no, forget I asked that."

"Okay, okay…no, no, no. Let's regroup. I'm not good at this. I'm trying my best but give me a minute here."

Scarlett laughs. "You're as bad as me. I see why he likes you. You remind me of me, actually."

Sloan smiles at the compliment. "So, wait, by everything…you mean," she leans in and whispers this time. "Like hand and mouth stuff then, right?"

Scarlett laughs at Sloan's use of hand gestures.

"Ah, promise you won't tell my dad? He finally trusts Johnny and he'll kill him if he knows this."

Sloan raises her hand as if she's being sworn in by a jury of her peers. "As long as you're not in danger, I promise I won't tell him."

"Alright," Scarlett lets out a huge breath. "Yeah, hand and um, mouth stuff."

Sloan shakes her head. "Mmm hmmm, okay. So, both of you with the hands and mouth then or…"

"Um, well, both with the hand stuff and just me with the mouth stuff. Johnny wants to but I haven't let him yet. He wants me to let him, you know, take my virginity too, but I'm scared it's going to hurt and I'm going to bleed all over the place. I promised him we'd do it on my birthday and now I'm freaking out. Ohmygod! I don't know what to do. My birthday is in a week" Scarlett admits all in one breath, close to hyperventilating.

"Calm down," Sloan says with a soothing hand to the teen's back. "Let's figure this out, okay?"

Scarlett nods then her phone vibrates again and she looks at the screen. "Johnny keeps texting me sweet things. He knows I'm nervous and he doesn't want me to back out again. I mean, he's not pressuring me. I want to do it but I'm scared too, you know?"

Sloan heaves in a deep breath of her own now. She hasn't had time to ease into this thing whatever this is, mothering, friending, or mentoring. Whatever the fuck it is, she's sure it would have been easier if it began with teething and potty training before moving on to oral sex and losing one's virginity.

"Okay, so here's the thing," Sloan begins. "I can't believe I'm going to say this and if your dad finds out, he's going to kill me. But...here's the deal. Let him, you know, with his mouth before he...with his" Sloan says using hand gestures again to get her thoughts across.

"I don't know" Scarlett says.

"Trust me, it'll help with the...it's going to hurt, Scarlett. I mean, is he ah..."

"My dad gave him some of his condoms."

"Wait, his? Like the ones he uses or he bought Johnny some?"

"He gave him a strip, not a box, so I'm guessing they're his and Johnny laughed because he said they're the same ones he used before. The same size so..."

"Oh," Sloan says. "Um, yeah, it's going to hurt the first time, honey. A lot."

Scarlett groans. "I'm not doing it. Fuc...sorry, um, forget that. No way. I keep telling him it's not going to fit but he just laughs and says it will."

Sloan chuckles. Scarlett will appreciate her boyfriend's apparent well-endowment soon enough but Sloan understands her concern as a virgin. "Listen, if you're having any second doubts then you should wait."

"They're not doubts about Johnny. I want to be with him, I want him to be my first, my only one, but I don't want it to hurt. It looks like it can really do some damage, Sloan."

Sloan laughs. "You'll stretch to accommodate him but it will hurt at first. The amount you bleed has nothing to do with his size, unless he's not easy with you. And the bleeding is out of your control so don't worry about it. Don't be embarrassed if it happens."

Scarlett nods. "What else?"

"He needs to make sure you're ready and um," she moans before finishing her sentence, unable to believe she's having this conversation with Scarlett only hours after they've met. "Wet and soft so that's why he should use his mouth first. Have you had an, has he made you, you know, um finish?"

Scarlett nods.

"With his hand? Wow, that's good. Hmmm, I guess boys are different today. Well, good for him, good for you, too. So, um yeah. He should do that first with his hands or his mouth before he puts it in and make sure he puts it in slowly and he's gentle with you, a little at a time. If it hurts too much, are you confident that he'll stop if you ask him to?"

"Yeah, he'd never hurt me like that on purpose. He's already promised me that he'd go slow and be gentle. He said he'd stop if I couldn't handle it but he seems to think that once he starts I'll be fine but I don't think he gets how," she clears her throat. "How big he is."

Sloan laughs. Ah, to be young, innocent, and naive again.

"So, where are you planning on doing this? Your first time should be special, Scarlett, not a quickie in the backseat of his car."

"Yeah, I know. He has it all worked out."

Sloan nods. "Your dad put you on the pill, you said, right?"

Scarlett shakes her head. "Yes, and gave him condoms remember?" she asks with a smile.

"Okay, that's good. You need to use them even though you're on the pill. Two forms of protection is best. The pill can fail if you're on antibiotics or you forget one and condoms do break. Don't forget that."

"I promise, Sloan. I don't want to end up like my mother."

"Scar, I didn't mean…"

"I know. Thanks for talking to me and the sandwich. I like you. I'm glad my dad let me meet you."

Sloan stands and hugs the girl before Scarlett bounds up to her room. She cleans the kitchen quickly so she can head to bed with Will. She knows Will is going to try his best to get this conversation out of her. She may even let him try his best for a little while. But she has no plans on betraying the girl she's grown to love in less than a day.

Chapter 25

"Really, Sloan?" Will asks. "Four orgasms and you're still not going to tell me what you two were talking about for two hours?"

Sloan moans, her body humming from the pleasure still coursing through her veins. "Nope. You're free to see if five is my breaking point but we really should get out of bed soon. We wouldn't want Scarlett to get the wrong impression."

Will chuckles, "Five it is" but as he's climbing on Sloan they hear squealing, the teenage girl and pig kind, coming from the hallway.

"The three little pigs have her wrapped around their snouts. Little assholes" Sloan laughs.

Will moans and stands, his erection not wanting to cooperate and get tucked away in his pajama bottoms, as Sloan runs a hand through her messy hair and grabs her clothes. They hear the laughter, Scarlett's and Aliana vibrating through the walls then the deep baritone of Johnny's and Jack's followed by the squealing of the three little pigs.

"I guess we need to go see what they're up to, huh?" Will asks.

Sloan nods and opens the door to find each pig paired up with one of the teenagers, Jack the only without a pink bundle in his arms. The pigs appear to be having the rides of their lives on pillows soaring down the flight of stairs. Teenagers can be mature one minute, talking to you about oral sex then the next…well, here they are sliding down a flight of stairs with pigs.

"Sloan!" Scarlett exclaims. "The three little pigs are never leaving!"

Sloan looks to Will who pulls her into his side. He leans in and whispers in her ear, "Maybe Scarlett is on to something."

Sloan pushes his comment aside and laughs then drags Will into the kitchen to make breakfast with bacon. That's what her pigs get for making her forgo her fifth orgasm.

*****

Will enters his master bedroom after hours of being banned while his girls got ready for the fundraiser. Sloan had returned with Katherine earlier in the day after spending the better part of the early afternoon in Manhattan. Sloan has spent hours with Katherine and his daughter doing their makeup and hair to finally be ready mere minutes before their ride was to arrive.

Sloan exits the bathroom first and Will is forced to catch his breath. She's wearing a long black gown, the one he bought her but never saw, Sloan insisting if he was buying it for her the least she could do was surprise him. She has another surprise for him under the gown too. Or lack thereof as she isn't wearing anything but the gown he sees. The gown hugs every curve and has a slit so far up one thigh he swears he can see her naked hip bone. His eyes don't stay there for long though because the neckline plunges into her cleavage creating a thin line to her naval. Will knows it's impossible for her to be wearing a bra and he reaches out a finger to swipe over a nipple without thinking.

Sloan closes her eyes and a moan escapes her as she grasps his wrist to stop his sweet torture knowing that Katherine and Scarlett are only inches away in the bathroom.

"Sloan," is all Will can manage before he's forced to adjust himself. "You are flawless. Jesus, sweetheart, come here."

Sloan smiles through her blushing and lowers her chin as she walks into his arms and wraps hers around his waist. "You look amazing too, Will. I mean, I love your scrub days, for obvious reasons, but this," She looks him up and down in his custom-made tuxedo. "This is just too much."

Will is careful not to destroy her makeup as he plants a sweet kiss to her lips but warns her that as soon as the night is over he plans to devour her properly. Starting with her exposed cleavage.

When Scarlett hears the chime of the doorbell, she comes bounding out of the bathroom to meet Johnny at the front door causing Will and Sloan to break apart. Will's breath stalls again when he sees his daughter but for a very different reason than when he saw Sloan. Scarlett is stunning in a light pink floor length gown, her hair and makeup making her look as if she's the same age as Sloan. The thought is disheartening for a few reasons but Will pushes them away to pay his daughter the compliment she deserves. "Scarlett, baby girl, you are stunning. Johnny is going to be out of his mind and have his hands full tonight. Promise me you'll stay near one of us. I don't need some doctor thinking you're an intern."

Before she plants a gentle kiss to his cheek and bounces out of the room to find her date, Scarlett chuckles, "Oh, Daddy!"

Katherine emerges a second later, just as Will has buried his face in Sloan's neck to inhale her familiar scent. "Caine just texted me that he and Johnny are here. The car is out front too."

"You look great as well Katherine," Will says approaching and kissing her on the cheek. "Caine is going to lose his shit as bad as I am by the end of the night."

Katherine giggles. "Yeah, he already has a plan. Need I explain?"

Will laughs. "Nope, I'm sure it's right along the lines of what I'm thinking. We'll have to take turns in the closest dark corner or closet."

Sloan bats his hand from her ass and walks from the room with a sly smile over her shoulder as she catches Will adjusting himself while he stares at her ass. "It's going to be a long night" he moans.

Will stands there in his room watching Sloan's tight ass sway in that dress, her body sinful, hopeful for the future.

*****

They enter the gala, housed inside a five-star hotel in the center of Manhattan, to find it transformed into an enchanted forest. Winter is still in full force outside but in here it feels like the patrons are princes and princesses floating in the spring breeze.

"Wow!" Sloan, Scarlett, and Katherine exclaim simultaneously. Each of their dates, with eyes only on them, agree.

"Let's find our table and see if Jessie is there," Caine suggests. "Maybe tonight is the night he'll finally fess up to what the fuck he's doing with Cindy. Apparently, I'm the only one who doesn't need to bang my co-workers."

"Do you think he really has something going on with Cindy or was he just in need of a date that wouldn't drop to her knees and call him

Master during the dinner portion of the evening?" Will wonders. "And you've 'banged' more than your fair share of co-workers."

"I don't know for sure but he's definitely banging the shit out of her. I heard them in his office and waited to see who would come out. Cindy looked like she'd just spent an hour on her knees followed by her back. I played it off like I had just gotten there and hadn't heard a thing. The poor girl looked like she was going to throw up."

"So, wait?" Sloan asks. "Master? As in Jessie is a hot alpha-male doctor who's into BDSM and spanks her and all that?" she asks, not letting on that Katherine has already filled her in on Dr. Jessie Holt's sexual preferences.

"Read much, Sloan?" Katherine laughs then sends her the friendship look telling her to play the information she's shared with her cool. "But um, yeah," she says when Sloan shoots her a death stare. "What she said."

Caine and Will laugh. "It's a long story," Caine says not wanting to elaborate any further about Jessie's sex life, that happens to have been tangled up in his own until very recently, and upset Katherine on this perfect evening. "But yes, Jessie likes control in the bedroom and he'd admit and call himself a Dom if asked."

"Huh, is that right?" Sloan says with a smile to Katherine. "Because you know the saying, right? Birds of a feather. Katherine, I think we've been getting the short end of that stick. And when I first started at the hospital, I heard rumors…"

"That's enough," Caine halts Sloan. "She's not missing out on anything, she's very satisfied, aren't you, Kitten?"

Will and Sloan raise eyebrows at Katherine and Caine at the use of his pet name for her but let it drop as they approach Jessie and Dr. Cindy Baxter sitting at their table. Will smiles at his parents and siblings who are sitting at the next table where Scarlett and Johnny have placed themselves. He takes Sloan's hand and brings her to his family for the formal introductions.

They make small talk with Chrissy and Brandon about their pregnancy first then Will brings Tommy in for a hug and a pat on the back. Will's younger brother leans in and kisses Sloan on the cheek in greeting before introducing her to his stunning date. "This is Bianca. She's my date for the evening."

Will growls at his brother and leans in to speak softly into his ear. "You still playing it like that?"

"She fucked some other guy, Will. She's lucky I'm playing it like anything" Tommy snaps at his brother with a smile on his face for the crowd.

"Whatever you two boys are talking about, stop it," Milly warns. "I see the look and I've no plans on dragging you both out of here by the ear for a time out like I used to have to do anywhere we went."

The brothers laugh as their dates look at them questionably. "Tommy was a handful" Will says in his defense.

"Bullshit, ass. You just used being sick as a way to be mom's favorite so you'd get away with murder."

"Exactly," Chrissy says. "Look at how he's saved in her contacts."

"Alright you two, enough," Milly protests. "You know I love you all the same. And I was not the one that entered that into my phone. I hadn't a clue how to even use it at the time."

"Call Will, my favorite son" Tommy says in a voice that mocks Will.

Will breaks out in a fit of giggles as he grabs his little brother around the neck and gives him a few good jabs for good measure. Tommy pushes him off and flips him the bird before sitting back down and wrapping his arm around Bianca's chair with a cocky grin sent in Will's direction.

When Will feels a hand on his back he knows it must be his mentor and friend, Rick Talbott, everyone else having already arrived and in their seats. "Will, my boy" he says in greeting then pulls Will in for an embrace.

"Hey, Doc" Will returns his hug then pulls the doctor's wife, Anita into his side and kisses her temple. He introduces them to Sloan and everyone takes their seats as the MC for the evening requests.

The night goes along smoothly, other than a few odd glances from Addison and Ollie but Will has long ago determined them nuts. He and

Sloan dance and eat, bid on a few items in the silent auction and mingle around the room.

Damian Stone and his wife Sydney are there with four tables of their closest friends. Damian looks better than ever, one would ever know what the man had endured only months prior. Sydney looks great as well, maybe a little tired now that she's a new mother again but flawless in her cream-colored sheath dress. Will and Sloan catch up with their patient and thank him for his generous donation to Will's department then excuse themselves with an acceptance to spend a long weekend with the Stone's at their cabin in the woods.

Everything is perfect. The company, the food and drinks, the music. Will knows the event has probably earned him a huge amount of money for his research and he is over the top thrilled to be able to put it to good use with Sloan by his side at work and in his life. Scarlett is happy too, her boyfriend is being a gentleman and even his younger brother seems to be heading in the right direction.

Everything is perfect or so Will had thought.

Until he hears his name on the lips of the woman he had never planned on seeing again, that is.

"Will?" he hears again before Addison and Ollie appear so he must not be asleep and having one of the worst nightmares of his life. Shit, he was hopeful there for a second.

"Oh my God!" Addison exclaims. "You two know each other?"

Will stands frozen, unable to stop the freight train as it barges into his world and takes no prisoners. He almost tries to move when he sees the look on Sloan's face as recognition dawns and Scarlett appears with her eyes that match the woman's who is saying his name again.

"Sloan," he begins. "I'm so sorry. I had no idea."

"Will?" Julia says his name a fourth time and it sounds sour to Will's ears. He wishes he could change his name, tainted now forever after hearing Julia saying it again after all these years.

"Julia," he states coldly. "It's been awhile."

Julia heaves in a breath when Scarlett appears next to Will.

"Daddy?" she questions as she looks her mother in the eyes for the first time in her life. "What's going on?"

"Scarlett, go find Grammy and Pop, ask them to take you home" he demands as he nods at Johnny to get his daughter as far away from the scene about to go down as possible.

As if having a connection to Will's state of being, Caine and Jessie appear at his side, each with their own eye roll and cold greeting to the woman who once held their best friend's heart in her hands then tossed it on the ground and stomped it to death before walking out of his life.

Caine, unable to hold back, begins. "Well, look what the cat dragged in. I'd say you look as good as you did the last time I saw you, but all I remember is your back as you ran away. Turn around, let me see if I recognize you from that familiar angle."

"Caine" Will warns. He feels Sloan try to slip her small fingers around his but he pulls back. He can't accept comfort from this perfect woman while his past stares him in the face. He can't make Sloan protect him when he knows he's doing a shitty job of protecting her right now.

"Yeah," Jessie agrees. "I recall begging you to get your shit together and think about what you were doing. That was when I assumed you had a heart. We all learned that wasn't true though, didn't we, Jules?" Jessie snarls while using the nickname they had used when she and Will had been together their senior year of college.

"Uncle Jessie," Scarlett questions knowing he'd be the easiest to break and find out what this was all about. Scarlett can tell by the group's demeanor that something isn't right and that this is huge. Johnny is still trying to tug her away from the carnage before it happens when the woman, clearly known by her father and uncles, speaks.

"Scarlett?" Julia tries her daughter's name out for the first time.

"Don't!" Will demands as he moves away from Sloan and stands in front of Julia. He looks down at her with pleading eyes then over his shoulder he glances one last time at Sloan. He tries to convey everything in that one look but knows he's failing miserably. He wishes their relationship were more solid, that it had had more time to mature. He doesn't have that luxury; he can only hope this won't destroy whatever little piece of happiness his future held with her. But that can't matter right now. All that matters is protecting his daughter from Julia and the pain that she's about to cause. "Scar, go with Johnny and go home. Right now! We'll talk later."

"But daddy…"

"Now!" he demands harsher than he means and he makes his daughter cry, her perfect makeup starting to smear on her face already. Johnny swoops in and finally drags her away.

Caine and Jessie approach Will, flanking him on either side, leaving Sloan to be flanked by Katherine and Cindy. She's thankful for that. If Katherine weren't supporting her weight, she'd be in a heap on the floor. Already her tears were flowing, no holding them back as she watches her future slip through her fingers.

"Take her home," Will begs his best friends. "Please."

"Will," Sloan cries.

"I can't…not now. I need…Sloan, just go, please."

"Are you fucking kidding me right now?"

Will turns with sadness in his eyes and simple states, "She's her mother. I have to go. I'm sorry."

Will leads Julia away with a hand on her elbow, going where, no one knows as Sloan stands and watches dumbstruck. Caine and Jessie are at her side as she hears Addison and Ollie chuckle. "Hope you've enjoyed your evening" Addison says.

Sloan tries to lash out at the off-kilter nurse but Caine already has her around the waist and off the ground. Jessie has the other two women pinned to his side and they all barrel through the gala in the direction of the exit.

Chapter 26

"How did you get here?" Will asks.

"A car service but I can…"

"Give me your address" he demands then enters the New Jersey information into his car's GPS.

"We need to talk, Will. It's something that should have happened a long time ago."

Will's temper is on the verge of exploding the way his life just has. He laughs like he imagines a crazy man would, no mirth in the sound. "Funny, I said those exact words to your back almost sixteen years ago."

Julia sighs. "The snow is really coming down. Maybe you should calm down and focus on driving?"

Will uses his voice activated feature on his car to text Milly asking her to tell Charles to be careful in this weather and for her to alert him when they're safely home with Scarlett. He doesn't mention whom he's with, he's sure Scarlett has pieced it together and told his mother. She's probably grilling Milly for information which will only make his mother angrier over the situation. She never liked Julia from the start. The way things ended had only proved her right. And when Milly is right, she likes to express that fact till it's beat like a dead horse on the ground.

"She's beautiful," Julia says. "She looks just like you."

Will rolls his eyes. "No, she doesn't."

"Is that your wife, are you married?"

"No." is all Will supplies on the topic of Sloan. The whole debacle is still way too raw. He has no idea what Sloan will be to him now. If he were her, and an ex had shown up, he'd be fuming pissed off and breaking shit right now. Like the face of that ex, especially if she had left with him. He'd understand if she was waiting at Julia's house to bitch slap them both. Hell, if she knew where Julia lived, he's sure she'd be there waiting to do just that. He also knows that he damn well deserves it. And if Sloan had left the gala tonight with an ex, Will would be homicidal. So, he can't blame her for whatever feelings she's having right now. He just wishes he knew what they were.

When Will's SUV slides and he almost loses control, Julia stops talking and they ride the rest of the way in silence until they reach her street. It's lined with nice homes, colonials with manicured lawns not much unlike Will's. It surprises him, he never pictured her in the suburbs, he'd always assumed she'd return to Boston and live in the city. Living in Connecticut with him and a baby, 'that life' as she called it, was one of the reasons she'd bolted.

"What do you do? Did you become a lawyer?" he asks.

Jesus, maybe she has a husband and kids. The life they talked about having until everything happened too quickly and she told him it wasn't what she wanted. Scarlett and him weren't what she wanted. But had she wanted another man and his child?

Julia shakes her head. "I'm a partner at the firm that represents your hospital. That's why I was there tonight."

"You've never been there before," Will states as he parks the car and cuts the engine. "Why tonight?"

"Someone on the planning committee called me directly and invited me. Said she'd done some research and found out that the doctor whose department was benefitting and I went to college together. I was intrigued, can't say you didn't immediately come to mind. Come inside and let's talk."

Will nods and steps out into the cold, his hair covered in snow in two seconds flat. Julia runs up her porch and unlocks the door then motions Will inside. She enters the foyer and begins to click on lights as she moves through her space. Will stands at the threshold feeling odd being with her in her home.

"Come in, have a seat," she offers. "Can I get you a drink?"

"Scotch. Probably more than one."

Julia smiles then heads towards the bar on the far side of the room.

"Your house is nice. Looks like you're doing well."

Will doesn't include the fact that nothing he sees reminds him of the girl he once knew.

"I am but…well, I was married. I got the interior designer decorated house, he took the vacation home" Julia says, omitting that the money she and her ex-husband had was primarily from her blackmail money from Will's best friends.

Will nods. "Kids?"

"No."

Will nods again, it seems to be the only action he's familiar with at the moment. "So you came tonight knowing I'd be there, that Scarlett would be there? You know you have no legal rights to her, there's nothing you can do…"

"I didn't come to stake a claim on our daughter."

"My daughter. Mine!" he roars as he raises to his feet.

"Calm down," Julia suggests. "Have a drink, relax. I came tonight out of curiosity, nothing else."

Will doesn't believe her. He trusted her in the past and look where that had gotten him. He won't make that mistake ever again. Not when the consequences affect his daughter.

"Are you healthy? You look good. Caine and Jessie haven't changed one bit, still standing guard over you, huh?"

"And you still sound jealous over them."

Julia laughs. "Whatever. Will, you didn't answer my question."

"I'm fine, Julia," Will glances out the window. The snow is coming down like crazy and he's afraid he's going to be stuck here for the night if he doesn't speed this along. "I'll be talking to my lawyers on Monday. I'll get a restraining order if I need to. You understand you're not to contact Scarlett?"

"Yeah, Milly spelled it out for me very clearly."

"Good. So…"

"Was that her boyfriend?"

"Julia" he warns.

She raises her hands in front of her. "Will, I came tonight to see you. I'm guessing if she were someone special, you wouldn't be here right now. So..."

"What are you talking about, Julia?"

"The pretty girl you were with. She's a bit younger than you but are you dating her?"

"Are you fucking kidding me? Are you judging me? That's a joke, Julia. And whom I date, fuck, am married to or not is absolutely none of your fucking business."

Julia laughs then tells Will to make himself at home while she starts a pot of coffee to take the chill off. He tries to stop her but she ignores him and leaves the room. She returns ten minutes later in sweats and a comfy shirt holding two mugs of steaming coffee.

"Julia, I need to go so let's get this over with."

He doesn't like the feelings stirring in the pit of his stomach over her and the way she's dressed, like she's still his college girlfriend with her hair in a messy knot on the top of her head and cozy in lounge clothes. She's bringing back way too many memories and emotions for him to process.

Will remembers her dressed in his sweats and t-shirt, laying on his bed after the first time they'd made love. She'd promised not to be clingy and tried to get up to leave. He'd pulled her back down and made love to her again. All night. Then in the light of day, he'd asked her to stay forever, asked her to be his girlfriend. She'd smiled and kissed him. He thought his life was finally perfect and on track. And it had been until that one spontaneous night when he didn't have a condom but was too horny to care and promised to pull out.

Will snaps out of his head when she speaks.

"I just heard on the radio, when I was getting the coffees, that New Jersey, New York, and Connecticut have closed their roads. I'm assuming you live in New York or Connecticut so it looks like you're stuck here."

"Fuck!" Will curses then pulls his cell out of his pants.

Missed calls and texts from Scarlett, Johnny, both of his parents, Caine, and Jessie taunt him because there's not one from Sloan. He hadn't expected there to be. He knows she's pissed and won't contact him. She'll wait for him to make the first move. If he doesn't, she'll assume the worst and this mess will only get bigger. But even though he knows he must make things right with her and explain everything, he can't do that over the phone from Julia's house. He needs to talk to Sloan in person. But first, he needs to figure out what the fuck Julia was up to with this stunt tonight. He has a very good idea who helped her and that's another layer to what this all means for him and Sloan.

"The person on the planning committee that contacted you, her name was Addison, wasn't it?"

"Yeah. She said she was one of your nurses."

Will laughs aloud. "Jesus Christ," he says. "She's fucking unhinged."

"What?"

"She's not my nurse. She's clumsy and a bit off actually. I've heard snickering and some rumors about her liking me but I ignored them. I only used her when my hand was forced in emergencies. The girl you saw tonight is my nurse."

Julia smiles and nods then chuckles a knowing sound. "Your nurse, huh? That all, Will? She's your nurse?"

"Yes, Julia, she's my nurse. Anything else between Sloan and I is none of your business."

"Sloan" Julia breathes, trying her name out on her lips for the first time.

Will heaves in a deep breath. "I need to call home. Is there somewhere I can…"

Julia nods in the direction of a hall. "Study, first door on the left."

"Thanks" Will says as he walks through her home and closes himself off for privacy.

He reads and responds to the texts from Milly first, making sure his parents are home safe and sound with Scarlett.

Will: *I can't explain now…don't flip. Julia showed up. I'm with her now trying to find out why. I'm stuck in NJ. Is Scar ok?*

It takes Milly a minute but she responds.

Milly: *Scar is fine. Roads are bad here too. Couldn't get Johnny home. He's here. We're staying as well. I don't like that you're with that girl! She's up to no good!!!*

Milly had always been protective of her children. If it weren't for her, Will knows his legal rights over his daughter would be shaky at best so he ignores the fact that his mother still treats him like a child from time to time.

Will: *I'm a big boy, I can handle her. Did Scar say anything? She saw her.*

Milly: *She's very upset! I didn't want to divulge too much but I refused to lie to her. She asked if that was her and I said it was. Her and Johnny are on the couch in the family room. She's upset but he's calming her down. I'll keep an eye on them.*

Will growls to himself. Sure, Milly will try to keep an eye on them but at some point, she and Charles will fall asleep and his distraught daughter will seek comfort in her horny boyfriend's arms.

He fires off a text to Johnny to warn him off.

Will: *Behave yourself tonight. She's upset and won't make good decisions. You better!*

A response doesn't come from Johnny, instead a call comes in from Scarlett but Will ignores it. This isn't something he can do now or over the phone with her either. She's home safe and hopefully Johnny won't let his dick make the decisions tonight.

Will reads the messages from Caine and Jessie and learns that they took Sloan and Katherine back to their apartment in the city. Sloan wasn't happy about leaving the three little pigs but she soon forgot about that issue once in the car with a wet bar. His friends asked where he was, what the hell happened, and why he's being a douche. He ignores them all and silences his phone after turning off his notification alerts.

Will returns to Julia's living space to find her wrapped in a blanket on the sofa, a fire roaring, and a drink in her hand. It's the picture of romance. Too bad it's with the wrong woman. And too bad Will isn't in the mood. He needs to figure Julia out and fast then figure out a way to drive home and straighten this shit out with the woman he's in love with.

Fuck! Yeah, he's in love with Sloan. Why the fuck hadn't he told her that? Why hadn't they made rules or some shit that couples do so they'd each feel safe and secure in their relationship if something like this were to happen? Now, he's stuck hoping that she'll believe him and understand why he did what he did tonight. It hadn't looked good, him leaving Sloan behind to take Julia home. He can't blame her for thinking the worst and he's sure that's exactly what she's doing right now. Well, that and drinking while planning his slow, painful castration no doubt.

"Have a seat," Julia offers. "You look like a teenager in a whorehouse. I'm not going to take your virginity!"

That comment has his head going directly to his home in Connecticut. More specifically his family room where his daughter might be losing hers as he stands here trying to figure out this woman from his past.

"What?" Julia asks. "You look like you're going to be sick."

Will shakes his head. "Scarlett is with her boyfriend and clearly upset over the events tonight. It's a recipe for disaster."

Julia laughs. "Will, she's what, almost sixteen? I'm sure the horse has been out of that barn for years."

"What the fuck are you up to Julia? Why did you come tonight?" Will asks not wanting to talk about his daughter's sex life with her. She hadn't earned the right to know a thing about Scarlett.

Julia stands and walks closer to Will. When she's standing only inches from him, her hands slide into his and she raises them to her hips, positioning herself closer to him.

Will pulls back. "That's it. I'll sleep in the car or risk driving home."

"Will, wait. I'm sorry," she apologizes. "It's been," she clears her throat. "A really, really long time. I'm…I'm just lonely but let me explain, okay? I didn't come tonight to seduce you. I didn't and I shouldn't have…"

"No, you shouldn't have" Will says putting more distance between them.

Julia spends the next few hours telling Will about her marriage that failed because of the ghosts from her past, her stressful work load, and her lack of a social life. She tells Will about law school and how her father recently passed away from a fatal heart attack. What she doesn't tell him is the secret she's been keeping from him for sixteen years. Seeing that he is still as thick as thieves with Caine and Jessie, she figures they haven't told him about the night they spent together either.

Will sits quietly and listens, never asking a single question or interjecting a story of his own. He's not here to learn more about her, to swap stories before they fall into bed and start a relationship. They'd done that already and look how it turned out. No, he's here to figure out if she's going to cause a problem for him and Sloan and if she's going to try to see Scarlett again. Then he's out of here.

"Julia," he begins with a yawn. "I'm really not interested in all of this. I want to know now what the fuck you were thinking tonight and if you're going to cause me trouble in the future because I won't tolerate it. You understand that, right?"

"Don't be so dramatic, Will. Honestly, when that nurse called it piqued my interest is all," she lies. Julia knew everything there was to know about Will. Well, almost everything. She'd missed this young girl sneaking into his life and crawling under his skin. "I just wanted to see you, get some closure like my therapist has been telling me so I can move on. I never expected Scarlett to be there. That's a pretty name, by the way. Did you choose it?"

"Yeah, I did because her mother deserted me in the fucking hospital" Will fumes.

"And left you with scars" Julia says, her breath a whisper.

Will nods. "Yeah."

"I'm…"

"Save it," Will demands. "I'm tired. I'll sleep here and leave as soon as the roads open. Don't contact me and stay away from my daughter."

Julia stands and sadly smiles at Will before she leaves the room in search of her own bed.

Will dozes off and when he awakes to Sloan's warm body pressed up against his, he grows hard, grinding into her back for relief with a groan. His arm wraps around her waist and pulls her in closer. He leans into the crook of her neck for a quick inhale of the smell of her and rears back, eyes flying open. "Jesus Christ," he yells. "What the fuck?"

Julia is curled around him, her hand lazily placed over his erection and she's naked. Will's eyes roam her body, still tight and enticing but he instantly loses his erection as his mind starts working out the fact that it's Julia he's looking at and not the woman he loves.

Julia slowly opens her eyes and tries to pull Will back down to the sofa but he recoils again, shifts in his trousers, and tosses a blanket over her exposed breasts. "Will, I…"

"Save it Julia. I know exactly what you were doing. You always did that, you know? Distracted me from problems in our relationship with sex. It's probably the main reason things went bad between us. We never talked, never opened up to each other. Not really anyway," Will sighs. "Shit! Get dressed. We need to…let's talk over a cup of coffee before I leave."

Julia looks sad, disappointed even but she nods and wraps the blanket around herself. "Can you start the pot? It's simple."

"Sure. And Julia," Will says over his shoulder. "No more tricks. We talk and I leave. End of story."

She nods again at his retreating back.

Chapter 27

Will's head is still reeling from the turn of events his life took over the past few hours when he pulls into his driveway. By the time he's parking the SUV in the garage, thankful that he pays to have his driveway plowed after a storm, he's not sure what kind of drama he's about to walk into. Has Sloan come back to wait for him? He doubts it. Will Milly and Charles be in parent mode even though he's a grown man? He'd bet money on it. And what about Scarlett? He's not even sure if he can guess where her head might be at. If other parts of her body haven't been anywhere near parts of Johnny's, he'll be fine.

He glances at his disheveled appearance and prays that Sloan isn't waiting for him. He looks like a man doing the walk of shame and Sloan seeing him now will only reinforce what he knows she must be suspecting. And he feels shame, it's not a good feeling nor is it one he's accustomed to, but it's written all over his face. He knows he hadn't handled the situation with Julia very well.

When he enters through the kitchen, he's relieved. Momentarily. Then he sees the woman that is waiting for him and it isn't Sloan, it's much worse.

Milly.

"Wilson," Milly says. "What in the hell were you thinking?"

Will raises a hand to silence her until he can retrieve a mug and fill it with coffee. He instantly notices that the three little pigs are not in the mudroom. Their stuff is still there so that's a good sign. Maybe Scarlett has them somewhere else in the house with her. Or, maybe Sloan has already been here and gone, grabbing her things and her pigs and rushing to leave before running into Will. He gulps down a large sip of the dark liquid then tops off his cup before answering his mother. "I wasn't thinking anything other than getting her away from Scarlett."

Milly sighs and plops herself back into a chair, having left it to stand when Will had finally walked through the door. "Sit down," she orders. "You look like shit and I won't mention that you look like a man coming home after a night in bed with a whore. I hope you had more sense than that, Wilson."

"The full name, huh, Ma? And twice? Wow! I haven't dealt with that since I was Scar's age."

"If I still had my wooden spoon in my purse" she warns.

Will laughs then sits down, running a hand through his crazy locks. "I didn't sleep with her," he states. "Not that my sex life should be any of your concern. I'm not sure why my sex life has all of a sudden become the hottest topic in this family."

Milly nods. She knows it isn't any of her business but once a child, always a child and Will has always been hers that told her everything, came to her for advice, and needed her the most. He might be an adult now with a daughter of his own but he will always be her child.

"I drove Julia home and we talked. I need to figure some shit out and until I do, I don't want to talk about it. Where's Scarlett?"

"She's in her room. Johnny's dad came by about an hour ago to get him. She's confused and upset. She's been crying non-stop."

"Where did Johnny sleep?"

"On the couch with her. She was hysterical and fighting over the logistics of that wasn't something I was up for. If he'd been in the guest room, he could have easily snuck into her room, Will. Or, trust me, Scarlett would have spent the night in there with him. She was inconsolable."

Will growls then stands, downs his coffee, and kisses his mother gently on the cheek. "I need a shower and a few hours of sleep to figure shit out before I talk to her. Thanks for taking her home. Where's dad?"

"He went to the market to grab a few things. The weather report says we're going to get hit with even more snow in a few hours and I don't have anything in the house. He'll be back by for me soon. Go get cleaned up and have a rest. I'll call you later and check in on you."

Will kisses Milly again then leaves her in the kitchen. On his way to his room, he stops outside of Scarlett's and listens at her door. He hears her shower running and the squealing of the three little pigs. Knowing Sloan will be back to get them propels him into his room and his own shower to try to wash off his regrets.

He must have fallen asleep after his shower, when he'd laid on his bed just for a second to rest his eyes, still naked, because he's startled awake by Scarlett pounding on his door. He jumps up and rushes to his dresser, throws on a pair of sweats, tucking himself inside and opens his door.

Scarlett stands there looking like a grown woman and a child all at the same time. Her hair is pulled up into a messy knot on the top of her head, still damp from her shower. She's wearing a tight sweater that accentuates her breasts and makes Will want to throttle the designer. Her lower half is clad in skin tight jeans that make him want to scream.

"Hey," Will says instead. "Do you want to talk in here or…"

"Here is fine" she answers.

"Alright, come sit down and I'll explain."

Scarlett walks over to his bed, her steps cautious then Will sees the slight wince when she sits down and he cringes. He debates whether he should address his concerns over the reason but quickly decides to drop it for the time being. If she's had sex, it's a done deal, there's no reason to cause more angst between them right now.

"I asked Grammy, I know that was my mom. Why was she there? Did you invite her?"

"No! Scar, I haven't seen or spoken to her since the day you were born."

Scarlett sighs. "It's my fault that she left you. If she hadn't gotten pregnant, you guys would have stayed together and then had a real family when you were both ready."

Will has her wrapped in his arms in a flash. He breathes in her scent, still that strawberry shampoo she's always loved, and then it's his turn to sigh. "It's not your fault. Don't ever think her leaving was your fault. She had a choice and she made the wrong one. That's on her, not you."

"What happened? You've never told me. I just know that she left us but I've always been afraid to hear you tell me why. I just thought…"

"Shhh," Will soothes. "It's complicated. But, baby, it's not your fault and we are a real family. You and I, right?"

"I didn't mean it that way. You know what I meant."

"Yeah, but don't ever feel like we had less because it was just us all these years."

"I don't" Scarlett says as she hugs Will tight, her tears wetting his bare chest.

Will gently places her back down on the bed, pushing aside his feelings as she winces again. Fuck, he wishes Sloan were here to talk to her about this. He wishes Sloan were here to talk to him about this and so much more but he's scared he may have fucked things up with her for good. Knowing he can't deal with both the situation with Scarlett and his troubles with Sloan, he focuses on his daughter like he's been doing for the past sixteen years, well, as of next week she'll be sixteen, and starts at the beginning. He laughs to himself when the age old saying, 'Sweet sixteen and never been kissed' crosses his mind. Why couldn't that be her?

"I met Julia in college. Uncle Caine and Uncle Jessie and I all went to the same school as you know. They've always felt like they needed to protect me. They warned me about her when we first started dating but I laughed them off. I thought they were jealous that I had gotten serious with a girl when they were still playing the field."

Scarlett laughs. "Playing the field? You mean hooking up with anything that walks?"

"Pretty much but don't tell them that I told you that."

"Dad, until about a second ago, they were still banging anything that walks."

"Scarlett," Will admonishes. "Don't talk about your uncles like that! And how the hell do you know that?"

Scarlett laughs and rolls her eyes.

"Okay, forget about them. So, I met Julia in school and we fell into a relationship fast. I hadn't had any serious girlfriends before and she didn't know my past. She didn't look at me with pity in her eyes. To her, I wasn't the kid who had had cancer."

"Oh, daddy," Scarlett sighs. "I'm sorry. I see what Mary is going through and I hate thinking about you…"

"It's over. Don't think about me like that. I'm fine. Promise."

Scarlett smiles at Will. "Good. Now…"

Will continues to tell his daughter about the young girl he met and fell in love with over the course of their time together. He debates about telling her about the night she was conceived but after what he figures she and Johnny did last night maybe it's about time he did tell her.

"I was stupid one night, Scar. I'll never regret it because I got you out of it but it was a dumb decision and I want you to promise me, you'll never make the same choice I did. Even though you're on the pill, promise me you'll never let Johnny not wear a condom."

"Dad!" she screeches.

"I'm not going to lecture you again about not having sex. You don't even need to tell me if you are, just promise that you'll be smart and safe. Please" he begs.

And she doesn't have to tell him. He's already seen the signs. There is no other reason for her movements to be cautious today. He knew when he'd left with Julia last night that Scar was going to be in a vulnerable position. He'd warned Johnny away, but in his heart, he knows the boy didn't use his daughter as a quick piece of ass. Will's been closely watching Johnny and there is no question about the kid's feelings for his daughter. He's sure they did what they did with Johnny's intent noble.

"Fine, yes, we'll always be safe."

"Good. So, I wasn't. Just one time. Once. About six weeks later, Julia started acting weird. It took her another three weeks to tell me why. She'd taken a pregnancy test but wouldn't go to the doctor. After she told me, I made an appointment and forced her to go. She was starting her second trimester by the time we saw the doctor."

Will remembers that day all too well. He'd been studying for finals and finishing up a few applications to medical school. Caine and Jessie, applying to the same institutions, had just left and his head was spinning from the stress. Caine and Jessie had seemed off as well and blamed it on graduation and their own medical school applications. Will wasn't so sure. His friends were clearly keeping a secret from him, he just wasn't quite sure what it was.

When Julia showed up at their apartment in tears, he'd figured she'd failed a test or had gotten a rejection letter from one of the law schools she was dreaming about attending. He wished for a moment that everyone around him would either keep their own shit to themselves or open the fuck up and include him. Instead, it seemed as if everyone still thought he was that weak kid with cancer that needs protecting and it was starting to piss him off.

He and Julia had been ignoring the talk about how they would survive four years in different cities, possibly across the country from one another. Will had his eyes on NYU, Julia was dreaming of Stanford. What Julia didn't know was that Will had come to the decision that it was time to end things and let the cards fall where they may. Wasn't that what fate was? If they were meant to be together in the end, they'd find each other again. Right? Or was he just looking for a nice way out?

"We need to talk" Julia sobbed into Will's strong chest.

"Shhh, baby," he consoled. "Did you fail a test? Tell me what's wrong and I'll make it all better" he said as he rubbed his growing erection on her leg. Yeah, he knows he's a dick for thinking about dumping her one minute then having an uncontrollable need to fuck her the next.

Julia batted him away then scoffed, "Yeah, I failed a test alright, you asshole! Will," she said. "I'm pregnant."

Will reared back. "Pregnant? How the fuck can you be pregnant?"

"I'll pull out," she imitated his pleas. "Just this once, come on, baby. I need you."

"I did pull out," he reminded her. "In more than enough time."

"Apparently not" she said and flung the positive test at the same chest she had just been crying into so Will never saw the smile cross her lips. Julia is aware of her situation. Yes, Will had pulled out but so had Caine and Jessie so anyone of the rich trust fund boys could be the father of this child she seems to be carrying. And Julia bets that Caine and Jessie will willingly share some of their money with her to protect their fragile best friend from finding out about their night of passion.

Will's head was ready to combust. Between all the talk lately of his, Caine, and Jessie's trust funds, Julia acting off every time it's mentioned, finals, medical school applications, and graduation, he couldn't handle one more thing. Not even a flat tire. And the bomb Julia had dropped on him was way bigger than car trouble.

"Daddy?" Scarlett questions, bringing Will out of his head.

"Sorry. So, we decided that Julia would continue the pregnancy. Scar, you must know that I never, not for one second didn't want you. Not having you or giving you up was never an option for me."

"No, but it was for her, wasn't it?"

Will looks sadly at his daughter. He doesn't want to share this part of the story but he knows the time has come. "Yes. Julia scheduled an abortion behind my back. I never would have even known but Uncle Caine happened to run into her on campus. She was acting weird and she said a few things that didn't sit right with him. He followed her to the shady clinic. By then, she was too far along for any reputable doctor to terminate."

Caine had called Jessie as he followed Julia, suspecting what she was up too, and told him to get Will and meet him as fast as they could. Julia was sitting in the waiting room when the three young men barged in the door. It was at that moment that Caine and Jessie vowed to be by Will's side every step of the way with his child like they had been when they thought his cancer had returned when they were teenagers. They took Julia back to their apartment, Will staying watch over her while his friends moved her stuff into Will's room. For the next few months, one of them was always with her, standing guard and protecting the unborn child that could be any of theirs.

Julia grew angry and depressed. Their relationship quickly changed, gone were the relaxed nights of pizza and beers on Friday with their friends or lazy sex alone in bed on a Saturday morning. Will, Caine, or Jessie followed her around and watched her like a hawk. She became resentful and moody as her pregnancy changed her body and her hormones wreaked havoc on her system. A tension, so huge it was palpable, between Caine, Jessie, and Julia formed and Will caught them many nights in a heated argument. They'd silence themselves when he'd come in the door. Caine and Jessie were always protecting him and Will didn't have the strength not to let them. So, he ignored his growing concern and went about his time as best as he could knowing he was about to be a father and he had no clue how in the world he was going to do that. Especially with a woman he'd recently realized he wasn't in love with. But he'd do the right thing and suck it up for his child. He didn't matter anymore, only his baby did.

By the time she went into labor, Julia and Will were barely speaking. The only conversations they had were about the baby. "Did you take your vitamin?" Will would ask. "The sonogram to determine the sex is at the end of the week. Are we going to find out the sex now or wait?" Julia questioned.

Julia would nod or shrug, never engaging in those conversations. She hadn't tried to terminate the pregnancy again; she'd promised it was a lapse in judgment. Will wasn't so sure and it came between them. He'd lost all trust and respect for the girl carrying his child, the girl he'd thought he'd one day marry. Now, he was just trying to get through one day at a time.

She did begin a conversation, not long before she went into labor, it's the one that changed Will's life forever. "Will," she began one morning as he was getting ready to leave for class, Caine scheduled to stand sentry for the day. "I got into Stanford and I accepted their offer."

Will froze in his spot. He had casually mentioned, when their relationship was stronger that she should apply to her dream school and he'd help her with the tuition. Now, how was he going to tell her that he wasn't feeling the same way? Without his financial assistance, Julia could never afford a school like Stanford.

Julia had grown up as poor as Will, Caine, and Jessie had grown up wealthy. Her mother had died when she was little and her father spent most of the money he made working blue-collar jobs on liquor to dull his pain.

He'd been waiting to tell her that he'd gotten into NYU and was planning on accepting their offer to begin in the fall. Caine and Jessie had also been admitted to the program, all had seemed to be working out for Will. Or so he thought.

"Um, what do you mean, Julia? That's California. I thought we talked about staying close by my parents so my mom could help?

Having a baby is going to be difficult enough, I'm not sure how law and medical school are even going to pan out. And the tuition now with a baby…"

"Yeah, here's the thing," Julia stated. "I'm going to California alone, Will. And my tuition is covered." She hadn't mentioned it was being funding by his best friend's hush money. Julia would be set for law school and well after. She figures she'll land herself a rich lawyer seeing as how the wealthy doctor she'd originally set her sights on wouldn't be working out. Well, not the way she'd planned. But things seemed to be working out just fine for her anyway.

"The fuck you are! You're not taking my baby across the coun…" he trailed off as recognition dawned. She'd said alone.

Julia nodded then left the room. A few days later, she walked out of the hospital and out of Will and Scarlett's lives.

Will clears his throat and realizes that he has tears running down his face. Scarlett does too. "I'm sorry. I never wanted to tell you that. I wish Julia had been different but not everyone is cut out to be a parent, especially not at twenty-one."

"And now?" Scarlett asks. "Does she want to be a parent now?"

Will doesn't answer her right away. He's not sure he knows the answer. Julia finally shared her story with him in the early morning hours while he waited for the roads to be opened. She admitted to wanting him but she hadn't seemed very interested in talking about Scarlett. "I don't know," he finally says. "Is that something that you want?"

Scarlett shrugs. "I'm not sure. I like Sloan," she takes in a deep breath. "I love Grammy and Ellie is great but Sloan felt like…I don't know how to explain it. Home, you know? The real thing and I just met her."

"Yeah, I know" Will says with a deep sigh.

"So, is she gone? Is she mad at you? She left the three little pigs."

"I'm sure she's furious. I'm not sure where I stand with her, Scar. Adult relationships are complicated. I need to get my head back on straight, it's still spinning over Julia, okay? I'm not sure about Sloan."

"If I say I want to have a relationship with her, my mother, will that change things for you and Sloan?"

Will heaves in a deep breath and shrugs. "Scar, I…I…I need to put you first, baby. That's not going to change. I'll figure my shit out after. First, I need to help you figure out yours."

Scarlett starts to cry again and lunges into Will's arms. "I want to meet her," she says. "My mother. I want to meet my mom."

Chapter 28

Monday morning arrives way too fast for Will but at the same time, it takes forever. He's not sure what he's walking into as he parks his car in the garage and enters the hospital. He knows he might find Sloan there, acting normal, and she might quietly warn him not to discuss their private life at work. Or maybe she'll tell him to shove his coffee up his ass in front of everyone and to leave her the fuck alone unless he needs her for a work-related task. Maybe, and this is the scenario Will fears the most, she's already put in for a transfer to another doctor.

He enters his office and boots up his computer to check his schedule for the day. He's early, Tonya, his secretary won't be in for at least another hour and with Sloan nowhere in sight and Will too afraid to ask her anything if she were there, he needs to know if he has any appointments today.

He's relieved to see that his entire week is clear. Having been gone for three weeks, he has no patients to follow up on and no new patients scheduled.

Strange that there aren't any new patients this week. He momentarily thinks that's odd but then brushes off his feelings and sifts through his emails. Sure, he and Sloan had been here a few times after visiting Mary but instead of getting much work done, they'd used their time in this office to have sex on his desk. He runs his hand over the hard surface as he remembers the last time.

Just as Will is growing hard at the memory of sinking into Sloan's invitingly warm body, her tight pussy clenching around him, Tonya taps at his door.

"Oh, hey, come on in," Will says as he adjusts himself in his trousers, thankful he didn't wear scrubs today and that he's sitting behind his desk. "You're here early."

Tonya looks at Will like he's out of his mind. "Well, um..." she stutters. "Did Miss Hale not speak to you first?"

"Fuck! Um, sorry. I...shit, what did she say?"

"She called me yesterday and told me that she wouldn't be in today. Or any day. She said you'd understand that she's put in for a transfer to another specialty. She didn't give me any details, but she said she'd be talking to HR and taking some time off before coming back to work for another doctor. I've been here for hours cancelling your patients for this week and moving the time sensitive ones for the next month to other doctors. I'll start calling nurses to fill in later but as of now I've cleared your week so we can try to find a replacement. I know you don't like to use Addison."

Will can't breathe. She's gone. He knew she'd be pissed but he hadn't thought she'd just cut him off and disappear without giving him a chance to explain.

"Thanks," Will mutters. "Don't replace Sloan and don't schedule me on anything yet. Tell the Chief I'll call him later. I…I have to go."

"Go? You just got back."

Will is out of his office door before Tonya can ask another question. He runs to the elevator while dialing Caine's number. Katherine should know where she is.

"Hey," Will says when Caine answers. "I need your help. Sloan is gone. I need to know where she is."

Caine laughs. "And this surprises you? Damn, you're worse than I am, aren't you?"

"Do you know where she is or not? I don't have time for this bullshit" he says as the elevator stops at the garage level and Will jogs to his car.

"I haven't a clue and thanks to you, this has caused a problem between me and my girl."

"Sorry," Will grumbles as his car roars to life and he screeches out onto the busy New York City streets heading to Sloan's apartment. "I'm going to their apartment now."

"She's not there. We dropped her and Katherine off after the 'episode' you pulled and Katherine refused to let me stay. She insisted they needed girl time without my dick in the way. I left, against my better judgement, only to lose track of her for the better part of twenty-four hours. When she finally showed up at my place, she told me Sloan wasn't going back to the hospital today and she warned me against asking any further questions about her location or anything else that I would then report back to you."

"I'm sorry" Will says again.

"Yeah, she spent some time thinking it over, ass pink over my knee, but she refused to cave. We fucked and made up and I agreed to let you and Sloan figure your own shit out and stay out of it. Katherine warned me not to bring it up if I knew what was good for me. You might want to question our boy, Jessie, though. He and Cindy are for sure fucking. Not sure if it's more than that but he's definitely tapping that fine piece of ass and she seemed nervous when I was speaking to him about Sloan leaving the hospital. You know she never hired a head nurse."

Will manages to laugh at the idea of Caine giving into a woman like he had caved with Katherine. The mighty Dr. Caine Cabrera has been taken down by a girl. Finally. "I just need to see her and explain" Will begs.

"Can't help you, brother. Honestly, if I could, I would, but the girls know how we are. Katherine has me on lockdown of all intel because she knows she can't trust me to not go to you with it."

"Fuck! The three little pigs are still at my house so maybe she'll go back there to get them. I'm going to still swing by her place first. I'll call you later."

"I'll come to you tonight after my shift. You have a lot of explaining to do to Jessie and I."

"Fine" Will says and disconnects the call as he tosses his keys to the valet, announcing that he's there to see Mr. Stone. That should get him access to the building in record speed.

As he suspected, within seconds, he's hurling himself through the main doors and asking Pedro to please let him up to Sloan's apartment. The man sends him a kind smile and addresses him by name, always taking his job seriously, knowing little things like that go a long way. "Dr. Anderson, Miss Hale isn't here. You just missed her. She was just here, didn't look so good. I asked if she needed anything but she refused my help."

"Fuck…sorry. Shit…whatever. Are you serious? Where did she go?"

"She didn't say, sir. She did tell me that she wasn't sure when she'd be back and thanked me for helping her. I fed those three little pigs of hers a few times."

"Not coming back? Jesus. Thanks, Pedro. I gotta go" Will says as he shakes the man's hand then runs back out to the valet to retrieve his car.

*****

Will tries Caine again on his way back to his house, hoping that maybe Sloan hasn't already been by to get her pigs, but he gets sent to voicemail. Then he leaves a message for Jessie after being sent to his voicemail as well. Sure, everyone else is working while his life is falling apart.

He pulls into his garage and enters his house through the now stripped bare mudroom, no signs of the three little pigs or their owner anywhere. He flies up to Scarlett's room where she'd had more of their stuff and finds it all gone as well. Before he leaves her room, a piece of paper sitting on her bed catches his eye. For a moment, he thinks it's probably a note from Johnny and not something he should read. Then he remembers that kids don't write anything by hand these days. If Johnny was going to send her something that Will should not read, he'd be sexting her, not writing it in a note.

He leans down and heaves in a sigh when he sees Sloan's handwriting.

Scarlett,
Thank you for taking care of the three little pigs for me. I'm glad I had the chance to meet you and I'm sorry that I had to leave without saying goodbye. Adults sometimes have things that happen that younger people might not fully understand so please don't be too hard on your father. He's a good man who is only trying to do what's best for you. Unfortunately, I need to also do what's best for me, and I think right now, that's walking away. If you ever need me for anything, you have my cell. Leave me a message and I promise I'll get back to you when I can.
Your Friend,
Sloan

Will places the note back on Scarlett's bed where he found it and heads to the main living space. He grabs a bottle of Scotch, liquid courage, and downs a few gulps before stalking to his room. He strips out of his work clothes and dons a pair of loose fitting sweats and a tight t-shirt. He runs his hands through his hair and plots out his next move. Before he knows it, his plans to call Sloan and explain have come and gone and Scarlett is standing over his bed. "You look like shit and smell worse. I'm guessing you read the note from Sloan?"

Will holds a finger in front of his mouth to quiet his daughter's voice. "Shhh," he says. "Headache."

"I'm sure. I have dance. Uncle Caine and Uncle Jessie stopped by but I told them you were sleeping. I guess I'll call Ellie for a ride. Or Johnny."

Will shakes his head. "Good idea" he says before rolling over and nodding off again. When he wakes the next time it's morning, the sun shining through his window. Will moans, he hasn't felt this awful since he had his last surgery as a teenager.

And that's how Will spends the next month and a half, drinking until he passes out. Scarlett and Milly force him to eat when they can. Charles empties the house of alcohol but Will calls and places an order for delivery. You have got to love the modern world, where after a quick phone call or a few clicks on a website, booze shows up at your door so you can drown in your sorrows. Caine and Jessie bitch at him and call him a pussy in hopes it'll piss him off enough to do something about it. It doesn't. The Chief of Staff at the hospital calls and puts him on extended administrative leave until further notice.

By late March, Will's a mess but agrees to allow Julia to come over one day while Scarlett is at school so they can discuss a visit between them. Will knows it's not the best of ideas right now but when would be a good time to introduce his sixteen-year-old daughter to the mother that deserted her at birth? Maybe it'll keep Scarlett's mind off Mary's worsening condition.

Mary was taken back into isolation after her last bout of chemo. Will has been trying to soften the inevitable blow that's coming but Johnny and Scarlett barely listen to a word he says. He can't blame them, most of his words are slurred drunken statements that most likely make little to no sense.

Will takes a shower, an activity he now hates because the space reminds him of Sloan. She forgot her body wash, or left it there to torture him, either way, he refuses to throw it away and inhales it every time he's in there. Today is no different except that when he pops the cap, a memory of them in the space comes hurling into his head. He'd laid off the booze for too long to try to be semi-coherent when Julia arrived. Big mistake. See what happens when he does. Fuck this. He'll be gulping down half a bottle to help take away the memories as soon as he leaves the shower. But first, he lets this memory assault him, bringing him to his knees on the wet tile floor.

In his mind, Sloan is there like she was the day he's remembering. The day he was also on his knees in this shower, Sloan standing, hand trying to grasp something to keep her upright while her leg draped over his shoulder and he brought her to an orgasm with his mouth then turned her around and fucked her from behind. The memory has Will growing hard and stroking his cock on the shower floor.

He stands, needing a better slide of his hand, and reaches for Sloan's body wash. He adds a dollop to his palm before grasping himself again, his thumb rolling over his head for extra lubrication. A groan escapes him as he closes his eyes and lets his mind believe that his hand is Sloan's.

He loves the way she gives hand jobs. His favorite is when she has him lie on his back and then she straddles his thighs. Then, her soft hand will gently rub lube on his cock, up and down his shaft until he's hard as granite and thrusting his hips for more. She makes him wait though, tortures him for a few extra minutes then firmly, but gently, she wraps her fingers around his dick and moves her fist up and down in a slow, steady motion.

Will moans as he jerks off, his cock solid and in need of a quick release. It's been way too long since he's come and he needs to relieve the pressure in his balls before dealing with the situation with Julia.

He pushes all thoughts of her out of his mind as he inhales Sloan's scent again. He closes his eyes and sees Sloan there on her knees giving him a moan-worthy hand job, mixing up her speed and pressure as his arousal grows. She always made sure to pay special attention to the super-sensitive ridge where the head of his cock meets the shaft and his favorite sweet spot, the thin ridge that runs the length of the underside of his dick. When Will remembers her fingers massaging those spots, he extends a hand to brace himself on the wall.

He remembers the feel of her hands, both hands as she uses them in tandem, doubling his pleasure. Will grasps his cock more firmly as he feels the tingle start in his lower back and his mind goes to the thought of Sloan forming a ring with her thumb and forefinger at the base of his throbbing shaft as she'd gently tug downward, while simultaneously fondling his craving balls with her other hand.

Will's other hand lowers and cups his balls at the memory. With his orgasm, only a few strokes away, Will increases the speed of his hand and rests his forehead against the cool tile wall. Sloan is there again, in his head, handling his cock with both tiny hands working in precision, first one hand scaling down his shaft followed directly by the other. She makes a gentle twisting motion on the way down each time, and when Will tries that move, his head begins to spin. He's close and Sloan's name escapes his lips on a groan of pleasure.

He knows what he needs to do to push himself over the cliff. Sloan's secret weapon as she called it when she'd tease him and make him beg to come in her hand. She'd wrap both hands around his cock and move them in opposite directions as she worked her way up and down his shaft. As he neared his release, she'd continue stroking his dick with one hand, while she gently massaged his nerve-packed stretch of skin between his ass and testicles, his other sweet spot, with the pointer and middle fingers of her other hand.

And that's all he has. Will comes into his own hand, hard and hot, covering the wall in front of him. As he reaches the height of his pleasure, the sensations overtake him and Will crumbles to the floor once more. He runs his palm over his cock to finish rubbing this one out and coats himself in his release before letting the spray of the shower wash it down the drain.

It takes Will a few minutes to pull himself together and finish his shower. He quickly dresses and by the time Julia is ringing his doorbell, Will has downed a good portion of Scotch and is back to feel nothing. Perfect for his meeting with the woman who has ruined his life twice.

"Julia," he slurs as he opens the door and motions her inside. "Scarlett will be home in about an hour. Let's set some ground rules."

"Ground rules?"

"Yeah, things you will not say to her."

"Are you drunk, Will?"

"Yep, as a matter of fact, I am. I've been placed on leave by the Chief so I have all the time on my hands I need to drink my sorrows away. Once again, thanks to you. Just sayin'."

Julia sends him a quizzical glance. "What's wrong? Did things not work out with the girl you were seeing?"

"Why Julia? Huh? If it didn't, you going to throw your hat back in the game? Let me take you upstairs and fuck your brains out like I used to before it all went to shit?"

"You're being a dick."

He was, but he couldn't seem to stop the wreckage he saw forming from his actions. Instead, he grabs his bulge and asks Julia if she thinks about his cock when she's alone in bed at night and earns himself a slap across the face.

"That was uncalled for" he laughs and downs another gulp of the amber liquid that has become a staple in his next to non-existent diet.

"No, it was exactly what was called for. Get your fucking head on straight, Wilson. This isn't my fault. This one is all on you. You could have stayed at that gala or fixed things with your girlfriend months ago. Instead, you decided to do what? Let her leave you? Did you fight for her even a little? Because you know what? You never fought for me. Maybe if you had, things would be very different now."

Julia wonders what would have happened if Will had fought for her instead of aligning himself with his best friends. Would Julia have stayed on the East Coast and given up law school for motherhood and the McMansion in the suburbs? Would she and Will have raised Scarlett together, her watching as she began to look more and more like the man she suspects is her biological father?

Yes, Caine and Will have a similar look to them. Both with the same coloring but Julia has her suspicions over Scarlett's paternity. Jessie, with his dark hair, dark eyes, and skin tone is out of the running for sure. But it's a toss-up between Will and Caine and she often wonders if Caine questions the fact that his best friend might be raising his daughter.

"Oh, so it's my fault that you didn't want a baby? Fine," he screams at her. "Yeah, it was my fault. I was fucking hard and horny that night and I wanted to bury myself deep in your fucking pussy. Is that what you want to hear? That I pulled the typical dick guy card and begged, telling you I had to have it and I'd pull out? Fine, but you know what? You didn't say no either, Julia. You let me fuck the shit out of you, you finally came for me, and I barely yanked my dick out in time to shoot my load on your stomach."

"That's enough" Will hears Scarlett's voice filled with tears coming from the doorway to the kitchen.

"Scar" he says and runs a hand through his hair.

"No!" she demands as she holds a hand up in his direction to stop him from crossing the room to get to her. "Your fucking drunk again like you've been since Sloan left you. I'm not staying here another minute. I'll be at Aliana's or Johnny's. If you sober up, call me but I'm not coming home until you do. And it sounds like all that fuss over Johnny being a dick to me, using me just to get laid, was you speaking from your own experience. You're an asshole and I'm not staying here!"

Scarlett turns on her heels and rushes from the house. She's gone before Will can move from the spot he is apparently glued to. Instead, he collapses to the floor and sobs like he should have done months ago. Julia approaches him and puts a gentle hand on his back. "That's not you Will. That's not how it happened and you know it."

Will shakes his head and lets Julia help him to the sofa. "I loved you, Jules. With everything I had and you destroyed me. I've hated you for so long, I'm not sure I know how not to hate you anymore."

If he only knew that he should hate her for what she'd done with his two best friends behind his back and the secret she's been keeping from him for sixteen years.

"It's about time you said that. Feel better?" Julia asks.

"Not really" Will chuckles.

"Come on," Julia offers. "I'll cook you something and we can make a plan about our daughter."

Julia leaves out the part about formulating a plan for her own future involving Will.

Chapter 29

The best laid plans are shot directly out of the water and straight to hell a few days later when Mary loses her battle. Will doesn't get the chance to find Sloan and try to repair everything he fucked up because when Mary dies all hell breaks loose with Johnny and Scarlett. As always, his priority must be his little girl. His relationship troubles can wait another day or two.

Mary dies peacefully in the hospital with her parents by her side. Her father tells Will that Mary looked into her mother's eyes one last time and smiled then turned her head and took her last breath. They called Johnny the following morning and he drove to Aliana's to tell Scarlett. Needing her father, Johnny took Scarlett home and she collapsed into Will's arms when he opened the front door.

"I'm sorry," she says. "I acted like a brat. Your relationships are none of my business."

"Your history is though, baby. I should have told you everything that happened between your mother and I a long time ago. But what you heard," Will clears his throat. "Wasn't how it happened. I said things to Julia to hurt her. Things I shouldn't have said. Things that were lies."

Scarlett nods sadly then hugs Will again. He stretches an arm out to Johnny and pulls him into their embrace, comforting the two teens.

"What happens now?" Johnny asks, wiping the tears from his face.

"The hospital will release her to her family. They'll take her to whatever funeral home they're using and make the arrangements. I'm sure they'll have a service" Will explains as he slumps down onto his sofa and thanks God that his daughter is healthy and safe once again in his home. It's a terrible thought after parents have lost their child, but he can't help it. He's lost enough already but if Scarlett is good, he can survive anything.

Johnny and Scarlett head up to her room to talk in private while Will calls Caine and Jessie to tell them the news. When he goes to Scarlett's room, Johnny's gone and she looks worse for the wear. "Oh, baby," Will says. "Come here," He wraps her in his arms again.

"Where's Johnny?" Scarlett sniffs then wipes her nose on Will's shirt like she used to do as a child. She smiles at him and apologizes when she realized what she just did. Will laughs it off then pats her leg. "You going to be okay?"

"Yeah, Johnny went to Mary's. Her mom called crying about a note she left for him in her room. I offered to go with him but he said her mom might not be up to company."

"I'm glad your home. We need to talk about your mother when you're ready, Scar."

"Maybe tomorrow, okay?"

"Sure," Will says. "I'll leave you alone. I'll be in the kitchen making you lunch if you need me."

"Thanks daddy," she smiles at the use of the term she used to use all the time but now never does. "And maybe you should call Sloan and tell her."

"Yeah, I'll see. We're kind of...well, so I'm going to go make lunch" Will clears his throat and leaves Scarlett's room.

They get through the next few days in a blur of sadness. The memorial service was beautiful but Johnny seemed off, distant with Scarlett in a way that has Will on high alert. His concerns are confirmed the night after they bury Mary when Scarlett enters the house like a basket case.

"Scar?" Will says as he leaps out of the chair and runs to his daughter's side. "What's going on?"

Scarlett heaves in a few breaths but Will can barely understand a word she's saying. She finally calms down enough for him to catch a word or two. "Letter...she loved him...wishes she had told him" Scar says through tears and wailing.

"Shhh," Will soothes. "Honey, I can't understand what you're talking about. Take a deep breath."

Scarlett heaves in a sob and flops into Will's lap as he sits on the sofa. He wraps his arms around his daughter and strokes her hair out of her wet, tear stained face. It takes her a few minutes but then she calms enough to explain.

"Mary's mom found a letter under her pillow addressed to Johnny. Remember she called him the other day and he went over there without me?"

Will nods and encourages her to continue.

"She read the letter. Promise me if anything ever happens to me, you won't read my private things."

"Scar, don't talk…"

"Just promise, okay?"

Will nods, not liking the thoughts forced into his brain and he makes a mental note to call one of his therapist friends and get Scarlett into counseling…tomorrow.

"So, she called Johnny and he went over there. Mary's mom gave him the letter. Mary was in love with him," Scarlett sobs. "She said she'd always loved him but knew he didn't return the feelings so she went along with their friendship to be close to him."

"Honey, maybe she was just really sad, knew the end was near, and confused their relationship in her mind."

"No, she loved him. I've always known. I saw the way she'd look at him from time to time, and when I'd tell her things," Scar clears her throat. "Um, about us being together, she'd get weird about it, like she was jealous and didn't want to hear it, not embarrassed because I was over-sharing, you know?"

"I'm sorry, Scar. I don't know what to say but just because she loved him or thought she did doesn't change how Johnny felt about her or how he feels about you."

"No? He dumped me. He fucking broke up with me, the prick. Said he needed time to think and," she looks at Will who has his mouth agape. "Sorry, but, well, you swear all the time. I grew up hearing Uncle Caine and Jessie talking you know? They have horrible language."

Will stifles a chuckle. She's right, his friends have terrible mouths and he's not much better. "Just don't make a habit out of it."

"I hate him. I told him he would regret it but he didn't say anything, just nodded and let me get out of the car. Daddy," she sobs. "He didn't even try to stop me."

"Oh, baby," Will says as he holds his daughter in his arms. Seems Johnny and he both had the same problem fighting for the girl they loved. "Give him some time. He's just lost a friend who has been a huge part of his life for as long as he can remember. Then he found out that their friendship wasn't what he thought it was. He's upset and confused. Let this rest for a few days then I'm sure he'll come around."

"Yeah, well, maybe I won't be here."

Will raises an eyebrow at her. Maybe Sloan won't be there for him now either. If he could manage to grow a pair of balls and find out that is.

"Maybe I'll be on a date with someone else."

"Scarlett," he warns. Will knows about rebounding girls. Caine and Jessie have always said they're the best to take to bed. Something to prove and a vendetta to settle make for great sex according to his pals. "Listen, I um…" Will stutters, grasping at straws. "Ah, maybe we…I was thinking of calling your mother and asking her over for dinner so we can talk. Maybe you should focus on having a relationship with her instead of dwelling on this drama for a while."

Scarlett rolls her eyes then stands. "Fine, call her to come over but maybe you should also call Sloan. It's been a long time. You owe her an explanation."

"Let's get you settled first then I'll worry about me, okay?"

Scarlett offers him a sad smile and heads to her room to be alone with her thoughts.

*****

Will and Julia spend the night with Scarlett and after she excuses herself to head up to bed, Julia agrees to spend more time with her.

Over the next few weeks, Will stops drinking and begins to piece his life back together. He still carries around an ache in his chest where Sloan resides but as more and more time passes, he feels like he's missed that boat and she wouldn't want to hear him out at this point anyway. He'd had his chance and he'd blown it. So instead of drowning himself in a bottle, Will begins to use exercise to clear his head. He runs a minimum of six miles a day and spends hours sculpting his muscles in his home gym. He's sober and able to make it through a day with his regret buried deep. He thinks about picking up the phone to call her only one hundred times a day now instead of a million so he sees that as a vast improvement.

He and Julia begin spending time together with Scarlett and eventually form a friendship with each other in the best interest of their daughter. One night, Scarlett upset over seeing Johnny at a party, comes home to find them laughing on the couch watching a sitcom together. The sight makes her wish they were a real family and she voices those thoughts before she can stop herself.

Will looks at Julia briefly then asks Scarlett why she came home so early.

"Johnny was at the party and I couldn't watch the parade of girls throwing themselves at the 'basketball god'. We got into a fight and he lost it. I wasn't about to stand there and let him yell at me when this whole thing is his fault. He's a dick and I hope his dick falls off. I can't wait for him to leave for college. Too bad he isn't going further away. Twelve hours is still too close."

Will growls and plans to call the boy tomorrow. He knows he should have done it weeks ago but he was trying to stay out of his daughter's business. No more. If Johnny is fucking everything that walks, which it sounds like he is, it's now Will's business because he knows that there's a chance, when all is said and done, and Johnny gets his head back on straight, he and Scarlett are going to be back together. And Will doesn't need his daughter getting a STD. But first, it's time to set Scarlett straight about relationships and boys. Something he should have done a long time ago.

"Scarlett, sit down," Will says. "It's time I said some things to you about guys and the way we think, the way we act without thinking."

Julia raises an eyebrow and Scarlett checks her phone quickly before giving Will her attention. "Fine, but your track record sucks so if Julia doesn't agree with what you say, I'm not listening."

"Fine," Will says with a look in Julia's direction saying that she'd better support him. "Just listen for a minute before you pass judgment."

"Have at it" Scarlett says.

"He's in love with you, Scarlett. I saw it the first time I met him. The way he looked at you made me want to choke him because I knew. He yelled at you tonight because he's in love with you. And I'm sure it killed him but…well, here's the thing. If yelling at you hadn't set his throat on fire like he had the worst case of strep throat known to man, then he doesn't love you. If your eyes didn't make him stop in his tracks and lose his breath tonight, then he isn't in love with you. If your laugh doesn't make him tense up and clench his fists when he hears someone else eliciting that sound from you, then he isn't in love with you. If he doesn't fixate over never hearing that sound again, he doesn't love you. If the sound of your voice doesn't calm his nerves and make him want to listen to anything and everything you say, even girly shit that he doesn't understand, then he's not in love with you. If your lips, your smile doesn't make his chest quake and his lungs shrink, he doesn't love you but…" Will pauses to look at Julia. "But, spending time with other girls, whether he's sleeping with them or not, doesn't mean he doesn't love you. Sometimes, guys use their…um, well, fine," Will says with a small laugh. "We use our dicks to mask our pain, forget things, pretty much for anything at all and it doesn't have to even make sense to us. We just go with what our dicks tell us to do and that's usually to use them to forget everything else. So, if he didn't love you, Scar, well…" Will trails off, catching himself thinking about Sloan. "Well, if he didn't love you, you'd know. You'd just know. Those girls mean nothing to him. He's hurting and using them to dull the pain."

Scarlett taps her phone again as she stands and kisses Will on the cheek. "Thanks, daddy. I'll think about it but maybe you should too" Scarlett turns towards her mother. "Good-night, Julia. See you in the morning?"

Julia nods apprehensively, wondering if Scarlett thinks and is implying that she and Will are sleeping together and that he's using her to mask his true pain over losing Sloan. Sure, they've been spending a lot of time together but Julia hopes she's made it appear to be for Scarlett's sake. And Julia has been doing it for Scarlett, the girl has grown on her yes, but she'd also like to have Will back in her life and her bed. Along with the comfort his wealth can bring her. But being here with them, like a family, has softened her and made her want that. But listening to what Will just said, a warning to Julia not to let him use her the same way, she knows she should be careful with her heart because unlike when she was a twenty-something in college with her whole life ahead of her, she's approaching a mid-life crisis as a divorcee who doesn't have many options left.

"Will," Julia begins, not knowing what she wants to say. "We should talk about…"

"Julia," Will interrupts. "I think you should move in."

Chapter 30

Will arrives, tail between his legs feeling like a fool, tired and hungover after three months of binge drinking and wallowing in his own mistakes and sorrows. The weather displays his emotions well, cool and raining. All in all a shit day and as he steps out of the car the wind picks up, mocking him and blowing his disheveled hair into further disarray.

He runs an apprehensive hand through his hair then impulsively takes his coat off, dropping it on the ground. He extends his arms to stand in the rain and let it soak through his clothes. He looks like a crazy man as his shirt soaks through to the skin and sticks to his body. He feels like one too.

Without her he's lost, has nothing, is nothing. He doesn't want to do this but he doesn't have a choice. He needs to make a clean break so he can focus on the choice he made for his daughter.

Sloan watches from the window of Damian Stone's cabin in the woods where she's been hiding out since the night of the gala when his life went to shit again thanks to Julia. Will's known this is where she's been for a while now but because he's a pussy, it took him until today to finally come here to see the woman who should be his. The only woman he needs. The only woman he wants. But the woman he can't have, the woman who's heart he must break…again.

He stands there, letting the rain assault him as he watches her in the window. He knows the irony, feeling like he's outside looking in on her when she's the one who's been an open book, he's the one who's held her at bay and kept her in the peripheral of his life. What the fuck had he been thinking? How things might have been different had he not waited to clear the air. Too late now. Scarlett's needs must come first.

Sloan had been a mystery to him from that first night he'd laid eyes on her in the restaurant, she overwhelmed him, made him feel things he kept telling himself he didn't deserve, couldn't have. He should have listened to himself back then. He could have saved himself and Sloan all this heartache. Because he can't have her.

When she sees Will standing outside in the rain, Sloan's hand goes to her mouth, the back of her palm masking the wail of agony as it threatens to escape her lips and meet his ears. He deserves to hear that sound. He deserves to suffer out in the cold and rain and watch her turn around and reject him, tell him to fuck off and stay out of her life. Instead, in her dark eyes, he sees a glimmer of hope and he knows that he'll have to rip that away from her too.

She runs her hand through her careless hair then disappears out of sight.

Will stands there, soaked through to the bone and freezing, trying to decide what to do next. Then the door opens. He doesn't see her; she must have opened the door and walked away. Is she inviting him in, expecting him to make the next move? Jesus, it's the least he can do. He's even fucking this up. He should have come after her that night. Fuck that. He should have never let her go to begin with. He should have chosen her and told Julia to fuck off but instead he'd made the biggest mistake of his life and hurt the woman who meant everything to him. But things are no longer as they seemed that night and now he must protect Scarlett at all costs, even if that means hurting Sloan.

And Will knows all too well what it's like to hurt. Caine and Jessie's confession had cut him to the bone and gutted him. He'd needed time to clear his head and process what he'd learned about their past. The last few days without his best friends, in his everyday life, had been brutal and foreign to Will but it was time he'd needed to be able to come to terms with what they had done. What they had kept from him and what it might mean for all of their futures.

He slowly approaches the cabin and makes his way up the porch. He stands in the doorway then discovers, when his eyes meet hers, he has nothing to say except, "Shitty weather, huh?"

"A comment about the weather? Really? Go fuck yourself, Will" Sloan says as she reaches to slam the door in his face. Will manages to react quick enough, which is surprising after all the time he recently spent being a drunk, and his hand connects with hers. They both feel the electrical charge that surges between them. Will would freeze time right here, right now if he could.

But Sloan rears back, flinching from his touch and stepping further into the house. Will, with not many options, follows and slams the cold and rain out.

"So, um, we need to talk. Sloan, please" he begs as he brushes a hand over his wet hair.

"Yeah, you think? I mean, it only took you forever to come up with that idea so I'm guessing, yeah, we should talk."

Sloan walks further into the house without welcoming him in but not throwing him out either. He follows her into the kitchen and slumps down in a chair at the island and watches her from the back. Sloan stretches up and retrieves two coffee mugs and pours them each an overflowing cup. She makes Will's the way he likes it, dark and sweet, same as her, then slides it in front of him. "You'll probably die from pneumonia" she says without thinking then apologizes for her careless comment. It's only been a short time since they'd buried his daughter's friend. Sloan had liked the girl and sent her condolences to her family, Scarlett, and Johnny but she hadn't been able to go to the services. She couldn't risk seeing Will with her...Scarlett's mother. The thought of him with Julia has kept her awake at night and a sobbing mess all day.

Sloan has spoken to Scarlett a few times and they text almost every day. Just yesterday Sloan had been taken aback by the video of Will lecturing her on Johnny's feelings that Scarlett sent with a message.

Scarlett: *He's talking about his feelings for you!*

Was he? Sloan doesn't know what to think about this surprise visit.

"Scarlett said you sent her a note," Sloan nods in his direction but remains silent. "That was nice of you," Will says as he stands in place and drips water onto the floor. "It meant a lot to her. She's not speaking to me by the way, well, she is sort of now. She only told me about the note when she was screaming at me and throwing shit in my face. Teenage girls are confusing."

"Teenagers can be dramatic."

"Good, I'm glad you feel that way. So, then you won't be throwing anything my way?"

"We'll see. I've had a reoccurring image of throwing a lot of things in your face, words weren't one of them though. I was thinking more along the lines of a brick or a chair. But that's just me, you know?"

"I deserve much worse, Sloan. What I did...I...I'm so sorry I hurt you. Please let me explain."

"Explain what, Will? I'm a big girl. I get it. You've moved on, I'm moving on. End of story."

"In case you failed to notice, I'm here. I'm not...fuck! It's so complicated, so much worse than I could ever have imagined."

"Well, in case you failed to notice, you broke my heart so I am moving on...without you. I'm going home for a while to visit my parents. My mom called last night, my dad needs to have some tests."

"Sloan, please," he begs as he stands and moves in front of her then falls to his knees and wraps his arms around her waist, his face pressing into her taunt belly. She feels her shirt getting wet. Is it from the rain or is Will crying? Sloan looks down into his tear-filled eyes.

"This is me down on my knees, breaking in front of you. I need you. I can't lose you. Please, let me explain, it's not what you think but we can't.... I can't..." Will tries to finish but his voice catches on a sob.

"Oh? So, my heart isn't bleeding? It wasn't torn from my body and stomped on in front of your ex-girlfriend and your friends, your family? You know what, Will? Your games are cruel, why did you even bother to come here?"

"I'm not trying to be cruel. What do you mean, why did I come here? I came here for you. Your mine, Sloan. Mine. But I..."

"Your words are breaking my heart; you are breaking my heart. Why are you doing this to me? I saw you, your face when she said your name. I saw the way she looked at you. You left with her, chose her over me. It's been fucking months since I've heard one fucking word from you. What, you fucked her and got her out of your system and now you want me back? Fuck off, Will! You know what, get the fuck out and leave me alone" she demands and rips away from him, dashing into the living space to gain some space.

Will chases after her then rips the band-aid off. "I asked Julia to move in with Scarlett and I."

"Get away from me. Leave" Sloan demands. "Why would you come here to tell me that?"

"Let me explain."

"Explain? What the fuck else could you possibly have to explain?"

"I don't love her. I'm not in love with her. She shared things with me about when she found out she was pregnant, why she felt like she had to leave and," Will huffs in a deep breath. He doesn't want to think about his conversation with Julia. He doesn't want to think about the argument that had followed between him, Caine, and Jessie. "Caine and Jessie are involved."

Sloan raises a curious eyebrow but remains silent to allow Will time to figure out if he wants to share his drama with her or not. He wishes he didn't have drama to share but his life has turned into a drama filled sitcom in the blink of an eye. Sad and laughable all at the same time.

"Caine and Jessie have a thing for ménages with girls. It was recently brought to my attention that they had sex with Julia around the same time…"

"No!" Sloan blurts then covers her mouth with her hand. "Sorry, continue."

Will sighs. "Unfortunately, yes. And there's more. Caine's condom broke and Jessie apparently pulled out but sometimes the mechanics of a threesome make for a difficult time maneuvering around certain situations. He'd already pulled out, taken off his condom and was jerking off to finish."

Sloan tries not to smile but the thought of that scene, the two hot doctors, one jerking off, the other exploding through his condom. Well…it's what great steamy romance novels are made of. "Wait, so…Caine?"

Will smiles for what feels like the first time since Julia appeared on the scene. "He was behind her. Yes, exactly where your mind is going. He pulled out and noticed it dripping into her too late."

Sloan nods. "Just so I understand this," she says but her true reason isn't only for clarities sake. Sloan might need this image during the long lonely nights she has in her future. "And Jessie was…"

"Julia was riding him; Jessie had pulled out and taken his condom off. He says he was jerking off with no plans to come anywhere near her but when Caine saw that his condom broke he flipped out and froze. Julia couldn't move, she was stuck between them and Jessie couldn't stop it by then" Will explains with a clearing of his throat.

"I don't mean to laugh, Will, but holy fucking shit. First, remove the pregnancy thing then the cheating on you with your two best friends and the situation is hot but how the fuck does shit always happen to you?"

Will runs a hand through his hair. "Wish I knew. As best as we all remember, that was two nights before Julia let me have sex with her without a condom. I pulled out but. Anyway," Will clears his throat again. Maybe he's already sick from standing in the rain and he'll be lucky enough to be dead before he makes it back to Connecticut. "We've all submitted a sample and should know in a week or so."

Realization finally dawns and Sloan slumps down on the sofa as the tears begin to flow for the young woman she's grown to love. "Scarlett" she states.

"Doesn't know anything and I'm not sure yet what, if anything, I am going to tell her. Caine and Jessie have both agreed to let me make that call regardless of…"

"Paternity," Sloan states. "I'm so sorry, Will."

Will shrugs. "Not your fault, sweetheart and not your problem. I'm sorry for dragging you into this. But I do have to ask you not to mention this to Scar. I need time to figure that out."

Sloan heaves in a deep breath. "You're taking her back, aren't you?" she asks. "Julia? You have your happily ever after. Either Scarlett is yours or she's not but you'll let her go on thinking she is. And, either way, you're planning on staying with Julia because you feel guilty about this? You know what? Forget it, Will. Have a nice life. See you around" she snarls and looks towards the door. "Don't let the door hit you on the ass on your way out."

"Sloan, please" Will begs but Sloan's crying halts him in his tracks. So does her hand.

"I fell in love with you," Sloan admits. "I thought we could be a family, you know? You, me, and Scar. But I can't do this. You're making a huge mistake with your daughter and with me. I won't tell her anything but you have an obligation to. I hope you'll see that and make the right choice. Good-bye, Will" Sloan says as she slowly turns and begins to walk out of the room.

"I love you, too. I'm in love with you too, but…"

"Yeah? But you can't, let me guess, what? You can't be with me?" Sloan questions, her back still turned to him. She can't look at him or she'll crack, after hearing his admission of love, and end up tangled in his arms and in his life. "Your plan is to live with Scarlett and Julia but what? Have me on the side? Fuck me in your office in between patients, hide me away in a hotel room on the weekends? Maybe fuck me one night a week at my apartment while Julia thinks you're working late and Scarlett is in the dark about everything? No thanks," she says as she turns to face him. She lifts her chin to indicate the door then says, "I thought you were a better man than this, Wilson, but I was wrong. Now, get out of this house and stay out of my life. We're over."

"Sloan," Will sighs then hangs his head. She was right. He should be a better man. But what else could he offer her? It isn't what she thinks between him and Julia but it taints their relationship all the same. He doesn't love her, isn't sleeping with her. Sloan wouldn't be his dirty little secret but she'd have to be his secret until he could determine Scarlett's paternity and she could handle the situation if he in fact decided to tell his daughter any of it. Will doesn't know when that will be.

If the results come out in his favor and he's Scarlett's dad, then he knows in his heart that he has no plans on telling her about Caine and Jessie's affair with her mother. If the results reveal that either Caine or Jessie are her father, then Will is going to have tough decisions to make. Maybe he'll wait until she's older and can better understand adult things like this. Then and only then would Will tell her anything. Until he knew how to best blend them all together, he wasn't telling Scarlett any of this. Could Sloan wait for him? Is it fair of him to even think she should?

Of course not but he's a selfish bastard when it comes to Sloan.

Maybe it was for the best for him to just walk away and leave Sloan out of this.

Of course it is but he doesn't know if he can do that.

"Please, just give me some time. Don't…" Will begs.

"No! I'm done. We're done" she says with her hand up in the air to silence him as she walks out of the room.

Will stands there for a minute. Waits until he hears the slam of the door. He hangs his head and turns to leave; still soaking wet and sure he'll be catching the cold of his life while driving home. This had not gone as he had planned at all.

*****

Will kisses Julia on the cheek and climbs into his car. She moved in and has been sleeping in the guest room since the day after he'd suggested they give it a shot for Scarlett's sake. She doesn't know that he'd gone to Sloan at Stone's cabin in the woods. No one does. He couldn't bear to discuss it. Not even with Caine or Jessie. He's spent the last few weeks trying to come to terms with his choices and his new life with Julia living in his home.

It hadn't been easy. Any of it. And Will doing it without his support system, the friends that have always been by his side, had been nearly impossible but he'd needed that time to heal after their argument.

Julia's been polite and helpful. Her and Scarlett have been spending time together and Scarlett seems to be handling things with Johnny better now that she has a woman in the house to turn to. At least Will thinks that's what has helped. He certainly can't for a minute believe he's been of any help to his daughter. He's barely off the bottle and lucid.

He drives into the city and parks in his familiar spot in the parking garage. It's been months since he's stepped foot into the hospital and he's worried about his feeling for Sloan resurfacing once he's inside where things will remind him of her.

He greets Tonya and is happy to hear that the interviews for his new nurse won't begin until the following day. The memories of the last time he met a new nurse almost brings him to his knees. Tonya knows him well enough to understand that he'll need today to come to terms with his shit.

He had texted Caine and Jessie last night and told them he'd be back to work today. So now he has lunch plans with them. After a few back and forth texts that held no emotion, he finally called them to meet and talk things through and even though he's nervous, he knows they should be together when they view the results he was handed earlier in the week but refused to look at until he had Caine and Jessie by his side.

While he waits for lunchtime to arrive, he tries to erase the memories of Sloan assaulting him. Sloan on his desk moaning his name as he sunk deep inside the wet heat of her tight pussy. Sloan laughing and spitting a gulp of her drink across his desk during lunch one day when Will had said something she'd found funny. He sees her everywhere in his mind.

However, he hadn't expected to see her in person but there she was walking down the corridor on her way into the cafeteria. Or maybe he was still out of his motherfucking mind and he was hallucinating. If Sloan was back working at the hospital, wouldn't Caine or Jessie have told him? They should know better than to hide anything else from him. Will had agreed to talk to them and try to put it all in the past but he's not sure if things between them will ever be the same again. Knowing that they've been keeping information about Sloan from him, isn't going to help their case.

Will wants to call out her name or chase after her but he can't speak, can't move. Instead he watches as a guy, dressed in scrubs, approaches her. He puts his hand in the dip of her back and leads her into the stairwell. In that moment, Will prays that he is bat-shit crazy and has imagined the whole thing.

He walks into the cafeteria and approaches the table where his two best friends sit. "What the fuck is all I am going to ask. Explain," Will demands. "Immediately."

"So, you've seen Sloan?" Jessie asks as his eyes fall on the envelope with the test results that can forever change his life. Jessie wasn't ready to be a father, far from it. But if he is Scarlett's biological father, will he be able to sit back and watch her raised by his best friend while she continues to think of him as her wild and crazy Uncle Jessie?

"I can't fucking believe you two. You both knew she came back to work? When?"

Caine raises a hand to Jessie, telling him to let Will take a seat before they begin. He needs the time too. Caine, even though he's ready to settle down with Katherine by his side, doesn't know if their relationship can survive if Scarlett is his. "After you went to Stone's cabin, she went home to get away from everything for a while. She spent time with her family and cleared her head. She got back about a month ago" Caine reports.

"And you've known this whole time?"

"Yes. She's living with Kathrine again but Will…"

Will stands and runs a frantic hand through his hair, the other still tightly holding that damn envelope. "But Will, what?" he demands.

"She's moved on. She's seeing someone and she made me promise to keep you away from her."

"The fuck is that about?" Will demands. "What, Katherine's pussy is more important to you than me? Fuck you, Cabrera. You too, Jessie. I'm sure you knew about this too."

This friendship that used to be easy and comfortable for Will is beginning to start to feel a lot like threes a crowd.

"I did," Jessie admits. "She's actually working for Cindy and I agree with Caine. She's moved on and so have you. Let it go, Will. You're going to need to find a way to deal with her being here though. Pull your shit together and man up. You're a big boy, you've made decisions, choices, and now is the time for you to live with them. We need to open that envelope and deal with whatever the outcome may be. You need to stop running away from this."

Will shakes his head at his best friends, shoves the envelope back in his pocket, then walks out of the cafeteria without eating or saying another word. He's made decisions, choices and now he must live with them. Well, fuck them both. It's their fault he's in this mess and he knows about his decisions, his choices. He made them in the best interest of his daughter. That doesn't mean they're what he wants. He wants Sloan. He wants to head to his office and pound back a bottle of Scotch too but instead he grabs his bag and heads to the gym in the hospital. It seems like Will never gets what he wants these days.

After two hours of working his body into exhaustion, Will hits the button for the elevator to take him back to his office. The doors open and two men in dark blue scrubs are inside, one of them with his back to Will the other looking like a wide-eyed resident.

"Thank fucking God I'm finally off his service. He's a train wreck and that nurse of his is a disaster, all hurky jerky. This next doctor has got to be better" the man with his back to Will says as he enters the elevator not looking like a doctor in his sweaty clothes. Will doesn't like to shower in the gym showers, preferring the privacy of his private bath in his office and the memories of he and Sloan in there.

"Yeah, I'd guess so, man" the other resident says and then he nods at Will, prompting the other man to turn and face him.

Will finds himself standing face to face with the doctor that had his hand on Sloan's back earlier. He nods back but keeps quiet.

"How are things with Sloan?" the one doctor asks.

"Fine. I mean, she's great but I don't know…skittish kind of."

Will closes his eyes and silently groans. He knows he should say something and stop these poor residents before they put their feet in their mouths but he doesn't. He waits it out to see what he can find out about this guy and Sloan.

"She's fucking hot, dude. Please tell me you're at least tapping that ass every chance you get."

The resident, that Will pictures strangling, laughs. "Oh, yeah. Of course," he jokes. "I had so much free time working with that idiot. I couldn't even squeeze in a nap let alone a quick fuck. But trust me, Felstead spends most of his day buried in that nurse of his."

"Well, Anderson is just getting back after a leave of absence so I'm sure you'll have a light case load with him and since Sloan went to the vagina squad, he doesn't have a nurse to fuck anymore so there's that. Tonya told you that she cancelled the interviews so now you're all he has."

"Yeah, thanks. That's so fucking helpful, Leapman. I hope you enjoy Felstead and Addison but knowing you, you'll agree to their weird ass propositions. And you're an asshole for reminding me that the doctor I start my six-month rotation with today used to fuck my girlfriend. Excellent job, dickhead."

The two nod at Will as they exit the elevator on Will's floor and Will remains inside, letting the doors close and the elevator take him one more floor up. He exits the elevator and uses the stairs to get back to his floor. He walks into his office and warns Tonya that they'll be having a conversation as soon as he showers.

He takes a shower as cold as he can stand and still his nerves are shot and he craves a glass of amber liquid. He tries to quench his thirst for alcohol by popping gum into his mouth before he summons Tonya into his office.

"Mrs. Hardiman, is there something you'd like to tell me?" he asks.

"Oh, stop it with the Mrs. crap, Will. I'm guessing you've seen Sloan?"

Will laughs. "That's all you're going to admit to? Knowing she's working for Cindy and my best friend?"

Tonya shrugs. "That was the plan but I'm guessing someone let the other cat out of the bag?"

"You could say that" Will says with a hand digging into his wet locks.

"He's a nice kid. I hear his surgical skills are great and he wants to specialize in neuro. I nabbed him for you before he was, well…nabbing Sloan," she tries a small giggle out but it's not well received. "Too soon?"

"Ya think?" Will huffs and plops himself in his chair and snaps his gum.

"When did you develop that habit? It's annoying."

Will raises his eyebrow. "Definitely too soon. But it's better than the other habit I'm trying to break so…"

Tonya smiles sadly at him. They've been friends since Will started his residency when she'd been Dr. Talbott's secretary. She knows how he's been struggling these last few months and she doesn't want to make things harder on him. "I can have Dr. Hotchkiss switched off your service and reschedule nurse interviews."

"Hotchkiss, huh?"

"Um, yeah. Carl Hotchkiss. He went to…"

"Don't say it," Will warns and sends Tonya a look. "Course he did. He's the new and improved me. When does he start?" Will groans.

Tonya looks at her watch as they hear a knock on Will's door.

"Um, Dr. Ander…oh, fuck," Carl says as he sees Will sitting behind his desk, recognizing him from the elevator. "Sir, I…I'm…fuck!"

"Dr. Hotchkiss. Nice mouth. Do you kiss Nurse Hale with it?"

"Wilson!" Tonya scolds.

"That'll be all Mrs. Hardiman," Will says, releasing her with a look. "Close the door on your way out please."

Tonya rolls her eyes and leaves the room, shutting the door behind her with a sad look to Carl.

Will remains sitting and an evil smirk crosses his face. "Sit down, Dr. Hotchkiss" he demands.

"Um, maybe I should talk to the Chief about…"

"Do you think that's wise? What are you going to say to him?" Will asks then starts to whine like a child, "I can't work for Dr. Anderson because he fucked Sloan first and she's all mine now."

"No, I wasn't going to…I mean, I'm not…I haven't…"

Will raises an eyebrow in question. "You haven't fucked her, have you?"

"Sir, with all due respect, I don't…"

Will punches his desk and the sound startles them both. "Answer the fucking question."

"No."

"No, you won't answer the question?"

"No, I haven't fucked Sloan. She's not over you. We're taking things slow. I just let Drew, um, the other doctor in the elevator and some of the others think what they wanted to get them off my back."

"Class act," Will says them mumbles, "Douche" under his breath.

"Sir, I…"

"I hear you're talented and have a desire to specialize in neuro?"

Carl shakes his head.

"Then I suggest you stay with me. I'm the best there is in the field. So, man up, Dr. Hot Kiss."

"Hotchkiss, Sir, it's Hotchkiss."

Will chuckles. "Course it is. You're dismissed. I'll see you in the training room in ten minutes."

"Sir, I haven't…"

Will cuts him off with an eye raise.

"Um, right, ten minutes. You're going to have a scalpel in your hand in there, aren't you?"

Will smiles. "Well, Dr.," he stresses the pronunciation of his name, "Hotchkiss. I am a surgeon. I cut, it's what I do and until I know that you have the balls to cut, you won't be of any use to me. Eight minutes. Go!"

Carl mumbles something under his breath and exits Will's office in a hurry to make it to the training room. He's not sure why he's in a rush, Will hasn't even stood up yet, instead he seems to be playing on his phone.

Will texts Caine and Jessie. He needs his friends and it's time to deal with this shit and get back to his life as it should be with his two best friends by his side and the woman he loves with him not his resident. They need to open that envelope and move forward, whatever the results are, Will knows they'll deal with them together.

Will: *Meet me at Stone Faced at 8pm. And yes, I'm still pissed off at both of you, but it's time I explain some shit to you too. I have the results. I haven't read them yet; we'll do it together so no girls.*

Caine and Jessie each reply simply saying they'll be there.

Will knows they'll be there ready to listen and offer their support regardless of the outcome of Scarlett's paternity. He only hopes that they can come up with a plan for him. One that will get Sloan back and keep Scarlett happy.

Chapter 31

Will walks into Stone Faced to find Damian Stone standing at the bar chatting with his brother-in-law, Mac. "Hey," Damian calls when he sees the doctor. "Will Anderson, get your good-looking ass over here."

"My favorite patient. Hello, Mr. Stone. How you feeling?"

"Perfect, Doc. Couldn't be better. And knock off the formalities."

Will smiles and nods at the multi-zillionaire.

Mac laughs. "Yeah, well that'd be true if the girls hadn't sent us guys out alone for the night."

Will raises an eyebrow at Mac and Damian, two men obsessed with their wives and not about to leave them for the night unless there was a payoff at the end of the evening.

"Oh, no," Damian says. "I see that look. It's nothing like that. They're just up to something. No good obviously but in the end, it'll work out for us when they're over our knees, asses in the air."

"Isn't he married to your sister?" Will asks, unable to picture his own sister in any kind of sexual act let alone a kinky one.

Damian and Mac laugh. "Yeah," Mac says. "He's lightened up about that over the years."

Damian reaches for his cell when he feels it buzz in his pocket and looks at the screen with a smile. "It would appear that the girls would like us to come home now."

"Giddy-up" Mac hoots as he gets to his feet and gulps back his shot of Petron.

"Have fun, Doc. It's all on the house," Damian says as he makes eye contact with his bartender. "Anything he wants, Dan."

The bartender nods and Damian shakes Will's hand then follows Mac out the door.

Will clears his throat to get Dan's attention. "I'm meeting my friends. Any chance there's an open table close by?"

Will checks his pocket for the envelope for the millionth time.

"For Mr. Stone's doctors? Sure. Just give me a minute. What can I get you while you're waiting?"

"Just water with ice for me tonight. I'm driving back to Connecticut."

Will needs something much stronger but he needs to be lucid for this conversation. He can't believe that in only a few minutes his whole life can change. Regardless of the results, he knows Scarlett will always be his little girl. But if he isn't her biological father, will she still feel the same for him? Will sighs at the thought of losing another woman from his life.

Dan nods, gives Will his drink, then heads to find a waitress to get him the table he requested.

As Will is siting, Caine and Jessie find and join him. They each order a drink and laugh at Will's choice of beverage.

"You're both douche bags for so many reasons" Will says teasingly, trying to keep the mood light as his nerves threaten to cripple him. He knows Caine and Jessie are only giving him a hard time out of love, they're nervous as hell too. They don't want to see him drinking any more than Will wants to live through those first days of cutting back again. "I still can't believe what you guys did and that you hid it from me all this time especially knowing that it effected Scarlett."

"We were young, Will, when we made our choice and decided it was best to keep our night with Julia from you," Jessie begins. "Then as time went on, we didn't see any other way to protect you. Caine and I paid her off, she took the money and left. We were in Scarlett's life, helping you," he shrugs. "We didn't know what else to do."

"So, you've only been like second dads to her because you think one of you is her father?"

"No!" Caine says. "I love Owl. I can care less what's in the envelope. I will always be in her life. I hope you'll always want me in yours and hers. Will, I hate that we're fighting."

"Me too," Will admits. He huffs in a deep sigh. "I can forgive you. I just need some time, okay?"

Caine and Jessie smile and nod. "Sure" they say in unison.

"You said you had shit you needed to unload on us," Jessie says sinking further down into the high-backed booth. "So, unload. You have the envelope? You want to do that first or…"

"Yeah, it's about time, man," Caine adds. "And we need to know those results so we can figure this shit out together. I don't like that we've been letting Julia come between us. I have my thoughts but let's put them aside until after we hear what you need to say then we open that" he says with a nod in the direction of Scarlett's paternity results.

Will huffs in a deep breath and tells them about his conversation with Julia that changed so much in his life. Caine and Jessie sit slacked jaw; they never would have guessed Julia to be a girl who suffered from depression and who had battled suicidal thoughts since she was a teen.

Actually, they call bullshit on all of it.

Julia's past might have led her to thoughts about her own pregnancy but the more Caine and Jessie think about it, the more they know that Julia had set them up. She'd planned the night with them. Caine wouldn't doubt that she'd tampered with the condom that she had conveniently handed him so he hadn't had to search in his pants that were across her room.

The more Will tells them, the more they think she's out for more money now and playing Will like a fiddle.

"I can't believe Julia kept all that from you," Jessie says as he makes eye contact with Caine to see if his thoughts are heading in the same direction. "Jesus, to have lived through your mom killing a baby then herself only to find yourself pregnant and having those same thoughts," Jessie says. "Julia might have saved Scarlett's life by walking away. What if she'd…"

"Don't say it," Will warns. "I know. It's all I've been thinking about since she told me."

"She's better now?" Caine asks, his eyes telling Jessie that the story about Julia's mom may be true and valid but he still thinks she's up to no good now and was up to no good sixteen years ago.

Will nods. "She's medicated and goes to therapy. Scarlett's not in any danger if that's what your implying."

"I'm not implying anything like that. You're a good dad, Will. That's never been in question. If you're good with her around Scarlett, then I'm sure it's fine. We trust your judgement but…" Caine says.

"But what?"

Jessie heaves in a deep breath then bites the bullet. "We think she's playing you."

Will chuckles. "You always think that I can't take care of myself, don't you?"

"We think she played all of us sixteen years ago," Caine admits. "The more we talk about it, I'm sure she fucked with my condom. I'd put money on the fact that she hid yours," Caine nods in Will's direction.

"If I hadn't taken mine off, I'm sure it would have broken too," Jessie says. "She was trying to get pregnant and she wanted us to not know who the father was."

Will frowns and tries to remember the events of that night that had altered his life.

"But why?" Will asks, confused as these are new ideas for him. Caine and Jessie have been throwing these thoughts around for sixteen years without including him.

"Julia has never really taken to either of you."

Another look crosses between Caine and Jessie. There was always some weird tension between them and Julia but Will hadn't thought much about it. Until now. Now, the pieces of this puzzle are falling into place.

Caine sees the look of recognition on Will's face first. "Will," he begins. "It was before you met her. That first time."

"Oh, fuck" Jessie says as he realizes that the cat is out of the bag after all these years.

"Julia was the first one wasn't she? The girl that night in college I heard you with? She framed us. She never really loved me. She's been using me from the start. Why?" Will wonders.

"Money is my guess" Caine says.

Jessie shakes his head.

"Fuck" Will's head makes contact with the back of the booth.

Jessie and Caine nod in unison. Julia had been the first girl to give them a taste of threesomes. A taste that they continued to quench until Katherine had appeared on the scene and Caine had refused to share her. Come to think of it, Jessie had never asked. Caine and Will knew Jessie had been acting strangely lately, but now Caine is curious if this thing Jessie's been hiding with Cindy is an honest relationship and not just Dom/sub fun in a club. Could the mighty Jessie Holt be hiding the fact that he's in love from them? In an honest to goodness relationship? Caine promises himself to find out once they clear up Will's troubles. One issue at a time.

"After you met her, we all decided it was best if we didn't tell you it was her. Well, Julia decided and we went along to protect you," Caine says. "We never thought it'd go as far as it did with you two."

"Yeah," Jessie says. "We thought you'd date her a little, fuck her a few times and move on. Will, you needed to get laid and she was…well, I mean you've fucked her."

Will laughs. "Really? Julia is your idea of a great lay?"

Caine laughs along with Will. "I thought so back then but now with Katherine? It's different. Better, you know?"

"Oh my fucking God, you are both women! Jesus, it's pussy, there's no difference from one to the other. I'm the pussy doctor, I know these things, remember?"

Caine and Will look at one another and smirk. Jessie Holt is going to go down, get taken to his knees by a woman someday soon and Caine and Will plan to be right there making his life miserable. He'll see just what they mean by different and they'll be sure to throw the 'pussy doctor's' little "it's pussy, there's no difference from one to the other" lecture back at him. Caine is pretty sure that day is coming soon, so a smile takes over his face then he turns to Will. "Open the envelope, Will."

Will nods and removes the test results from his pocket. He looks at his friends one last time. This can be the last time that he thinks of them as his daughter's uncles. In one minute, either of them can forever be known as her father and where will that put Will?

"Do you want me to open it?" Jessie asks.

"No," Will says. "I need to be the one that does it. I'll read the results."

Will slides his finger through the seal and opens the flap. He removes the paper and keeps his eyes locked with Caine and Jessie's as he unfolds it. His eyes leave theirs to scan the paper and a smile crosses his face.

"Thank fuck" Jessie sighs before Will can even read the results, the look on his face told Jessie all he needed to know.

"You're her father" Caine states with confidence. "But those results wouldn't have changed that either way."

Will nods and tears fall from his eyes. Caine and Jessie each reach out and grab one of his hands.

"So, we're cool?" Caine asks Will.

"Yeah, it's water far under the bridge and I have another problem I need your help with before we take Julia down" Will states with a smile to get them back on track. This bullet dodged until they need to deal with Julia.

"Dr. Hot Kiss?" Jessie asks.

"You call him that too?"

"The girls do" Jessie admits then reaches down to rub his shin after Caine kicks him under the table. Jessie sends his friend a warning glare.

"The girls?" Will asks but before Caine or Jessie can answer, Will gets his answer in living color when he hears the familiar chuckling coming from his right.

Sloan, Katherine, and Cindy are sitting at the bar pounding back shots.

"I'm with Holt," Will says when he sees the girls. "You're fucking pussy whipped, man. You couldn't come out for one fucking drink without having your girl an inch away from your dick?"

"I didn't tell Katherine I'd be here," Caine says. "This is a very interesting turn of events for her and I though. With that lunatic trying to get his hands on my girl, she's been told she's not to go anywhere without my knowledge and one of Mac's men. She's grown into a stubborn, confident woman. I'm glad for that but not when her safety is in question. She's getting her ass spanked for this stunt. Maybe that'll make her think twice about continuing to pull this shit."

Will sees the look in Caine's eye, the twitch of his palm and knows Katherine had better brace herself and good.

Jessie laughs. "Novice," he states. "She's being purposefully bratty. She wants over your knee. We'll talk later. I've told you a million times you need to let me school you in Dom life but whatever, man."

The men sit back and watch as the girls drink well beyond their limit. Caine and Will take notice to Jessie's eyes as they travel along his partner. His tongue darts out to moisten his lower lip and he shifts in his pants to cover his growing erection as he watches Cindy giggle, throwing her head back to expose her long, slender neck. Dr. Cindy Baxter might just be the woman Caine and Will have been waiting for, the one to bring Jessie to his knees. They smirk at each other, Jessie's eyes glued to Cindy so he doesn't notice that his friends are on to him.

After about half an hour, when Katherine begins to get loud and Sloan can barely stand erect, they head to the table behind the men. Caine, Will, and Jessie out of sight by the high back of the booth, sit back, now able to hear the girl's conversation without straining their necks.

"It's like having a cut that won't heal," Sloan moans. "Just when I was moving on, he's back, ripping the stiches out and opening me up again. I mean, fuck him! He's a doctor, isn't his job to heal people not fuck them up worse? I know he took an umph, oath...whatever" she slurs then takes a sip of her beer.

"If he's going to open anyone up, it'll be Carl. I heard he had him in the practice room for hours with a scalpel," Cindy says. "He threatened to never let him in his OR right after he told him he'd castrate him."

"Ugh," Sloan slurs. "He asked him if he kisses me with his mouth."

"What?"

Caine and Jessie look at Will and start laughing, hands covering their mouths so the girls won't hear them. Caine mouths, "Castrate?"

Will sends him the one finger salute then mouths back, "Shut the fuck up!"

"I don't know," Sloan says. "Carl was barely explaining anything rationally. Something about swearing and Dr. Dick Fuck asking him about kissing me."

Will leans in across the table and whispers to Caine and Jessie, "Wait, what the fuck is that? He's Dr. Hot Kiss and I'm Dr. Dick Fuck now? Jesus!"

Caine and Jessie smile, nod, and laugh at their friend's expense before the trio grows quiet again to hear the girls. Jessie grabs his bulge and mouths, "Dr. Dick Fuck, that's golden."

"It's their cocks," Katherine begins. "Stupid guy cocks!"

Jessie raises an eyebrow at Caine over his girl's comment and Caine rubs his itchy palms together. "What?" Caine asks, his voice barely a whisper. "She loves my stupid guy cock. And she's going to get it good in about an hour for that mouth and the fact that she's here without my knowledge or her bodyguard."

Will rolls his eyes then tells them to be quiet so he can hear Sloan.

"Yes!" Sloan says, pointing an unsteady finger at her friends. "Yes! It's their stupid guy cocks all long and thick and hard and…wait, what was I saying?"

"You need to get laid" Cindy adds.

"Yes! You are both so smart. My doctor friend and my so super pretty model friend. See, you're not stupid," Sloan slurs. "Because you don't have stupid guy cocks. You guys both have a smart who-ha!"

"I have a pretty vagina. Caine tells me all the time" Katherine says without thinking. Her filter clogged by alcohol.

Jessie laughs aloud, unable to hold back at that one. "Pretty? Oh, man," he says. "You really are a pussy."

Caine flips him off as they hear the girl's laughter.

"Exactly," Cindy says. "Stupid guy cocks are bad. We all need smart cock."

"But Caine's cock is amazing," Katherine says as a smile covers her face from ear to ear. "But I agree, it makes him stupid as fuck but it's…" she trails off fanning herself.

Caine smirks at his friends and mouths, "Amazing cock" while he points to his crotch.

"The problem is estrogen," Jessie explains using his professional voice but keeping it low so the girls won't hear. "It fucks the shit out of them and there's no warning signs. Just BAM! and we're all fucked. I need to find a safe way to halt their periods and stop the PMS madness."

When Jessie accentuates his words with a pound of his fist on the table, the girls take notice of them and Sloan freezes as her eyes lock with Will's. "Oh, fuck this. I'm out" she says as she raises from the table and quickly walks to the exit with Will calling her name and chasing her out into the rain.

"Sloan," he yells. "Stop!"

Sloan turns to face him, her hair already soaked from the rain, water running down her face to mix with her tears. "What, Will? Huh, what can you possibly have to say to me?"

"We should talk," he says. "We should discuss this," He points between them. "And um, she's my daughter! Scarlett is mine!"

"This?" she screeches at him. "There is no this," she says, pointing between them like he just had. "You know about Carl and I and you clearly plan on being a douche to him. Fine. I don't fucking care what you do. He's a good doctor, he can take your shit. So, bring it on, Dr. Dick Fuck and yes, that's what I call you now." Then Sloan clears her throat and adds, "I'm glad about Scarlett."

Will smirks. It's a horrible nickname but at least it lets him know she's been thinking about him. If she put thought into a name, he was on her mind. He prefers when she calls him Wills or Willis but he's a desperate man and will take whatever this woman will give him.

"Why are you smiling at me? Don't look at me like that!"

"Like what?" Will asks and ventures an inch closer to her.

She doesn't back up but her voice is filled with venom. "Like you're going to say something that's going to mind-fuck me worse than you already have."

"We need to talk, Sloan. There's things I need to tell you so you'll understand why I did what I had to do. Things are not always as they seem. Caine and Jessie think Julia set us up sixteen years ago. They paid her off to leave. They think she's after money from us again."

"Oh," she screams at him. "You're a piece of work. Leave me alone. I'm not listening to any of your excuses. I gotta go," She holds up a hand. "And don't follow me, Will. Let this go. It's best for both of us that way."

Sloan stumbles closer to the curb, almost falling off into the busy New York City streets, a heel snapping off in the process. "Fuck me!" she moans. She attempts to hail a cab as Will grabs her wrist. The heat of his touch scalds her and she whirls around to face him. "Get your hands off me," she warns as she pulls her arm back and crashes into his broad chest. "You lost the right to touch me a long time ago. Go home and touch Julia. I'm sure she has no idea what you're doing."

Sloan instinctively inhales his familiar scent as she presses her nose into his chest. She doesn't want to do it but she just can't seem to help herself. God, he smells so fucking good she wishes she could lick his neck and taste him.

"Sloan," Will says as he holds her close to his warm body. If he lets go she's going to fall in a heap on the dirty concrete. "Julia and I…we're not together. It's not like…"

"Oh, you're a bigger dick than I thought. Save the bullshit for the next stupid girl that falls for that, Will, because it ain't gonna be me."

Sloan pushes him away and spins around to climb into a cab that has parked at the curb in hopes of getting her fare, but the alcohol and slippery sidewalk don't mix and this time she finds herself sprawled out on the hard concrete. Will scoops her up, throwing her over his shoulder, and waves the taxi away. He walks her to his car, all the while, Sloan punching at his back. "You've been working out? You've gotten bigger" she slurs then a yawn takes over. Will bounces her and juggles her body into a cradle hold, her head falls to his shoulder on its own accord and a soft sigh escapes her. And there's his scent again, damn it.

Will laughs. "I have a lot of aggression I need to work out. Hitting the gym is better for me than the bottle I took to for the first few months."

"I don't want to talk to you," she says without any conviction to her words but she inhales his neck to get another whiff of him. "I can take the subway. Put me down."

"Like hell. You're drunk, it's late, and you're soaking wet. I'm driving you home and seeing you safely inside."

Sloan sighs again but doesn't bother to fight. She doesn't have any fight left inside her, she's drunk and tired, and too confused by her own feelings to do much of anything other than let Will carry her away. And smell him. Why does she insist on smelling him?

"Whatever" she says as Will places her in the passenger seat of his SUV and buckles her in. Sloan turns her head to face the window as Will climbs in and starts the engine.

"Sloan, I need you to listen to me. Julia told me things I didn't know. She left for the hush money that Caine and Jessie gave her but there was also another reason why she left Scar and I all those years ago. She did it to protect her, not to hurt me."

"What are you talking about? I'm drunk remember? I can't understand a thing you're saying."

Will drives the rest of the way in silence knowing she's right. Sloan is drunk and his words will fall on deaf ears. He needs to get her home and into a hot shower than sober her up before he explains.

He throws his keys to the valet at Stone Towers and leads Sloan into her building. Pedro smiles at the couple then sends Will a confused look as he takes in their soaking wet clothes and Sloan's drunken posture. Will greets him with a smile and a handshake to ease his concerns. Pedro sends Will a thumbs up as they pass and Will smiles back. He leads Sloan into the elevator, she'd never make it up even the one flight of stairs to her apartment. He pulls her wet body into his for warmth and support as the doors slide shut. She doesn't fight him this time. He notices that she does take yet another sniff of the crook of his neck.

It's a quick ride up one floor and Will has her into her apartment in no time. The three little pigs come squealing up to him, nudging his ankles with their snouts. He bends down and pets them all then picks them up and kisses them, putting them back down when Sloan groans, "Traitors. I'm having bacon in the morning, just so you three know."

The pigs go squealing away at their owner's empty threat and Will heads into Sloan's kitchen and starts a pot of coffee. "Go get off those wet clothes and take a hot shower before you get sick. I'll make you something to eat and then you're going to listen to me."

Sloan rolls her eyes but does as he asks and heads into her bedroom while Will sends Caine a text.

Will: *You have any clothes at Katherine's?*

Caine: *Shit! Yes, top drawer, right side. What are you doing, Will?*

Will: *What I should have done months ago*

Caine: *Call me in the morning. Katherine will sleep at my place tonight. Be careful with her. You hurt her bad, Will. Don't do it again. This thing with Julia is complicated. You know there's a chance that we're wrong about her. I don't know, I don't think we are, she could have changed. I'm just saying take things slow with Sloan until we figure this shit out.*

Will: *Thanks, and I know.*

Will heads into Katherine's room and strips out of his wet clothes. He dries off as best as he can then pulls on a pair of Caine's grey sweatpants and a white t-shirt. He runs his hands through his wet hair and returns to the kitchen to start the eggs he needs to help Sloan sober up.

Sloan clears her throat when she sees him looking better than she remembers. Her eyes travel up and down his body, pausing a second too long on the bulge in his pants, before she catches herself and turns around. "You should go, Will. Nothing good can possibly come from this."

"I'll go after I explain. Sit. I'll make you eggs and you need to drink this" he says pouring her a cup of coffee then placing a glass of juice next to it with a few pills.

"Thanks" she mutters.

Will smiles and gets to work on the eggs. He adds toast to the toaster and jokes about her not having any bacon in the house. They both chuckle when they hear the pigs protest from the other room.

Will places a portion of the meal on a plate and pushes it across the island to Sloan. He makes a plate for himself and joins her, sitting across from her and digging into the eggs. "Eat," he orders. "It's good, I promise."

Sloan closes her eyes and moans at the first taste of the food Will cooked for her. Why does it taste so much better when he cooks for her?

"Good, right?" he asks.

"Yeah," she admits. "Thanks."

Will nods and they eat in silence. When Will reaches for her plate their fingers touch and their eyes meet. "Go sit on the sofa, I'll clean up then we'll talk."

Sloan doesn't bother to argue; she heads to the sofa and cuddles up with a throw that she keeps on the back for when she watches movies or reads. She pulls her legs under her and waits for him to sit down across from her in the chair he always liked. "Will, I don't see how this is going to change anything."

"Shhh, just hear me out. Please. I'm not sure about anything anymore. I'm pretty sure at this point that Julia set us up and got pregnant on purpose. I think she was after our money and she always had this strange jealousy of my relationship with Caine and Jessie. I don't think she ever cared about me. She used me but now…I'm not sure what's going on in her head."

Sloan nods and then sits silently as Will explains Julia's history with depression and suicidal thoughts. He tells her about Julia's mother and her sibling that she took before killing herself. Sloan sits riveted to the story and her concern for Scarlett mounts before Will expresses his own.

"She's shaken up over Mary's death," Will admits. "And Johnny breaking up with her hasn't helped any but she's in therapy and in a good place now. Having Julia there has helped her, I think. This thing with Julia, regardless of her motivation where I'm concerned," Will sighs. "I have to do what I have to do for Scarlett."

Sloan nods, her heart breaking now that she understands. She knows Will did the right thing. Well, maybe he hadn't gone about it in the right way but he'd made the right choice for his daughter. If he hadn't put Scarlett first, he wouldn't be the man Sloan had fallen in love with. Is still in love with.

"I need you to know something else," Will says. "I was broken for a very long time after Julia left us. I focused on med school and Scarlett. I didn't date, I barely fucked even though Caine and Jessie tried their hardest to get me laid. When I started dating occasionally, I didn't feel anything so I gave up and took to my own devices for pleasure and buried myself in work and my daughter. Before I knew it, fifteen years had passed and then I met you."

"You met me," Sloan says with a smile at the memory of that first night at the restaurant, then in Damian Stone's gentleman's club, and finally in that hotel room where she and Will had had sex for the first time. "What was I to you, Will?"

"That night?" he asks. "The first time? Honestly, a good time. A distraction. Well, that was what I wanted you to be. But, within an hour of meeting you, you were so much more. By the time I had you naked and in bed, you were like oxygen to me. I had been drowning for a long time and hadn't even noticed. You were like coming up for air. Sweet air that filled my lungs and made me want to live. You saved me from myself, Sloan."

"Will" she breathes.

"Sloan" he sighs and gets up to stand in front of her. He reaches down and pulls her to stand then his hands go into her hair and he pulls her lips to his.

He kisses her softly at first but as his tongue tries to make her open for him she pulls back and her hands push at his hard pecs. He looks down at her with a question written on his face.

"It's not enough," she says. "It's too late, Will, and I can't" she heaves out in one gulp of air. "You made the right choice for Scarlett and I won't...I can't. Will, we..."

Will sighs. "I know. I know, Sloan but I..."

"Yeah. Me too."

They stand and look at each other for what feels like an eternity before she speaks again, Sloan gaining control over her emotions first. "You should go. It's late and Scarlett..."

"Yeah. Scarlett," Will sighs. "So, um, I'll see you at the hospital?"

"Yeah, Wills," she says using one of her nicknames for him. One he likes better than Dr. Dick Fuck. "I'll see you around."

"Sloan," he sighs as he opens her door. "I'm sorry it has to be this way. Maybe in a few..."

Sloan holds up a hand to stop his words. "Good-bye, Will" she says and turns and walks into her bedroom. She closes the door so she doesn't have to hear Will leave.

Will arrives home, more broken than he felt before unloading it all on Sloan, to find Johnny drunk on his front lawn, yelling for Scarlett to let him in to talk.

Fuck!

The last thing he wants to do is stand out in the rain and get wet all over again but he stops his SUV in the driveway and climbs out.

"What in the hell are you doing?" he asks the teen. "It's pouring and you're soaking wet."

"I need her to talk to me. I need to fix this and she won't listen" Johnny calls over the wind and rain, flipping his long, dark, wet hair out of his red-rimmed eyes. He stumbles, falls to the ground, and puts his face in his hands, his jeans now covered in mud and grime from the front lawn.

"Are you drunk?" Will asks. "How did you get here?"

"Jack dropped me off and yeah, I might have had a drink to calm down before I came over."

"A drink or a few?"

"A lot," Johnny admits. "I'm losing my shit. I need her."

Will moans. "Fuck. Alright, let's go. Come inside and dry off and I'll try to get her to hear you out but no promises. If she refuses, I'm taking you home. And let me go on record as saying that I'm not happy that you're drunk."

Johnny tries to stand up but can't manage on his own, his legs failing to hold him upright. Will grabs him around the shoulders and leads him into the house where he finds Julia standing. "She doesn't want to see him, Will. She refused to let him in. He's been out there for an hour."

Will looks at Johnny for confirmation and he nods his head then lowers it in embarrassment.

"Go to my room, take off your wet clothes and take a hot shower," Will instructs and those similar words he spoke to Sloan only a few hours ago hit him in the chest. "Put on something dry of mine and I'll try to talk some sense into her."

"Sense into her?" Julia yells. "He dumped her."

"Julia," Will warns. "Stay out of this. It's been a long night already and I'm not in the mood for anymore drama."

She eyes his appearance and raises an eyebrow. "Where have you been?" Will looks at her and she knows she shouldn't ask again but she does. "I asked you where you've been. You should have been home hours ago. And why are you dressed like that?"

"Drop it, Jules. We have an understanding and at no time have I ever made you think this was any more than just that. I don't owe you an explanation and I've been working through some things in my head. Caine and Jessie have been helping to fill in a few things along the way. We need to talk about the money you took from them."

Julia starts to defend her character but Will silences her with a hand held up in the air. "Don't," he demands. "I'm not ready to hear it yet. But the way I see things, you used me, Jules. You never loved me. You picked me, not Caine or Jessie because you saw me as the weak one. You planned your pregnancy then maybe things got too much for you. I don't know. I'm guessing things with your mom came back and fucked up your head. Regardless, what you did is unforgiveable and I'm not sure what your motives are now. But know one thing Julia, you will not hurt my daughter."

Julia raises an eyebrow as Will admits to Scarlett's paternity.

"Yes, she's mine" Will states.

Julia sadly nods at him, knowing full well that he's right about everything he's just called her out on. She had used him, thought he was the weakest link of their little rich boy trio, and planned her pregnancy. He was also right about her past coming back to haunt her once her hormones had kicked in. What he was wrong about was her feelings for him. Yes, when she started out with her plan, she hadn't loved him. But, by the time she was leaving him, she had deep feelings for him that have remained all these years.

But Julia also knows that if he wouldn't answer her earlier question about his whereabouts, he's been with another woman. Most likely Sloan Hale. Julia turns on her heel and heads up the stairs. Will jumps when he hears the slamming of the guest room door then Scarlett's feet pounding down the stairs.

Women. Jesus Christ, how on Earth is this his life?

"What are you thinking letting him in this house. I told you I didn't want to see him ever again. You know he broke my heart. Whose side are you on?" Scarlett screeches.

"Yours, baby. You've been in a funk since Mary died then worse since Johnny ended things. Hear him out, it might help if nothing else."

"Fine, but you better warn him first that I'm pissed off and have the potential to rip his balls off."

Will laughs at her spunk. "I'm sure he knows, but I'll talk to him."

Will heads to his room and opens the door as Johnny is pulling a pair of Will's drawstring pants over his hips. "I hope…are these are okay for me to wear?" he asks.

Will takes one look at the athletic teen in the prime of his life, his man V prominent and he laughs. "Yeah, those are fine. Maybe a shirt too though."

"Yeah, sure whatever" he says shrugging his broad, sculpted shoulders.

Will fishes a shirt out of a drawer and tosses it to Johnny. "She wanted me to warn you that she's pissed and there's a great possibility that she might rip your balls off."

"As long as she touches me, I don't care what she does."

Will sighs, knowing that feeling all too well.

"Sit down and let me talk to you for a minute before you fuck this up worse with her."

Johnny sits and places his head in his hands again then sends Will a look of panic before he hops off the bed and rushes to vomit in the toilet. He emerges a few minutes later smelling like mouthwash and looking like shit if not a bit sobered up.

"Feel better?"

"Not really"

"Good," Will says. "Let that be a lesson to you. You're too young to drink and if I see you drunk again, we're going to have a problem, understand?"

"Yeah. Sorry. I don't know what came over me. I'm just so fucking desperate, Will. Tell me what to do to fix this. Please" he begs.

Will smiles and thinks about what he wants to say for a minute, what he wants for his daughter. What he wishes he could be for Sloan. "You hurt her, Johnny. You're the first boy she's ever loved, the only boy and you broke her heart."

"I know. I didn't mean any of it. I was just so fucked up over Mary dying then that fucking letter she wrote me."

"I know but…the other girls she found out about didn't help you, man."

Johnny groans. "Ugh, she told you about that?"

Will smirks. "Yeah. I hope I don't need to ask you if you were safe."

Johnny blushes. "Yeah, I wrapped it and just for the record, it sucked every time."

"Good. That's what it's like to just fuck someone. Hope you see the difference and learn that lesson young."

"I did. I mean, with Scar…oh, fuck! Will, I…" Johnny stutters once he catches himself admitting to having sex with Scarlett.

Will holds up a hand. "I already know. I knew the morning after."

Johnny nods. "Does Scar know that you know? She never mentioned that you guys talked about it."

Will shrugs. "I didn't tell her I noticed she winced every time she sat down so…"

"Shit! I made her promise she'd tell me if I hurt her."

Johnny falls onto the bed and runs a frustrated hand through his long locks of hair.

"She's fine but you need to fix the damage you've done."

"I know but she won't hear me out. She's blocked me on every social media site and she won't take my calls. Aliana is like a fortress around her that even Jack can't get through. This girl code shit is ridiculous."

"Tell me about it" Will commiserates. He hasn't heard the end of Caine's complaining about Sloan forcing Katherine to keep him in the dark over their damn girl code. Caine had ended up getting a few good-natured swats to his ass from his girl over him telling Will Sloan's whereabouts when she was at Damian Stone's cabin in the woods. Jessie and Will had had a good laugh at Caine's expensive over that story.

Will pats him on the back and paces the room as he talks. "Here's the thing. You need to be the guy who will play with her hair while watching a movie for no other reason than it's there and you can't help but touch it. Hold her hands even when you'd rather put on gloves in the snow because her hands warm you more than any piece of material ever could. Get on your knees and beg her for forgiveness, be honest with her. Tell her about every girl and how empty they made you feel. Explain your feelings for Mary and how it felt to hear she'd loved you. You need to be Scar's best friend not just her boyfriend and to do that, she needs to trust you again. That's not going to happen overnight. You're going to have to earn her trust back. Take her for walks and have serious emotional conversations with her but show her that you remember how to have fun. Make her laugh and make love to her. As much as I hate to say that, that's what she'll need to lose the image in her head of you with all those other girls."

"You think she sees that? Fuck!"

"Yup, I'm sure of it. Put yourself in her shoes. What if she'd been with a bunch of guys?"

"Will," he warns. "Seriously, don't right now."

Will laughs. Yeah, he might be the only one who hates that thought more than Johnny.

"Tell her that. That right there," Will says pointing to the expression of anger on Johnny's face. "The way you feel about her, tell her."

Johnny nods. "Yeah, okay. I'll tell her everything. Do you think she'll hear me out?"

"You'll only know if you give it a try. She's in her room," Will nods towards the door. "If you work it out, call your parents and tell them I said it was okay for you to stay on the couch tonight and I'll bring you home in the morning on my way to work."

"Thanks and if I don't?" Johnny asks as he heads to Scarlett's room and Will sends up a prayer to the powers that be that he gave the kid the right advice.

"Worry about that if it happens but I think she's ready to listen to you."

"Thanks again, Will and um," Johnny pauses at the threshold of Will's room. "Maybe you should take some of your own advice and try again with Sloan."

Will nods as Johnny leaves him with thoughts of how things had just ended with Sloan.

Chapter 32

Will stands and waits for the main elevator to arrive to take him up to his office. He wishes he had his own private lift to carry him up to his floor so he wouldn't have to stress out over who might climb into this box with him each time he's waiting for it.

As he stands there, his mind drifts to his daughter. He thanks his lucky stars that he had found Scarlett and Johnny cuddled up together last night, their fight long over and apologies accepted. When he drove Johnny home on his way to work, the teen told him that Scarlett's not ready to let him off the hook for his atrocious behavior just yet but she was finally ready to listen to him and give him another chance. He promised Scarlett then Will that he'd never do anything to hurt her again. Will warned him that he planned to hold him to that promise.

Will glances to the right, instinctively, as if his body is drawn to her presence, to see Sloan approaching with Cindy. The elevator arrives and he props the door open with his strong arm. Sloan slides in, her arm brushing over the muscle in his and she shivers then looks into his eyes before moving her gaze to the floor and clearing her throat.

"Miss Hale," Will says in greeting. "How are you feeling today?"

"Empty" Sloan whispers.

"Empty? What the fuck does that..."

"Will," Cindy warns, cutting him off midsentence. "Just leave it. Sometimes, in the morning things don't always look better, okay?"

Again, what the fuck?

Will nods as the elevator doors open. He looks up to see his resident, Dr. Hotchkiss and his sidekick. Carl pauses when he sees both Will and Sloan in the elevator. "Fuck," he grunts. "This is a great way to start my day."

"What was that Dr. Hot Kiss?" Will smiles and Sloan shoots him a look to kill.

Drew, Carl's friend and fellow intern, laughs at his expense then quiets when Cindy shoots him a silencing look. Dr. Leapman apparently either wants to be a pussy doctor or he wants to fuck one.

Either way, Will has a feeling that Jessie is not going to take to this young doctor any more than he's enjoying his own resident's presence.

"I was just saying…"

"Don't," Sloan warns. "Just let him act like a child."

"I'm not being a child, Miss Hale and I thought we discussed…"

Sloan's head snaps up as if to tell Will not to mention their conversation or the mere fact that they were together last night in front of her new boyfriend.

"Oh, yeah, I'm the one acting like a child," Will says then turns to Carl. "Let's go" he demands.

"Will" Sloan begins but stops herself as Cindy places a hand on her arm.

Will goes about his day, finally interviewing nurses for the position that he only wants Sloan to fill. He'd let Tonya talk him into it after he'd had time to accept that Sloan would not be returning to his service and he'd need more help than Carl in assisting him.

Now, if he's being honest, the position he wants Sloan to fill would get him fired for conducting interviews during hospital time. He knows being a nurse in his department had never been for Sloan and he's accepted that maybe they had a better chance of a relationship if she wasn't his nurse.

Carl is helpful throughout the interview process and by the end of the day, Will has himself a new nurse. This time she's well into her fifties, married with kids, and free from all impending drama.

After warning Carl to get a good night's sleep, so he won't fuck up his first real incision in the morning, Will finds himself in the elevator again. He stands with his back against the wall and thinks over his brilliant plan to keep Carl extremely busy and so tired that he'll never have a chance to see Sloan. And if he does? Well, Will figures if he manages to make time to see her, he'll still never have enough energy to fully enjoy himself. Or more importantly, to help Sloan enjoy herself.

Will smiles to himself and as the doors open a chuckle forms in his throat. His merriment is halted when he sees Sloan standing there waiting to climb in. Will quickly stifles that chuckle. His face lights up when he sees her. She steps on and smiles at him then as the doors close she turns to look at Will straight on. "Stop!" she warns. "Are you stalking me?"

"What? I work here. I'm not stalking you."

"Mmmm Hmmm, whatever, Wills."

"Did we not just talk last night?"

"Yes, we talked," Sloan says and Will touches her arm. She pulls back saying, "And I told you it wasn't enough."

"I agree but if you could just give me a little time. Scar…"

"A little time? What, till Scarlett leaves for college? You're out of your fucking mind. And if she…oh, forget it."

The elevator arrives on the main floor and as the doors open Sloan flings herself out into the lobby, thankful when she sees Katherine there waiting for her. Will lets Sloan walk away but as he passes her and Katherine, he leans in to Katherine's ear and whispers, "Look out for her." Katherine nods and glances at her friend then to the bulky Hunter King, who is obviously overseeing her safety today, before they watch Will exit to the parking garage.

And so is his life. Every day Will trains Carl to be a great brain surgeon like himself while wondering if the kid spent the previous night fucking the woman he loves. Carl doesn't poke the bear; he tries to remain as professional as he can and never brings Sloan into their conversations. It makes Will wonder if Sloan and Carl are still not sleeping together. When the curiosity over that fact grows too great, Will tries a new tactic with Sloan.

Sloan is sitting alone in the cafeteria looking tired when Will enters and his eyes immediately land on her. He walks over and plops down in the chair across from her. "Hey, you look like you could use a friend. Have you eaten?" he asks handing her a cookie from his stash, the doctor has always had a sweet tooth.

"A friend? Really, that's where this is going now?"

"Well, I don't want to be enemies so if I can't have what I want," Will shrugs. "I guess for now, yeah. Friends."

"Friends," Sloan sighs. "Fine, Will, friends."

"So, you were right about Carl. He's going to be a great doctor. He's dedicated and eager to learn from me. I just hope he learns from my mistakes too."

"Don't do that," Sloan warns. "Don't talk to me like you're my person or my boyfriend or whatever. Just...Aargh!" she moans. "Just stop talking to me."

Will raises an eyebrow but before he can say anything more, Sloan reaches into her pocket and looks at the screen of her cell. "I have to go" she says and jumps to her feet.

"Sloan," Will calls as she runs from the cafeteria, never looking back.

They spend the next few days each finding themselves thinking about the other.

Will stands in the atrium and stares out into the courtyard, his thoughts on Sloan until he's interrupted by a 911 page and runs into surgery to save someone's life while her boyfriend watches.

Sloan's thoughts drift to Will while she sits in the nurse's room and a new batch of interns enter, each excited for their new tasks. All Sloan can think about is her first day there, when she walked into Will's office to find she'd slept with her boss without knowing.

The days go by, Will continues to make his peace with his best friends and he and Sloan see each other in passing. Now that Caine is back in his life, Will keeps tabs on Sloan through him and Katherine and he interrogates Carl every chance he gets. When Will gets a text from Caine telling him that Sloan's in the ER waiting for her father to be brought in, Will races down eight flights of stairs to get to her.

When he flings himself through the ER doors, she's nowhere to be found. He flies out the front door to see if she's waiting outside for the ambulance, that's carrying her father, to arrive. Will wonders what the fuck could have happened to him as he hurls himself out into the noise of the concrete jungle of New York City. Maybe a car accident. Jesus, he hopes he's going to be okay. Or, being that he obviously needs serious medical attention, he hopes it's a neuro case so he can make this all better for Sloan. Yes, he's cocky but is it being cocky if you are that good? Because Dr. Wilson Anderson is in fact that good at his job.

He finds Sloan slumped down on the curb, her head in her hands and he can tell by the tremors running through her body that she's crying. "Sloan, sweetheart, what's happened?"

Sloan cries harder at his presence as she stands but keeps her back to him. It's like when you're at a loved one's funeral. You're standing there sad but doing okay. Then you see someone, your person, a friend, and you lose it. That's what Will's presence does to her now. He affects her. He is her person, the one, the only one. She must fight those feelings; she can't act on them any longer but that fact doesn't change how she feels. "Please," she begs. "Please, just please. Please don't say anything" she sobs, tears streaming down her face as she heaves in as much air into her lungs as she can manage. It's not enough. Within seconds she's collapsing into his arms, lightheaded.

"Sloan," he screams as he catches her and takes her back to the ground. He cradles her in his lap and does a quick neuro assessment. She's fine, the events leading up to this moment have just finally taken their toll. "Shhh, I've got you."

"Yes, you do," she admits. "That's part of the problem, Will."

Will nods but refuses to let up on his grip. He knows he should be a better man and walk away, walk completely out of her life and let her heal. Give her a fair shot of moving on and finding someone but he can't. He just can't leave her.

"Caine texted me that your father was coming in. What happened?"

"Heart attack. I don't know anything else really. They took him up to Dr. Williams so he's in good hands, right?"

"Yes, Christian is one of the best in the country. If it were my dad, I'd call Chris in."

Sloan nods. "Ok, that's good then."

"Is your mom here?"

"She's upstairs. I just couldn't…"

"I know. It's going to be okay. I'm here. You're entitled to freak out. Let me take you to my office so you can have some privacy."

"Thanks" she says as she lets Will help her to her feet and take her to his office where he settles her on his couch.

"Do you need me to stay? I mean, I can call Katherine or Cindy if you'd prefer. Or Carl, I guess."

"No, you'll do for now," she says with a sad smile. "Thanks, Will. I'm better now. I'll probably just stay here a few more minutes then go check on my mom, see how long my dad will be in surgery."

Will wants to be helpful but he wants to stay with her, comfort her in his arms. He knows that's not his role in her life any longer and so he tries his best to push his own desires aside and do whatever it is that Sloan needs.

"I'll check on that. I want to be sure they don't need a neuro consult anyway."

"Thank you, that's nice of you."

"Sloan, you're…"

"Don't, okay? You're complicated, that's what you are and I can't do complicated right now."

"Complicated? Really, me?" Will jokes.

"Ah, yeah. Your ex is back and she's living with you, you have a daughter that you kept from me and you're a workaholic brain surgeon. Comp-li-fucking-cated!"

"Thanks for not mentioning that little issue I had with Caine and Jessie."

Sloan sadly smiles then wipes her face, pulls her long hair back into a messy bun at the nape of her neck, and raises to her feet.

"I'll go check with Dr. Williams. If I'm not back for a bit, don't think the worst. I'll find you as soon as I know anything."

Sloan nods and they exit Will's office together then go their separate ways. Will heads to the OR and Sloan goes in search of her mother. As much as it pains Will, he sends a text to Carl and tells him what's happened and where he can find Sloan. He tells him he can clear his schedule for the rest of the day to be sure she's alright.

*****

"What the hell are you doing in my OR, Anderson? This isn't a neuro case," Dr. Christian Williams says. "Get out. I didn't ask for nor do I need a consult and I'm well aware of your affiliation with my patient so don't even attempt to go there. You know you shouldn't be in here asking what you're about to ask."

Chris Williams is one of Will's colleagues that he also considers a friend. He's a great guy and an even better surgeon. But Chris knows that Will shouldn't be in his OR for more than one reason and he's called him out on it. He also knows that this is a touch and go case and he needs to focus on his patient laying on the table with his chest cracked open but if the tables were turned and Will had his father-in-law on this table, Chris would be in here demanding information too.

"I'm not in the mood to measure dicks with you. You'd lose anyway. Just tell me what's going on with Sloan's dad" Will demands.

Chris laughs. "I'd slap my dick down and win...easily, but I don't have two free hands right now and I need both to lift it."

"Chris" Will says, his voice no longer light. The banter of their friendship evaporates and Chris knows he needs to give Will something.

Chris sighs. "It's not good. I'm doing my best but I'm not sure if that's going to be enough, okay? Even if I can repair...Will, you need to warn her. He might make it out of surgery because yes, I am that good but honestly, I'm not sure if that's going to be enough."

Will heaves in a deep breath then blows it out. "If you need me..."

"I'll have you paged."

"Thanks. And..."

"Don't," Chris warns. "Go prepare her for the worst and let me do my job."

Will leaves the OR and rips his mask off then the bonnet covering his head. He flings them both to the ground and heaves himself against the wall. How the fuck is he supposed to go and tell Sloan that there's a chance, a good chance, that her father is not going to make it? That's not what he wanted to hear. He wanted Chris to tell him that everything was going to be fine so he could relay that to Sloan and have her jump in his arms and thank him.

"Fuck!" he mutters as he pulls himself from the wall and goes in search of Sloan. It takes him a few tries to find her but after half an hour he walks into the nurses' room and hears her sobbing. Will finds her crying on the floor next to her locker and he sits down next to her and puts a strong hand on her knee. He expects Sloan to pull away from his touch but she remains still for a minute then places a hand over his and squeezes.

"I don't want my dad to die but that's what you're in here to tell me isn't it? I can tell, I see the look on your face."

Before Will can confirm or deny her suspicions Sloan begins to hyperventilate, her sobbing stealing every breath she tries to take in.

"Take a deep breath, come on. Sloan, sweetheart, you can do it. Nice deep breathes like me. Let's breathe together," he soothes. "In and out, nice and easy. That's my girl. Good. A few more."

Sloan begins to settle down, her breathing no longer threatening to make her pass out. Will continues to hold her hand, his thumb rubbing her knuckles. She lowers her head to his shoulder and Will engulfs her in his arms. They cuddle for a few minutes until Sloan sighs, "I'm okay."

"Yeah, sweetheart, you are" Will says as he wipes the hair out of her eyes so he can stare into them. His eyes fall to her lips as her gaze goes to his. They're frozen in time, each wanting what the other needs. Then they hear someone clearing their throats. When they look up they find Carl watching them.

"I came to find you," he says. "Your dad is out of surgery. You'll be able to go in to see him soon."

"Oh. Okay, thanks," Sloan says as she stands up then turns to Will. "Will, I um…"

"Go," he says. "Go see your dad. Call me if you need anything. Carl will stay with you."

Will nods at Carl who sends him a confused look before following Sloan out the door.

Will spends the next two weeks miserable without Sloan in his life. Sloan feels the same way about Will but with her father still clinging to life, she pushes those feelings aside and lets Carl take care of her.

He brings her coffee while she sits by her father's bed and strokes his hand. She feels guilty because all she can think of when he hands it to her is how he doesn't know her. Not like Will does. He hands her a coffee cup every time from the cafeteria. Will would know better; he'd get Sloan her favorite from the popular chain down the street.

Carl sits with her and listens as she talks to her father. He talks to the doctors and nurses and fills her in on his condition. She knows she should be grateful for him but all she can think about is how she wishes he were Will instead.

Scarlett calls Sloan when she hears about her dad but Sloan lets it go to voicemail then forgets to listen to it for days. When she does, she's confused by the message and perplexed enough that she texts Scarlett back and heads into Connecticut to see the girl. They meet in a privately-owned coffee shop and Sloan sucks it up and drinks more of the dark brew she doesn't prefer while Scarlett picks at a muffin.

"I'm glad you came to meet me," Scarlett says. "How's your dad?"

"The same, not good. The doctors aren't very hopeful. My mom is there now. I can't stay long but, Scar, you said things that concerned me. I wanted to see you and talk face to face."

"Have you seen my dad?" Scarlett asks as she pushes her plate with the chocolate chip muffin on it that she'd been poking at with her finger.

"Yeah, I'm working at the hospital again. For Cindy now. I see him there."

Scarlett nods. "Yeah, he mentioned that."

"He talks about me to you? What about your mom? Does she know, I mean does he…"

"Sloan," Scarlett begins on a sigh. "They're not together like that. You know that, right?"

"What do you mean?"

"Julia sleeps in the guest room and they barely communicate. My dad only asked her to move in for me which I didn't even want or need but you know how he is and he flipped out over some shit."

Sloan sits dumbfounded for a minute then recovers because her main goal for this visit, even though she wants this information about Will and Julia, is to be sure Scarlett is alright. "Your dad told me about why Julia left when you were born."

Scarlett nods then takes a sip of her coffee and cringes. "This is awful."

"I know," Sloan laughs. "We should have gone to my fav. Tell me what happened, Scar. I'm worried about you. Why did your dad flip out?"

Scarlett shares her feelings over Mary's death and then Johnny leaving her after her mother told him about a letter Mary had left confessing her true feelings for him. She explains, as Will had, Julia's history with depression and her maternal grandmother's post-partem issues. Scarlett then shares the part of the story Will hadn't told Sloan.

"He flipped out because I wasn't eating. I refused to get out of bed for school or dance and I was crying all the time and couldn't stop. Before I knew about Julia's issues, I may have made a comment about wishing I were dead and he took it literally. I know it was a stupid thing to say and that suicide is a real thing, not to be joked about, but I wasn't joking. I just wasn't serious about it either, you know?"

Sloan nods. She gets it. She remembers being a teenage girl and devastated over a break-up or two. She'd locked herself in her room for days once, blasting sad songs and thinking about ways to get the boy back. Hell, she hadn't reacted much differently as an adult when Will left her.

"Are you better now?" Sloan asks.

"Yeah, Johnny and I are back together. I'm still a little pissed off at him but I was better before he came back. He was an asshole, by the way. I don't even want to talk about what he did," Scarlett clears her throat then with an eye roll says, "Or who more like it."

"Oh, Scar. I'm sorry he was a jerk. Have you guys…" Sloan wiggles her eyebrows.

Scarlett blushes red. "Um, yeah. The night of the gala. When we left, it was snowing bad and my grandfather just wanted to get us home so he brought Johnny to my house. I was upset over everything with you and my dad. Johnny was there. He held me and made it all fade away. He didn't try anything. It was me. I...I wanted, well, I asked him."

"Please tell me you were safe" Sloan says.

Scarlett laughs, "After dad giving him his condoms, do you think either of us would want the lecture if we weren't?"

Sloan and Scarlett laugh together.

"I'm glad you guys were smart about it."

"Sloan," Scarlett jumps topics. "What's going on with you and my dad? He still loves you. There's nothing going on with him and my mom. I've heard them arguing a lot lately over their relationship. I probably shouldn't tell you this but she's in love with him. She told him that she always has been. I'm not sure what went down but I heard them fighting. He said he was trying his best for my sake but that all he sees is you. They were in her room at the time and when he came out, I saw him through my door. He looked disheveled but I don't think anything happened between them."

"Scarlett," Sloan warns. "First, you shouldn't be spying on your parents to see if they're having sex and secondly, you shouldn't be reporting back to me. They're adults, what they do in their relationship is no one's business but theirs."

"But that's the thing. They don't have a relationship. The next morning, Julia told my father that she was sorry then I heard him on the phone with Uncle Caine. He told him what happened the night before with Julia."

Sloan raises her eyebrows. "I'm afraid to ask and I know I shouldn't. If you ever tell your father I will kill you but..."

"Yeah, I'm not going to tell him. Telling you is bad enough. It's gross."

Sloan looks at her with a confused expression.

"Julia apparently tried to hook up with my dad and he couldn't," she clears her throat then scrunches up her face. "Get it up with her. That's so freaking gross, does that really happen? I mean, Johnny is..."

"Alrighty then," Sloan interrupts. "Moving on."

Scarlett laughs. "Yeah, so my dad told Julia they should try to work things out and keep living together for me, he said he'd try harder. Something about stability and being consistent for me. I think he's worried I'm going to be upset if they're not together. I don't know what he's thinking. I grew up with just him. I don't need them to be together. I like knowing Julia but I don't need her to live with us especially if they're not hooking up, you know? I'd actually rather have him with you so he's happy," Scarlett catches herself and laughs. "Oh, I don't mean…I love you, Sloan. Honest. I want him to be happy but I also want him with you because I really do like you."

"I know, honey. I really like you too. I'm just not sure about your dad and I. It's complicated, he's complicated."

"He's sad all the time now, Sloan. Like he was before he met you. I just didn't notice it back then because it was how he'd always been. After seeing how he was with you, I'm sad for him now because he's a mess. He spent the first few months after you guys broke up drunk. He didn't even talk to my uncles for a long time. Then he got obsessed with working out and now he's just…sad."

Sloan groans and takes a sip of her coffee which makes her groan again. "This is terrible," she chuckles. "And I um, I need to get back to the city to make sure my dad's okay. Can we talk again? Maybe in a day or two, after I think about things?"

"I'd like that. Don't tell my dad we met up, okay?"

"It's our secret" Sloan says offering Scarlett her pinkie finger.

*****

Will meets up with Caine and Jessie at Stone Faced again a few days later only this time he succumbs to a few drinks and by the time they hear the familiar sound of Sloan, Katherine, and Cindy, Will is the one drunk. He slurs his words as he glances in the direction of the bar where the girls are throwing back a few shots. Sloan occasionally looking in his direction. "Everythink is going to be five," he says. "Right?"

Caine laughs at Will's question then turns to scan the room to be sure that Graham King is watching over Katherine. The King brothers have been rotating their shifts watching over her since she told Caine that Mike had continued to try to work things out with her.

"Yeah, man. Things have a way of working out for the best" Jessie mumbles, barely paying attention to the conversation.

"I was talking to Caine," Will states. "My dick, please telp me it's going to work again" he says then chuckles at his error. "Tell, tell me."

Jessie, not knowing what Will is talking about, looks at Caine who shrugs.

"Um, yeah, I guess it'll work again. Why? Has it been not working?" Caine asks. "I thought you weren't with Julia. I thought she was sleeping in your guest room, only there for Scarlett's benefit, and until we can figure out what she's playing at with you this time around."

Will downs another shot and raises his hand to get the bartender's attention and request another beer.

"Maybe you should slow down" Jessie says.

"Julia's hot, right? Sexy as fuck? My dick should ducking work, no? Fuck! Fucking work."

"What's this all about?" Jessie asks, still confused about what Will is talking about.

"I'm so lonely. I miss Sloan so muck," Will slurs again. "And that Carl with his stupid millennial beard, gifted hands, and smart cock."

"Okay," Caine says. "Did Carl try to jack you off and you couldn't get it up with him? What the fuck does he have to do with any of this? I thought the plan was to see if Jules would sleep with you. What the fuck are you trying to say? You're making little to no sense, man."

Will sighs as they hear the girls getting a bit loud a few feet away.

"He fixes brains, brains. He's a fucking brain surgeon, how can he be so fucking stupid?" Sloan asks Katherine and Cindy after describing what she'd learned earlier that day from Scarlett.

Cindy and Katherine shrug their shoulders then both take a sip of their wine as Sloan downs a few more gulps of her beer. "I don't know. Caine is a brilliant doctor but he's clueless in most everything else."

"How?" Sloan continues to rant about Will. "Seriously, how? How can he possibly be that dumb? No, really, I'm asking. How? Is it his stupid guy cock? It is, right?"

It's Cindy's turn to answer. "Well, there's this saying, birds of a feather, right? Because Jessie is the most clueless of them all. I've all but written out my feelings for him and he still hasn't made a move since that night at The Society."

"I still can't believe he's," Katherine whispers. "A sexual Dominant."

Sloan laughs aloud then covers her mouth when she realizes she's just gained the attention of Will, Caine, and Jessie. "Oh, come on. He has that Alpha-Male thing in spades. I would have been shocked if he wasn't into it."

"They're looking at us," Will says. "And no, Carl didn't jack me off, idiot. Do you think they're talking about my dick? Fuck, what if Sloan finds out it's broke? She'll never want me again. She'll stay with Hot Kiss and his hard, working, smart dick."

"Will," Jessie asks. "Did you try to hook up with Julia but couldn't get an erection?"

"Oooo, listen to the pussy doctor with his fancy terms," Will laughs. "Yeah. Okay, kind of. She tried to…I don't know. She tried to hook up with me the other night. She admitted to still being in love with me and wanting us to try for real. I was about to tell her I couldn't when she kissed me. Before I came to my senses her hand was in my pants and I couldn't get hard. All I saw was the look on Sloan's face that night at the gala when I left her."

"Do you want to fuck Julia?" Caine asks.

"No. I want Sloan. I'm in love with Sloan but," he sighs. "I thought the plan was to see if Julia was playing me again. She still hasn't given you guys back the money?"

"Nope." Caine says.

"Not a dime," Jessie adds. "And that is the plan you idiot. To *see* if she's playing you. Not to fuck her or let her jack you off or whatever the fuck vanilla shit it is you do."

"So, she's still sticking to her story that she's actually in love with you?" Caine asks.

Will rolls his eyes. "Is it that hard to believe that a woman might be in love with me?"

"Not a woman," Caine says. "That woman. She's not capable of love, Will. It's just not in her DNA."

"Alright, back to the original topic of your limp dick. You're fucking stupid," Jessie states. "You couldn't get it up because you felt guilty and probably because you're not attracted to Julia anymore. If you're in love with Sloan and you want her, what the fuck are you doing with Julia in your house and letting her get in your pants?"

"I don't fucking know," Will yells then bangs his head on the table when his eyes meet with Sloan's from across the room. "I gotta get home. Can one of you bring me? I can't drive."

The following day, Will enters the elevator wearing dark glasses and nursing a coffee from Sloan's favorite chain. She steps on behind him looking worse for the wear as well.

"Rough night?" she asks, her voice soft due to the pounding in her own head.

"Night?" Will asks. "Nah. Not a rough night, sweetheart. It's been a rough few months."

Will traps her body against the elevator door then stretches his arm. He presses the stop button and suspends them between floors.

"What the fuck are you doing?" she asks.

"What I should have done a long time ago."

Will leans in and captures her mouth. His lips moving slowly over hers, his tongue seeking and being granted entry. He smiles into the kiss when he feels the hardening of his dick in his pants. Thank fucking God!

Sloan presses her palms to his chest and breaks their embrace. "I'm not going to be that girl, Will. You know the one? The one that makes you choose or plays along as your dirty little secret on the side. I love you. I'm still in love with you but I'm not going to be the girl that takes Scarlett's dad away from her mother, a family, if you think that's what she needs. But, Will, you should be sure that's what she needs and what you want before it's too late because I won't be that girl."

Sloan reaches across him and hits the button to set the elevator in motion again. When it stops on the next floor, she exits without saying another word.

As the weeks go by, Will can't catch a break. Every time he enters a fucking elevator or an empty corridor, he finds Sloan there. Each time their eyes meet, Sloan retreats before Will can decide what to do. He knows he's running out of time but he can't seem to get his balls out of his ass.

He slides up behind her while she's writing in a patient's chart and inhales her familiar scent.

"What are you doing?" she asks in a whisper.

"I miss you" he says then walks away as Carl appears and senses the sexual tension between them.

Sloan finds herself sitting on a gurney, exhausted from her twelve-hour shift and sneaking in visits with her dad. Will appears in the dark corner and plops down next to her.

"You look tired. You can sleep in my office if you want."

"I'm fine. I just talked to Dr. Williams. We're giving my dad till the end of the week then we're taking him off life support."

"Oh, sweetheart. I'm sorry."

Sloan cries into Will's chest as he rubs soothing circles on her back to help calm her. They hear Carl's voice and break apart. "It's funny how I'm always finding you two sharing a moment. For a couple who broke up and are with other people, you two spend a lot of time together."

"Didn't I give you enough shit to keep you busy until our surgery? If you fuck up the incision or the closure on this kid, you're going to be the one to tell the parents. Go practice, you need it" Will orders.

"Sloan," Carl asks. "Am I out of my mind?"

She doesn't make eye contact or answer the question. She remains with her chin down, eyes intent on her lap.

"You could at least acknowledge my presence," he says. "You know what? Fuck this!"

Sloan lets him storm away without trying to explain. What could she say? He was right. Her and Will have been finding every opportunity to sneak away and be alone even if only for a few minutes to talk. They haven't taken it further than that since that one kiss in the elevator.

"Maybe I should take you up on your offer and try to get some sleep."

Will takes Sloan by the hand and walks her to his office. He settles her in on the sofa with a blanket and a glass of water before turning out the lights and stepping out into the waiting area. He walks directly into Julia. "Jules?" he asks. "Is Scarlett good? What are you doing here?"

"We need to talk."

Will looks around, not sure where to take her for privacy. Certainly, not into his office where Sloan is cuddled up on his couch. "Um, my office...yeah, ah, let's go into here instead."

Will leads her into the parent room, thankful that he's not seeing patients today and they're alone. Carl should be busy preparing for their surgery that starts in an hour and Tonya has the day off. Will knows that the office is silent and the walls are thin. If Sloan is still awake, there's a good chance she'll hear every word they say but he's out of options.

"What do you need Julia?" he asks.

"I've been doing a lot of thinking about us."

Will raises an eyebrow. "Alright. Like what?"

"I think we have two choices here, Will. One, we're together. Like really together. We sleep together, we fuck, you know? Together. Or two, I need to move out. And before you say anything, if you're leaning towards option one, then you need to stop seeing Sloan because we both know that's why you responded to me the way you did, or weren't able to respond as it was."

"Julia, I...I can get it up. I was just surprised and tired and this surgery I have..."

Julia interrupts him. "You talk in your sleep, Will," she states. "Or you get yourself off to her when you're alone. Either way, I hear you in your room."

"What the fuck, Julia?"

"Exactly, Will. I'm right there in the next room, naked and waiting for you and you're alone jacking off to memories of some girl you haven't been with…"

Julia sends him a questioning look.

"I haven't fucked anyone Julia. And I can't do this here. Not now. I have surgery," he says dismissing her. "We'll talk at home…later."

"What? You mean at two in the morning when you sneak in so you don't have to see me before you go jerk off in your bed?"

"Good-bye Julia" Will says and nods towards his door. Julia huffs and storms out.

Will sinks down onto the sofa and places his head in his hands. He fires off a group text to Caine and Jessie.

Will: *It's time to figure out what in the hell Julia is up to.*

Caine: *I couldn't agree more. You have every right to toss her out and get the girl you love back. Julia is playing for money, man. Sorry but…*

Jessie: *Of course she is, she's heartless. Is Scarlett strong enough?'*

Caine: *Owl is fine. Julia has no legal rights to her so we're not looking at a custody battle, she's old enough to decide if she wants to see her mother or not.*

Jessie: *Milly did good with that years ago.*

Will: *She did.*

"Do you love her?" he hears Sloan ask and he looks up to find her standing in the doorway that Julia just exited. Sloan is wrapped in the blanket from his couch and he doesn't think she's ever looked sexier in her life. Not even in that ball gown he never had the chance to strip from her body.

He doesn't answer. He's not sure what he'd say if he opened his mouth.

"It's good that you're trying with her, Wills. You know, for Scarlett. That's the kind of dad I knew you were. If you weren't doing this, you wouldn't be the man I fell in love with. I just wish…"

"What? What do you wish, Sloan?"

She smiles at him and hands him his blanket. "Cindy needs me. Thanks for the sofa. I gotta go. See ya around, Wills."

Chapter 33

Everyone in the hospital sees what's happening between Will and Sloan. They've each caught them at least once, most of them way more. Alone in an elevator, having a private conversation in the atrium, sharing a cup of coffee from their favorite place, or even whispering while sitting together on a gurney in a dark corridor.

Will and Sloan know they're the talk of the hospital but neither one can muster up a fuck. They laugh over giving no fucks what people think. Sloan has been keeping Carl at bay, stringing him along. He's busy and doesn't have the time to go looking for anyone else so he lets it slide. He accepts what she gives, which is minimal affection at best. She won't let him emotionally close to her and she certainly isn't putting out. Will is doing the same with Julia. He hasn't been home enough lately to have a conversation with her about their lack of a relationship let alone have a physical one with her but he knows when she does finally corner him again, he's going to have to make some decisions.

Caine and Jessie are convinced that she's only there for Will's money and lifestyle and Will is starting to believe that they're right. Sloan never asked him for anything. Not a dress to wear to the gala, not a date at a fancy restaurant, or even an expensive piece of jewelry when they went window shopping on Fifth Avenue to see them decorated for the holidays. Julia has asked for all that and then some.

Katherine and Cindy offer Sloan their silent support while Caine and Jessie rib Will over the situation every chance they get. That's the difference between the sexes. Women protect one another while men look for the chance to tease their closest friends until they bring them to their breaking point and someone ends up rolling on the ground punching someone else. Will, Caine, and Jessie have clocked in more hours on a floor punching each other than they care to reminisce about. But each time after their rumble, they stand up and man hug the other as if nothing has happened. Even that hit to the jaw Jessie took, when Will learned about his,

Caine's, and Julia's night of sexual debauchery, has since been forgiven and forgotten.

Will finds himself with some much-needed free time on his hands one day when a surgery is cancelled and he's assigned Carl research on their next case. He can't go home in the fear that Julia is there and will want to talk or worse still…fuck. He wants to do neither with her so his new method of avoidance is the only way to go.

He wants things with her to be over but he's never been one for confrontations. Will sees himself as a failure once more but this time the stakes are higher because his daughter will judge him for his short comings this time around. She'll listen as her mother, a female role model, cuts him down and makes him look like a pathetic excuse for a man. If Scarlett were to look at him and see a failure, he wouldn't be able to ever look her in the eyes again. So, that is why he doesn't want to accept the fact that Julia is using him and doesn't have nor ever did have feelings for him. Julia's one love, where Will is concerned, is his bank account and the wealthy lifestyle he could provide her.

He steps into the elevator thinking that maybe he'll go for a run then spend a few hours working out but then Sloan steps on behind him and the air crackles around them. It sizzles like lightening meeting an inferno.

"Are you leaving?" Sloan asks. "It's mid-morning. Is everything alright with Scar?"

"Yeah, Scar's great. My surgery got cancelled so I have a free day now."

"Where's um, what's Carl doing? He says you've been great about giving him extra training hours lately."

Will nods then laughs. Of course, he's been giving him extra training hours. He's doing everything in his power to keep his resident busy so he'll be as far away from Sloan as possible. Training Carl is also another thing to do to avoid going home to Julia which should tell him something. He'd rather spend time with the other man in Sloan's life than go home to Julia.

"Yeah, he shows a lot of promise. He's researching something for me now that our surgery was cancelled. You want to go get a coffee?"

"A real coffee? Don't fuck with me and take me to some shit-ass place."

Will puts his hand over his heart, stricken at the thought. "I'd never!"

"Don't look at me with that face either" Sloan warns.

"What face?"

"Our look. I know what's going through your mind. You're looking at me like you want to pour coffee on my tits and lick it off instead of just drinking it like you should."

"Fuck, Sloan," Will says as he adjusts himself. "Why? Why did you have to do that? That visual is…well, it has potential for me…for later."

Sloan laughs. "I'm over you, your blue balls aren't my problem anymore."

"Are you over me?"

"No, are you over me?"

Will looks at her then grabs the painful bulge in his pants. "Do I look over you?"

"You're fucking with me, Wills."

"I'd like to be over you, fucking with you" he says with a wiggle of his eyebrows.

"Isn't Julia waiting for you at home?" she asks.

Will shrugs. "I haven't a clue."

"I'm guessing she doesn't know your surgery got cancelled?"

"She doesn't need to know that. She doesn't need to know anything."

Will holds the door open to his and Sloan's favorite coffee chain, his hand slides to the dip in her lower back and he leads her to the counter. He places their order and flashes his phone to make his payment then leads her over to a table where they plant themselves for the next hour. They find themselves sitting in comfortable silence, a silence you can only have with someone that you have a level of confident intimacy with. And then Katherine happens upon them and breaks their spell.

"Will" Katherine says in greeting, looking like the cat that ate the canary for a reason unknown to him.

"Katherine" he returns with a smirk, wondering if maybe she knows about his stolen moments with Sloan. Will knows she's been like a vault for Sloan and refuses to offer up anything even to Caine. He also knows as Sloan's best friend and his best friend's girl, she's been trying to shake Caine down for intel just as hard as he's been doing to her. Katherine's expression clearly means she's either up to something or knows something and if she knows something, Will is sure she used sex to take Caine down.

Sloan sends Katherine a warning glance that goes unnoticed as they each stand their ground and Katherine and Sloan stare at the other with smirks on their faces. "Um, I'm going to pop in the bathroom really quick then I should probably head back to see my dad. You two can whip your dicks out while I'm gone. Katherine, just a warning, he's going to win that contest."

Will nods with a smirk on his face and watches her as she walks away.

"You broke her heart, you know?" Katherine begins. "And just when she was getting herself back together, you slide back into her life?" She raises her eyebrows at him. "You asked me to watch out for her. I've been trying, but you're the one who keeps hurting her. You need to stop doing that and figure your shit out."

"I'm not trying to hurt her."

Katherine nods and smiles as Sloan returns. "Yeah maybe, but I'm her person and if you hurt her again, I'll be the one picking up the pieces so I'll know. I won't be as forgiving the next time, just so we understand each other" she says.

"Will" Sloan says.

"Sloan" Will returns as they stand there locking eyes.

"I'm walking away now," Sloan says with a smile. "I'll take her with me before she claws your eyes out."

"You too with the nickname? So what?" Katherine asks her hands landing on her hip in defiance. "He calls me Kitten, so what? We went to a sex club one time and that's all anyone can talk about. Jessie's into much worse, can't we focus on that?"

"Bye, Kitten" Will says as Sloan pulls her out of the franchise and onto the busy New York City streets.

Before Will makes it to his car in the parking garage he gets a text from Sloan.

Sloan: *Please come back to the hospital. Oh, god, Will, I need you. It's my dad*

He replies as he runs back into the hospital and up the flight of stairs until he reaches the floor where Sloan's dad is.

Will: *On my way*

As a doctor, or maybe it's because he grew up as a kid around sickness and death, Will has a twisted sixth sense about it. He knows every time he steps into his OR if it's going to end in him losing his patient. It's a look he sees on others, a feeling he gets in his chest and in the pit of his stomach. It's the feeling he has as he flies through the door of Sloan's father's room.

"You okay?" he asks as her mother turns to see who has spoken into the dead silence of the room.

Sloan turns as well and runs into his arms, burying her face in the front of his shirt. She inhales his familiar scent then whispers, "I have this weird feeling."

"It'll pass," he says with confidence and experience. "I get it too when..."

"He's going to die, isn't he?" she asks.

"Sloan, I don't know, I…"

"Tell me the feeling you get. Describe it."

Will huffs in a deep breath. "It started when I was a kid in treatment. I didn't understand it back then but I knew somehow, had a feeling about the kids that weren't going to make it. I was never wrong. It's a look, a smell when I walk into the OR that alerts me when it's coming."

"Have you been wrong, ever?"

"Never. I'm sor…" he begins as her father's machines begin to alert his team that his heart has stopped.

Will jumps into action and begins to assess him. The nurses fly into the room with a crash cart as Sloan's mother collapses on the floor. He orders someone to take care of her and then yells at another nurse to get Sloan out of the room.

"Fuck that," she cries. "I'm staying."

Dr. Chris Williams slides into the room and shoves Will aside, grabbing the paddles from his hands before he can deliver a shock to jump start Tom Hale's heart. "Clear" he states and the room grows silent as they watch the patient's body bounce from the table.

Chris works on his patient for five minutes, shocking him, trying to bring the man back to life. But back to what kind of life? He'd already spent the better part of two weeks in a coma on life support, unable to breathe on his own.

Will grabs Sloan from behind, around the waist, and holds her secure in his embrace as she screams. It's a howling sound, like an animal dying in the wild. "I'm scared" she admits.

"You can do this. Lean on me. I've got you."

Sloan turns in his arms and lets him rock her body back and forth as Chris calls her father's time of death.

*****

"Hey," Sloan says as her eyes flutter open.

"Hey."

"Where am I?" What happened? My dad" she moans as she begins to remember.

"He's gone, sweetheart. I gave you something to relax and you fell asleep. You're okay now. We're in my office."

"My mom, she passed out and then I…"

"She's fine too. She woke up seconds after she blacked out. She's with Chris making arrangements for your dad."

"I was dreaming about you," she mutters. "Our last time together. I can't remember the last time we made love. I'm forgetting you, us, the way I'll forget him. I don't want to forget him. I don't want to forget us, Will. I don't want to forget" she cries and her breathing grows erratic again.

"Shhh," he soothes. "You're okay, sweetheart. Breathe with me. In and out," he instructs. "That's my good girl."

Will rubs soothing circles on her back, holding her against his body as she sits up on the sofa in his office.

"Do you remember?" she asks. "Our last time?"

"I remember. It was a Friday morning. We had a surgery scheduled last minute even though we were on vacation. Scarlett was due back later that day but I had slept at your place the night before. You took a shower while I ran out to get us coffees. I knew it was going to be a quick surgery then we had plans to head to my house and get ready to pick up Scarlett."

She smiles. "We didn't sleep much the night before."

"No, we didn't. I came into your bedroom and you were in a towel, your hair wet around your shoulders. You smiled at me then pulled your hair up into one of those messy bun things you do. I kissed behind your ear then your neck as I handed you your coffee."

"You said something about the way I smelled."

"You smelled like your shampoo and body wash. That scent drives me wild."

"You were running late and I touched your chest to push you along."

"I love when you touch my chest, it's an aphrodisiac of mine," Will states with a smile, placing her opened palms on his pectorals. "I leaned in and gently kissed your lips then I couldn't help myself and I bit your bottom one. You looked up at me with fire in your eyes then let them slowly close as a moan left your lips," Will's thumb brushes over her lips. "You said, "See you later, Wills" softly into my ear while you stood on your tippy toes to reach and your hand trailed away, down my arm. I grabbed your hand before you could walk away then my finger pulled your towel from between your breasts and it fall to the floor."

"You sank to your knees and kissed my belly then lifted my leg and placed it on your shoulder."

"See, you remember," Will states. "Just like you'll remember your dad."

"Thank you for taking care of me."

"My pleasure, sweetheart."

"I should go find my mom, see if she needs my help."

Will nods and stands, taking her hand in his. "I'll come with you."

"No," she says with a gentle shake of her head. "I should go see her alone. I'll text you later, okay?"

"Sloan," Will calls as she begins to exit his office. "That doesn't have to be the last time we make love. We can make more memories, new ones you'll never forget."

Sloan leaves without responding.

Will attends Tom Hale's services with Scarlett, Johnny, Caine and Katherine, Jessie and Cindy. Carl is there with Drew and surprisingly Ollie and Addison stop by to pay their respects. Sloan is cautious with them, her guard up since their stunt at the hospital gala all those months ago. They smile kindly at her and leave, all's well that ends well. Well, if it ends well. That's still debatable when it comes to her and Will.

After the services conclude, Will heads to find a bathroom but instead finds Sloan alone slumped in a chair in a dark room. He enters and sits down next to her. "Hey" he says.

"Hey, Willy."

Will laughs at the nickname then smiles sadly at the girl who, still after all this time and everything that's happened, holds his heart. "Why are you in here all alone?"

Sloan shrugs a shoulder. "Just needed a minute to regroup I guess."

"Want me to leave you alone then?"

"Nope. I'd actually like you to stay and talk to me about anything other than the fact that my father is gone."

Will starts to make a comment about the weather then decides against it. He heaves in a deep breath and tells her something he should have a very long time ago. "It wasn't all Julia's fault that we broke up."

Sloan looks up through her tears and stares into Will's eyes. "Why do you think she left you if it wasn't all her fault? I thought you said her mental instability and everything with the pregnancy…"

"All true and all factors but," Will sighs deeply. "I…"

"Were you different then?" Sloan asks. "A shitty boyfriend?"

"I don't know. Yes. I guess. Kind of. Maybe."

Sloan doesn't speak, she waits for him to elaborate.

Another deep sigh escapes Will before he caves and begins to explain what he means. "I was self-absorbed. I was a workaholic, studying and fixated on getting into med school. What I've never told anyone, not even my parents, not Caine or Jessie, was that I was having migraines and thought I had another tumor. I figured the cancer had come back and well, I kind of checked out."

A worried expression crosses Sloan's face and her hand migrates to his thigh. "It hadn't though?"

"No. No tumor, no cancer. Just me stressed out over everything. Then, Julia got pregnant and I was dealing with her turmoil."

"Are you trying to tell me that if she hadn't gotten pregnant, you think things would have been different? That you'd still be with her?"

"Yes and no. Yes, things would have been different, of course. But, no, I don't think we would have lasted. She needs a lot more attention than I can provide her. She's not a strong, independent woman like someone else I know."

Sloan laughs. "I don't feel like the same person I was when I met you, Willy."

"You're an even better version and I like when you call me Willy, it does things to me" Will admits with a wiggle of his eyebrows.

"Thanks," she laughs. "But...I don't know if I can keep doing this 'friends' thing with you."

"You can. You'd miss me, you're lucky to have me, you know? I'm loyal like a pig."

Sloan laughs from her belly for the first time in ages and Will loves that it's him that made her do that.

"How can we be friends? Does Julia know we're friends?"

"Julia and I are..."

"Well, big surprise," Carl says when he finds Sloan and Will together. "I knew I'd find you wherever she was."

Will stands up and approaches his resident. "Do you have something you want to say to me? We're not in the hospital. I'm not your attending here, just a guy with a girl trying to cheer her up. You're free to speak your mind."

Carl laughs. "Classic. Whatever, man. Call it what you like but it's obvious to me that you're not over her."

"Carl, please," Sloan begs. "Not now, not here."

He nods, mumbles something under his breath that sounds a lot like a complaint over Sloan saying a similar comment about sex, then leaves the room with a huff.

"See, how can we be friends?"

"Are you sleeping with him?"

"Are you sleeping with Julia?"

Neither will answer the other. Will finally breaks and clears his throat. "I was heading to find a bathroom. I should probably round up my crew and head out soon."

Sloan nods but doesn't make a move to stand. "See ya, Willy."

*****

Sloan returns to work a few days later a different woman and Will hates what he sees. She barely acknowledges him and her distance begins to eat at him by the second day.

He overhears her talking to Katherine the following day in the cafeteria. Sloan tells her best friend about her first time with Carl and how after all these months, they finally had sex. Will sits there, hidden from Sloan's view and listens to her describing another man's hands on her flesh, him inside her body. Will leaves the cafeteria and storms into his office, heads straight for his bathroom and spends the next ten minutes vomiting. He's never understood the expression 'see red' until now. After he empties his stomach, he considers breaking everything in his sight, which, ironically looks red through his bloodshot eyes.

Yeah, he gets the meaning now.

To make matters in his life worse, Julia has decided to ramp up her game. She made arrangements with Ellie and Frank to take the girls, Johnny and Jack in tow, to the beach house Wills parents own. With the house to themselves for the weekend, Julia begins her plans of mass seduction.

Will arrives home on Friday night, after a long week of being ignored by Sloan and Carl looking way too pleased for his own good, to find the house lit only by candles. As he enters the living space he sees Julia move in the shadows. She's naked and her hair is cascading over her shoulders and covering a bare breast. Just what he needs. Fuck!

"Julia," he heaves in as his eyes rake over her body. Against his own will and better judgement, he grows hard and shifts in his trousers. It pisses him off. He doesn't want to be hard for her, anyone except Sloan, but his body has finally reached its breaking point and is begging to be given the female attention it's grown accustomed to.

"Finally getting the reaction I want" she giggles as she approaches him, smiling at the tenting of his pants. Julia reaches for his hand and Will doesn't pull back as she places his palm over her exposed breast. His thumb runs over her nipple and Julia moans as it hardens. Will shifts again as he further lengthens in his pants, his erection now straining to be let free.

"Julia, we can't…we're not…fuck" he moans as her hand cups the tip of his erection fighting to escape.

"Yes, we can. Let me make you feel good. For tonight at the very least. We're both lonely. How long has it been Will, since you've felt a woman? Hmm? Your body is wound so tight you feel like a volcano."

He moans as her hand strokes up and down the front of his pants. "My feelings for Sloan," he begins and his erection starts to subside at the thought of him being with another woman. Then Julia lowers to her knees in front of him and he sighs, his hands tangle into her hair. "Where's Scar?"

"Ellie and Frank took them all to your parent's beach house. We have the house to ourselves until Sunday night."

"Julia, I need you to understand what this is before we…if we…it's just comfort from an old friend. Sex to fill a physical need. Nothing more. Can you handle that?" he asks, unable to believe he's considering doing this. But as she reaches into his pants and frees his erection, stroking him to full hardness, he remembers that Sloan is probably on her knees about to do the same for Carl. And it's been so long. Julia's right, he needs to feel a woman, her pussy fluttering around him as he comes, instead of his own fist pumping himself to get off then feeling empty once he has. "We can't ever be a couple again, you understand that, right?"

"I'm fine. Don't worry about me. I know what this is and I'm a big girl. I can handle it, Will. You don't have to wear kid gloves with me. We fuck and get it out of our systems. It's all good."

Will heaves Julia to her feet and crashes his lips over hers. His brain stops working and Will goes with the lead of his dick. It isn't until they come up for air an hour later, sweaty and sated on the floor that Will processes what he's done. "Fuck," he mutters. "Julia, we…"

"Listen," Julia begins. "We did nothing wrong. We're both consenting adults with a history. We let that get the best of us in a moment of weakness. We used protection and no one needs to know, no one will unless we tell them. I'm leaving, Will. I was offered a job in Washington that I applied for long before this started up and it's not something I want to turn down."

"So, that was a pity fuck? A good-bye? Jesus, Julia, you have a way of fucking up my life like a pro. I can't believe I...fuck. Sloan..."

"Doesn't have to know and is fucking your resident. Maybe if she did know, she'd come to her senses and see how much you love her. You said her name, you know?"

"What?" Will asks, confused by that information. "When?"

Julia sends Will a look. "Take a guess."

"Jesus."

"My leaving will be the best thing for all of us. I love you, I do and Scarlett too but this isn't working, Will, and you know it. I need more than convincing you to fuck me because you've been without sex for months." Will opens his mouth to speak but Julia silences him with a hand. "Let me finish," she begs. "Caine and Jessie were wrong about me, you know?"

Will raises a curious eyebrow.

Julia chuckles slightly then continues. "Okay, they were wrong this time. Here," she says handing him an envelope filled with cash.

"What is this?" Will asks.

"Give this to them for me. Caine and Jessie. And tell them that I do love you and it wasn't all for the money. Not this time anyway."

Will places the envelope on the table and nods at Julia. He can't deny that what just happened between them hadn't felt like a pity fuck. Maybe Julia does love him and this time around maybe it's his fault because he knows without a shadow of a doubt that he's in love with another woman.

The feelings of emptiness have already settled into his gut and he's having all he can do not to regurgitate his last meal when they hear a car in the driveway.

Julia scurries around to help Will find his clothes then she bolts for her room. Will runs a hand through his damp hair just as Caine and Katherine tap on the door then walk right in, Caine not used to Will living with anyone but Scarlett. He takes one look at his best friend and knows exactly what he's been doing. Caine just hopes for Will's sake and his own that Katherine doesn't take notice. Will makes eye contact and silently pleads with his best friend not to mention what he knows just occurred on his living room floor.

"What are you doing here?" Will asks after clearing his throat and hoping their surprise visit doesn't have anything to do with Sloan. It'd be just his luck after fucking another woman that his best friend would be here to drop a bomb on him. Gee, maybe Sloan has run off to elope with his resident. Sounds about right, that's Will's luck.

"We need to talk about Jessie and Cindy," Caine says. "He's fucking her. I'm just not sure about the BDSM shit and if he's serious about her or not but this secret fucking around between all of us," Caine says shooting a serious look to Will. "Has to stop. Right now, right here."

Will throws his eyebrows up into his hairline at that declaration. "Maybe it's best if we did that with just us guys. No disrespect, Katherine but..."

"I told him the same thing," she admits. "You should know that Julia called him and said you'd need to see him."

"Kitten!" Caine scolds. He hadn't wanted Katherine to reveal that piece of information.

"Jesus, she's a fucking piece of work and you," Will says pointing a finger at his best friend. "You could have warned me that she had something up her sleeve."

Caine shrugs, little does Will know he, Katherine, Jessie and Cindy are all in on a mission get Will and Sloan back together. "You needed the closure amongst other things," he states with a smirk to Will. "It's done and she'll be gone in the morning. Now, we can make a plan to help you get Sloan back. That's where my kitty cat comes in," Caine says pulling Katherine into his side and kissing her on the temple. "Plus I don't like to be without her for too long."

"You've turned into some kind of pussy, haven't you?" Will teases, shocking himself that he can joke as his life is falling apart.

"That I am, my friend. When it comes to her, that I am. And you're no different, Jessie, apparently either. So, here's how this is going to work. Seeing as how I am the only one of the three of us that has their shit together, you will do as I say. Pack your bags, we're taking a guy's only trip. We'll drop Katherine off at home and she'll deal with your girl. I have the security detail on call. They'll look after the girls while we're gone."

Will smiles at Katherine as she approaches him and wraps him in a hug. "I've always liked you, Will. You're her guy person and I'm going to help you get her back."

"Thanks," Will says. "I've always liked you too, Kitten" he says with a smirk then chuckles as Katherine swats at his bicep.

Katherine laughs and Will pulls her into his side and kisses her temple then leaves the room to do as he's told and pack a bag. Knowing that Scarlett is with Ellie and Frank and surely having a blast with Johnny by her side, a last hurrah before the boy is off to college twelve hours away, he doesn't need to worry about planning for her.

After packing a bag, he stops at his guest room door. Julia opens it after the first knock.

"You'll be gone when I get back?" he speculates correctly.

"It's best that way."

"You planned this?"

"We both needed the closure. I'll call Scarlett tomorrow from D.C. and give her my new address. Maybe she'll want to look at schools there, you never know, right?"

Will sucks in a deep breath. He can't think about his little girl going to college yet. He still has plenty of time before that happens. First, he'll have to survive this coming school year with her moping around the house with Johnny gone. He's leaving for college in only a few days. The drama surrounding that is about to hit full force and Will isn't prepared.

He nods at Julia then opens his arms for her to walk into them. He hugs her then kisses her gently on the lips one last time. "Good-bye, Julia. Take care of yourself."

"Thanks. I hope things work out for you and Sloan. Truly, I do."

Will laughs. "Sloan," he huffs. "I don't know about us, Jules."

Julia smiles. "It'll work out. You really love her, don't you?"

"More than I can explain but it's too late, she's…"

"It's never too late. Well," she sighs thinking about their broken relationship. "For the one you're meant to be with, it isn't. You need to fight for her, Will. Tell her how you feel and fix this. If you don't, you're going to be a very lonely man and I can't be running back here to fuck you all the time. I'm going to be too busy."

Will laughs at that. "God, you make me sound pathetic."

"There was nothing pathetic about that performance."

Will nods, says one last good-bye to Julia and closes the door behind him.

Caine and Katherine are waiting in the living room and when Will returns, Caine grabs one of his bags and leads them to the car. They drop Katherine off at her apartment then plan their ambush on Jessie while Katherine begins hers on Sloan.

Chapter 34

"Stone has the life" Jessie says as he leisurely sinks into the hot tub outside on the back deck of Damian Stone's cabin.

"You should know, you live a similar lifestyle, right?"

Jessie smirks and makes a chuckling sound. "You want a lesson on getting laid, man?"

Will looks to Caine for help then he sends Jessie the one finger salute. He doesn't need help getting laid, he knows he's a good-looking guy who could walk into any bar and leave with a one-night stand on his arm. That's not what he wants. What Will wants is Sloan. Only Sloan.

Caine sinks into the hot tub then raises his hips and removes his swim trunks with a smirk.

"Oh, hey! What the fuck?" Jessie asks.

"It feels better this way. I'm confident enough in my manhood for this. Apparently, you're not, Holt, but it's not my issue so deal."

Jessie scoffs. "I'm more than confident enough and I've seen your 'manhood' more times than I care to remember."

Will clears his throat. "Should I feel left out that I never had a woman with either of you?"

Caine and Jessie both laugh at the thought of fucking a girl with Will. They love him and all but neither can picture Will in a threesome.

"I'm not sure you'd know where to put your hands, dude" Jessie laughs.

Will raises his eyebrows. "Have you guys accidently touched the other's dick when you were fucking some girl?"

Caine and Jessie look at each other and start laughing again. Yes, yes they have and it wasn't fun.

"Maybe by accident once or twice before we knew what we were doing."

"Wait," Will says with a puzzled expression. "But you let go, right?"

"No," Caine says sliding closer to Jessie. "I put it in my mouth and finished him off while the girl watched."

Jessie pushes Caine to the other side of the hot tub where he bumps into Will. "He's an asshole. Don't listen to him" Jessie says.

"Speaking of assholes," Caine begins. "Katherine mentioned Cindy had a date last weekend with a real douche."

"It wasn't a date" Jessie says faster than he should have if Cindy was truly just a friend. "And he's not a douche. Wait, did she say the guy was a douche?"

Caine and Will smile at him. They know exactly whom Cindy finally got to take her out on a full-fledged date. A date in a real restaurant, not a night of hot sex strapped to a spanking bench in a sex club. Yes, Jessie Holt's fall into coupledom has begun.

"Hmmm," Caine says. "Well, Katherine said they went to dinner at a fancy place then to a musical before hitting Stone's club together where they scened. Too bad the guy didn't last long. Waste of her time."

"What the fuck? I lasted through three of her orgasms with a room full of people watching. She's going over my knee for…" Jessie stops speaking realizing Caine led him right into that trap. "Fuck!"

"So, you're fucking your partner at The Society?"

Jessie huffs in a breath. Might as well go for broke. "Yeah, but it's way more than that and I'm freaking the fuck out over it so leave me alone."

Will laughs. "And the mighty one falls."

"I said drop it. I'm not ready to think about it yet. But, um…what exactly did Cindy tell Katherine?"

She better not have said anything negative about his sexual abilities or Jessie was going to have her over his knee with a paddle in his hand.

Caine rolls his eyes. "And dare you have it wadies and gentlemen, the big, bad Dom wants to know what his wittle submissive thinks about his fucking skills" he says in the voice he used to use on Scarlett when she was a baby.

Jessie splashes Caine who covers his face with his beer bottle and belly laughs at his friend.

The trio spends the rest of their weekend drunk, teasing each other about their relationships with their girls. Caine and Jessie make Will see the error of his ways and finally breaks down in a puddle of tears over his true feelings for Sloan. After he composes himself, they agree to help him do whatever it takes to get her back.

It isn't until Sunday night when they're heading back home that Caine flies into a barrage of curses.

"What's the problem?" Will asks.

"Fucking Katherine."

Jessie throws their bags into the trunk of Will's car. "What happened?"

"She's not answering my texts or calls."

"Maybe she's sleeping. You said her friends were spending the weekend at Stone Towers. Maybe she's catching up on some sleep" Jessie offers.

Caine growls. Mike had been contacting Katherine over the last few weeks and the sweet model couldn't just ignore him. She insisted that she no longer had feelings for him and his control over her was long gone since Caine entered her life and showed her what true love was. Caine had reluctantly dropped the argument and gotten her security but she'd proven time and time again that she was a headstrong female who would pull a stunt like sneaking out if she got the idea into her pretty little head.

"Or maybe she didn't follow directions and snuck off to have another "closure session" with Mike."

"Mike as in the ex-fiancé that was an abusive dick?" Jessie asks.

"Where's Sloan? Did she go with her?" Will worries that Sloan will end up covered in the dude's blood again. On second thought, that would be fun to watch. Will knows his girl can hold her own.

"I don't fucking know but when I get home, Katherine's not going to have time to explain anything before I paddle her ass bright red! And this time won't be for fun!"

"I just bought a new one," Jessie says. "We can stop by my place and grab it."

Caine growls. "Just drive fast, Will" he orders as the air in the car fills with an unease.

By the time Will pulls into the city limits, Caine is out of his mind, after sending Katherine a strand of texts that all go unanswered. They head to her apartment, it's empty, not even a little piggy squealing on the other side of the door. Caine calls her no less than five times, each call going directly to voicemail. Will texts Sloan to see if she knows anything about Katherine seeing Mike but she doesn't respond either. Jessie calls Cindy but she says she hasn't talked to either of the girls since Saturday when she was forced to cancel on them, being held up at the hospital.

Will drops Jessie off at Cindy's and neither he nor Caine give him a hard time. Caine is too upset over his own problems to worry about teasing Jessie over fucking his partner and admitting to having feelings for the woman. There'll be plenty of time for that later. Right now, from the screaming Will hears coming from his passenger seat, he guesses Caine is reaming out Mac.

"You need to take a deep breath and calm the fuck down. I'm sure Mac will find her. What the hell happened?"

"I have no motherfucking idea. The last he saw of her, she was in the apartment. She fucking promised me!"

Will heads to Caine's building and leaves him to wait for Mac and hope that Katherine resurfaces sooner than later and with apologies and a damn good explanation.

"I'll let you know if I hear from Sloan but after everything…"

"Thanks" Caine says and runs up his stoop and into his brownstone.

Will heads back to Connecticut and finds his house free of Julia. It's a relief but a stressor all the same. With Julia gone, he hasn't an excuse in the world not to make amends with Sloan. Except for Carl.

What if Sloan would rather be with him and she tells Will it truly is too late for them? He might have lost his chance for good this time and he doesn't want to face facts.

"Hey," Will says to Scarlett as he walks into the house. "Have you spoken to your mom?"

"Yeah. She called me when she got to D.C. She said she told you she was taking a job there. She said I could go visit whenever I want."

"You okay?"

"Yeah, I'm fine. I'm not sure what you were trying to do in the first place. It's obvious that you don't love her. It's clear you want to be with Sloan so…"

Will huffs. "It's complicated."

"Yeah, that's what Sloan said too" Scarlett says then covers her mouth with her hand when she realizes that she just admitted to Will that she's been talking to Sloan.

"When did you talk to Sloan?" Will asks as he sits down on the sofa across from his daughter who looks more like a woman every day.

Scarlett smiles her best innocent smile at her father. "Um…"

"Scar" he warns with a voice he reserves for when she's in deep shit with him. She couldn't be in any deeper than in this moment.

"Fine," she says. "I've spoken to her a few times. We went for coffee once and we text every few days. I like her, okay? I wish you had asked me what I wanted before moving Julia in here for whatever dumb ass reason you did."

"I was trying to," Will stands and begins to pace the room. He runs his hands through his hair and considers the bar. He rethinks that idea when Scarlett rolls her eyes at him. He drank enough this weekend with Caine and Jessie and it's not a habit he wants to fall back into. "I don't know what the fuck I was trying to do. I love Sloan. I need to fix this."

"Yes you do," Scarlett says. "But she's with that resident of yours now. He was texting her non-stop the last time I was on the phone with her. I think they've grown," Scarlett clears her throat. "Closer recently, if you get what I mean."

Will swears and flings himself back down, this time into the chair that's his favorite. He remembers sitting in this chair naked, Sloan cradled in his lap then turning herself around to straddle him and ride him until he was moaning her name and coming so hard he saw stars. He clears his throat and leans forward to block his growing erection from his daughter. "Maybe I should call her" he says.

"Good luck, dad. I'm going to Johnny's later. I'll be home early though, okay?"

"Sure, baby. Be careful driving. Tell Johnny to stop by and say hi before he heads off to school."

It doesn't matter how many times he watches his daughter leave in her new car, Will will never be able to wrap his head around the fact that Scarlett is almost all grown up. In a year, she'll be in college.

Scarlett smiles at Will and leaves him to his thoughts.

Will is surprised a few minutes later as he's flopping down on his bed to think through his life, when his phone rings and he sees Sloan's face on his screen. He answers on the first ring but she isn't there. He says hello and calls her name. No response. She must have butt dialed him. Then he hears her voice muffled in the background. Before he has time to shout her name, in the hopes that she'll realize he's on the line, he hears Carl and his world comes crashing down on top of him.

"That feels so fucking good, Sloan. Yeah, lick it just like that, baby."

Motherfucker!

Will should hang up. The last thing he should do is stay on the line and listen to this. Just knowing that Sloan is having sex with his resident has been enough, more than enough. But listening to it? He probably won't survive. But he can't hang up when he hears her moan. It's a familiar sound but different all at the same time.

"That's it, open wide," Carl says, his voice laced with pleasure. "Suck my cock hard, baby."

Shit!

Will listens as Carl moans through what Will knows is the best thing on earth. Sloan giving him a blow job was one of his favorite things and now Carl is enjoying the pleasures that Will had thrown away. And for what? Sloan was right, he should have talked to Scarlett before he moved Julia into his house and left Sloan like someone who didn't hold every piece of his heart in her hand.

"Lay down, I'm close and I want to fuck you," Will hears Carl grunt out. "But first, let me have a taste of that pussy. Mmmmm."

Are you fucking kidding me? Will can't believe the Universe has it out for him this bad.

He stays on the line and listens as Sloan cries out and he knows Carl's lips must be on her pussy, his pussy. His. Damn it.

He listens and waits for her orgasm sounds but they never come. Instead, he hears Carl grunting and his breathing growing ragged. Then Carl calls out her name and tells her he's going to come. Will hangs up and flings the lamp from his bedside table across the room before heading downstairs to pour himself a drink. Or maybe ten.

*****

Monday morning hits Will in the face with a hangover and he's thankful that he doesn't have any patients today. What he does have is a full day of torture planned for his horny resident that apparently has no idea that it's bad form as a guy to come first and not take care of your woman. Well, so be it. Better for him in the long run. And Sloan is his woman anyway and he plans on reclaiming her as soon as possible.

Will decides to take the stairs and burn off some of his aggression before he's forced to come face to face with the man he listened to having sex with Sloan only hours ago. Maybe he'll rethink this whole intern, resident, fellow shit for the future. They're proving to be nothing but trouble for him.

He opens the door and starts to jog up the stairs then, as he's approaching, the door on the next floor opens almost hitting him, and there she is. Sloan is standing right in front of him.

An annoyed sound escapes him and he gives her an eye roll then a laugh that lets her know he's mad at her about something. Sloan can't think of anything for him to be mad about so she says his name in greeting and starts to walk up the stairs next to him.

"You feeling okay today?" Will asks with a laugh that doesn't hold any joy.

Sloan stops and looks at him with a confused expression. "Um, yeah. I guess."

"Not frustrated? That's funny. I'd think you'd be a little antsy."

"What the hell are you talking about?"

Will laughs again then stops and looks at Sloan with an expression she can't make out.

"Stop looking at me like that" she demands.

"Like what?" he asks. "I called you, Caine is nuts. He can't find Kat."

Sloan shrugs, obviously not concerned over her friend so she either knows where she is or doesn't think she's in any danger wherever she may have gone. "You watch me, you know? While I'm doing charts or when I'm walking by you. You look at me like," she points at his face. "Like that. I can't breathe when you…"

"You think I want to look at you? I have responsibilities in this hospital and instead of being able to focus on them, all I can think about is you fucking blowing my resident. I'm sick to my stomach right now thinking about Carl's hands touching you. Making you moan, eating that sweet pussy that should only be for me. Jesus, Sloan, he didn't even make you come!"

Sloan rears back and places her hand over her mouth as the tears start to flow. "How do you…Did you ask him about…Did he tell you?"

Will grabs Sloan by the upper arms to stop her ascent up the stairs. He places her against the wall gently then closes her in with his body. "You butt dialed me last night. I had called you earlier when Caine was freaking the fuck out over Katherine not answering him. You must have hit a button and your phone called back your last missed call. I heard the whole thing."

Sloan slaps his face. Hard. Leaving a red mark, she says, "How dare you? You left me. You choose Julia. I loved you. I thought you were the one I'd be with forever. I thought I had finally found the guy that would treat me right and take care of me. Stay with me. But I was wrong. I was done with other guys but you walked away. You," Sloan raises her voice and presses her finger into his chest with every word. "You. Left. Me."

Will grabs her hand and Sloan pulls it back. "Sloan" he says.

"No! You left me! I will not apologize for who I date or how I fuck them. It's none of your business what I do anymore."

Sloan runs up the next flight of stairs, leaving Will to collapse on the floor of the stairwell as she opens the door and steps out on the next floor.

An hour later, Will steps into an elevator to find her standing there. She rolls her eyes and steps further into the corner. They make eye contact. Will opens his mouth to speak, apologize maybe but for what? Listening to her not come with her boyfriend? Mentioning it? Leaving her for Julia, a woman he didn't love? The list was endless. In the end, he doesn't say anything.

Sloan looks at him and reacts the same. Her lips curl as if she's holding something back, something she wants to say but decides against it.

The elevator stops and Sloan steps out without a word.

Will is paged to an exam room for a neuro consult. It's a little off the beaten path, a room usually reserved in the ER for drunk, belligerent patients on a Friday night and Will momentarily thinks that it's odd that it's being used on a Monday morning.

Will walks into the room to find Jessie waiting for him. "Where's the neuro consult patient? I don't have time for your bullshit today, Holt" Will states. Yeah, he's a real dick to be around today.

"They took him down to run a quick scan," Jessie says as the door opens and Sloan walks in.

Will heaves in a deep breath. "What the fuck? So this neuro consult happens to also be an OB-GYN case? That's why you're both here, right?"

"Cindy paged me to come here for a patient that's in labor. She's in surgery so she said...fuck" Sloan mutters when realization dawns.

"Text me when you're good" Jessie says as he exits the room and Will and Sloan hear the click of the lock before they can respond.

"Stop looking at me," Sloan demands. "And why is there a lock on that door?"

"This room is usually reserved for the drunk and disorderly after a Friday night bar fight when they get their skulls bashed in and I have to relieve the pressure on their brains before they die."

"You're still looking at me," Sloan says. "Stop fucking looking at me like that, Will" she demands, her voice light, giving away her true feelings.

"I can't. I can't stop looking at you. I can't stop thinking about you. I'm losing my fucking mind, Sloan" Will says as he grabs her face, his lips mere inches from hers.

"Get off me" she demands while her hands grasp the back of his neck then her fingers sink into his hair.

Will crashes his lips over hers and Sloan moans a contented sound. A sound he never heard her make once during that phone call when he listened to her have sex with another man.

Will's tongue seeks immediate entry and Sloan obliges, opening for him. She runs her tongue over his as his hands cup her ass. Will lifts her and flings her onto the exam table, his lips never leaving hers. His fingers go to the hem of her shirt and lifts, taking the top off and exposing her pink lace bra. He breaks their kiss for a quick look then goes back to devouring her mouth once more. Sloan's fingers only leave his hair long enough to unhook her bra and fling it to the floor.

Will's kisses move to her neck, behind her ear and she gives him full access. Leaning back and bracing herself on her hands, she exposes her neck and offers up her breasts. Will flicks a nipple with his tongue then returns to her neck. His fingers work the drawstring of her scrubs as his tongue finds her other nipple.

"Yes," she sighs.

"Shhh," he says with a smile. "I've got you. Raise your hips for me so I can get these off."

Sloan lifts her hips and Will reveals her pink lace covered pussy. His finger touches then rubs the wet spot on the front of them and he moans along with her. "Your wet for me" he states confidently. Facts are facts and he has all the evidence he needs right under his touch.

"I have been since that night in the restaurant" she shamelessly admits as he rips her panties off and brings them to his face. She loves the dirtiness of the act coming from this clean-cut man. It drives her mad, makes her want to do things with him that she knows are probably illegal in a few states.

Will inhales her scent and moans. "I've missed you so fucking much. We need to talk but…fuck! I…first I need to fuck you for hours. Maybe days."

"Will" she sighs.

"Open your legs for me or I'll open them for you," he demands. "I need to taste you on my tongue. Feel you come for me. You need that too, sweetheart?"

"Yes," she says as she widens her legs. "Please."

"So pretty" he praises. "I love your pussy."

Will crosses his arms in front of him, grabs the hem of his shirt and rips it off over his head. He flings it to the floor as he sinks to his knees and latches his lips onto her pussy. Sloan's body arches off the table as she feels his warm mouth cover her. As his tongue swipes over her clit, Sloan cries out, "I'm close already. Jesus, how is that possible?"

Will smiles up at her. "Watch me make you come in my mouth, then I'm going to fuck you like never before."

"I'm coming" she cries as Will's tongue enters her, his finger circling her clit.

He licks her through every twitch of her body, extending her pleasure into something almost painful but oh so good. He stands and smiles at her, his eyes locked on hers as he licks his lips. "Best taste ever" he says and that's all it takes for Sloan to crave more.

Will pulls the drawstring on his own scrubs then leans down and licks her throat. It's the most erotic sensation and Sloan purrs from deep in her belly. Will sinks his hands into her hair and crashes his lips over hers again. Sloan moans once more when she tastes herself on his lips. Will pulls back and smiles at her. He removes his erection after pushing down his briefs. He smiles at her again as he sinks deep inside her hot, tight body in one long push. "Oh my God," he grunts. "You feel so fucking good. So perfect."

Will makes slow, passionate love to her. He whispers her name in between the grunting he can't seem to control while Sloan claws at his chest as her release builds again. Then as Will senses her orgasm, his own on the brink, his head falls back and they come together.

"Jesus," Will moans into her neck as he inhales her sweet perfume. "Sloan, I need to tell you something."

Sloan is only half coherent, her orgasms clouding her understanding of the spoken word. "Hmmm" she moans.

"I love you, sweetheart," Will says. "I'm in love with you. I want you, us, forever. Julia's gone and the thing with her was never…"

Sloan interrupts him with a heated kiss to his lips then she pulls back and says, "I know. Carl is a great guy but he isn't you. For me, it's only ever been you."

"You're it for me too, sweetheart. You have ruined me for all womankind."

Well, that brings her back to reality real quick.

"Will" she sighs.

"Yeah, sweetheart, tell me what you're thinking."

"We never made any rules. The first time we were together, we didn't have rules. Maybe we need rules."

"Rules?" he asks. "What kind of rules?"

"You know," Sloan begins as Will slowly leaves her body and pulls his scrubs up then kisses her nose. "Rules about other people. I…um, well you know that Carl and I…"

"Don't remind me. We'll deal with him later."

Will pulls his shirt on and hands Sloan her bra. He hates the thought of them being forced to get dressed and return to reality. He wishes they were alone in a warm bed somewhere. A place where he could keep her all to himself until they were solid enough to withstand any outside force that might try to break them apart again.

"Can I ask you something?"

Will nods and hands Sloan her shirt.

"Did you and Julia, um, you know?"

Will sighs. "Julia didn't mean anything to me. I haven't had feelings for her in a long time. You're all that I want, sweetheart. You don't need to worry about me being with anyone else," Will chuckles. "I spent months so drunk I couldn't see straight and then the thing with Julia…it wasn't like that with her. She tried once and to be honest, I couldn't get it up. Then I…" Will sighs as Sloan reaches for her pants that he hands her. "I was so lonely and she was there. I'm sorry. I shouldn't have done it but I…"

"I know" Sloan says.

"But that's all behind us. Do you love me, Sloan? Are you in love with me?"

Sloan shakes her head yes. "You won't have time to fuck anyone else anyway. I'm a handful as it is, you might remember."

"Oh, I remember."

Sloan hits Will's chest and he grasps her hand and pulls her into his body.

"I want you all to myself. Is that going to be a problem?"

"Um, I just need a little time to let Carl down easy, okay? He's a good guy and this is going to be uncomfortable" she says as the door to the room is unlocked and opens to reveal none other than Carl standing there.

"Dr. Baxter said there was a neuro consult in here. I guess she was wrong."

"Carl, wait" Sloan calls out.

"What, Sloan? Huh? Listen, I'm not equipped to deal with this shit while doing my residency and he's my attending. You need to decide. Him or me. I can't do this anymore. So, who's it going to be?"

Before Sloan can say another word, Caine appears. His eyes are red rimmed, from crying by the looks of him, and his hair is wild. "Will," he cries. "I need a consult. Please, it's Katherine."

"Katherine?" Sloan asks. She just now remembers Will's earlier concerns over Caine not hearing from her. When Sloan had woken up on Sunday, Katherine had been asleep in her room or so she'd assumed. Sloan, Rose, and Amber had let her sleep and Sloan took their friends to the train station before working a shift then spending the night at Carl's. She never checked back in with Katherine.

"Sloan?" Carl questions.

"What the fuck happened?" Will asks.

"Mike beat the shit out of her," Caine cries. "I told her to stay in the fucking apartment but she couldn't fucking listen to me. Will, I need you to fix this. Please, help me."

Will wraps his best friend into an embrace then looks at Sloan over Caine's shoulder.

"Sloan?" Carl repeats.

"Sloan?" Will asks.

Sloan stands looking at both men unable to respond, decide. She also wants to rush to Katherine's side, make sure her friend is okay, but is unable to make her feet move.

"Sloan" Carl says again and it sounds like he's asking her to decide. At a time like this, when her best friend needs the top neurosurgeon in the world?

"Sloan" Will says but it sounds like he's telling her to move, join him.

When both men realize that she's not going to be the one to make the decision, one of them makes it for her and takes her by the hand.

TO BE CONTINUED...

Coming Soon...

Dissection of Love

(The Anatomy of Love Trilogy)

Book 2

Dr. Caine Cabrera

The second book (The Dissection of Love) will focus on Wilson Anderson's best friend and colleague, Dr. Caine Cabrera.

Caine Cabrera is a ladies' man, a different flavor of the week in his bed every night and never one twice. But Caine's life is in desperate need of a change. Unfortunately, only the love of the right woman will be able to make that happen. Lucky for him, Katherine Mills is about to crash into his world and cause Caine to question everything he's ever known about women, relationships, and love.

Katherine Mills is a model, she's confident in her looks, but timid when it comes to men until Caine Cabrera crosses her path and makes her understand her true value. Now, with her self-esteem restored, she must decide if a marriage to the wrong man is still what she deserves or is she should take a chance with the confident doctor and find out what it finally means to find love.

There's only one problem, is Caine truly ready to open his heart and explore the Dissection of Love?

Sutures of Love

(The Anatomy of Love Trilogy)

Book 3

Dr. Jessie Holt

The third and final book in The Anatomy of Love Trilogy.

Dr. Jessie Holt, the world's leading fertility specialist began his sexual experiences early in life, quickly learning the art of bringing women to their knees while convincing himself that he wasn't built for long-term relationships.

Now Jessie must examine his actions of long ago if he's to have any hope of a future. But is Jessie is ready to repair his heart and explore the Sutures of Love?

About the Author

Kitty Berry grew up an only child who never wished for a sibling in a small town in Connecticut. After graduating with a degree in Early Childhood Special Education, she began teaching in the field and started to raise a family. Her literary influences happened later in life when she stumbled upon The Pilot's Wife by Anita Shreve after seeing it featured on the Oprah Show. It was her late mother's (whose name she uses as a pen name) desire of becoming a writer that prompted Kitty to create a contemporary romantic series.

Being a creative person by nature who came into writing during a time in her life when the busy balance of career and family made her crave an escape into the world of romance, Kitty took that desire and turned it into a romantic series that offers the reader multidimensional characters.

In 2013, she published her first novel from The Stone Series, Sliding. Since then she has written 9 other novels in that series, among them Stoned, Second Chances, Surrender, Starting Over, and Silence. The final installment, Survivor, was released in 2016. Her new Trilogy, Anatomy of Love, is scheduled to release in 2017 and Berry is currently working on a stand-alone that will be a carry-over from her other series. This stand-alone should release in 2018.

Because angst-ridden, plot-driven, women's contemporary romances mesmerize Kitty, Berry writes only in that genre. While each book in The Stone Series can stand alone with its own story,

Berry's intention was to create carry-over characters to satisfy the need of the reader to know more after each novel concludes. As an avid reader, Kitty enjoys the feeling of being there with the characters inside the story and often finds herself wanting to know more about them, missing them when the story is over, and becoming excited all over again when she discovers those familiar characters in subsequent novels. It is her hope that The Stone Series will do the same for her readers.

Kitty is married to a man she met in graduate school. She has three teenage boys, which makes her the only woman in a house of screaming sport fanatics! During any given evening, you can find Kitty curled up in bed reading unless she is driving carpools, attending basketball games, Cross Country races or Track meets. When she is done coordinating the social lives of her three adolescent children (who have way better social lives than she does), Kitty plans to also enjoy traveling.

Visit Kitty's website @ www.kittyberryauthor.com

Made in the USA
Middletown, DE
21 January 2019